THE ROBERT SHECKLEY OMNIBUS

THE ROBERT SHECKLEY OMNIBUS

Edited and Introduced

by

ROBERT CONQUEST

LONDON
VICTOR GOLLANCZ LTD
1973

ISBN 0 575 01677 9

PRINTED IN GREAT BRITAIN BY
NORTHUMBERLAND PRESS LIMITED
GATESHEAD

CONTENTS

INTRODUCTION

SHECKLEY'S REPUTE IN the science fiction world goes without saying. But it is also true that many who seldom or never read science fiction in the ordinary way should find him irreplaceably interesting and entertaining.

The recent vogue for sf (and let us note that the solecism "sci-fi" is a merely voguish one, never used by genuine devotees) has meant that by now those who do not read it are mainly those who have decided it is not for them. But from time to time a genre produces a writer who, if they did but know it, would be attractive to many besides its addicts. It is a welcome task to introduce such authors to the wider audience, as Hilaire Belloc introduced Ernest Bramah, or as E. C. Bentley introduced Damon Runyon. As Belloc put it, there may be "lack of communication between those who desire to find good stuff and those who produce it. It is in the attempt to build a bridge between the one and the other that men who have the privilege of hearing a good thing betimes write such words as I am writing here."

The short story, in the traditional sense, is now comparatively uncommon in "mainstream" writing. There one still finds, it is true, many short pieces of fiction but they are seldom short *stories*. They depict a mood, adumbrate an attitude and so on; but they do not tell a tale. Science fiction, as Sheckley's pieces demonstrate, is one of the more important of the remaining strongholds in which this art-form survives in its old freshness and vigour.

Sheckley is, of course, a stylist. That is to say he writes in good clear English with an unmistakable personal tone, and salted with adult irony. In a period when so many works seek a sort of stylishness in contortion this may be specially welcome. It is often said that Henry James was more of an artist than H. G. Wells, largely because every sentence of James' is ostentatiously insistent on the point. But, in fact, let us assert at once that Wells not only writes just as well but is subtler and more effective even in evocativeness. And James is, of course, a model of unpretentious clarity compared with many more recent literary phenomena. Yet where "mainstream" literature has, in modern times, tended excessively towards first introspection and later the disruption of sense and the achievement of significance by frenzy, essential elements—especially intellectual concern, objectivity and a sense of the phenomena—have found an important refuge in science fiction, as this collection so clearly shows.

Some of Sheckley's tales have strong affinities with the fable, and even the fairy story. But the resemblance to the fairy story is formal rather than essential, as in *Something For Nothing*. At a superficial glance this is simply a rejargoning of old stories about wishing caps and such, even as to its unfortunate *dénouement*, with the moral that everything has to be paid for in the end. But this is in some ways even more forceful for the very reason that it is not due to arbitrary magic beyond human control but to the operation of an intertemporal credit system. It is, in fact, one of the clearest illustrations not only of the resemblances, but also of the final differences between science fiction and fantasy.

Other pieces may be no more than enjoyable and ingenious tales: for Sheckley is wonderfully ingenious. Look, for example, at the events depending upon mere gadgetry in the unpretentious *Hands Off*. Or, again, at the first Sheckley story I read—*Specialist*. I was instantly delighted. This story has, indeed, one characteristic rather rare in science fiction—it is built round an entirely new idea. Amateurs reading, and even more writing, science fiction, often think that they have found a surprising and novel theme. The stories thus produced often have a considerable air of self-congratulation at such supposed originality. But in fact it is very rare indeed for any true novelty to emerge as it does here—and (in a different sense) in *Immortality Inc*.

However, that is not the only virtue of *Specialist*; (nor does it make it Sheckley's best story). It is, indeed, a notable locus of Sheckley's virtues—stylishness, ease, high spirits. But above all, it demonstrates these in a context of science fiction pure and simple, stripped to the bone and using virtually none of the resources it shares with any other genre. There is virtually no sex or tragedy, only the most perfunctory social comment or "characterization". It shows how much can be done without them.

Those are, indeed, ingredients which may be acceptable, and even admirable, in certain styles of science fiction—(except for character-ization, or at any rate too much in the way of characterization. For science fiction is a form of writing in which the essence is the manipulation of the context, a writing in which excessive introspec-tion or preoccupation with the nuances of individuals is almost always out of place and destructive of the effect.)

But social satire, though minimal or absent in such stories as *Specialist* and *Ghost V*, is one of those themes which finds a natural home in science fiction. Indeed, *Gulliver's Travels* could reasonably be described as science fiction. In those days, undiscovered islands in the Pacific were legitimate speculation. And Swift's ships played the part which nowadays must be allotted to the interplanetary or interstellar rocket. Sheckley works in the Swiftian tradition of satire, like Samuel Butler, Aldous Huxley and others, having nothing in common with the abusive self-righteousness that has passed for "satire" in these latter days. The delightful *A Ticket to Tranai* is the *Erewhon* of the space age, comically destructive, a devastating comment on particular notions, rather than a piece of preaching.

It is a thoroughly endearing point about Sheckley that he so clearly enjoys what he is doing. He does not come to science fiction from outside with the aim of turning it into a vehicle for sermonizing. Nor does he make of it a stage-set for the sort of silly-cleverness which attracts some readers by indulging them in the feeling that they are doing something superior, that they and the author are one up on all those peasants. Science fiction is, rather, his natural element; and he is thoroughly at home in the future.

"At home", because there are many established traditions about the future, paradoxical as it may seem. Such traditions are not, of course, binding: there are many science fiction writers who ignore them, or create totally different universes. The fact that they exist is, nevertheless, of the greatest help to the type of story best set up within an accepted background. This is true even as to detail. For example, the hand weapon in Sheckley is the "blaster", the currency is the "credit". These, and a number of other properties, have long since become established. The advantage is—on "blaster" for example—that it is unnecessary to go through the whole rigmarole of explaining at length how it works, or describing it in technical terms which, however valid, are as unlikely in real speech as who should call a revolver a "multiple lead projector". In Sheckley's usage, moreover, as Bentley wrote of Runyon, (purveyor of a milieu as strange to most Englishmen as any Mars), "Even if a term or a phrase is unfamiliar, the context tells you instantly what it means".

This may not be essential to, but it certainly contributes to, the easy matter-of-factness which is Sheckley's usual mode of achieving credibility. Note, for example, the way in which he gets one of his heroes right across the galaxy in *A Ticket To Tranai*. Many good science fiction writers would deal with the immensities of space, the glare of strange suns, the feelings of enormous isolation. Sheckley's method is dryly factual, as in Gulliver's outward voyages, conveying the familiarity as well as the hugeness of the interstellar.

For even within the traditions of classical clarity in science fiction, a wide variety of tones is possible. As has often been noted, such writers as James H. Schmitz and Jack Vance, who almost equally attain their effects through careful "realism" (rather than through the high-paced obsessiveness which is the other main science fiction method), normally convey much more of terror and wonder than is usual for Sheckley. Or, to look at it another way, they recount the legends, rather than the fables, of the future.

But though this is Sheckley's most typical method, he is not limited to it. The quiet astringence of *The Store Of The Worlds*, the poetic touches in *Ask A Foolish Question*, are only the most obvious signs of a more complex set of feelings which underlie and give extra depths and flavours even to the driest and simplest of these pieces. For, of course, an arid or a simple mind cannot produce a dry and easy story of any excellence. It is the all-too-rarely-found combination of ebullient creativity and tight control, of art and discipline, which has produced this work.

Veteran science fiction readers will, we are sure, be delighted to repeat and renew their pleasure in a writer who has been called (by Kingsley Amis) "science fiction's premier gadfly". At the same time, we welcome the broader public to the certain enjoyment of good writing and high spirits, in the ingenious, sardonic, intelligent and entertaining work of Robert Sheckley.

ROBERT CONQUEST

Part One

IMMORTALITY INC.

I

AFTERWARDS, THOMAS BLAINE thought about the manner of his dying and wished it had been more interesting. Why couldn't his death have come while he was battling a typhoon, meeting a tiger's charge, or climbing a windswept mountain? Why had his death been so tame, so commonplace, so ordinary?

But an enterprising death, he realized, would have been out of character for him. Undoubtedly he was meant to die in just the quick, common, messy, painless way he did. And all his life must have gone into the forming and shaping of that death—a vague indication in childhood, a fair promise in his college years, an implacable certainty at the age of thirty-two.

Still, no matter how commonplace, one's death is the most interesting event of one's life. Blaine thought about his with intense curiosity. He had to know about those minutes, those last precious seconds when his own particular death lay waiting for him on a dark New Jersey highway. Had there been some warning sign, some portent? What had he done, or not done? What had he been thinking?

Those final seconds were crucial to him. How, exactly, had he died?

He had been driving over a straight, empty white highway, his headlights probing ahead, the darkness receding endlessly before him. His speedometer read seventy-five. It felt like forty. Far down the road he saw headlights coming towards him, the first in hours.

Blaine was returning to New York after a week's vacation at his cabin on Chesapeake Bay. He had fished and swum and dozed in the sun on the rough planks of his dock. One day he sailed his sloop to Oxford and attended a dance at the yacht club that night. He met a silly, pert-nosed girl in a blue dress who told him he looked like a South Seas adventurer, so tanned and tall in his khakis. He sailed back to his cabin the next day, to doze in the sun and dream of giving up everything, loading his sailboat with canned goods and heading for Tahiti. *Ah Raiatea, the mountains of Moorea, the fresh trade wind...*

But a continent and an ocean lay between him and Tahiti, and other obstacles besides. The thought was only for an hour's

dreaming, and definitely not to be acted upon. Now he was returning to New York, to his job as a junior yacht designer for the
famous old firm of Mattison & Peters.

The other car's headlights were drawing near. Blaine slowed to
sixty.

In spite of his title, there were few yachts for Blaine to design.
Old Tom Mattison took care of the conventional cruising boats. His
brother Rolf, known as the Wizard of Mystic, had an international
reputation for his ocean-racing sailboats and fast one-designs. So
what was there for a junior yacht designer to do?

Blaine drew layouts and deck plans, and handled promotion,
advertising and publicity. It was responsible work, and not without
its satisfactions. But it was not yacht designing.

He knew he should strike out on his own. But there were so many
yacht designers, so few customers. As he had told Laura, it was
rather like designing arboglasts, scorpions and catapults. Interesting
creative work, but who would buy your products?

"You could find a market for your sailboats," she had told him,
distressingly direct. "Why not make the plunge?"

He had grinned boyishly, charmingly. "Action isn't my forte. I'm
an expert on contemplation and mild regret."

"You mean you're lazy."

"Not at all. That's like saying that a hawk doesn't gallop well,
or a horse has poor soaring ability. You can't compare different
species. I'm just not the go-getter type of human. For me, dreams,
reveries, visions, and plans meant only for contemplation, never for
execution."

"I hate to hear you talk like that," she said with a sigh.

He *had* been laying it on a bit thick, of course. But there was a lot
of truth in it. He had a pleasant job, an adequate salary, a secure
position. He had an apartment in Greenwich Village, a hi-fi, a car,
a small cabin on Chesapeake Bay, a fine sloop, and the affection of
Laura and several other girls. Perhaps, as Laura somewhat tritely
expressed it, he was caught in an eddy on the current of life ... But
so what? You could observe the scenery better from a gently revolving eddy.

The other car's headlights were very near. Blaine noticed, with a
sense of shock, that he had increased speed to eighty miles an hour.

He let up on the accelerator. His car swerved freakishly,
violently, towards the oncoming headlights.

Blowout? Steering failure? He twisted hard on the steering wheel.
It wouldn't turn. His car struck the low concrete separation between
north and south lanes, and bounded high into the air. The steering
wheel came free and spun in his hands, and the engine wailed like
a lost soul.

The other car was trying to swerve, too late. They were going to meet nearly head-on.

And Blaine thought, yes, I'm one of them. I'm one of those silly bastards you read about whose cars go out of control and kill innocent people. Christ! Modern cars and modern roads and higher speeds and the same old sloppy reflexes...

Suddenly, unaccountably, the steering wheel was working again, a razor's edge reprieve. Blaine ignored it. As the other car's headlights glared across his windshield, his mood suddenly changed from regret to exultance. For a moment he welcomed the smash, lusted for it, and for pain, destruction, cruelty and death.

Then the cars came together. The feeling of exultance faded as quickly as it had come. Blaine felt a profound regret for all he had left undone, the waters unsailed, movies unseen, books unread, girls untouched. He was thrown forward. The steering wheel broke off in his hands. The steering column speared him through the chest and broke his spine as his head drove through the thick safety glass.

At that instant he knew he was dying.

An instant later he was quickly, commonly, messily, painlessly dead.

2

He woke in a white bed in a white room.

"He's alive now," someone said.

Blaine opened his eyes. Two men in white were standing over him. They seemed to be doctors. One was a small, bearded old man. The other was an ugly red-faced man in his fifties.

"What's your name?" the old man snapped.

"Thomas Blaine."

"Age?"

"Thirty-two. But—"

"Marital status?"

"Single. What—"

"Do you see?" the old man said, turning to his red-faced colleague. "Sane, perfectly sane."

"I would never have believed it," said the red-faced man.

"But of course. The death trauma has been overrated. Grossly overrated, as my forthcoming book will prove."

"Hmm. But rebirth depression—"

"Nonsense," the old man said decisively. "Blaine, do you feel all right?"

"Yes. But I'd like to know—"

"Do you see?" the old doctor said triumphantly. "Alive again, and sane. *Now* will you co-sign the report?"

"I suppose I have no choice," the red-faced man said. Both doctors left.

Blaine watched them go, wondering what they had been talking about. A fat and motherly nurse came to his bedside. "How do you feel?" she asked.

"Fine," Blaine said. "But I'd like to know—"

"Sorry," the nurse said, "no questions yet, doctor's orders. Drink this, it'll pep you up. That's a good boy. Don't worry, everything's going to be all right."

She left. Her reassuring words frightened him. What did she mean, *everything's going to be all right*? That meant something was wrong! What was it, what was wrong? What was he doing here, what had happened?

The bearded doctor returned, accompanied by a young woman. "Is he all right, doctor?" the young woman asked.

"Perfectly sane," the old doctor said. "I'd call it a good splice."

"Then I can begin the interview?"

"Certainly. Though I cannot guarantee his behaviour. The death trauma, though grossly overrated, is still capable of—"

"Yes, fine." The girl walked over to Blaine and bent over him. She was a very pretty girl, Blaine noticed. Her features were clean-cut, her skin fresh and glowing. She had long, gleaming brown hair pulled too tightly back over her small ears, and there was a faint hint of perfume about her. She should have been beautiful; but she was marred by the immobility of her features, the controlled tenseness of her slender body. It was hard to imagine her laughing or crying. It was impossible to imagine her in bed. There was something of the fanatic about her, of the dedicated revolutionary; but he suspected that her cause was herself.

"Hello, Mr. Blaine," she said. "I'm Marie Thorne."

"Hello," Blaine said cheerfully.

"Mr. Blaine," she said, "where do you suppose you are?"

"Looks like a hospital. I suppose—" He stopped. He had just noticed a small microphone in her hand.

"Yes, what do you suppose?"

She made a small gesture. Men came forward and wheeled heavy equipment around his bed.

"Go right ahead," Marie Thorne said. "Tell us what you suppose."

"To hell with that," Blaine said moodily, watching the men set up their machines around him. "What is this? What's going on?"

"We're trying to help you," Marie Thorne said. "Won't you co-operate?"

Blaine nodded, wishing she would smile. He suddenly felt very unsure of himself. Had something happened to him?

"Do you remember the accident?" she asked.

"What accident?"

"Do you remember being hurt?"

Blaine shuddered as his memory returned in a rush of spinning lights, wailing engine, impact and breakage.

"Yes. The steering wheel broke. I got it through the chest. Then my head hit."

"Look at your chest," she said softly.

Blaine looked. His chest, beneath white pyjamas, was unmarked.

"Impossible!" he cried. His own voice sounded hollow, distant, unreal. He was aware of the men around his bed talking as they bent over their machines, but they seemed like shadows, flat and without substance. Their thin, unimportant voices were like flies buzzing against a window.

"*Nice first reaction.*"

"*Very nice indeed.*"

Marie Thorne said to him, "You are unhurt."

Blaine looked at his undamaged body and remembered the accident. "I can't believe it!" he cried.

"*He's coming on perfectly.*"

"*Fine mixture of belief and incredulity.*"

Marie Thorne said, "Quiet, please. Go ahead, Mr. Blaine."

"I remember the accident," Blaine said. "I remember the smashing. I remember—dying."

"*Get that?*"

"*Hell, yes. It really plays!*"

"*Perfectly spontaneous scene.*"

"*Marvellous! They'll go wild over it!*"

She said, "A little less noise, please. Mr. Blaine, do you remember dying?"

"Yes, yes, I died!"

"*His face!*"

"*That ludicrous expression heightens the reality.*"

"*I just hope Reilly thinks so.*"

She said, "Look carefully at your body, Mr. Blaine. Here's a mirror. Look at your face."

Blaine looked, and shivered like a man in fever. He touched the mirror, then ran shaking fingers over his face.

"It isn't my face! Where's my face? Where did you put my body and face?"

He was in a nightmare from which he could never awaken. The flat shadow men surrounded him, their voices buzzing like flies against a window, tending their cardboard machines, filled with vague menace, yet strangely indifferent, almost unaware of him. Marie Thorne bent low over him with her pretty, blank face, and from her small red mouth came gentle nightmare words.

"Your body is dead, Mr. Blaine, killed in an automobile accident. You can remember its dying. But we managed to save that part of you that really counts. We saved your mind, Mr. Blaine, and have given you a new body for it."

Blaine opened his mouth to scream, and closed it again. "It's unbelievable," he said quietly.

And the flies buzzed.

"*Understatement.*"

"*Well, of course. One can't be frenetic forever.*"

"*I expected a little more scenery-chewing.*"

"*Wrongly. Understatement rather accentuates his dilemma.*"

"*Perhaps, in pure stage terms. But consider the thing realistically. This poor bastard has just discovered that he died in an automobile accident and is now reborn in a new body. So what does he say about it? He says, 'It's unbelievable.' Damn it, he's not really reacting to the shock!*"

"*He is! You're projecting!*"

"Please!" Marie Thorne said. "Go on, Mr. Blaine."

Blaine, deep in his nightmare, was hardly aware of the soft, buzzing voices. He asked, "Did I really die?"

She nodded.

"And I am really born again in a different body?"

She nodded again, waiting.

Blaine looked at her, and at the shadow men tending their cardboard machines. Why were they bothering him? Why couldn't they go pick on some other dead man? Corpses shouldn't be forced to answer questions. Death was man's ancient privilege, his immemorial pact with life, granted to the slave as well as the noble. Death was man's solace, and his right. But perhaps they had revoked that right; and now you couldn't evade your responsibilities simply by being dead.

They were waiting for him to speak. And Blaine wondered if insanity still retained its hereditary privileges. With ease he could slip over and find out.

But insanity is not granted to everyone. Blaine's self-control returned. He looked up at Marie Thorne.

"My feelings," he said slowly, "are difficult to describe. I've died, and now I'm contemplating the fact. I don't suppose any man fully believes in his own death. Deep down he feels immortal. Death seems to await others, but never oneself. It's almost as though—"

"*Let's cut it right here. He's getting analytical.*"

"I think you're right," Marie Thorne said. "Thank you very much, Mr. Blaine."

The men, solid and mundane now, their vague menace disappeared, began rolling their equipment.

"Wait—" Blaine said.

"Don't worry," she told him. "We'll get the rest of your reactions later. We just wanted to record the spontaneous part now."

"*Damn good while it lasted.*"

"*A collector's item.*"

"Wait!" Blaine cried. "I don't understand. Where am I? What happened? How—"

"I'll explain everything tomorrow," Marie Thorne said. "I'm terribly sorry, I must hurry now and edit this for Mr. Reilly."

The men and equipment were gone. Marie Thorne smiled reassuringly, and hurried away.

Blaine felt ridiculously close to tears. He blinked rapidly when the fat and motherly nurse came back.

"Drink this," said the nurse. "It'll make you sleep. That's it, take it all down like a good boy. Just relax, you had a big day, what with dying and being reborn and all."

Two big tears rolled down Blaine's cheeks.

"Dear me," said the nurse, "the cameras should be here now. Those are genuine spontaneous tears if I ever saw any. Many a tragic and spontaneous scene I've witnessed in this infirmary, believe me, and I could tell those snooty recording boys something about genuine emotion if I wanted to, and they thinking they know all the secrets of the human heart."

"Where am I?" Blaine asked drowsily. "Where is this?"

"You'd call it being in the future," the nurse said.

"Oh," said Blaine.

Then he was asleep.

3

After many hours he awoke, calm and rested. He looked at the white bed and white room, and remembered.

He had been killed in an accident and reborn in the future. There had been a doctor who considered the death trauma overrated, and men who recorded his spontaneous reactions and declared them a collector's item, and a pretty girl whose features showed a lamentable lack of emotion.

Blaine yawned and stretched. Dead. Dead at thirty-two. A pity, he thought, that this young life was snuffed in its prime. Blaine was a good sort, really, and quite promising...

He was annoyed at his flippant attitude. It was no way to react. He tried to recapture the shock he felt he should feel.

Yesterday, he told himself firmly, I was a yacht designer driving back from Maryland. Today I am a man reborn into the future. The future! Reborn!

No use, the words lacked impact. He had already grown used to the idea. One grows used to anything, he thought, even to one's death. *Especially* to one's death. You could probably chop off a man's head three times a day for twenty years and he'd grow used to it, and cry like a baby if you stopped...

He didn't care to pursue that train of thought any further.

He thought about Laura. Would she weep for him? Would she get drunk? Or would she just feel depressed at the news, and take a tranquillizer for it? What about Jane and Miriam? Would they even hear about his death? Probably not. Months later they might wonder why he never called any more.

Enough of that. All that was past. Now he was in the *future*.

But all he had seen of the future was a white bed and a white room, doctors and a nurse, recording men and a pretty girl. So far, it didn't offer much contrast with his own age. But doubtless there were differences.

He remembered magazine articles and stories he had read. Today there might be free atomic power, undersea farming, world peace, international birth control, interplanetary travel, free love, complete desegregation, a cure for all diseases, and a planned society in which men breathed deep the air of freedom.

That's what there should be, Blaine thought. But there were less pleasant possibilities. Perhaps a grim-faced Oligarch had Earth in his iron grasp, while a small, dedicated underground struggled towards freedom. Or small, gelatinous alien creatures with outlandish names might have enslaved the human race. Perhaps a new and horrible disease marched unchecked across the land, or possibly the Earth, swept of all culture by hydrogen warfare, struggled painfully back to technological civilization while human wolfpacks roamed the badlands; or a million other equally dismal things could have happened.

And yet, Blaine thought, mankind showed an historic ability to avoid the extremes of doom as well as the extremes of bliss. Chaos was forever prophesied and utopia was continually predicted, and neither came to pass.

Accordingly, Blaine expected that this future would show certain definite improvements over the past, but he expected some deteriorations as well; some old problems would be gone, but certain others would have taken their places.

"In short," Blaine said to himself, "I expect that this future will be like all other futures in comparison with their pasts. That's not very specific; but then, I'm not in the predicting *or* the prophesying business."

His thoughts were interrupted by Marie Thorne walking briskly into his room.

*   *   *

"Good morning," she said. "How do you feel?"

"Like a new man," Blaine said, with a perfectly straight face.

"Good. Would you sign this, please?" She held out a pen and a typed paper.

"You're very damned efficient," Blaine said. "What am I signing?"

"Read it," she said. "It's a release absolving us from any legal responsibility in saving your life."

"*Did* you save it?"

"Of course. How did you think you got here?"

"I didn't really think about it," Blaine admitted.

"We saved you. But it's against the law to save lives without the potential victim's written consent. There wasn't opportunity for the Rex Corporation lawyers to obtain your consent beforehand. So we'd like to protect ourselves now."

"What's the Rex Corporation?"

She looked annoyed. "Hasn't anyone briefed you yet? You're inside Rex headquarters now. Our company is as well known today as Flyier-Thiess was in your time."

"Who's Flyier-Thiess?"

"No? Ford, then?"

"Yeah, Ford. So the Rex Corporation is as well known as Ford. What does it do?"

"It manufactures Rex Power Systems," she told him, "which are used to power spaceships, reincarnation machines, hereafter drivers, and the like. It was an application of the Rex Power Systems that snatched you from your car at the moment after death and brought you into the future."

"Time travel," Blaine said. "But how?"

"That'll be hard to explain," she said. "You don't have the scientific background. But I'll try. You know that space and time are the same thing, aspects of each other."

"They are?"

"Yes. Like mass and energy. In your age, scientists knew that mass and energy were interchangeable. They were able to deduce the fission-fusion processes of the stars. But they couldn't immediately duplicate those processes, which called for vast amounts of power. It wasn't until they had the knowledge *and* the available power that they could break down atoms by fission and build up new ones by fusion."

"I know this," Blaine said. "What about time travel?"

"It followed the same pattern," she said. "For a long time we've known that space and time are aspects of the same thing. We knew that either space or time could be reduced to fundamental units and transformed into the other by a power process. We could deduce the warping of space-time in the vicinity of supernovae, and we were able to observe the disappearance of a Wolf-Rayet star when its time-conversion rate accelerated. But we had to learn a lot more. And we had to have a power source exponentially higher than you needed to set off the fusion process. When we had all this, we could interchange time units for space units—which is to say, time distances for space distances. We could then travel the distance of, say, a hundred years instead of the interchangeable distance of a hundred parsecs."

"I see, after a fashion," Blaine said. "Would you mind running through it again, slowly?"

"Later, later," she said. "Will you please sign the release?"

The paper stated that he, Thomas Blaine, agreed not to bring suit against the Rex Corporation for their unauthorized saving of his life in the year 1958 and the subsequent transporting of that life to a Receptacle in the year 2110.

Blaine signed. "Now," he said, "I'd like to know—"

He stopped. A teenage boy had come into the room holding a large poster. "Pardon me, Miss Thorne," he said, "the Art Department wants to know will this do?"

The boy held up the poster. It showed an automobile at the moment of smash-up. A gigantic stylized hand was reaching down from the sky and plucking the driver from the burning wreck. The caption read: REX DID IT!

"Not bad," Marie Thorne said, frowning judiciously. "Tell them to brighten the reds."

More people were coming into the room. And Blaine was growing angry.

"What's going on?" he asked.

"Later, later," Marie Thorne said. "Oh, Mrs. Vaness! What do you think of this poster for a teaser?"

There were a dozen people in his room now, and more coming. They clustered around Marie Thorne and the poster, ignoring Blaine completely. One man, talking earnestly to a grey-haired woman, sat down on the edge of his bed. And Blaine's temper snapped.

"Stop it!" Blaine shouted. "I'm sick of this damned rush act. What's the matter with you people, can't you behave like human beings? Now get the hell out of here!"

"Oh lord," Marie Thorne sighed, closing her eyes, "he would have to be temperamental. Ed, talk to him."

A portly, perspiring middle-aged man came to Blaine's bedside. "Mr. Blaine," he said earnestly, "didn't we save your life?"

"I suppose so," Blaine said sullenly.

"We didn't have to, you know. It took a lot of time, money and trouble to save your life. But we did it. All we want in return is the publicity value."

"Publicity value?"

"Certainly. You were saved by a Rex Power System."

Blaine nodded, understanding now why his rebirth in the future had been accepted so casually by those around him. They had taken a lot of time, money and trouble to bring it about, had undoubtedly discussed it from every possible viewpoint, and now were conscientiously exploiting it.

"I see," Blaine said. "You saved me simply in order to use me as a gimmick in an advertising campaign. Is that it?"

Ed looked unhappy. "Why put it that way? You had a life that needed saving. We had a sales campaign that needed sparking. We took care of both needs, to the mutual benefit of you and the Rex Corporation. Perhaps our motives weren't completely altruistic; would you prefer being dead?"

Blaine shook his head.

"Of course not," Ed agreed. "Your life is of value to you. Better alive today than dead yesterday, eh? Fine. Then why not show us a little gratitude? Why not give us a little co-operation?"

"I'd like to," Blaine said, "but you're moving too fast for me."

"I know," Ed said, "and I sympathize. But you know the advertising game, Mr. Blaine. Timing is crucial. Today you're news, tomorrow nobody's interested. We have to exploit your rescue right now, while it's hot. Otherwise it's valueless to us."

"I appreciate your saving my life," Blaine said, "even if it wasn't completely altruistic. I'll be glad to co-operate."

"Thank you, Mr. Blaine," Ed said. "And please, no questions for a while. You'll get the picture as we go along. Miss Thorne, it's all yours."

"Thanks, Ed," Marie Thorne said. "Now, everybody, we have received a provisional go-ahead from Mr. Reilly, so we'll continue as planned. Billy, you figure out a release for the morning papers. 'Man from Past' sort of thing."

"It's been done."

"Well? It's always news, isn't it?"

"I guess once more won't hurt. So. Man from 1988 snatched—"

"Pardon me," Blaine said. "1958."

"So from 1958 snatched from his smashed car at the moment after death and set into a host body. Brief paragraph about the host body. Then we say that Rex Power Systems performed this snatch over one hundred and fifty-two years of time. We tell 'em how many ergs of energy we burned, or whatever it is we burn. I'll check with an engineer for the right terms. OK?"

"Mention that no other power system could have done it," Joe said. "Mention the new calibration system that made it possible."

"They won't use all that."

"They might," Marie Thorne said. "Now, Mrs. Vaness. We want an article on Blaine's feelings when Rex Power Systems snatched him from death. Make it emotional. Give his first sensations in the amazing world of the future. About five thousand words. We'll handle placement."

The grey-haired Mrs. Vaness nodded. "Can I interview him now?"

"No time," Miss Thorne said. "Make it up. Thrilled, frightened, astonished, surprised at all the changes that have taken place since his time. Scientific advances. Wants to see Mars. Doesn't like the new fashions. Thinks people were happier in his own day with less gadgets and more leisure. Blaine will OK it. Won't you, Blaine?"

Blaine nodded dumbly.

"Fine. Last night we recorded his spontaneous reactions. Mike, you and the boys make that into a fifteen minute spin which the public can buy at their local Sensory Shop. Make it a real connoisseur's item for the prestige trade. But open with a short, dignified technical explanation of how Rex made the snatch."

"Gotcha," said Mike.

"Right. Mr. Brice, you'll line up some solido shows for Blaine to appear on. He'll give his reactions to our age, how it feels, how it compares to his own age. See that Rex gets a mention."

"But I don't know anything about this age!" Blaine said.

"You will," Marie Thorne told him. "All right, I think that's enough for a start. Let's get rolling. I'm going to show Mr. Reilly what we've planned so far."

She turned to Blaine as the others were leaving.

"Perhaps this seems like shabby treatment. But business is business, no matter what age you're in. Tomorrow you're going to be a well-known man, and probably a wealthy one. Under the circumstances, I don't think you have any cause for complaint."

She left. Blaine watched her go, slim and self-confident. He wondered what the penalty was, in this day and age, for striking a woman.

4

The nurse brought him lunch on a tray. The bearded doctor came in, examined him and declared him perfectly fit. There was not the slightest trace of rebirth depression, he declared, and the death trauma was obviously overrated. No reason why Blaine shouldn't be up and about.

The nurse came back with clothing, a blue shirt, brown slacks, and soft, bulbous grey shoes. The outfit, she assured him, was quite conservative.

Blaine ate with good appetite. But before dressing, he examined his new body in the full-length bathroom mirror. It was the first chance he'd had for a careful appraisal.

His former body had been tall and lean, with straight black hair and a good-humoured boyish face. In thirty-two years he had grown used to that quick, deft, easy-moving body. With good grace he had accepted its constitutional flaws, its occasional illnesses, and had glorified them into virtues, into unique properties of the personality that resided within them. For his body's limitations, far more than its capabilities, seemed to express his own particular essence.

He had been fond of that body. His new body was a shock.

It was shorter than average, heavily muscled, barrel chested, broad shouldered. It felt top-heavy, for the legs were a little short in proportion to the herculean torso. His hands were large and calloused. Blaine made a fist and gazed at it respectfully. He could probably fell an ox with a single blow, if an ox were procurable.

His face was square and bold, with a prominent jaw, wide cheekbones and a Roman nose. His hair was blond and curly. His eyes were a steely blue. It was a somewhat handsome, slightly brutal face.

"I don't like it," Blaine said emphatically. "And I hate curly blond hair."

His new body had considerable physical strength; but he had always disliked sheer physical strength. The body looked clumsy, graceless, difficult to manage. It was the kind of body that bumped into chairs and stepped on people's toes, shook hands too vigorously, talked too loudly, and sweated profusely. Clothes would always bulge and constrict this body. It would need continual hard exercise. Perhaps he would even have to diet; the body looked as though it had a slight tendency towards fat.

"Physical strength is all very well," Blaine told himself, "if one has a purpose for it. Otherwise it's just a nuisance and a distraction, like wings on a dodo."

The body was bad enough. But the face was worse. Blaine had never liked strong, harsh, rough-hewn faces. They were fine for sandhogs, army sergeant, jungle explorers and the like. But not for a man who enjoyed cultured society. Such a face was obviously incapable of subtlety of expression. All nuance, the delicate interplay of line and plane, would be lost. With this face you could grin or frown; only gross emotions would show.

Experimentally he smiled boyishly at the mirror. The result was a satyr's leer.

"I've been gypped," Blaine said bitterly.

It was apparent to him that the qualities of his present mind and his new body were opposed. Co-operation between them seemed impossible. Of course, his personality might reshape his body; on the other hand, his body might have some demands to make on his personality.

"We'll see," Blaine told his formidable body, "we'll see who's boss."

On his left shoulder was a long, jagged scar. He wondered how the body had received so grievous a wound. Then he began wondering where the body's real owner was. Could he still be lodged in the brain, lying doggo, waiting for a chance to take over?

Speculation was useless. Later, perhaps, he would find out. He took a final look at himself in the mirror.

He didn't like what he saw. He was afraid he never would.

"Well," he said at last, "you takes what you gets. Dead men can't be choosers."

That was all he could say, for the moment. Blaine turned from the mirror and began dressing.

Marie Thorne came into his room late in the afternoon. She said, without preamble, "It's off."

"Off?"

"Finished, over, through!" She glared bitterly at him, and began pacing up and down the white room. "The whole publicity campaign around you is off."

Blaine stared at her. The news was interesting; but much more interesting were the signs of emotion on Miss Thorne's face. She had been so damnably controlled, so perfectly and grotesquely businesslike. Now there was colour in her face, and her small lips were twisted bitterly.

"I've worked on this idea for two solid years," she told him. "The company's spent I don't know how many millions to bring you here. Everything's set to roll, and that damned old man says drop the whole thing."

She's beautiful, Blaine thought, but her beauty gives her no pleasure. It's a business asset, like grooming, or a good head for liquor, to be used when necessary, and even abused. Too many hands reached to Marie Thorne, he imagined, and she never took any. And when the greedy hands kept reaching she learned contempt, then coldness, and finally self-hatred.

It's a little fanciful, Blaine thought, but I'll keep it until a better diagnosis comes along.

"That damned stupid old man," Marie Thorne was muttering.

"What old man?"

"Reilly, our brilliant president."

"He decided against the publicity campaign?"

"He wants it hushed up completely. Oh God, it's just too much! Two years!"

"But why?" Blaine asked.

Marie Thorne shook her head wearily. "Two reasons, both of them stupid. First, the legal problem. I told him you'd signed the

release, and the lawyers had the rest of the problem in hand, but
he's scared. It's almost time for his reincarnation and he doesn't
want any possible legal trouble with the government. Can you
imagine it? A frightened old man running Rex! Second, he had a
talk with that silly, senile old grandfather of his, and his grandfather doesn't like the idea. And that clinched it. After two years!"
    "Just a minute," Blaine said. "Did you say his *reincarnation?*"
    "Yes. Reilly's going to try it. Personally I think he'd be smarter
to die and get it over with."
    It was a bitter statement. But Marie Thorne didn't sound bitter
making it. She sounded as though she were making a simple statement of fact.
    Blaine said, "You think he should die instead of trying for rein-
carnation?"
    "*I* would. But I forgot, you haven't been briefed. I just wish he'd
make up his mind earlier. That senile old grandfather butting in
now—"
    "Why didn't Reilly ask his grandfather earlier?" Blaine asked.
    "He did. But his grandfather wouldn't talk earlier."
    "I see. How old is he?"
    "Reilly's grandfather? He was eighty-one when he died."
    "*What?*"
    "Yes, he died about sixty years ago. Reilly's father is dead, too,
but he won't talk at all, which is a pity because he had good business
sense. Why are you staring at me, Blaine? Oh, I forgot you don't
know the set-up. It's very simple, really."
    She stood for a moment, brooding. Then she nodded emphatically,
whirled and walked to the door.
    "Where are you going?" Blaine asked.
    "To tell Reilly what I think of him! He can't do this to me!
He promised!"
    Abruptly her control returned.
    "As for you, Blaine, I suppose there's no further need of you
here. You have your life, and an adequate body in which to live it.
I suppose you can leave at any time you desire."
    "Thanks," Blaine said, as she left the room.

    Dressed in his brown slacks and blue shirt, Blaine left the
infirmary and walked down a long corridor until he reached a door.
A uniformed guard was standing beside it.
    "Excuse me," Blaine said, "does this door lead outside?"
    "Huh?"
    "Does this door lead outside the Rex Building?"
    "Yeah, of course. Outside and on to the street."
    "Thank you," Blaine hesitated. He wanted the briefing he had

had been promised but never given. He wanted to ask the guard what New York was like, and what the local customs and regulations were, and what he should see, and what he should avoid. But the guard apparently hadn't heard about the Man from the Past. He was staring pop-eyed at Blaine.

Blaine hated the idea of plunging into the New York of 2110 like this, without money or knowledge or friends, without a job or a place to stay, and wearing an uncomfortable new body. But it couldn't be helped. Pride meant something, after all. He would rather take his chances alone than ask assistance from the porcelain-hard Miss Thorne, or any of the others at Rex.

"Do I need a pass to get out?" he asked hopefully.

"Nope. Just to get back in." The guard frowned suspiciously. "Say, what's the matter with you?"

"Nothing," Blaine said. He opened the door, still not believing that they would let him leave so casually. But then, why not? He was in a world where men talked to their dead grandfathers, where there were spaceships and hereafter drivers, where they snatched a man from the past as a publicity stunt, then lightly discarded him.

The door closed. Behind him was the great grey mass of the Rex Building. Before him lay New York.

5

At first glance, the city looked like a surrealistic Baghdad. He saw squat palaces of white and blue tile, and slender red minarets, and irregularly shaped buildings with flaring Chinese roofs and spired onion domes. It looked as though an oriental fad in architecture had swept the city. Blaine could hardly believe he was in New York. Bombay perhaps, Moscow, or even Los Angeles, but not New York. With relief he saw skyscrapers, simple and direct against the curved Asiatic structures. They seemed like lonely sentinels of the New York he had known.

The streets were filled with miniature traffic. Blaine saw motor cycles and scooters, cars no bigger than Porsches, trucks the size of Buicks, and nothing larger. He wondered if this was New York's answer to congestion and air pollution. If so, it hadn't helped.

Most of the traffic was overhead. There were vane and jet operated vehicles, aerial produce trucks and one-man speedsters, helicopter taxis and floating buses marked "Skyport 2nd Level" or "Express to Montauk." Glittering dots marked the vertical and horizontal lanes within which the traffic glided, banked, turned, ascended and descended. Flashing red, green, yellow and blue lights seemed to regulate the flow. There were rules and conventions; but to Blaine's inexperienced eye it was a vast fluttering confusion.

Fifty feet overhead there was another shopping level. How did people get up there? For that matter, how did anyone live and retain his sanity in this noisy, bright, congested machine? The human density was overpowering. He felt as though he were being drowned in a sea of flesh. What was the population of this super-city? Fifteen million? Twenty million? It made the New York of 1958 look like a country village.

He had to stop and sort his impressions. But the sidewalks were crowded, and people pushed and cursed when he slowed down. There were no parks or benches in sight.

He noticed a group of people standing in a line, and took a place on the end. Slowly the line shuffled forward. Blaine shuffled with it, his head pounding dully, trying to catch his breath.

In a few moments he was in control of himself again, and slightly more respectful of his strong, phlegmatic body. Perhaps a man from the past needed just that sort of fleshy envelope if he wanted to view the future with equanimity. A low-order nervous system had its advantages.

The line shuffled silently forward. Blaine noticed that the men and women standing in it were poorly dressed, unkempt, unwashed, They shared a common look of sullen despair.

Was he in a breadline?

He tapped the shoulder of the man in front of him. "Excuse me," he said, "where is this line going?"

The man turned his head and stared at Blaine with red-rimmed eyes. "Going to the suicide booths," he said, jerking his chin towards the front of the line.

Blaine thanked him and stepped quickly out of the line. What a hell of an inauspicious way to start his first real day in the future. Suicide booths! Well, he would never enter one willingly, he could be absolutely sure of that. Things surely couldn't get *that* bad.

But what kind of a world had suicide booths? And free ones, to judge by the clientele ... He would have to be careful about accepting free gifts in this world.

Blaine walked on, gawking at the sights and slowly growing accustomed to the bright, hectic, boisterous, overcrowded city. He came to an enormous building shaped like a Gothic castle, with pennants flying from its upper battlements. On its highest tower was a brilliant green light fully visible against the fading afternoon sun.

It looked like an important landmark. Blaine stared, then noticed a man leaning against the building, lighting a thin cigar. He seemed to be the only man in New York not in a tearing hurry. Blaine approached him.

"Pardon me, sir," he said, "what is this building?"

"This," said the man, "is the headquarters of Hereafter, Incorporated." He was a tall man, very thin, with a long, mournful weatherbeaten face. His eyes were narrow and direct. His clothes hung awkwardly on him, as though he were more used to levis than tailored slacks. Blaine thought he looked like a westerner.

"Impressive," Blaine said, gazing up at the Gothic castle.

"Gaudy," the man said. "You aren't from the city, are you?"

Blaine shook his head.

"Me neither. But frankly, stranger, I thought everybody on Earth and all the planets knew about the Hereafter building. Do you mind my asking where you're from?"

"Not at all," Blaine said. He wondered if he should proclaim himself a man from the past. No, it was hardly the thing to tell a perfect stranger. The man might call a cop. He'd better be from somewhere else.

"You see," Blaine said, "I'm from—Brazil."

"Oh?"

"Yes. Upper Amazon Valley. My folks went there when I was a kid. Rubber plantation. Dad just died, so I thought I'd have a look at New York."

"I hear it's still pretty wild down there," the man said.

Blaine nodded, relieved that his story wasn't being questioned. But perhaps it wasn't a very strange story for this day and age. In any event, he had found a home.

"Myself," the man said, "I'm from Mexican Hat, Arizona. The name's Orc, Carl Orc. Blaine? Glad to meet you, Blaine. You know, I came here to cast a look around this New York and find out what they're always boasting about. It's interesting enough, but these folks are just a little too up and roaring for me, if you catch my meaning. I don't mean to say we're pokey back home. We're not. But these people bounce around like an ape with a stick in his line."

"I know just what you mean," Blaine said.

For a few minutes they discussed the jittery, frantic, compulsive habits of New Yorkers, comparing them with the sane, calm, pastoral life in Mexican Hat and the Upper Amazon Valley. These people, they agreed, just didn't know how to live.

"Blaine," said Orc, "I'm glad I ran into you. What say we get ourselves a drink?"

"Fine," Blaine said. Through a man like Carl Orc he might find a way out of his immediate difficulties. Perhaps he could get a job in Mexican Hat. He could plead Brazil and amnesia to excuse his lack of present-day knowledge.

Then he remembered that he had no money.

He started a halting explanation of how he had accidentally left his wallet in his hotel. But Orc stopped him in mid-sentence.

"Look here, Blaine," Orc said, fixing him with his narrow blue eyes, "I want to tell you something. A story like that wouldn't cut marge with most people. But I figure I'm somewhat of a judge of character. Can't say I've been wrong too often. I'm not exactly what you'd call a poor man, so what say we have the evening on me?"

"Really," Blaine said, "I couldn't—"

"Not another word," Orc said decisively. "Tomorrow evening is on you, if you insist. But right now, let us proceed to inspect the internal nocturnal movements of this edgy little old town."

It was, Blaine decided, as good as any other way of finding out about the future. After all, nothing could be more revealing than what people did for pleasure. Through games and drunkenness, man exhibits his essential attitudes towards his environment, and shows his disposition towards the questions of life, death, fate and free will. What better symbol of Rome than the circus? What better crystallization of the American West than the rodeo? Spain had its bullfights and Norway its ski-jumps. What sport, recreation or pastime would similarly reveal the New York of 2110? He would find out. And surely, to experience this in all its immediacy was better than reading about it in some dusty library, and infinitely more entertaining.

"Suppose we have a look at the Martian Quarter?" Orc asked.

"Lead away," Blaine said, well-pleased at the chance to combine pleasure with stern necessity.

Orc led the way through a maze of streets and levels, through underground arcades and overhead ramps, by foot, escalator, subway and helicab. The interlocking complexity of streets and levels didn't impress the lean Westerner. Phoenix was laid out in the same way, he said, although admittedly on a smaller scale.

They went to a small restaurant that called itself the "Red Mars", and advertised a genuine South Martian cuisine. Blaine had to confess he had never eaten Martian food. Orc had sampled it several times in Phoenix.

"It's pretty good," he told Blaine, "but it doesn't stick to your ribs. Later we'll have a steak."

The menu was written entirely in Martian, and no English translation was included. Blaine recklessly ordered the Number One Combination, as did Orc. It came, a strange-looking mess of shredded vegetables and bits of meat. Blaine tasted, and nearly dropped his fork in surprise.

"It's exactly like Chinese food!"

"Well, of course," Orc said. "The Chinese were the first on Mars, in '97 I think. So anything they eat up there is Martian food. Right?"

"I suppose so," Blaine said.

"Besides, this stuff is made with genuine Martian-grown vegetables and mutated herbs and spices. Or so they advertise."

Blaine didn't know whether to be disappointed or relieved. With good appetite he ate the C'kyo-Ourher, which tasted just like shrimp chow mein, and the Trrdxat, or egg roll.

"Why do they give it such weird names?" Blaine asked, ordering the Hggshrt for dessert.

"Man, you're really out of touch!" Orc said, laughing. "Those Martian Chinese went all the way. They translated the Martian rock-carvings and suchlike, and started to talk Martian, with a strong Cantonese accent I presume, but there wasn't no one around to tell them different. They talk Martian, dress Martian, think Martian. You call one of them a Chinese now, he'd up and hit you. He's a *Martian*, boy!"

The Hggshrt came, and turned out to be an almond cookie.

Orc paid the check. As they left, Blaine asked, "Are there many Martian laundries?"

"Hell yes. Country's filled with them."

"I thought so," Blaine said, and paid a silent tribute to the Martian Chinese and their firm grip on traditional institutions.

They caught a helicab to the Greens Club, a place that Orc's Phoenix friends had told him not to miss. This small, expensive, intimate little club was world-famous, an absolute must for any visitor to New York. For the Greens Club was unique in presenting an all-vegetable floor show.

They were given seats on a little balcony, not far from the glass-fenced centre of the club. Three levels of tables surrounded the centre, and brilliant spotlights played upon it. Behind the glass fence was what looked like a few square yards of jungle, growing in a nutrient solution. An artificial breeze stirred the plants, which were packed tight together, and varied widely in size, shape and hue.

They behaved like no plants Blaine had ever seen. They grew rapidly, fantastically, from tiny seeds and root tendrils to great shrubs and rough-barked trees, squat ferns, monstrous flowers, dripping green fungus and speckled vines; grew and quickly completed their life-cycle and fell into decay, casting forth their seeds to begin again. But no species seemed able to reproduce itself. Sports and mutants sprang from the seeds and swollen fruit, altered and adapted to the fierce environment, battled for root space below and air space above, and struggled towards the artificial suns that glowed above them. Unsuccessful shrubs quickly moulded themselves into parasites, clung to the choked trees, and discovered new adaptations clinging to them in turn. Sometimes, in a burst of creative ambition, a plant would surmount all obstacles, put down the growths around it, strangle the opposition, conquer all. But new species already grew from its body, pulled it down and squabbled over the corpse. Sometimes a blight, itself vegetable, would attack the jungle and carry everything before it in a grand crescendo of mould. But a courageous sport would at last take root in it, then another, and on went the fight. The plants changed, grew larger or smaller, transcended themselves in the struggle for survival. But no amount of determination, no cunning, no transcendence helped. No species could prevail, and every endeavour led to death.

Blaine found the spectacle disturbing. Could this fatalistic pageant of the world be the significant characteristic of 2110? He glanced at Orc.

"It's really something," Orc told him, "what these New York labs can do with quick-growing mutants. It's a freak show, of course. They just speed up the growing rate, force a contra-survival situation, throw in some radiation, and let the best plant try to win. I hear these plants use up their growth potential in about twenty hours, and have to be replaced."

"So that's where it ends," Blaine said, watching the tortured but ever-optimistic jungle. "In replacements."

"Sure," said Orc, blandly avoiding all philosophical complications. "They can afford it, at the prices they charge here. But it's freak stuff. Let me tell you about the sandplants we grow in Arizona."

Blaine sipped his whiskey and watched the jungle growing, dying and renewing itself. Orc was saying, "Right on the burning face of the desert. Fact. We've finally adapted fruit and vegetable-bearing plants to real desert conditions, without increasing their bulk water supply, and at a price which allows us to compete with the fertile areas. I tell you, boy, in another fifty years the entire concept of *fertile* is going to change. Take Mars, for example..."

They left the Greens Club and worked their way from bar to bar, towards Times Square. Orc was showing a certain difficulty in focusing, but his voice was steady as he talked about the lost Martian secret of growing on sand. Someday, he promised Blaine, we'll figure out how they produced the sandplants without the added nutrients and moisture-fixatives.

Blaine had drunk enough to put his former body into a coma twice over. But his bulky new body seemed to have an inexhaustible capacity for whiskey. It was a pleasant change, to have a body that could hold its liquor. Not, he added hastily, that such a rudimentary ability could offset the body's disadvantages.

They crossed Times Square's garish confusion and entered a bar on 44th Street. As their drinks were served, a furtive-eyed little man in a raincoat stepped up to them.

"Hey, boys," he said tentatively.

"Whatcha want, podner?" Orc asked.

"You boys out looking for a little fun?"

"You might say so," Orc said expansively. "And we can find it ourselves, thank you kindly."

The little man smiled nervously. "You can't find what *I'm* offering."

"Speak up little friend," Orc said. "What exactly are you offering?"

"Well, boys, it's—hold it! Flathats!"

Two blue-uniformed policemen entered the bar, looked around and left.

"OK," Blaine said. "What is it?"

"Call me Joe," the little man said with an ingratiating grin. "I'm a steerer for a Transplant game, friends. The best game and highest jump in town!"

"What in hell is Transplant?" Blaine asked.

Both Orc and Joe looked at him. Joe said, "Wow, friend, no insult but you must *really* be from down on the farm. Never heard of Transplant? Well I'll be griped!"

"OK, so I'm a farmboy," Blaine growled, thrusting his fierce, square, hard-planed face close to Joe's. "What is Transplant?"

"Not so loud!" Joe whispered, shrinking back. "Take it easy, farmer, I'll explain. Transplant is the new switch game, buddy. Are you tired of living? Think you've had all the kicks? Wait 'til you try Transplant. You see, farmer, folks in the know say that straight sex is pretty mouldy potatoes. Don't get me wrong, it's fine for the birds and the bees and the beasts and the brutes. It still brings a thrill to their simple animal hearts, and who are we to say they're wrong? As a means of propagating the species, old nature's little sex gimmick is still the first and the best. But for real kicks, sophisticated people are turning to Transplant.

"Transplant is democratic, friends. It gives you the big chance to switch over into someone else and feel how the other ninety-nine per cent feels. It's educational, you might say, and it takes up where straight sex leaves off. Ever get the urge to be a high-strung Latin, pal? You can, with Transplant. Ever wonder what a genuine sadist feels? Tune in with Transplant. And there's more, more, so much more! For example, why be a man all your life? You've proved your point by now, why belabour it? Why not be a woman for a while? With Transplant you can be aboard for those gorgeous moments in the life of one of our specially selected gals."

"Voyeurism," Blaine said.

"I know them big words," Joe said, "and it ain't true. This is no peeping-Tom's game. With Transplant *you are there*, right in the old corpus, moving those exotic muscles, experiencing those sensations. Ever get the urge to be a tiger, farmboy, and go loping after a lady tiger in the old mating season? We *got* a tiger, friend, and a lady tiger too. Ever ask yourself what thrill a man could possibly find in flagellation, shoe-fetishism, necrophilia, or the like? Find out with Transplant. Our catalogue of bodies reads like an encyclopedia. You can't go wrong at Transplant, friends, and our prices are set ridiculously—"

"Get out," Blaine said.

"What, buddy?"

Blaine's big hand shot out and grabbed Joe by the raincoat front. He lifted the little pusher to eye level and glared at him.

"You take your perverted little notions out of here," Blaine said. "Guys like you have been selling off-beat kicks since the days of Babylon, and guys like me haven't been buying. Get out, before I break your neck for a quick sadistic thrill."

He released him. Joe smoothed his raincoat and smiled nervously. "No offence, buddy, I'm going. Don't feel like it tonight. There's always another night. Transplant's in your future, farmboy. Why fight it?"

Blaine started to move forward, but Orc held him back. The little pusher scuttled out of the door.

"He isn't worth dropping," Orc said. "The flathats would just take you in. It's a sad, sick, dirty world, friend. Drink up."

Blaine threw down his whiskey, still seething. Transplant! If that was the characteristic amusement of 2110 he wanted no part of it. Orc was right, it was a sad, sick, dirty world. Even the whiskey was beginning to taste funny.

He grabbed at the bar for support. The whiskey tasted *very* funny. What was wrong with him? The stuff seemed to be going to his head.

Orc's arm was around his shoulder. He was saying, "Well, well, my old buddy's taken himself that one too many. Guess I'd better take him back to his hotel."

But Orc didn't know where his hotel was. He didn't even have an hotel to be taken to. Orc, that damned quick-talking straight-eyed Orc, must have put something in his drink while he was talking to Joe.

In order to roll him? But Orc knew he had no money. Why then?

He tried to shake the arm off his shoulders. It was clamped in place like an iron bar. "Don't worry," Orc was saying, "I'll take care of you, old buddy."

The bar-room revolved lazily around Blaine's head. He had a sudden realization that he was going to find out a great deal about 2110 by the dubious method of direct experience. Too much, he suspected. Perhaps a dusty library would have been better after all. The bar-room began to revolve more rapidly. Blaine passed out.

6

He recovered consciousness in a small, dimly lighted room with no furniture, no doors or windows, and only a single screened ventilation outlet in the ceiling. The floors and walls were thickly padded, but the padding hadn't been washed in a long time. It stank.

Blaine sat up, and two red-hot needles stabbed him through the eyes. He lay down again.

"Relax," a voice said. "Them knock drops take a while to wear off."

He was not alone in the padded room. There was a man sitting in a corner, watching him. The man was wearing only shorts. Glancing at himself, Blaine saw that he was similarly dressed.

He sat up slowly and propped himself against a wall. For a moment he was afraid his head would explode. Then, as the needles drove viciously in, he was afraid it wouldn't.

"What is this?" he asked.

"End of the line," the man said cheerfully. "They boxed you, just like me. They boxed you and brought you in like fabrit. Now all they got to do is crate you and label you."

Blaine couldn't understand what the man was saying. He was in no mood to decipher 2110 slang. Clutching his head, he said, "I don't have any money. Why did they box me?"

"Come off it," the man said. "Why *would* they box you? They want your body, man!"

"My body?"

"Right. For a host."

A host body, Blaine thought, such as he was now occupying. Well of course. Naturally. It was obvious when you came to think about it. This age needed a supply of host bodies for various and sundry purposes. But how do you get a host body? They don't grow on trees, nor can you dig for them. You get them from people. Most people wouldn't take kindly to selling their own bodies; life is so meaningless without one. So how to fill the supply?

Easy. You pick out a sucker, dope him, hide him away, extract his mind, then take his body.

It was an interesting line of speculation, but Blaine couldn't continue it any longer. It seemed as though his head had finally decided to explode.

Later, the hangover subsided. Blaine sat up and found a sandwich in front of him on a paper plate, and a cup of some dark beverage.

"It's safe to eat," the man told him. "They take good care of us. I
hear the going black market price for a body is close to four
thousand dollars."

"Black market?"

"Man, what's wrong with you? Wake up! You know there's a
black market in bodies just like there's an open market in bodies."

Blaine sipped the dark beverage, which turned out to be coffee.
The man introduced himself as Ray Melhill, a flow-control man off
the spaceship *Bremen*. He was about Blaine's age, a compact, red-
headed, snub-nosed man with slightly protruding teeth. Even in his
present predicament he carried himself with a certain jaunty
assurance, the unquenchable confidence of a man for whom something always turns up. His freckled skin was very white except for a
small red blotch on his neck, the result of an old radiation burn.

"I should of known better," Melhill said. "But we'd been transit-
ing for three months on the asteroid run and I wanted a spree. I
would of been fine if I'd stuck with the boys, but we got separated.
So I wound up in a dog kennel with a greasy miranda. She knocked
my drink and I wound up here."

Melhill leaned back, his hands locked behind his head. "Me, of all
people! I was always telling the boys to watch out. Stick with the gang
I was always telling them. You know, I don't mind the thought of
dying so much. I just hate the idea of those bastards giving my
body to some dirty fat decrepit old slob so he can play around for
another fifty years. That's what kills me, the thought of that fat
old slob wearing my body. Christ!"

Blaine nodded sombrely.

"So that's my tale of woe," Melhill said, growing cheerful again.
"What's yours?"

"Mine's a pretty long one," Blaine said, "and a trifle wild in spots.
Do you want to hear it all?"

"Sure. Plenty of time. I hope."

"OK. It starts in the year 1958. Wait, don't interrupt me. I was
driving my car..."

When he had finished, Blaine leaned back against the padded wall
and took a deep breath. "Do you believe me?" he asked.

"Why not? Nothing so new about time travel. It's just illegal and
expensive. And those Rex boys would pull anything."

"The girls, too," Blaine said, and Melhill grinned.

They sat in companionable silence for a while. Then Blaine
asked, "So they're going to use us for host bodies?"

"That's the score."

"When?"

"When a customer totters in. I've been here a week, close as I can figure. Either of us might be taken any second. Or it might not come for another week or two."

"And they just wipe our minds out?"

Melhill nodded.

"But that's murder!"

"It sure is," Melhill agreed. "Hasn't happened yet, though. Maybe the flathats will pull a raid."

"I doubt it."

"Me too. Have you got hereafter insurance? Maybe you'll survive after death."

"I'm an atheist," Blaine said. "I don't believe in that stuff."

"So am I. But life after death is a fact."

"Get off it," Blaine said sourly.

"It is! Scientific fact!"

Blaine stared hard at the young spacemen. "Ray," he said, "how about filling me in? Brief me on what's happened since 1958."

"That's a big order," Melhill said, "and I'm not what you'd call an educated guy."

"Just give me an idea. What's this hereafter stuff? And reincarnation and host bodies? What's *happening*?"

Melhill leaned back and took a deep breath. "Well, let's see. 1958. They put a ship on the moon somewhere around 1960, and landed on Mars about ten years later. Then we had that quickie war with Russia over the asteroids—strictly a deep-space affair. Or was it with China?"

"Never mind," Blaine said. "What about reincarnation and life after death?"

"I'll try to give it to you like they give it to me in high school. I had a course called Survey of Psychic Survival, but that was a long time ago. Let's see." Melhill frowned in deep concentration. "Quote. 'Since earliest times man has sensed the presence of an invisible spirit world, and has suspected that he himself will participate in that world after the death of his body.' I guess you know all about that early stuff. The Egyptians and Chinese and the European alchemists and those. So I'll skip to Rhine. He lived in your time. He was investigating psychic phenomena at Duke. Ever hear of him?"

"Sure," Blaine said. "What did he discover?"

"Nothing, really. But he got the ball rolling. Then Kralski took over the work at Vilna, and shoved it ahead some. That was 1987, the year the Pirates won their first World Series. Around 2000 there was Von Leddner. Outlined the general theory of the hereafter, but didn't have any proofs. And finally we come to Professor Michael Vanning.

"Professor Vanning is the boy who pinned it all down. He *proved* that people survive after death. Contacted them, talked with them, recorded them, all that stuff. Offered absolute sure-enough concrete scientific proof of life after death. So of course there were big arguments about it, a lot of religious talk. Controversy. Headlines. A big-time professor from Harvard named James Archer Flynn set out to prove the whole thing was a hoax. He and Vanning argued back and forth for years.

"By this time Vanning was an old man and decided to take the plunge. He sealed a lot of stuff in a safe, hid stuff here and there, scattered some code words and promised to come back, like Houdini promised but didn't. Then—"

"Pardon me," Blaine interrupted, "if there *is* life after death, why didn't Houdini come back?"

"It's very simple, but please, one thing at a time. Anyhow, Vanning killed himself, leaving a long suicide note about man's immortal spirit and the indomitable progress of the human race. It's reprinted in a lot of anthologies. Later they found out it was ghost-written, but that's another story. Where was I?"

"He suicided."

"Right. And damned if he didn't contact Professor James Archer Flynn after dying and tell him where to find all that hidden stuff, the code words, and so forth. That clinched it, buddy. Life after death was *in*."

Melhill stood up, stretched, and sat down again. "The Vanning Institute," he said, "warned everybody against hysteria. But hysteria there was. The next fifteen years are known as the Crazy Forties."

Melhill grinned and licked his lips. "Wish I'd been around then. Everybody just sort of let go. 'Doesn't matter what you do,' the jingle ran, 'pie in the sky is waitin' for you.' Saint or sinner, bad or good, everybody gets a slice. The murderer walks into the hereafter just like the archbishop. So live it up, boys and girls, enjoy the flesh on Earth while you're here, 'cause you'll get plenty of spirit after death. Yep, and they really lived it up. Anarchy it was. A new religion popped up calling itself 'Realization'. It started telling people that they owed it to themselves to experience *everything*, good or bad, fair and foul, because the hereafter was just a long remembrance of what you did on Earth. So *do* it, they said, that's what you're put on Earth for, *do* it, or you'll be short-changed in the after-life. Gratify every desire, satisfy every lust, explore your blackest depths. Live high, die high. It was wacky. The real fanatics formed torture clubs, and wrote encyclopedias on pain, and collected tortures like a housewife would collect recipes. At each meeting, a member would voluntarily present himself as a victim, and they'd kill him in the most excruciating damned ways they could find. They wanted to experience the absolute most in pleasure and pain. And I guess they did.

Melhill wiped his forehead and said, more sedately, "I've done a little reading on the Crazy Years."

"So I see," Blaine said.

"It's sort of interesting stuff. But then came the crusher. The Vanning Institute had been experimenting all this time. Around 2050, when the Crazy Years were in full swing, they announced that there was a hereafter, sure enough; *but not for everyone.*"

Blaine blinked, but made no comment.

"A real crusher. The Vanning Institute said they had certain proof that only about one person in a million got into the hereafter. The rest, the millions and millions, just went out like a light when they died. Pouf! No more. No afterlife. Nothing."

"Why?" Blaine asked.

"Well, Tom, I'm none too clear on that part myself," Melhill told him. "If you asked me something about flow-mechanics, I could really tell you something; but psychic theory isn't my field. So try to stick with me while I struggle through this."

He rubbed his forehead vigorously. "What survives or doesn't survive after death is the mind. People have been arguing for thousands of years about what a mind is, and where and how it interacts with the body, and so forth. We haven't got all the answers, but we do have some working definitions. Nowadays, the mind is considered a high-tension energy web that emanates from the body, is modified by the body, and itself modifies the body. Got that?"

"I think so. Go on."

"So, the way I got it, the mind and body interact and intermodify. But the mind can also exist independently of the body. According to a lot of scientists, the independent mind is the next stage of evolution. In a million years, they say, we won't even need a body except maybe for a brief incubation period. Personally I don't think this damned race will survive another million years. It damn well doesn't deserve to."

"At the moment I agree with you," Blaine said. "But get back to the hereafter."

"We've got this high-tension energy web. When the body dies, that web *should* be able to go on existing, like a butterfly coming out of a cocoon. Death is simply the process that hatches the mind from the body. But it doesn't work that way because of the death trauma. Some scientists think the death trauma is nature's ejecting mechanism, to get the mind free of the body. But it works too hard and louses up everything. Dying is a tremendous psychic shock, and most of the time the energy web gets disrupted, ripped all to hell. It can't pull itself together, it dissipates, and you're but completely dead."

Blaine said, "So that's why Houdini didn't come back."

"Him and most others. Right. A lot of people did some heavy thinking, and that ended the Crazy Years. The Vanning Institute went on working. They studied Yoga and stuff like that, but on a scientific basis. Some of those Eastern religions had the right idea, you know. Strengthen the mind. That's what the Institute wanted; a way to strengthen the energy web so it would survive the death process."

"And they found it?"

"In spades. Along about that time they changed their name to Hereafter, Inc."

Blaine nodded. "I passed their building today. Hey, wait a minute! You say they solved the mind strengthening problem? Then no one dies! Everyone survives after death!"

Melhill grinned sardonically. "Don't be a farmer, Tom. You think they give it away free? Not a chance. It's a complex electrochemical treatment, pal, and they charge for it. They charge *plenty*."

"So only the rich go to heaven," Blaine said.

"What else did you expect? Can't have just *anyone* crashing in."

"Sure, sure," Blaine said. "But aren't there other ways, other mind-strengthening disciplines? What about Yoga? What about Zen?"

"They work," Melhill said. "There are at least a dozen government tested and approved home-survival courses. Trouble is, it takes about twenty years of really hard work to become an adept. That's not for the ordinary guy. Nope, without the machines to help you, you're dead."

"And only Hereafter, Inc. has the machines?"

"There's one or two others, the Afterlife Academy and Heaven, Ltd., but the price stays about the same. The government's getting to work on some death-survival insurance, but it won't help us."

"I guess not," Blaine said. The dream, for a moment, had been dazzling; a relief from mortal fears; the rational certainty of a continuance and existence after the body's death; the knowledge of an uninterrupted process of growth and fulfilment for his personality to its own limits—not the constricting limits of the frail fleshy envelope that heredity and chance had imposed on him.

But that was not to be. His mind's desire to expand was to be checked, rudely, finally. Tomorrow's promises were forever not for today.

"What about reincarnation and host bodies?" he asked.

"You should know," Melhill told him. "They reincarnated you and put you in a host. There's nothing complicated about mind-switching, as the Transplant operators will gladly tell you. Transplant is only temporary occupancy, however, and doesn't involve full dislodgement of the original mind. Hosting is for keeps. First, the original mind must be wiped out. Second, it's a dangerous game for the mind attempting to enter the host body. Sometimes, you see, that mind can't penetrate the host and breaks itself up trying. Hereafter conditioning often won't stand up under a reincarnation attempt. If the mind doesn't make it into the host—pouf!"

Blaine nodded, now realizing why Marie Thorne had thought it better for Reilly to die. Her advice had been entirely in his best interests.

He asked, "Why would any man with hereafter insurance still make the attempt at reincarnation?"

"Because some old guys are afraid of dying," Melhill said. "They're afraid of the hereafter, scared of that spirit stuff. They want to stay right here on Earth where they know what's going on. So they buy a body legally on the open market, if they can find a good one. If not, they buy one on the black market. One of *our* bodies, pal."

"The bodies on the open market are offered for sale voluntarily, then?"

Melhill nodded.

"But who would sell his body?"

"A very poor guy, obviously. By law he's supposed to receive compensation in the form of hereafter insurance for his body. In actual fact, he takes what he can get."

"A man would have to be crazy!"

"You think so?" Melhill asked. "Today like always, the world is filled with unskilled, sick, disease-ridden and starving people. And like always, they all got families. Suppose a guy wants to buy food for his kids? His body is the only thing of value he has to sell. Back in your time he didn't have anything to sell."

"Perhaps so," Blaine said. "But no matter how bad things got, I'd never sell my body."

Melhill laughed with good humour. "Stout fellow! But Tom, they're taking it for nothing!"

Blaine could think of no answer for that.

7

Time passed slowly in the padded cell. Blaine and Melhill were given books and magazines. They were fed often and well, out of paper cups and plates. They were closely watched, for no harm must come to their highly marketable bodies.

They were kept together for companionship; solitary men sometimes go insane, and insanity can cause irreparable damage to the valuable brain cells. They were even granted the right to exercise, under strict supervision, to relieve boredom and to keep their bodies in shape for future owners.

Blaine began to experience an exceeding fondness for the sturdy, thick-set, well-muscled body he had inhabited so recently, and from which he would be parted so soon. It was really an excellent body, he decided, a body to be proud of. True, it had no particular grace; but grace could be overrated. To counterbalance that lack, he suspected the body was not prone to hay fever like the former body he had tenanted; and its teeth were very sound.

On the whole, all considerations of mortality aside, it was not a body to be given up lightly.

One day, after they had eaten, a padded section of wall swung away. Looking in, protected by steel bars, was Carl Orc.

"Howdy," said Orc, tall, lean, direct-eyed, angular in his city clothes, "how's my Brazilian buddy?"

"You bastard," Blaine said, with a deep sense of the inadequacy of words.

"Them's the breaks," Orc said. "You boys gettin' enough to eat?"

"You and your ranch in Arizona!"

"I've got one under lease," Orc said. "Mean to retire there some day and raise sandplants. I reckon I know more about Arizona than many a native-born son. But ranches cost money, and hereafter insurance costs money. A man does what he can."

"And a vulture does what *he* can," Blaine said.

Orc sighed deeply. "Well, it's a business, and I guess it's no worse than some others I could think of if I set my mind to it kinda hard. It's a wicked world we live in. I'll probably regret all this sometime when I'm sitting on the front porch of my little desert ranch."

"You'll never get there," Blaine said.

"I won't?"

"No. One night a mark is going to catch you spiking his drink. You're going to end in the gutter, Orc, with your head caved in. And that'll be the end of you."

"Only the end of my body," Orc corrected. "My soul will march on to that sweet life in the by and by. I've paid my money, boy, and heaven's my next home!"

"You don't deserve it!"

Orc grinned, and even Melhill couldn't conceal a smile. Orc said, "My poor Brazilian friend, there's no question of *deserving*. You should know better than that! Life after death just isn't for the meek and humble little people, no matter how worthy they are. It's the bright lad with the dollar in his pocket and his eyes open for number one whose soul marches on after death."

"I can't believe it," Blaine said. "It isn't fair, it isn't just."

"You're an idealist," Orc said, interestedly, as though he were studying the world's last moa.

"Call it what you like. Maybe you'll get your hereafter, Orc. But I think there's a little corner of it where you'll burn forever!"

Orc said, "There's no scientific evidence of hell-fire But there's a lot we don't know about the hereafter. Maybe I'll burn. And maybe there's even a factory up there in the blue where they'll reassemble your shattered mind ... But let's not argue. I'm sorry, I'm afraid the time's come."

Orc walked quickly away. The steel-barred door swung open, and five men marched into the room.

"No!" Melhill screamed.

They closed in on the spaceman. Expertly they avoided his swinging fists and pinioned his arms. One of them pushed a gag in his mouth. They started to drag him out of the room.

Orc appeared in the doorway, frowning. "Let go of him," he said. The men released Melhill.

"You idiots got the wrong man," Orc told them. "It's *that* one." He pointed at Blaine.

Blaine had been trying to prepare himself for the loss of his friend. The abrupt reversal of fortune caught him open-mouthed and unready. The men seized him before he had time to react.

"Sorry," Orc said, as they led Blaine out. "The customer specified your particular build and complexion."

Blaine suddenly came to life and tried to wrench free. "I'll kill you!" he shouted at Orc. "I swear it, I'll kill you!"

"Don't damage him," Orc said to the men, wooden-faced.

A rag was pushed over his mouth and nose, and Blaine smelled something sickeningly sweet. Chloroform, he thought. His last recollection was of Melhill, his face ashen, standing at the barred door.

8

Thomas Blaine's first act of consciousness was to find out whether he was still Thomas Blaine, and still occupying his own body. The proof was there, apparent in the asking. They hadn't wiped out his mind yet.

He was lying on a divan, fully dressed. He sat up and heard the sound of footsteps outside, coming towards the door.

They must have overestimated the strength of the chloroform! He still had a chance!

He moved quickly behind the door. It opened, and someone walked through. Blaine stepped out and swung.

He managed to check the blow. But there was still plenty of force left when his big fist struck Marie Thorne on the side of her shapely chin.

He carried her to the divan. In a few minutes she recovered and looked at him.

"Blaine," she said, "you're an idiot."

"I didn't know who it was," Blaine said. Even as he said it he realized it wasn't true. He *had* recognized Marie Thorne a fractional instant before the blow was irretrievably launched; and his well-machined, responsive body could have recalled the punch even then. But an unperceived, uncontrollable fury had acted beneath his sane, conscious, morally aware level; fury had cunningly used urgency to avoid responsibility; had seized the deceiving instant to smash down the cold and uncaring Miss Thorne.

That act hinted at something Blaine didn't care to know about himself. He said, "Miss Thorne, who did you buy my body for?"

She glared at him. "I bought it for you, since you obviously couldn't take care of it yourself."

So he wasn't going to die after all. No fat slob was going to inherit his body, scattering his mind to the wind. Good! He wanted very much to live. But he wished anyone but Marie Thorne had saved him.

"I might have done better if I'd known how things work here," Blaine said.

"I was going to explain. Why didn't you wait?"

"After the way you talked to me?"

"I'm sorry if I was brusque," she said. "I was quite upset after Mr. Reilly cancelled the publicity campaign. But couldn't you understand that? If I'd been a man—"

"You aren't a man," Blaine reminded her.

"What difference does it make? I suppose you have some strange old-fashioned ideas about woman's role and status."

"I don't consider them strange," Blaine said.

"Of course not." She fingered her jaw, which was discoloured and slightly swollen. "Well, shall we consider ourselves even? Or do you want another clout at me?"

"One was enough, thank you," Blaine said.

She stood up, somewhat unsteadily. Blaine put an arm around her to steady her, and was momentarily disconcerted. He had visualized that trim body was whipcord and steel; but in fact it was flesh, firm, resilient, and surprisingly soft. So close, he could see stray hairs escaping her tight coiffure, and a tiny mole on her forehead near the hairline. At that moment Marie Thorne ceased as an abstraction for him, and took shape as a human being.

"I can stand by myself," she said.

After a long moment, Blaine released her.

"Under the circumstances," she said, looking at him steadily, "I think our relationship should remain on a strictly business level."

Wonder after wonder! *She* had suddenly begun viewing *him* as a human being too; she was aware of him as a man, and disturbed by it. The thought gave him great pleasure. It was not, he told himself, that he liked Marie Thorne, or even desired her particularly. But he wanted very much to throw her off balance, scratch enamel off the façade, jar that damnable poise.

He said, "Why of course, Miss Thorne."

"I'm glad you feel that way," she told him. "Because frankly, you're not my type."

"What is your type?"

"I like tall, lean men," she said. "Men with a certain grace, ease and sophistication."

"But—"

"Shall we have lunch?" she said easily. "Afterwards, Mr. Reilly would like a word with you. I believe he has a proposal to make."

He followed her out of the room, raging inwardly. Had she been making fun of him? Tall, lean, graceful, sophisticated men! Damn it, that's what he had been! And under this beefy blond wrestler's body he still was, if only she had eyes to see it!

And who was jarring who's poise?

As they sat down at a table in the Rex executive dining-room, Blaine suddenly said, "Melhill!"

"What?"

"Ray Melhill, the man I was locked up with! Look, Miss Thorne, could you possibly buy him, too? I'll pay for it as soon as I can. We were locked up together. He's a damned nice guy."

She looked at him curiously. "I'll see what I can do."

She left the table. Blaine waited, rubbing his hands together, wishing he had Carl Orc's neck between them. Marie Thorne returned in a few minutes.

"I'm very sorry," she said. "I contacted Orc. Mr. Melhill was sold an hour after you were removed. I really am sorry. I didn't know."

"It's all right," Blaine said. "I think I'd like a drink."

9

Mr. Reilly sat erect and almost lost in a great, soft, thronelike chair. He was a tiny, bald, spiderlike old man. His wrinkled translucent skin was stretched tight across his skull and clawed hands, and bone and tendon showed clearly through the leathery, shrunken flesh. Blaine had the impression of blood coursing sluggishly through the brittle, purple varicosed veins, threatening momentarily to stop. Yet Reilly's posture was firm, and his eyes were lucid in his humorous monkey's face.

"So this is our man from the past!" Mr. Reilly said. "Please be seated, sir. You too, Miss Thorne. I was just discussing you with my grandfather, Mr. Blaine."

Blaine glanced around, almost expecting to see the fifty-years-dead grandfather looming spectrally over him. But there was no sign of him in the ornate, high-ceilinged room.

"He's gone now," Mr. Reilly explained. "Poor grandfather can maintain an ectoplasmic state for only a brief time. But even so, he's better off than most ghosts."

Blaine's expression must have changed, for Reilly asked, "Don't you believe in ghosts, Mr. Blaine?"

"I'm afraid I don't."

"Of course not. I suppose the word has unfortunate connotations for your twentieth-century mind. Clanking chains, skeletons, all that nonsense. But words change their meaning, and even reality is altered as mankind alters and manipulates nature."

"I see," Blaine said politely.

"You consider that doubletalk," Mr. Reilly said good-naturedly. "It wasn't meant to be. Consider the manner in which words change their meaning. In the twentieth century, 'atoms' became a catch-all word for imaginative writers with their 'atom-guns' and 'atom-powered ships'. An absurd word, which any level-headed man would do well to ignore, just as you level-headedly ignore 'ghosts'. Yet a few years later, 'atoms' conjured a picture of very real and imminent doom. No level-headed man could ignore the word!"

Mr. Reilly smiled reminiscently. "'Radiation' changed from a dull textbook term to a source of cancerous ulcers. 'Space-sickness' was an abstract and unloaded term in your time. But in fifty years it meant hospitals filled with twisted bodies. Words tend to change, Mr. Blaine, from an abstract, fanciful, or academic use to a functional, realistic, everyday use. It happens when manipulation catches up with theory."

"And ghosts?"

"The process has been similar. Mr. Blaine, you're old-fashioned! You'll simply have to change your concept of the word."

"It'll be difficult," Blaine said.

"But necessary. Remember, there was always a lot of evidence in their favour. The prognosis for their existence, you might say, was favourable. And when life after death became fact instead of wishful thinking, ghosts became fact as well."

"I think I'll have to see one first," Blaine said.

"Undoubtedly you will. But enough. Tell me, how does our age suit you?"

"So far, not too well," Blaine said.

Reilly cackled gleefully. "Nothing endearing about body snatchers, eh? But you shouldn't have left the building, Mr. Blaine. It was not in your best interests, and certainly not in the company's best interests."

"I'm sorry, Mr. Reilly," Marie Thorne said. "That was my fault."

Reilly glanced at her, then turned back to Blaine. "It's a pity, of course. You should, in all honesty, have been left to your destiny in 1958. Frankly, Mr. Blaine, your presence here is something of an embarrassment to us."

"I regret that."

"My grandfather and I agreed, belatedly I fear, against using you for publicity. The decision should have been made earlier. Still, it's made now. But there may *be* publicity, in spite of our desires. There's even a possibility of the government taking legal action against the corporation."

"Sir," Marie Thorne said, "the lawyers are confident of our position."

"Oh, we won't go to jail," Reilly said. "But consider the publicity. *Bad* publicity! Rex must stay respectable, Miss Thorne. Hints of scandal, innuendoes of illegality ... No, Mr. Blaine should not be here in 2110, a walking proof of bad judgment. Therefore, sir, I'd like to make you a business proposition."

"I'm listening," Blaine said.

"Suppose Rex buys you hereafter insurance, thus ensuring your life after death? Would you consent to suicide?"

Blaine blinked rapidly for a moment. "No."

"Why not?" Reilly asked.

For a moment, the reason seemed self-evident. What creature consents to take its own life? Unhappily, man does. So Blaine had to stop and sort his thoughts.

"First of all," he said, "I'm not fully convinced about this hereafter."

"Suppose we convince you," Mr. Reilly said. "Would you suicide then?"

"No!"

"But how shortsighted! Mr. Blaine, consider your position. This age is alien to you, inimical, unsatisfactory. What kind of work can you do? Who can you talk with, and about what? You can't even walk the streets without being in deadly peril of your life."

"That won't happen again," Blaine said. "I didn't know how things worked here."

"But it will! You can never know how things work here! Not really. You're in the same position a caveman would be, thrown haphazardly into your own 1958. He'd think himself capable enough, I suppose, on the basis of his experience with sabre-tooth tigers and hairy mastodons. Perhaps some kind soul would even warn him about gangsters. But what good would it do? Would it save him from being run over by a car, electrocuted on a subway track, asphyxiated by a gas stove, falling through an elevator shaft, cut to pieces on a power saw, or breaking his neck in the bathtub? You have to be born to those things in order to walk unscathed among them. And even so, these things happened to people in your age when they relaxed their attention for a moment! How much more likely would our caveman be to stumble?"

"You're exaggerating the situation," Blaine said, feeling a light perspiration form on his forehead.

"Am I? The dangers of the forest are as nothing to the dangers of the city. And when the city becomes a super-city—"

"I won't suicide," Blaine said. "I'll take my chances. Let's drop the subject."

"Why can't you be reasonable?" Mr. Reilly asked petulantly. "Kill yourself now and save us all a lot of trouble. I can outline your future for you if you don't. Perhaps, by sheer nerve and animal cunning, you'll survive for a year. Even two. It won't matter, in the end you'll suicide anyhow. You're a suicide type. Suicide is written all over you—you were born for it, Blaine! You'll kill yourself wretchedly in a year or two, slip out of your maimed flesh with relief—but with no hereafter to welcome your tired mind."

"You're crazy!" Blaine cried.

"I'm never wrong about suicide types," Mr. Reilly said quietly. "I can always spot them. Grandfather agrees with me. So if you'll only—"

"No," Blaine said. "I won't kill myself. I'm afraid you'll have to hire it done."

"That's not my way," Mr. Reilly said. "I won't coerce you. But come to my reincarnation this afternoon. Get a glimpse of the hereafter. Perhaps you'll change your mind."

Blaine hesitated, and the old man grinned at him.

"No danger, I promise you, and no tricks! Did you fear I might steal your body? I selected my host months ago, from the open market. Frankly, I wouldn't *have* your body. You see, I wouldn't be comfortable in anything so gross."

The interview was over. Marie Thorne led Blaine out.

10

The reincarnation room was arranged like a small theatre. It was often used, Blaine learned, for company lectures and educational programmes on an executive level. Today the audience had been kept small and select. The Rex board of directors was present, five middle-aged men sitting in the back row and talking quietly among themselves. Near them was a recording secretary. Blaine and Marie Thorne sat in front, as far from the directors as possible.

On the raised stage, under white floodlights, the reincarnation apparatus was already in place. There were two sturdy armchairs equipped with straps and wires. Between the chairs was a large glossy black machine. Thick wires connected the machine to the chair, and gave Blaine the uneasy feeling that he was going to witness an execution. Several technicians were bent over the machine, making final adjustments. Standing near them was the bearded old doctor and his red-faced colleague.

Mr. Reilly came on the stage, nodded to the audience and sat down in one of the chairs. He was followed by a man in his forties with a frightened, pale, determined face. This was the host, the present possessor of the body that Mr. Reilly had contracted for. The host sat down in the other chair, glanced quickly at the audience and looked down at his hands. He seemed embarrassed. Perspiration beaded his upper lip, and the armpits of his jacket were stained black. He didn't look at Reilly, nor did Reilly look at him.

Another man came on the stage, bald and earnest-looking, wearing a dark suit with a cleric's collar and carrying a little black book. He began a whispered conversation with the two seated men.

"Who's that?" Blaine asked.

"Father James," Marie Thorne told him. "He's a clergyman of the Church of the Afterlife."

"What's that?"

"It's a new religion. You know about the Crazy Years? Well, during that time there was a great religious controversy..."

The burning question of the 2040's was the spiritual status of the hereafter. It became even worse after Hereafter, Inc. announced the advent of the *scientific* hereafter. The corporation tried desperately hard to avoid any religious involvement; but involvement couldn't very well be avoided. Most churchmen felt that science was unfairly pre-empting their territory. Hereafter, Inc., whether they liked it or not, was considered the spokesman for a new scientific religious position: That salvation lay, not through religious, moral or ethical considerations, but through an applied, impersonal, invariant scientific principle.

Convocations, meetings and congresses were held to decide the burning question. Some groups adopted the view that the newly revealed scientific hereafter was obviously *not* heaven, salvation, nirvana or paradise; because the soul was not involved.

Mind, they held, is not synonymous with soul; nor is the soul contained in or a part of the mind. Granted, science had found a means of extending the existence of one portion of the mind-body entity. That was fine, but it didn't affect the soul at all, and certainly didn't mean immortality or heaven or nirvana or anything like that. The *soul* could not be affected by scientific manipulation. And the soul's disposition after the eventual and inevitable death of the mind in its scientific hereafter would be in accordance with traditional moral, ethical and religious practices.

"Wow!" Blaine said. "I think I get what you mean. They were trying to achieve a co-existence between science and religion. But wasn't their reasoning a little subtle for some people?"

"Yes," Marie Thorne said, "even though they explained it much better than I've done, and backed it up with all sorts of analogies. But that was only one position. Others didn't attempt co-existence. They simply declared that the scientific hereafter was sinful. And one group solved the problem by joining the scientific position and declaring that the soul *is* contained in the mind."

"I suppose that would be the Church of the Afterlife?"

"Yes. They splintered off from other religions. According to them, the mind contains the soul, and the hereafter is the soul's rebirth after death, with no spiritual ifs and buts."

"That's keeping up with the times," Blaine said. "But morality—"

"In their view, this didn't dispense with morality. The Afterlifers say that you can't impose morals and ethics on people by a system of spiritual rewards and punishments; and if you could, you shouldn't. They say that morality must be good in its own right, first in terms of the social organism, second in terms of the individual man's best good."

To Blaine this seemed a lot to ask of morality. "I suppose it's a popular religion?" he asked.

"Very popular," Marie Thorne answered.

Blaine wanted to ask more, but Father James had begun speaking.

"William Fitzsimmons," the clergyman said to the host, "you have come to this place of your own free will, for the purpose of discontinuing your existence upon the earthly plane and resuming it upon the spiritual plane?"

"Yes, Father," the pale host whispered.

"And the proper scientific instrumentality has been performed so that you may continue your existence upon the spiritual plane?"

"Yes, Father."

Father James turned to Reilly. "Kenneth Reilly, you have come to this place of your own free will for the purpose of continuing your existence upon Earth in the body of William Fitzsimmons?"

"Yes, Father," Reilly said, small and hard-faced.

"And you have made possible for William Fitzsimmons an entrance into the hereafter; and have paid a sum of money to Fitzsimmons' heirs; and have paid the government tax involved in transactions of this kind?"

"Yes, Father," Reilly said.

"All these things being so," Father James said, "no crime is involved, civic or religious. Here there is no taking of life, for the life and personality of William Fitzsimmons continues unabated in the hereafter, and the life and personality of Kenneth Reilly continues unabated upon Earth. Therefore, let the reincarnation proceed!"

To Blaine it seemed a hideous mixture of wedding ceremony and execution. The smiling clergyman withdrew. Technicians secured the men to their chairs, and attached electrodes to their arms, legs and foreheads. The theatre grew very still, and the Rex directors leaned forward expectantly in their seats.

"Go ahead," Reilly said, looking at Blaine and smiling slightly.

The chief technician turned a dial on the black machine. It hummed loudly, and the floodlights dimmed. Both men jerked convulsively against the straps, then slumped back.

Blaine whispered. "They're murdering that poor Fitzsimmons bastard."

"That poor bastard," Marie Thorne told him, "knew exactly what he was doing. He's thirty-seven years old and he's been a failure all his life. He's never been able to hold a job for long, and had no previous chance of survival after death. This was a marvellous opportunity for him. Furthermore he has a wife and five children for whom he has not been able to provide. The sum Mr. Reilly paid will enable the wife to give the children a decent education."

"Hurray for them!" Blaine said. "For sale, one father with slightly used body in excellent condition. Must sell! Sacrifice!"

"You're being ridiculous," she said. "Look, it's over."

The machine was turned off, and the straps were removed from the two men. Reilly's wrinkled, grinning old corpse was ignored as the technicians and doctors examined the body of the host.

"Nothing yet!" the bearded old doctor called.

Blaine could sense apprehension in the room, and a hint of fear. The seconds dragged by while the doctors and technicians clustered around the host.

"Still nothing!" the old doctor called, his voice going shrill.

"What's happening?" Blaine asked Marie Thorne.

"As I told you, reincarnation is tricky and dangerous. Reilly's mind hasn't been able to possess the host-body yet. He doesn't have much longer."

"Why not?"

"Because a body starts dying the moment it's untenanted. Irreversible death processes start if a mind isn't at least dormant in the body. The mind is essential. Even an unconscious mind controls the automatic processes. But with no mind at all—"

"Still nothing!" the old doctor shouted.

"I think it's too late now," Marie Thorne whispered.

"A tremor!" the doctor said. "I felt a tremor!"

There was a long silence.

"I think he's in!" the old doctor cried. "Now, oxygen, adrenalin!"

A mask was fitted over the host's face. A hypodermic was slipped into the host's arm. The host stirred, shivered, slumped back, stirred again.

"He's made it!" the old doctor cried, removing the oxygen mask.

The directors, as though on cue, hurried out of their chairs and went up on the stage. They surrounded the host, which was now blinking its eyes and retching.

"Congratulations, Mr. Reilly!"

"Well done, sir!"

"Had us worried, Mr. Reilly!"

The host stared at them. It wiped its mouth and said, "My name is not Reilly."

The old doctor pushed his way through the directors and bent down beside the host. "Not Reilly?" he said. "Are you Fitzsimmons?"

"No," said the host, "I'm not Fitzsimmons, the poor damned fool! And I'm not Reilly. Reilly tried to get into this body but I was too quick. I got into the body first. It's my body now."

"Who are you?" the doctor asked.

The host stood up. The directors stepped away from him, and one man quickly crossed himself.

"It was dead too long," Marie Thorne said.

The host's face now bore only the faintest and most stylized resemblance to the pale, frightened face of William Fitzsimmons. There was nothing of Fitzsimmons' determination, nothing of Reilly's petulance and good humour in that face. It resembled nothing but itself.

The face was dead white except for black dots of stubble on its cheeks and jaw. The lips were bloodless. A lock of black hair was plastered against its cold white forehead. When Fitzsimmons had been in residence the features had blended pleasantly, harmoniously, nondescriptly. But now the individual features had coarsened and grown separate. The unharmonious white face had a thick and unfinished look, like iron before tempering or clay before firing. It had a slack, sullen, relaxed look because of the lack of muscle tone and tension in the face. The calm, flaccid, unharmonious features simply existed, revealing nothing of the personality behind them.

The face seemed no longer completely human. All humanity now resided in the great, patient, unblinking Buddha's eyes.

"It's gone zombie," Marie Thorne whispered, clinging to Blaine's shoulder.

"Who are you?" the old doctor asked.

"I don't remember," it said. "I don't." Slowly it turned and started walking down the stage. Two directors moved tentatively to bar its path.

"Get away," it said to them. "It's my body now."

"Leave the poor zombie alone," the old doctor said wearily.

The directors moved out of its way. The zombie walked to the end of the stage, descended the steps, turned, and walked over to Blaine.

"I know you!" it said.

"What? What do you want?" Blaine asked nervously.

"I don't remember," the zombie said, staring hard at him. "What's your name?"

"Tom Blaine."

The zombie shook its head. "Doesn't mean anything to me. But I'll remember. It's you, all right. Something ... My body's dying, isn't it? Too bad. I'll remember before it gives out. You and me, you know, together. Blaine, don't you remember me?"

"No!" Blaine shouted, shrinking from the suggested relationship, the idea of some vital link between him and this dying thing. It couldn't be! What shared secret was this thief of corpses, this unclean usurper hinting at, what black intimacy, what sniggering knowledge to be shared like a dirty crust of bread for just Blaine and himself?

Nothing, Blaine told himself. He knew himself, knew what he was, knew what he had been. Nothing like this could arise legitimately to confront him. The creature had to be crazy, or mistaken.

"Who are you?" Blaine asked.

"I don't know!" The zombie flung his hands into the air, like a man caught in a net. And Blaine sensed how his mind must feel, confused, disoriented, nameless, wanting to live and caught in the fleshy dying embrace of a zombie body.

"I'll see you again," the zombie said to Blaine. "You're important to me. I'll see you again and I'll remember all about you and me."

The zombie turned and walked down the aisle and out of the theatre. Blaine stared after him until he felt a sudden weight on his shoulder.

Marie Thorne had fainted. It was the most feminine thing she had done so far.

Part Two

11

The head technician and the bearded doctor were arguing near the reincarnation machine, with their assistants ranged respectfully behind them. The battle was quite technical, but Blaine gathered that they were trying to determine the cause of the reincarnation failure. Each seemed to feel that the fault lay in the other's province.

The old doctor insisted that the machine settings must have been faulty, or an uncompensated power drop had occurred. The head technician swore the machine was perfect. He felt certain that Reilly hadn't been physically fit for the strenuous attempt.

Neither would yield an inch. But being reasonable men, they soon reached a compromise solution. The fault, they decided, lay in the nameless spirit who had fought Reilly for possession of Fitzsimmons' body, and had supplanted him.

"But who was it?" the head technician asked. "A ghost, do you think?"

"Possibly," the doctor said, "though it's damned rare for a ghost to possess a living body. Still, he talked crazy enough to be a ghost."

"Whoever he was," the head technician said, "he took over the host too late. The body was definitely zombie. Anyhow, no one could be blamed for it."

"Right," said the doctor. "I'll certify to the apparent soundness of the equipment."

"Fair enough," said the head technician. "And I'll testify to the apparent fitness of the patient."

They exchanged a look of perfect understanding.

The directors were holding an immediate conference of their own, trying to determine what the short-range effects would be upon the Rex corporate structure, and how the announcement should be made to the public, and whether all Rex personnel should be given a day off to visit the Reilly Family Palace of Death.

Old Reilly's original body lay back in its chair, beginning to stiffen, wearing a detached, derisive grin.

Marie Thorne recovered consciousness. "Come on," she said, leading Blaine out of the theatre. They hurried down long grey corridors to a street door. Outside, she hailed a helicab and gave the driver an address.

"Where are we going?" Blaine asked, as the helicab climbed and banked.

"To my place. Rex is going to be a madhouse for a while." She began rearranging her hair.

Blaine settled back against the cushions and looked down on the glittering city. From that height it looked like an exquisite miniature, a multi-coloured mosaic from the Thousand and One Nights. But somewhere down there, walking the streets and levels was the zombie, trying to remember—him.

"But why me?" Blaine asked out loud.

Marie Thorne glanced at him. "Why you and the zombie? Well, why not? Haven't you ever made any mistakes?"

"I suppose I have. But they're finished and done with."

She shook her head. "Maybe mistakes ended for good in your time. Today nothing ever dies for certain. That's one of the great disadvantages of a life after death, you know. One's mistakes sometimes refuse to lie decently dead and buried. Sometimes they follow you around."

"So I see," Blaine said. "But I've never done anything that would bring up *that*!"

She shrugged indifferently. "In that case, you're better than most of us."

Never had she seemed more alien to him. The helicab began a slow descent. And Blaine brooded over the disadvantages inherent in all advantages.

In his own time he had seen the control of disease in the world's backward areas result in an exploding birthrate, famine, plague. He had seen nuclear power breed nuclear war. Every advantage generated its own specific disadvantages. Why should it be different today?

A certified, scientific hereafter was undoubtedly an advantage to the race. Manipulation had again caught up with theory! But the disadvantages ... There was a certain inevitable weakening of the protective barrier around mundane life, some rips in the curtain, a few holes in the dike. The dead refused to lie decently still, they insisted upon mingling with the quick. To whose advantage? Ghosts, too—undoubtedly logical, operating within the boundaries of known natural laws. But that might be cold comfort to a haunted man.

Today, Blaine thought, a whole new stratum of existence impinged upon man's existence on Earth. Just as the zombie impinged uncomfortably on *his* existence.

The helicab landed on the roof of an apartment building. Marie Thorne paid, and led Blaine to her apartment.

* * *

It was a large airy apartment, pleasingly feminine, and furnished with a certain dramatic flair. There was more bright colour than Blaine would have thought compatible with Miss Thorne's sombre personality; but perhaps the vivid yellows and sharp reds expressed a wish of some sort, a compensation for the restraint of her business life. Or perhaps it was just the prevailing style. The apartment contained the sort of gadgetry that Blaine associated with the future; self-adjusting lighting and air-conditioning, self-conforming armchairs, and a pushbutton bar that produced an adequate Martini.

Marie Thorne went into one of the bedrooms. She returned in a high-collared housedress and sat down on a couch opposite him.

"Well, Blaine, what are your plans?"

"I thought I'd ask you for a loan."

"Certainly."

"In that case my plan is to find a hotel room and start looking for a job."

"It won't be easy," she said, "but I know some people who might—"

"No thanks," Blaine said. "I hope this doesn't sound too silly, but I'd rather find a job on my own."

"No, it doesn't sound silly. I just hope it's possible. How about some dinner?"

"Fine. Do you cook, too?"

"I set dials," she told him. "Let's see. How would you like a genuine Martian meal?"

"No thanks," Blaine said. "Martian food is tasty, but it doesn't stick to your ribs. Would you happen to have a steak around the place?"

Marie set the dials and her auto-chef did the rest, selecting the foods from pantry and freezer, peeling, unwrapping, washing and cooking them, and ordering new items to replace those used. The meal was perfect; but Marie seemed oddly embarrassed about it. She apologized to Blaine for the completely mechanical operation. After all, he came from an age in which women had opened their own cans, and done their own tasting; but they'd probably had more leisure time, too.

The sun had set by the time they finished their coffee. Blaine said, "Thank you very much, Miss Thorne. Now if you could loan me that money, I'll get started."

She looked surprised. "At night?"

"I'll find a hotel room. You've been very kind, but I wouldn't want to presume any further—"

"That's all right," she said. "Stay here tonight."

"All right," Blaine said. His mouth was suddenly dry, and his heart was pounding with suspicious rapidity. He knew there was nothing personal in her invitation; but his body didn't seem to understand. It insisted upon reacting hopefully, expectantly even, to the controlled and antiseptic Miss Thorne.

She gave him a bedroom and a pair of green pyjamas. Blaine closed the door when she left, undressed and got into bed. The light went out when he told it to.

In a little while, just as his body had expected, Miss Thorne came in wearing something white and gossamer, and lay down beside him.

They lay side by side in silence. Marie Thorne moved closer to him, and Blaine slipped an arm under her head.

He said, "I thought you weren't attracted to my type."

"Not exactly. I said I *preferred* tall, lean men."

"I was once a tall, lean man."

"I suspected it," she said.

They were both silent. Blaine began to grow uncomfortable and apprehensive. What did this mean? Had she some fondness for him? Or was this simply a custom of the age, a sort of Eskimo hospitality?

"Miss Thorne," he said, "I wonder if—"

"Oh be quiet!" she said, suddenly turning towards him, her eyes enormous in the shadowy room. "Do you have to question everything, Tom?"

Later she said, dreamily, "Under the circumstances, I think you can call me Marie."

In the morning Blaine showered, shaved and dressed. Marie dialled a breakfast for them. After they had eaten she gave him a small envelope.

"I can loan you more when you need it," she said. "Now about finding a job—"

"You've helped me very much," Blaine said. "The rest I'd like to do on my own."

"All right. My address and telephone number are on the envelope. Please call me as soon as you have a hotel."

"I will," Blaine said, watching her closely. There was no hint of the Marie of last night. It might have been a different person entirely. But her studied self-possession was reaction enough for Blaine. Enough, at least, for the moment.

At the door she touched his arm. "Tom," she said, "please be careful. And call me."

"I will, Marie," Blaine said.

He went into the city happy and refreshed, and intent upon conquering the world.

12

Blaine's first idea had been to make a round of the yacht-design offices. But he decided against it simply by picturing a yacht designer from 1806 walking into an office in 1958.

The quaint old man might be very talented; but how would that help him when he was asked what he knew about metacentric shelf analysis, flow diagrams, centres of effort, and the best locations for RDF and sonar? What company would pay him while he learned the facts about reduction gears, exfoliating paints, tank testing, propeller pitch, heat exchange systems, synthetic sailcloth...

Not a chance, Blaine decided. He couldn't walk into a design office 152 years behind the times and ask for a job. A job as *what*? Perhaps he could study and catch up to 2110 technology. But he'd have to do it on his own time.

Right now, he'd take anything he could get.

He went to a newsstand and purchased a microfilm *New York Times* and a viewer. He walked until he found a bench, sat down and turned to the classified ads. Quickly he skipped past the skilled categories, where he couldn't hope to qualify, and came to unskilled labour. He read:

"Set-up man wanted in auto-cafeteria. Requires only basic knowledge of robotics."

"Hull wiper wanted, Mar-Coling liner. Must be Rh positive and fortified anticlaustrophobiac."

"List man needed for hi-tensile bearing decay work. Needs simple jenkling knowledge. Meals included."

It was apparent to Blaine that even the unskilled labour of 2110 was beyond his present capacity. Turning the page to Employment for Boys, he read:

"Wanted, young man interested in slic-trug machinery. Good future. Must know basic calculus and have working knowledge Hootean Equations."

"Young Men wanted, salesmen's jobs on Venus. Salary plus commission. Knowledge basic French, German, Russian and Ourescz."

"Delivery, Magazine, Newspaper boys wanted by Eth-Col agency. Must be able to drive a Sprening. Good knowledge of city required."

So—he couldn't even qualify as a newsboy!

It was a depressing thought. Finding a job was going to be more difficult than he had imagined. Didn't anyone dig ditches or carry packages in this city? Did robots do all the menial work, or did you need a Ph.D. even to lug a wheelbarrow? What sort of world was this?

He turned to the front page of the *Times* for an answer, adjusted his viewer, and read the news of the day:

A new spacefield was under construction at Oxa, New South Mars.

A poltergeist was believed responsible for several industrial fires in the Chicago area. Tentative exorcism proceedings were under way.

Rich copper deposits had been discovered in the Sigma-G sector of the asteroid belt.

Doppelganger activities had increased in Berlin.

A new survey was being made of octopi villages in the Mindanao Deep.

A mob in Spenser, Alabama, lynched and burned the town's two local zombies. Legal action was being taken against the mob leaders.

A leading anthropologist declared the Tuamoto Archipelago in Oceania to be the last stronghold of 20th century simplicity.

The Atlantic Fish Herders' Association was holding its annual convention at the Waldorf.

A werewolf was unsuccessfully hunted in the Austrian Tyrol. Local villages were warned to keep a twenty-four hour watch for the beast.

A bill was introduced into the House of Representatives to outlaw all hunts and gladiatorial events. It was defeated.

A berserker took four lives in downtown San Diego.

Helicopter fatalities reached the one million mark for the year.

Blaine put the newspaper aside, more depressed than ever. Ghosts, doppelgangers, werewolves, poltergeists ... He didn't like the sound of those vague, grim, ancient words which today seemed to represent actual phenomena. He had already met a zombie. He didn't want to encounter any more of the dangerous side-effects of the hereafter.

He started walking again. He went through the theatre district, past glittering marquees, posters advertising the gladiatorial events at Madison Square Garden, billboards heralding solidovision programmes and sensory shows, flashing signs proclaiming overtone concerts and Venusian pantomime. Sadly Blaine remembered that *he* might have been part of this dazzling fairyland if only Reilly hadn't changed his mind. He might be appearing at one of those theatres now, billed as the Man from the Past...

Of course! A Man from the Past, Blaine suddenly realized, had a unique and indisputable novelty value, an inherent talent. The Rex Corporation had saved his life in 1958 solely in order to use that talent. But they had changed their minds. So what was to prevent him from using his novelty value for himself? And for that matter, what else could he do? Show business looked like the only possible business for him.

He hurried into a gigantic office building and found six theatrical agents listed on the board. He picked Barnex, Scofield & Styles, and took the elevator to their offices on the 19th floor.

He entered a luxurious waiting-room panelled with gigantic solidographs of smiling actresses. At the far end of the room, a pretty receptionist raised an inquiring eyebrow at him.

Blaine went up to her desk. "I'd like to see someone about my act," he told her.

"I'm so sorry," she said. "We're all filled."

"This is a very special act."

"I'm really terribly sorry. Perhaps next week."

"Look," Blaine said, "my act is really unique. You see, I'm a man from the past."

"I don't care if you're the ghost of Scott Merrivale," she said sweetly. "We're *filled*. Try us next week."

Blaine turned to go. A short, stocky man breezed past him, nodding to the receptionist.

"Morning, Miss Thatcher."

"Morning, Mr. Barnex."

Barnex! One of the agents! Blaine hurried after him and grabbed his sleeve.

"Mr. Barnex," he said, "I have an act—"

"Everybody has an act," Barnex said wearily.

"But this act is unique!"

"Everybody's act is unique," Barnex said. "Let go my sleeve, friend. Try us next week."

"I'm from the past!" Blaine cried, suddenly feeling foolish. Barnex turned and stared at him. He looked as though he might be on the verge of calling the police, or Bellevue. But Blaine plunged recklessly on.

"I really am!" he said. "I have absolute proof. The Rex Corporation snatched me out of the past. Ask them!"

"Rex?" Barnex said. "Yeah, I heard something about that snatch over at Lindy's ... Hmm. Come into my office, Mister—"

"Blaine, Tom Blaine." He followed Barnex into a tiny, cluttered cubicle. "Do you think you can use me?" he asked.

"Maybe," Barnex said, motioning Blaine to a chair. "It depends. Tell me, Mr. Blaine, what period of the past are you from?"

"1958. I have an intimate knowledge of the nineteen thirties, forties and fifties. By way of stage experience I did some acting in college, and a professional actress friend of mine once told me I had a natural way of—"

"1958? That's 20th Century?"

"Yes, that's right."

The agent shook his head. "Too bad. Now if you'd been a 6th Century Swede or a 7th Century Jap, I could have found work for you. I've had no difficulty booking appearances for our 1st Century

Roman or our 4th Century Saxon, and I could use a couple more like them. But it's damned hard finding anyone from those early centuries, now that time travel is illegal. And B.C. is completely out."

"But what about the 20th Century?" Blaine asked.

"It's filled."

"Filled?"

"Sure. Ben Therler from 1953 gets all the available stage appearances."

"I see," Blaine said, getting slowly to his feet. "Thanks anyhow, Mr. Barnex."

"Not at all," Barnex said. "Wish I could help. If you'd been from any time or place before the 11th Century, I could probably book you. But there's not much interest in recent stuff like the 19th and 20th Centuries ... Say, why don't you go see Therler? It isn't likely, but maybe he can use an understudy or something." He scrawled an address on a piece of paper and handed it to Blaine.

Blaine took it, thanked him again, and left.

In the street he stood for a moment, cursing his luck. His one unique and indisputable talent, his novelty value, had been usurped by Ben Therler of 1953! Really, he thought, time travel should be kept more exclusive. It just wasn't fair to drop a man here and then ignore him.

He wondered what sort of man Therler was. Well, he'd find out. Even if Therler didn't need an understudy, it would be a pleasure and relief to talk to someone from home. And Therler, who had lived here longer, might have some ideas on what a 20th century man could do in 2110.

He flagged a helicab and gave him the address. In fifteen minutes he was in Therler's apartment building, pressing the doorbell.

The door was opened by a sleek, chubby, complacent-looking man wearing a dressing gown.

"You the photographer?" he asked. "You're too early."

Blaine shook his head. "Mr. Therler, you've never met me before. I'm from your own century. I'm from 1958."

"Is that so?" Therler asked, with obvious suspicion.

"It's the truth," Blaine said, "I was snatched by the Rex Corporation. You can check my story with them."

Therler shrugged his shoulders. "Well, what is it you want?"

"I was hoping you might be able to use an understudy or something—"

"No, no, I never use an understudy," Therler said, starting to close the door.

"I didn't think so," Blaine said. "The real reason I came was

just to talk to you. It gets pretty lonely being out of one's century. I
wanted to talk to someone from my own age. I thought maybe you'd
feel that way, too."

"Me? Oh!" Therler said, smiling with sudden stage warmth. "Oh,
you mean about the good old twentieth century! I'd love to talk to
you about it sometime, pal. Little old New York! The Dodgers and
Yankees, the hansoms in the park, the roller-skating rink in Rockefeller Plaza. I sure miss it all! Boy! But I'm afraid I'm a little busy
now."

"Certainly," Blaine said. "Some other time."

"Fine! I'd really love to!" Therler said, smiling even more brilliantly. "Call my secretary, will you, old man? Schedules, you know.
We'll have a really great old gab some one of these days. I suppose
you could use a spare dollar or two—"

Blaine shook his head.

"Then, 'bye," Therler said heartily. "And do call soon."

Blaine hurried out of the building. It was bad enough being
robbed of your novelty value; it was worse being robbed by an out-
and-out phony, a temporal fraud who'd never been within a hundred
yards of 1953. The Rockefeller *roller*-skating rink! And even that
slip hadn't been necessary. Everything about the man screamed
counterfeit.

But sadly, Blaine was probably the only man in 2110 who could
detect the imposture.

That afternoon Blaine purchased a change of clothing and a
shaving kit. He found a room in a cheap hotel on Fifth Avenue. For
the next week, he continued looking for work.

He tried the restaurants, but found that human dishwashers were
a thing of the past. At the docks and spaceports, robots were doing
most of the heavy work. One day he was tentatively approved for a
position as package-wrapping inspector at Gimbel-Macy's. But the
personnel department, after carefully studying his personality pro-
file, irritability index and suggestibility rating, vetoed him in favour
of a dull-eyed little man from Queens who held a master's degree in
package design.

Blaine was wearily returning to his hotel one evening when he
recognized a face in the dense crowd. It was a man he would have
known instantly, anywhere. He was about Blaine's age, a compact,
red-headed, snub-nosed man with slightly protruding teeth and a
small red blotch on his neck. He carried himself with a certain
jaunty assurance, the unquenchable confidence of a man for whom
something always turns up.

"Ray!" Blaine shouted. "Ray Melhill!" He pushed through the
crowd and seized him by the arm. "Ray! How'd you get out?"

The man pulled his arm away and smoothed the sleeve of his jacket. "My name is not Melhill," he said.

"It's not? Are you sure?"

"Of course I'm sure," he said, starting to move away.

Blaine stepped in front of him. "Wait a minute. You look exactly like him, even down to the radiation scar. Are you *sure* you aren't Ray Melhill, a flow-control man off the spaceship *Bremen*?"

"Quite certain," the man said coldly. "You have confused me with someone else, young man."

Blaine stared hard as the man started to walk away. Then he reached out, caught the man by a shoulder and swung him around.

"You dirty body-thieving bastard!" Blaine shouted, his big right fist shooting out.

The man who so exactly resembled Melhill was knocked back against a building, and slid groggily to the pavement. Blaine started for him, and people moved quickly out of his way.

"Berserker!" a woman screamed, and someone else took up the cry. Blaine caught sight of a blue uniform shoving through the crowd towards him.

A flat-hat! Blaine ducked into the crowd. He turned a corner quickly, then another, slowed to a walk and looked back. The policeman was not in sight. Blaine started walking again to his hotel.

It had been Melhill's body; but Ray no longer occupied it. There had been no last-minute reprieve for him, no final chance. His body had been taken from him and sold to the old man whose querulous mind wore the jaunty body like a suit of ill-fitting, too-youthful clothes.

Now he knew his friend was really dead. Blaine drank silently to him in a neighbourhood bar before returning to his hotel.

The clerk stopped him as he passed the desk. "Blaine? Got a message for you. Just a minute." He went into the office.

Blaine waited, wondering who it could be from. Marie? But he hadn't called Marie yet, and wasn't planning to until he found work.

The clerk came back and handed him a slip of paper. The message read: "There is a Communication awaiting Thomas Blaine at the Spiritual Switchboard, 23rd Street Branch. Hours, nine to five."

"I wonder how anybody knew where I was?" Blaine asked.

"Spirits got their ways," the clerk told him. "Man I know, his dead mother-in-law tracked him down through three aliases, a Transplant and a complete skin job. He was hiding from her in Abyssinia."

"I don't have any dead mother-in-law," Blaine said.

"No? Who you figure's trying to reach you?" the clerk asked.

"I'll find out tomorrow and let you know," Blaine said. But his sarcasm was wasted. The clerk had already turned back to his correspondence course on Atomic Engine Maintenance. Blaine went up to his room.

13

The 23rd Street Branch of the Spiritual Switchboard was a large greystone building near Third Avenue. Engraved above the door was the statement: "Dedicated to Free Communication Between Those on Earth and Those Beyond."

Blaine entered the building and studied the directory. It gave floor and room numbers for Messages Incoming, Messages Outgoing, Translations, Abjurations, Exorcisms, Offerings, Pleas, and Exhortations. He wasn't sure which classification he fell under, or what the classifications signified, or even the purpose of the Spiritual Switchboard. He took his slip of paper to the information booth.

"That's Messages Incoming," a pleasant, grey-haired receptionist told him. "Straight down the hall to room 32A."

"Thank you." Blaine hesitated, then said, "Could you explain something to me?"

"Certainly," the woman said. "What do you wish to know?"

"Well—I hope this doesn't sound too foolish—what *is* all this?"

The grey-haired woman smiled. "That's a difficult question to answer. In a philosophical sense I suppose you might call the Spiritual Switchboard a move towards greater oneness, an attempt to discard the dualism of mind and body and substitute—"

"No," Blaine said. "I mean literally."

"Literally? Why, the Spiritual Switchboard is a privately endowed, tax-free organization, chartered to act as a clearing house and centre for communications to and from the Threshold plane of the Hereafter. In some cases, of course, people don't need our aid and can communicate directly with their departed ones. But more often, there is a need for amplification. This centre possesses the proper equipment to make the deceased audible to our ears. And we perform other services, such as abjurations, exorcisms, exhortations and the like, which become necessary from time to time when flesh interacts with spirit."

She smiled warmly at him. "Does that make it any clearer?"

"Thank you very much," Blaine said, and went down the hall to room 32A.

It was a small grey room with several armchairs and a loudspeaker set in the wall. Blaine sat down, wondering what was going to happen.

"Tom Blaine!" cried a disembodied voice from the loudspeaker.

"Huh? What?" Blaine asked, jumping to his feet and moving towards the door.

"Tom! How are you, boy?"

Blaine, his hand on the doorknob, suddenly recognized the voice. "Ray Melhill?"

"Right! I'm up there where the rich folks go when they die! Pretty good, huh?"

"That's the understatement of the age," Blaine said. "But Ray, *how?* I thought you didn't have any hereafter insurance."

"I didn't. Let me tell you the whole story. They came for me maybe an hour after they took you. I was so damned angry I thought I'd go out of my mind. I stayed angry right through the chloroforming, right through the wiping. I was still angry when I died."

"What was dying like?" Blaine asked.

"It was like exploding. I could feel myself scattering all over the place, growing big as the galaxy, bursting into fragments, and the fragments bursting into smaller fragments, and all of them were *me.*"

"And what happened?"

"I don't know. Maybe being so angry helped. I was stretched as far as I could go—any further and it wouldn't be me—and then I just simply came back together again. Some people do. Like I told you, a few out of every million have always survived without hereafter training. I was one of the lucky ones."

"I guess you know about me," Blaine said. "I tried to do something for you, but you'd already been sold."

"I know," Melhill said. "Thanks anyhow, Tom. And say, thanks for popping that slob. The one wearing my body."

"You saw that?"

"I been keeping my eyes open," Melhill said. "By the way, I like that Marie. Nice looking kid."

"Thanks. Ray, what's the hereafter like?"

"I don't know."

"You don't?"

"I'm not *in* the hereafter yet, Tom. I'm in the Threshold. It's a preparatory stage, a sort of bridge between Earth and the hereafter. It's hard to describe. A sort of greyness, with Earth on one side and the hereafter on the other."

"Why don't you cross over?" Blaine asked.

"Not yet," Melhill said. "It's a one-way street into the hereafter. Once you cross over, you can't come back. There's no more contact with Earth."

Blaine thought about that for a moment, then asked, "When are you going to cross over, Ray?"

"I don't rightly know. I thought I'd stay in Threshold for a while and keep an eye on things."

"Keep an eye on me, you mean."

"Well..."

"Thanks a lot, Ray, but don't do it. Go into the hereafter. I can take care of myself."

"Sure you can," Melhill said. "But I think I'll stick around for a while anyhow. You'd do it for me, wouldn't you? So don't argue. Now look, I suppose you know you're in trouble?"

Blaine nodded. "You mean the zombie?"

"I don't know who he is or what he wants from you, Tom, but it can't be good. You'd better be a long way off when he finds out. But that wasn't the trouble I meant."

"You mean I have more?"

"Afraid so. You're going to be haunted, Tom."

In spite of himself, Blaine laughed.

"What's so funny?" Melhill asked indignantly. "You think it's a *joke* to be haunted?"

"I suppose not. But is it really so serious?"

"Lord you're ignorant," Melhill said. "Do you know anything about ghosts? How they're made and what they want?"

"Tell me."

"Well, there are three possibilities when a man dies. First, his mind can just explode, scatter, dissipate; and that's the end of him. Second, his mind can hold together through the death trauma; and he finds himself in the Threshold, a spirit. I guess you know about those two."

"Go on," Blaine said.

"The third possibility is this: His mind breaks during the death trauma, but not enough to cause dissipation. He pulls through into the Threshold. But the strain has been permanently disabling. He's insane. And that, my friend, is how a ghost is born."

"Hmm," Blaine said. "So a ghost is a mind that went insane during the death trauma?"

"Right. He's insane, and he haunts."

"But why?"

"Ghosts haunt," Melhill said, "because they're filled with twisted hatred, anger, fear and pain. They won't go into the hereafter. They want to spend as much time as they can on Earth, where their attention is still fixed. They want to frighten people, hurt them, drive them insane. Haunting is the most asocial thing they can do, it's their madness. Look Tom, since the beginning of mankind..."

Since the beginning of mankind there have been ghosts, but their numbers have always been small. Only a few out of every million people managed to survive after death; and only a tiny percentage of those survivors went insane during the transition, and became ghosts.

But the impact of those few was colossal upon a mankind fascinated by death, awed by the cold uncaring mobility of the corpse so recently quick and vital, shocked at the ghastly inapropos humour of the skeleton. Death's elaborate, mysterious figure seemed infinitely meaningful, its warning finger pointed towards the spirit-laden skies. So for every genuine ghost, rumour and fear produced a thousand. Every gibbering bat became a ghost. Marsh-fires, flapping curtains and swaying trees became ghosts, and St. Elmo's fire, great-eyed owls, rats in the walls, foxes in the bush, all became ghostly evidence. Folklore grew and produced witch and warlock, evil little familiars, demons and devils, succubi and incubi, werewolf and vampire. For every ghost a thousand were suspected, and for every supernatural fact a million were assumed.

Early scientific investigators entered this maze, trying to discover the truth about supernatural phenomena. They uncovered countless frauds, hallucinations and errors of judgment. And they found a few genuinely inexplicable events, which, though interesting, were statistically insignificant.

The whole tradition of folklore came tumbling down. Statistically there were no ghosts. But continually there was a sly, elusive *something* which refused to stand still and be classified. It was ignored for centuries, the occasional *something* which gave a basis and a reality to tales of incubi and succubi. Until at last scientific theory caught up with folklore, made a place for it in the realm of indisputable phenomena, and gave it respectability.

With the discovery of the scientific hereafter, the irrational ghost became understandable as a demented mind inhabiting the misty interface between Earth and the hereafter. The forms of ghostly madness could be categorized like madness on Earth. There were the melancholics, drifting disconsolately through the scenes of their great passion; the whispering hebephrenic, chattering gay and random nonsense; the idiots and imbeciles who returned in the guise of little children; the schizophrenics who imagined themselves to be animals, prototypes of vampire and Abominable Snowman, werewolf, weretiger, werefox, weredog. There were the destructive stone-throwing and fire-setting ghosts, the poltergeists, and the grandiloquent paranoids who imagined themselves to be Lucifer or Beelzebub, Israfael or Azazael, the Spirit of Christmas Past, the Furies, Divine Justice, or even Death itself.

Haunting was madness. They wept by the old watch tower, these few ghosts upon whose gossamer shoulders rested the entire great structure of folklore, mingled with the mists around the gibbet, jabbered their nonsense at the seance. They talked, cried, danced

and sang for the delectation of the credulous, until scientific obser-
vers came with their sober cold questions. Then they fled back to
the Threshold, terrified of this onslaught of reason, protective of
their delusions, fearful of being cured.

"So that's how it was," Melhill said. "You can figure out the rest.
Since Hereafter, Inc. a hell of a lot more people are surviving after
death. But of course a lot more are going insane on the way."

"Thus producing a lot more ghosts," Blaine said.

"Right. One of them is after you," Melhill said, his voice growing faint. "So watch your step. Tom, I gotta go now."

"What kind of ghost is it?" Blaine asked. "Whose ghost? And
why do you have to go?"

"It takes energy to stay on Earth," Melhill whispered. "I'm just
about used up. Have to recharge. Can you still hear me?"

"Yes, go on."

"I don't know when the ghost will show himself, Tom. And I
don't know who he is. I asked, but he wouldn't tell me. Just watch
out for him."

"I'll watch out," Blaine said, his ear pressed to the loudspeaker.
"Ray! Will I speak to you again?"

"I think so," Melhill said, his voice barely audible. "Tom, I know
you're looking for a job. Try Ed Franchel, 322 West 19th Street. It's
rough stuff, but it pays. And watch yourself."

"Ray!" Blaine shouted. "What *kind* of a ghost is it?"

There was no answer. The loudspeaker was silent, and he was
alone in the grey room.

14

322 West 19th Street, the address Ray Melhill had given him, was
a small, dilapidated brownstone near the docks. Blaine climbed the
steps and pressed the ground-floor buzzer marked *Edward J.
Franchel Enterprises.* The door was opened by a large, balding man
in shirtsleeves.

"Mr. Franchel?" Blaine asked.

"That's me," the balding man said, with a resolutely cheerful
smile. "Right this way, sir."

He led Blaine into an apartment pungent with the odour of
boiled cabbage. The front half of the apartment was arranged as an
office, with a paper-cluttered desk, a dusty filing cabinet and several
stiff-backed chairs. Past it, Blaine could see a gloomy living-room.
From the inner recesses of the apartment a solido was blaring out a
daytime show.

"Please excuse the appearance," Franchel said, motioning Blaine
to a chair. "I'm moving into a regular office uptown just as soon as

I find time. The orders have been coming in so fast and furious ...
Now sir, what can I do for you?"

"I'm looking for a job," Blaine said.

"Hell," said Franchel, "I thought you were a customer." He turned
in the direction of the blaring solido and shouted, "Alice, will you
turn that goddamned thing down?" He waited until the volume
had receded somewhat, then turned back to Blaine. "Brother, if
business doesn't pick up soon I'm going back to running a suicide
booth at Coney. A job, huh?"

"That's right. Ray Melhill told me to try you."

Franchel's expression brightened. "How's Ray doing?"

"He's dead."

"Shame," Franchel said. "He was a good lad, though always a bit
wild. He worked for me a couple times when the space pilots were
on strike. Want a drink?"

Blaine nodded. Franchel went to the filing cabinet and removed
a bottle of rye whiskey labelled "Moonjuice". He found two shot
glasses and filled them with a practised flourish.

"Here's to old Ray," Franchel said. "I suppose he got himself
boxed?"

"Boxed and crated," Blaine said. "I just spoke to him at the
Spiritual Switchboard."

"Then he made Threshold!" Franchel said admiringly. "Friend,
we should only have his luck. So you want a job? Well, maybe I can
fix it. Stand up."

He walked around Blaine, touched his biceps and ran a hand
over his ridged shoulder muscles. He stood in front of Blaine, nodding to himself with downcast eyes, then feinted a quick blow at his
face. Blaine's right hand came up instantly, in time to block the
punch.

"Good build, good reflexes," Franchel said. "I think you'll do.
Know anything about weapons?"

"Not much," Blaine said, wondering what kind of job he was
getting into. "Just—ah—antiques. Garands, Winchesters, Colts."

"No kidding?" Franchel said. "You know, I always wanted to
collect antique recoil arms. But no projectile or beam weapons are
allowed on this hunt. What else you got?"

"I can handle a rifle with bayonet," Blaine said, thinking how
his basic-training sergeant would have roared at that overstatement.

"You can? Lunges and parries and all? Well I'll be damned, I
thought bayonetry was a lost art. You're the first I've seen in fifteen
years. Friend, you're hired."

Franchel went to his desk, scribbled on a piece of paper and
handed it to Blaine.

"You go to that address tomorrow for your briefing. You'll be paid standard hunter's salary, two hundred dollars plus fifty a day for every working day. Have you got your own weapons and equipment? Well, I'll pick the stuff up for you, but it's deducted from your pay. And I take ten per cent off the top. OK?"

"Sure," Blaine said. "Could you explain a little more about the hunt?"

"Nothing to explain. It's just a standard hunt. But don't go around talking about it. I'm not sure if hunts are still legal. I wish Congress would straighten out the Suicide and Permitted Murder Acts once and for all. A man doesn't know where he's at any more."

"Yeah," Blaine agreed.

"They'll probably discuss the legal aspects at the briefing," Franchel said. "The other hunters will be there, and the Quarry will tell you all you need to know. Say hello to Ray for me if you speak to him again. Tell him I'm sorry he got killed."

"I'll tell him," Blaine said. He decided not to ask any more questions for fear his ignorance might cost him the job. Whatever hunting involved, he and his body could surely handle it. And a job, any job, was as necessary now for his self-respect as for his dwindling wallet.

He thanked Franchel and left.

That evening he ate dinner in an inexpensive diner, and bought several magazines. He was elated at the knowledge of having found work, and sure that he was going to make a place for himself in this age.

His high spirits were dampened slightly when he glimpsed, on the way back to his hotel, a man standing in an alley watching him. The man had a white face and placid Buddha eyes, and his rough clothes hung on him like rags on a scarecrow.

It was the zombie.

Blaine hurried on to his hotel, refusing to anticipate trouble. After all, if a cat can look at a king, a zombie can look at a man, and where's the harm?

This reasoning didn't prevent him from having nightmares until dawn.

Early the next day, Blaine walked to 42nd Street and Park Avenue, to catch a bus to the briefing. While waiting, he noticed a disturbance on the other side of 42nd Street.

A man had stopped short in the middle of the busy pavement. He was laughing to himself, and people were beginning to edge away from him. He was in his fifties, Blaine judged, dressed in quiet tweeds, bespectacled, and a little overweight. He carried a small briefcase and looked like ten million other businessmen.

Abruptly he stopped laughing. He unzipped his briefcase and

removed from it two long, slightly curved daggers. He flung the briefcase away, and followed it with his glasses.

"Berserker!" someone cried.

The man plunged into the crowd, both daggers flashing. People started screaming, and the crowd scattered before him.

"Berserker, berserker!"

"Call the flathats!"

"Watch *out*, berserker!"

One man was down, clutching his torn shoulder and swearing. The berserker's face was fiery red now, and spittle came from his mouth. He waded deeper into the dense crowd, and people knocked each other down in their efforts to escape. A woman shrieked as she was pushed off balance, and her armload of parcels scattered across the pavement.

The berserker swiped at her left-handed, missed, and plunged deeper into the crowd.

Blue-uniformed police appeared, six or eight of them, sidearms out. "Everybody down!" they shouted. "Flatten! Everybody down!"

All traffic had stopped. The people in the berserker's path flung themselves to the pavement. On Blaine's side of the street, people were also getting down.

A freckled girl of perhaps twelve tugged at Blaine's arm. "Come on, Mister, get down! You wanna get beamed?"

Blaine lay down beside her. The berserker had turned and was running back towards the policemen, screaming wordlessly and waving his knives.

Three of the policemen fired at once, their weapons throwing a pale yellowish beam which flared red when it struck the berserker. He screamed as his clothing began to smoulder, turned, and tried to escape.

A beam caught him square in the back. He flung both knives at the policemen and collapsed.

An ambulance dropped down with whirring blades and quickly loaded the berserker and his victims. The policemen began breaking up the crowd that had gathered around them.

"All right, folks, it's all over now. Move along!"

The crowd began to disperse. Blaine stood up and brushed himself off. "What was that?" he asked.

"It was a berserker, silly," the freckled girl said. "Couldn't you *see*?"

"I saw. Do you have many?"

She nodded proudly. "New York has more berserkers than any other city in the world except Manila where they're called amokers. But it's all the same thing. We have maybe fifty a year."

"More," a man said. "Maybe seventy, eighty a year. But this one didn't do so good."

A small group had gathered near Blaine and the girl. They were discussing the berserker much as Blaine had heard strangers in his own time discuss an automobile accident.

"How many did he get?"

"Only five, and I don't think he killed any of them."

"His heart wasn't in it," an old woman said. "When I was a girl you couldn't stop them as easily as that. Strong they were."

"Well, he picked a bad spot," the freckled girl said, "42nd Street is filled with flathats. A berserker can't hardly get started before he's beamed."

A big policeman came over. "All right, folks, break it up. The fun's over, move along now."

The group dispersed. Blaine caught his bus, wondering why fifty or more people chose to berserk in New York every year. Sheer nervous tension? A demented form of individualism? Adult delinquency?

It was one more of the things he would have to find out about the world of 2110.

15

The address was a penthouse high above Park Avenue in the Seventies. A butler admitted him to a spacious room where chairs had been set up in a long row. The dozen men occupying the chairs were a loud, tough, weatherbeaten bunch, carelessly dressed and ill at ease in such rarefied surroundings. Most of them knew each other.

"Hey, Otto! Back in the hunting game?"

"Yah. No money."

"Knew you'd come back, old boy. Hi, Tim!"

"Hi, Bjorn. This is my last hunt."

"Sure it is. Last 'til next time."

"No, I mean it. I'm buying a seed-pressure farm in the North Atlantic Abyss. I just need a stake."

"You'll drink up your stake."

"Not this time."

"Hey, Theseus! How's the throwing arm?"

"Good enough, Chico. Que tal?"

"Not too bad, kid."

"There's Sammy Jones, always last in."

"I'm on time, ain't I?"

"Ten minutes late. Where's your sidekick?"

"Sligo? Dead. That Asturias hunt."

"Tough. Hereafter?"

"Not likely."

A man entered the room and called out, "Gentlemen, your attention please!"

He advanced to the centre of the room and stood, hands on his hips, facing the row of hunters. He was a slender sinewy man of medium height, dressed in riding breeches and an open-necked shirt. He had a small, carefully tended moustache and startling blue eyes in a thin, tanned face. For a few seconds he looked the hunters over, while they coughed and shifted their feet uncomfortably.

At last he said, "Good morning, gentlemen. I am Charles Hull, your employer and Quarry." He gave them a smile of no warmth. "First, gentlemen, a word concerning the legality of our proceedings. There has been some recent confusion about this. My lawyer has looked into the matter fully, and will explain. Mr. Jensen!"

A small, nervous-looking man came into the room, pressed his spectacles firmly against his nose and cleared his throat.

"Yes, Mr. Hull. Gentlemen, as to the present legality of the hunt: In accordance with the revised statutes to the Suicide Act of 2102, any man protected by Hereafter insurance has the right to select any death for himself, at any time and place, and by any means, as long as those means do not constitute cruel and unnatural abuse. The reason for this fundamental 'right to die' is obvious: The courts do not recognize physical death as death *per se*, if said death does not involve the destruction of mind. Providing the mind survives, the death of the body is of no more moment, legally, than the sloughing of a fingernail. The body, by the latest Supreme Court decision, is considered an appendage of the mind, its creature, to be disposed of as the mind directs."

During this explanation Hull had been pacing the room with quick, catlike steps. He stopped now and said, "Thank you, Mr. Jensen. So there is no questioning my right to suicide. Nor is there any illegality in my selecting one or more persons such as yourselves to perform the act for me. And your own actions are considered legal under the Permitted Murder section of the Suicide Act. All well and good. The only legal question arises in a recent appendage to the Suicide Act."

He nodded to Mr. Jensen.

"The appendage states," Jensen said, "that a man can select any death for himself, at any time and place, by any means, etcetera, *so long as that death is not physically injurious to others.*"

"That," said Hull, "is the troublesome clause. Now, a hunt is a legal form of suicide. A time and place is arranged. You, the hunters, chase me. I, the Quarry, flee. You catch me, kill me. Fine! Except for one thing."

He turned to the lawyer. "Mr. Jensen, you may leave the room. I do not wish to implicate you."

After the lawyer had left, Hull said, "The one problem remaining is, of course, the fact that I will be armed and trying my very best to kill *you*. Any of you. All of you. And *that* is illegal."

Hull sank gracefully into a chair. "The crime, however, is mine, not yours. I have employed you to kill me. You have no idea that I plan to protect myself, to retaliate. That is a legal fiction, but one which will save you from becoming possible accessories to the fact. If I am caught trying to kill one of you, the penalty will be severe. But I will not be caught. One of you will kill me, thus putting me beyond the reach of human justice. If I should be so unfortunate as to kill *all* of you, I shall complete my suicide in the old-fashioned manner, with poison. But that would be a disappointment to me. I trust you will not be so clumsy as to let that happen. Any questions?"

The hunters were murmuring among themselves:

"Slick fancy talking bastard."

"Forget it, all Quarries talk like that."

"Thinks he's better than us, him and his classy legal talk."

"We'll see how good he talks with a bit of steel through him."

Hull smiled coldly. "Excellent. I believe the situation is clear. Now, if you please, tell me what your weapons are."

One by one the hunters answered.

"Mace."

"Net and trident."

"Spear."

"Morning star."

"Bola."

"Scimitar."

"Bayoneted rifle," Blaine said when his turn came.

"Broadsword."

"Battleaxe."

"Sabre."

"Thank you, gentlemen," Hull said. "I will be armed with a rapier, naturally, and no armour. Our meeting will take place Sunday, at dawn, on my estate. The butler will give each of you a paper containing full instructions on how to get there. Let the bayonet man remain. Good morning to the rest of you."

The hunters left. Hull said, "Bayonetry is an unusual art. Where did you learn it?"

Blaine hesitated, then said, "In the army, 1943 to 1945."

"You're from the past?"

Blaine nodded.

"Interesting," Hull said, with no particular sign of interest.

"Then this, I daresay, is your first hunt?"

"It is."

"You appear a person of some intelligence. I suppose you have your reasons for choosing so hazardous and disreputable an employment?"

"I'm low on funds," Blaine said, "and I can't find anything else to do."

"Of course," Hull said, as though he had known it all along. "So you turned to hunting. Yet hunting is not a thing merely to turn to; and hunting the beast Man is not for everyone. The trade calls for certain special abilities, not the least of which is the ability to kill. Do you think you have that innate talent?"

"I believe so," Blaine said, though he hadn't considered the question until now.

"I wonder," Hull mused. "In spite of your bellicose appearance, you don't seem the type. What if you find yourself incapable of killing me? What if you hesitate at the crucial moment when steel grates on steel?"

"I'll chance it," Blaine said.

Hull nodded agreeably. "And so will I. Perhaps, hidden deep within you, a spark of murder burns. Perhaps not. This doubt will add spice to the game—though you may not have time to savour it."

"That's my worry," Blaine said, feeling an intense dislike for his elegant and rhetorical employer. "Might I ask you a question?"

"Consider me at your service."

"Thank you. Why do you wish to die?"

Hull stared at him, then burst into laughter. "Now I *know* you're from the past! What a question!"

"Can you answer it?"

"Of course," Hull said. He leaned back in his chair, and his eyes took on the dreamy look of a man forming rhetoric.

"I am forty-three years old, and weary of nights and days. I am a wealthy man, and an uninhabited one. I have experimented, contrived, laughed, wept, loved, hated, tasted and drunk—my fill. I have sampled all Earth has to offer me, and I choose not to tediously repeat the experience. When I was young, I pictured this excellent green planet revolving mysteriously around its flamboyant yellow luminary as a treasure-trove, a brass box of delights inexhaustible in content and immeasurable in their effect upon my ever-eager desires. But now, sadly, I have lived longer and have witnessed sensation's end. And now I see with what bourgeois complacency our fat round Earth circles, at wary distance and unvarying pace, its gaudy dreaded star. And the imagined treasure chest of the Earth seems now a child's painted toy box, shallow in its contents and mediocre in its effect upon nerves too quickly deadened to all delight."

Hull glanced at Blaine to note the effect of his words, and then went on.

"Boredom stretches before me now like a vast, arid plain—and I choose not to be bored. I choose, instead, to move on, move forward, move out; to sample Earth's last and greatest adventure—the adventure of Death, gateway to the afterlife. Can you understand that?"

"Of course," Blaine said, irritated yet impressed by Hull's theatricals. "But what's the rush? Life might have some good things still in store for you. And death is inevitable. Why rush it?"

"Spoken like a true 20th Century optimist," Hull said, laughing. "'Life is real, life is earnest...' In your day, one *had* to believe that life was real and earnest. What alternative was there? How many of you really believed in a life after death?"

"That doesn't alter the validity of my point," Blaine said, hating the stodgy, cautious, reasonable position he was forced to assume.

"But it does! The perspective on life and death has changed now. Instead of Longfellow's prosy advice, we follow Nietzsche's dictum —to die at the right time! Intelligent people don't clutch at the last shreds of life like drowning men clinging to a bit of board. They know that the body's life is only an infinitesimal portion of man's total existence. Why shouldn't they speed the body's passing by a few years if they so desire? Why shouldn't those bright pupils skip a grade or two of school? Only the frightened, the stupid, the un-educated grasp at every possible monotonous second on Earth."

"The frightened, stupid and uneducated," Blaine repeated. "And the unfortunates who can't afford Hereafter insurance."

"Wealth and class have their privileges," Hull said, smiling faintly, "and their obligations as well. One of those obligations is the necessity of dying at the right time, before one becomes a bore to one's peers and a horror to oneself. But the deed of dying tran-scends class and breeding. It is every man's patent of nobility, his summons from the king, his knightly adventure, the greatest deed of his life. And how he acquits himself in that lonely and perilous enterprise is his true measure as a man."

Hull's blue eyes were fierce and glittering. He said, "I do not wish to experience this crucial event in bed. I do not wish a dull, tame, commonplace death to sneak over me disguised as sleep. I choose to die—fighting!"

Blaine nodded in spite of himself, and felt regret at his own prosaic death. A car accident! How dull, tame, and commonplace! And how strange, dark, atavistic and noble seemed Hull's lordly selection of death. Pretentious, of course; but then, life itself was a pretension in the vast universe of unliving matter. Hull was like an ancient Japanese nobleman calmly kneeling to perform the ceremonial act of hara-kiri, and emphasizing the importance of life in the very selection of death. But hara-kiri was a passive Eastern avowal; while Hull's manner of dying was a Western death, fierce, violent, exultant.

It was admirable. But intensely irritating to a man not yet prepared to die.

Blaine said, "I have nothing against you or any other man choosing his death. But what about the hunters you plan to kill? They haven't chosen to die, and they won't survive in the hereafter."

Hull shrugged his shoulders. "They choose to live dangerously. In Nietzsche's phrase, they prefer to run risk and danger, and play dice with death. Blaine, have you changed your mind?"

"No."

"Then we will meet Sunday."

Blaine went to the door and took his paper of instructions from the butler. As he was leaving, he said, "I wonder if you've considered one last thing."

"What is that?" Hull asked.

"You must have thought of it," Blaine said. "The possibility that this whole elaborate set-up—the scientific hereafter, voices of the dead, ghosts—are merely a gigantic hoax, a money-making fraud perpetrated by Hereafter, Inc."

Hull stood perfectly still. When he spoke there was a hint of anger in his voice. "That is *quite* impossible. Only a very uneducated man could think such a thing."

"Maybe," Blaine said. "But wouldn't you look silly if it *were* a hoax! Good morning, Mr. Hull."

He left, glad to have shaken up that smooth, smug, fancy, rhetorical bastard even for a moment—and sad that his own death had been so dull, tame, and commonplace.

16

The following day, Saturday, Blaine went to Franchel's apartment for his rifle, bayonet, hunter's uniform and pack. He was given half his salary in advance, less ten per cent and the cost of the equipment. The money was very welcome, for he had been down to three dollars and change.

He went to the Spiritual Switchboard, but Melhill had left no further messages for him. He returned to his hotel room and spent the afternoon practising lunges and parries.

That evening Blaine found himself tense and despondent, and nervous at the thought of the hunt beginning in the morning. He went to a small West Side cocktail lounge that had been designed to resemble a 20th Century bar, with a dark gleaming bar, wooden stools, booths, a brass rail, and sawdust on the floor. He slid into a booth and ordered beer.

The classic neon lights glowed softly, and a genuine antique juke box played the sentimental tunes of Glenn Miller and Benny Goodman. Blaine sat, hunched over his glass of beer, drearily asking himself who and what he was.

Was it truly *he* taking casual employment as a hunter and killer of men?

Then what happened to *Tom Blaine*, the former designer of sail-boats, former listener to high-fidelity music, former reader of fine books, former viewer of good plays? What happened to that quiet, sardonic, non-aggressive man?

Surely that man, housed in his slender, nervous, unassuming body, would never choose to kill!

Would he?

Was that familiar and regretted Blaine defeated and smothered by the large, square-muscled, quick-reflexed fighter's body he had acquired? And was that body, with its own peculiar glandular secretions dripping into the dark bloodstream, its own distinct and configurated brain, its own system of nerves and signals and responses —was that domineering body responsible for everything, dragging its helpless owner into murderous violence?

Blaine rubbed his eyes and told himself that he was dreaming nonsense. The truth simply was: He had died through circumstances beyond his control, been reborn in the future, and found himself unemployable except as a hunter. Q.E.D.

But that rational explanation didn't satisfy him, and he no longer had time to search out the slippery and elusive truth.

He was no longer a detached observer of 2110. He had become a biased participant, an actor instead of an onlooker, with all of an actor's thoughtless sweep and rush. Action was irresistible, it generated its own momentary truth. The brakes were off, and the engine Blaine was rolling down the steep hill Life, gathering momentum but no moss. Perhaps this, now, was his last chance for a look, a summing up, a measured choice...

But it was already too late, for a man slid into the booth opposite him like a shadow across the world. And Blaine was looking into the white and impassive face of the zombie.

"Good evening," the zombie said.

"Good evening," Blaine said steadily. "Would you care for a drink?"

"No, thank you. My system doesn't respond to stimulation."

"Sorry to hear it," Blaine said.

The zombie shrugged his shoulders. "I have a name now," he said. "I decided to call myself Smith, until I remember my real name. Smith. Do you like it?"

"It's a fine name," Blaine said.

"Thank you. I went to a doctor," Smith said. "He told me my body's no good. No stamina, no recuperative powers."

"Can't you be helped?"

Smith shook his head. "The body's definitely zombie. I occupied it much too late. The doctor gives me another few months at most."

"To bad," Blaine said, feeling nausea rise in his throat at the sight of that sullen, thick-featured, leaden-skinned face with its unharmonious features and patient Buddha's eyes. Smith sat, slack and unnatural in rough workman's clothes, his black-dotted white face close-shaven and smelling of strong lotion. But he had changed. Already Blaine could see a certain leathery dryness in the once-pliant skin, certain striations in the flesh around the eyes, nose and mouth, minute creases in the forehead like tool-marks in old leather. And, mingled with the heavy after-shaving lotion, Blaine thought he could sense the first faint odour of dissolution.

"What do you want with me?" Blaine asked.

"I don't know."

"Then leave me alone."

"I can't do that," Smith said apologetically.

"Do you want to kill me?" Blaine asked, his throat dry.

"I don't know! I can't remember! Kill you, protect you, maim you, love you—I don't know yet! But I'll remember soon, Blaine, I promise!"

"Leave me alone," Blaine said, his muscles tensing.

"I can't," Smith said. "Don't you understand? I know nothing except you. Literally nothing! I don't know this world or any other, no person, face, mind or memory. You're my only landmark, the centre of my existence, my only reason for living."

"Stop it!"

"But it's true! Do you think I *enjoy* dragging this structure of flesh through the streets? What good is life with no hope before me and no memory behind me? Death is better! Life means filthy decaying flesh, and death is pure spirit! I've thought about it, dreamed about it, beautiful fleshless death! But one thing stops me. I have *you*, Blaine, to keep me going!"

"Get out of here," Blaine said, nausea bitter in his mouth.

"*You*, my sun and moon, my stars, my Earth, my total universe, my life, my reason, my friend, enemy, lover, murderer, wife, father, child, husband—"

Blaine's fist shot out, striking Smith high on the cheekbone. The zombie was flung back in the booth. His expression did not change, but a great purple bruise appeared on his lead-coloured cheek-bone.

"*Your* mark!" Smith murmured.

Blaine's fist, poised for another blow, dropped.

Smith stood up. "I'm going. Take care of yourself, Blaine. Don't die yet! I need you. Soon I'll remember, and I'll come to you."

Smith, his sullen, slack, bruised face impassive, left the bar.

Blaine ordered a double whiskey and sat for a long time over it, trying to still the shaking in his hands.

17

Blaine arrived at the Hull estate by rural jetbus, an hour before dawn. He was dressed in a traditional hunter's uniform—khaki shirt and slacks, rubber-soled shoes and wide-brimmed hat. Slung over one shoulder was his field pack; over the other he carried his rifle and bayonet in a plastic bag.

A servant met him at the outer gate and led him to the low, rambling mansion. Blaine learned that the Hull estate consisted of ninety wooded acres in the Adirondack Mountains between Keene and Elizabethtown. Here, the servant told him, Hull's father had suicided at the age of fifty-one, taking the lives of six hunters with him before a sabre man slashed his head off. Glorious death! Hull's uncle, on the other hand, had chosen to berserk in San Francisco, a city he had always loved. The police had to beam him twelve times before he dropped, and he took seven bystanders with him. The newspapers made much of the exploit, and accounts of it were preserved in the family scrapbook.

It just went to show, the garrulous old retainer pointed out, the difference in temperaments. Some, like the uncle, were friendly, fun-loving men who wanted to die in a crowd, attracting a certain amount of attention. Others, like the present Mr. Hull, were more given to the love of solitude and nature.

Blaine nodded politely to all this and was taken to a large, rustic room where the hunters were assembled, drinking coffee and honing a last razor edge to their weapons. Light flashed from the blued-steel broadsword and silvery battleaxe, wavered along the polished spearhead and glinted frostily from the diamond-points of the mace and morning star. At first glance, Blaine thought it looked like a scene from medieval times. But on second thought he decided it was more like a movie set.

"Pull up a chair, pal," the axeman called. "Welcome to the Benevolent Protective Society of Butchers, Slaughterhouse Men, and Killers-at-Large. I'm Sammy Jones, finest axeman in the Americas and probably Europe, too."

Blaine sat down and was introduced to the other hunters. They represented half a dozen nationalities, although English was their common tongue.

Sammy Jones was a squat, black-haired, bull-shouldered man, dressed in patched and faded khakis, with several old hunting scars across his craggy, thick-browed face.

"First hunt?" he asked, glancing at Blaine's neat pressed khakis. Blaine nodded, removed his rifle from its plastic bag and fitted the bayonet to its end. He tested the locking mechanism, tightened the rifle's strap, and removed the bayonet again.

"Can you really use that thing?" Jones asked.

"Sure," Blaine said, more confidently than he felt.

"Hope so. Guys like Hull have a nose for the weak sisters. They try to cut 'em out of the pack early."

"How long does a hunt usually last?" Blaine asked.

"Well," Jones said, "longest I was ever on took eight days. That was Asturias, where my partner Sligo got his. Generally a good pack can pin down a Quarry in a day or two. Depends on how he wants to die. Some try to hang on as long as they can. They run to cover. They hide in caves and ravines, the dirty treacherous dogs, and you have to go in for them and chance a thrust in the face. That's how Sligo got it. But I don't think Hull's that way. He wants to die like a great big fire-eating he-man hero. So he'll stalk around and take chances, looking to see how many of us he can knock off with his pigsticker."

"You sound as if you don't approve," Blaine said.

Sammy Jones raised his bushy eyebrows. "I don't hold with making a big fuss about dying. Here comes the hero himself."

Hull entered the room, lean and elegant in khaki-coloured silk, with a white silk bandanna knotted loosely around his neck. He carried a light pack, and strapped to one shoulder was a thin, wicked-looking rapier.

"Good morning, gentlemen," he said. "Weapons all honed, packs straight, shoelaces firmly tied? Excellent!"

Hull walked to a window and drew the curtains aside.

"Behold the first crack of dawn, a glorious streak in our eastern skies, harbinger of our fierce Lord Sun who rules the chase. I shall leave now. A servant will inform you when my half-hour grace is done. Then you may pursue, and kill me upon sight. If you are able! The estate is fenced. I will remain within its confines, and so shall you."

Hull bowed, then walked quickly and gracefully out of the room.

"God, I hate these fancy birds!" Sammy Jones shouted, after the door was closed. "They're all alike, every one of them. Acting so cool and casual, so goddamned *heroic*. If they only knew how bloody *silly* I think they are—me that's been on twenty-eight of these things."

"Why do you hunt?" Blaine asked.

Sammy Jones shrugged. "My father was an axeman, and he taught me the business. It's the only thing I know."

"You could learn a different trade," Blaine said.

"I suppose I could. The fact is, I *like* killing these aristocratic gentlemen. I hate every rich bastard among them with their lousy hereafter a poor man can't afford. I take pleasure in killing them, and if I had money I'd pay for the privilege."

"And Hull enjoys killing poor men like you," Blaine said. "It's a sad world."

"No, just an honest one," Sammy Jones told him. "Stand up, I'll fasten your pack on right."

When that was done, Sammy Jones said, "Look Tom, why don't you and me stick together on this hunt? Mutual protection, like?"

"*My* protection, you mean," Blaine said.

"Nothing to be ashamed of," Jones told him. "Every skilled trade must be learned before it can be practised. And what better man to learn from than myself, the finest of the fine?"

"Thanks," Blaine said. "I'll try to hold up my end, Sammy."

"You'll do fine. Now, Hull's a fencer, be sure of it, and fencers have their little tricks which I'll explain as we go along. When he—"

At that moment a servant entered, carrying an old, ornate chronometer. When the second hand passed twelve, he looked sharply at the hunters.

"Gentlemen," he said, "the time of grace is passed. The chase may begin."

The hunters trooped outside into the grey, misty dawn. Theseus the tracker, balancing his trident across his shoulders, picked up the trail at once. It led upwards, towards a mist-wreathed mountain.

Spread out in a long single file, the hunters started up the mountain's side.

Soon the early morning sun had burned away the mists. Theseus lost the trail when it crossed bare granite. The hunters spread out in a broken line across the face of the mountain, and continued advancing slowly upward.

At noon, the broadsword man picked a fragment of khaki-coloured silk from a thornbush. A few minutes later, Theseus found footprints on moss. They led down, into a narrow thickly wooded valley. Eagerly the hunters pressed forward.

"Here he is!" a man shouted.

Blaine whirled and saw, fifty yards to his right, the man with the morning star running forward. He was the youngest of the hunters, a brawny, self-confident Sicilian. His weapon consisted of a stout handle of ash, fixed to which was a foot of chain. At the end of the chain was a heavy spiked ball, the morning star. He was whirling this weapon over his head and singing at the top of his lungs.

Sammy Jones and Blaine sprinted towards him. They saw Hull break from the bushes, rapier in hand. The Sicilian leaped forward and swung a blow that could have felled a tree. Hull dodged lightly out of the way, and lunged.

The morning star man gurgled and went down, pierced through the throat. Hull planted a foot on his chest, yanked the rapier free, and vanished again into the underbrush.

"I never could understand why a man'd use a morning star," Sammy Jones said. "Too clumsy. If you don't hit your man the first lick, you never recover in time."

The Sicilian was dead. Hull's passage through the underbrush was clearly visible. They plunged in after him, followed by most of the hunters, with flankers ranged on either side.

Soon they encountered rock again, and the trail was lost.

All afternoon they searched, with no luck. At sundown they pitched camp on the mountainside, posted guards, and discussed the day's hunting over a small campfire.

"Where do you suppose he is?" Blaine asked.

"He could be anywhere on the damned estate," Jones said. "Remember, he knows every foot of ground here. We're seeing it for the first time."

"Then he could hide from us indefinitely."

"If he wanted to. But he wants to be killed, remember? In a big, flashy, heroic way. So he'll keep on trying to cut us down until we get him."

Blaine looked over his shoulder at the dark woods. "He could be standing there now, listening."

"No doubt he is," Jones said. "I hope the guards stay awake."

Conversation droned on in the little camp, and the fire burned low. Blaine wished morning would come. Darkness reversed the roles. The hunters were the hunted now, stalked by a cruel and amoral suicide intent upon taking as many lives with him as possible.

With that thought, he dozed off.

Sometime before dawn he was awakened by a scream. Grabbing his rifle, he sprang to his feet and peered into the darkness. There was another scream, closer this time, and the sound of hurried movement through the woods. Then someone threw a handful of leaves on the dying fire.

In the sudden yellow glow, Blaine saw a man staggering back to

the camp. It was one of the guards, trailing his spear behind him.
He was bleeding in two places, but his wounds didn't appear fatal.

"That bastard," the spearman sobbed, "that lousy bastard."

"Take it easy, Chico," one of the men said, ripping open the
spearman's shirt to clean and bandage the wound. "Did you get
him?"

"He was too quick," the spearman moaned. "I missed."

That was the end of the sleeping for the night.

The hunters were moving again at the first light of dawn, widely
scattered, looking for a trace of the Quarry. Theseus found a broken
button and then a half-erased footprint. The hunt veered again,
winding up a narrow-faced mountain.

At the head of the pack, Otto gave a sudden shout. "Hey! Here!
I got him!"

Theseus rushed towards him, followed by Blaine and Jones. They
saw Hull backing away, watching intently as Otto advanced swinging the bola around his cropped head. The Argentinian lasso hissed
in the air, its three iron balls blurring. Then Otto released it.
Instantly Hull flung himself to the ground. The bola snaked through
the air inches above his head, wrapped itself around a tree limb and
snapped it off. Hull, grinning broadly, ran towards the weaponless
man.

Before he could reach him Theseus had arrived, flourishing his
trident. They exchanged thrusts. Then Hull whirled and ran.

Theseus lunged. The Quarry howled with pain but continued
running.

"Did you wound him?" Jones asked.

"A flesh wound in the rump," Theseus said. "Probably most painful to his pride."

The hunters ran on, panting heavily, up the mountain's side. But
they had lost the Quarry again.

They spread out, surrounding the narrowing mountain, and
slowly began working their way towards the peak. Occasional noises
and footprints told them the Quarry was still before them, retreating
upward. As the peak narrowed they were able to close their ranks
more, lessening any chance of Hull slipping through.

By late afternoon the pine and spruce trees had become sparse.
Above them was a confused labyrinth of granite boulders, and past
that the final peak itself.

"Careful now!" Jones called to the hunters.

As he said it, Hull launched an attack. Springing from behind a
rock pinnacle, he came at old Bjorn the mace man, his rapier hiss-
ing, trying to cut the man down quickly and escape the throttling
noose of hunters.

But Bjorn gave ground only slowly, cautiously parrying the rapier thrusts, both hands on his mace as though it were a quarterstaff. Hull swore angrily at the phlegmatic man, attacked furiously, and threw himself aside just in time to avoid a blow of the mace.

Old Bjorn closed—too rapidly. The rapier darted in and out of his chest like a snake's flickering tongue. Bjorn's mace dropped, and his body began rolling down the mountainside.

But the hunters had closed the circle again. Hull retreated upward, into a maze of boulders.

The hunters pressed forward. Blaine noticed that the sun was almost down; already there was a twilight hue to the air, and long shadows stretched across the grey rocks.

"Getting towards evening," he said to Jones.

"Maybe half an hour more light," Jones said, squinting at the sky. "We better get him soon. After dark he could pick every man of us off this rock."

They moved more quickly now, searching among the high boulders.

"He could roll rocks on us," Blaine said.

"Not him," Jones said. "He's too damn proud."

And then Hull stepped from behind a high rock near Blaine.

"All right, rifleman," he said.

Blaine, his rifle at high port, just managed to parry the thrust. The blade of the rapier rasped along the gun barrel, past his neck. Automatically he deflected it. Something drove him to roar as he lunged, to follow the lunge with an eager disembowelling slash and then a hopeful butt stroke intended to scatter his enemy's brains across the rocks. For that moment, Blaine was no longer a civilized man operating under a painful necessity; he was a more basic creature joyously pursuing his true vocation of murder.

The Quarry avoided his blows with quick silken grace. Blaine stumbled after him, anger sapping his skill. Suddenly he was shoved aside by Sammy Jones.

"Mine," Jones said. "All mine. I'm your boy, Hull. Try me with the pigsticker."

Hull, his face expressionless, advanced, his rapier flashing. Jones stood firm on slightly bowed legs, the battleaxe turning lightly in his hands. Hull feinted and lunged. Jones parried so hard that sparks flew, and the rapier bent like a green stick.

The other hunters had come up now. They chose seats on nearby rocks and caught their wind, commenting on the duel and shouting advice.

"Pin him against the cliff, Sammy!"

"No, over the edge with him!"

"Want some help?"

"Hell no!" Jones shouted back.

"Watch out he don't nip a finger, Sammy."

"Don't worry," Jones said.

Blaine watched, his rage ebbing as quickly as it had come. He had assumed that a battleaxe would be a clumsy weapon requiring a full backswing for each stroke. But Sammy Jones handled the short, heavy axe as though it were a baton. He took no backswing but let drive from any position, recovering instantly, his implacable weight and drive forcing Hull towards the cliff's sheer edge. There was no real comparison between the two men, Blaine realized. Hull was a gifted amateur, a dilettante murderer; Jones was a seasoned professional killer. It was like matching a ferocious house dog against a jungle tiger.

The end came quickly in the blue twilight of the mountaintop. Sammy Jones parried a thrust and stamped forward, swinging his axe backhanded. The blade bit deep into Hull's left side. Hull fell screaming down the mountain's side. For seconds afterward they heard his body crash and turn.

"Mark where he lies," Sammy Jones said.

"He's gotta be dead," the sabre man said.

"He probably is. But it isn't a workmanlike job unless we make sure."

On the way down they found Hull's mangled and lifeless body. They marked the location for the burial party and walked on to the estate.

18

The hunters returned to the city in a group and threw a wild celebration. During the evening, Sammy Jones asked Blaine if he would join him on the next job.

"I've got a nice deal lined up in Omsk," Jones said. "A Russian nobleman wants to hold a couple of gladitorial games. You'd have to use a spear, but it's the same as a rifle. I'd train you on the way. After Omsk, there's a really big hunt being organized in Manila. Five brothers want to suicide together. They want fifty hunters to cut them down. What do you say, Tom?"

Blaine thought carefully before answering. The hunter's life was the most compatible he had found so far in this world. He liked the rough companionship of men like Sammy Jones, the straight, simple thinking, the life outdoors, the action that erased all doubts.

On the other hand there was something terribly pointless about wandering around the world as a paid killer, a modern and approved version of the bully, the bravo, the thug. There was something futile about action just for action's sake, with no genuine intent or purpose behind it, no resolution or discovery. These considerations might not arise if he were truly what his body seemed; but he was not. The hiatus existed, and had to be faced.

And finally there were other problems that this world presented, other challenges more apropos to his personality. And those had to be met.

"Sorry, Sammy," he said.

Jones shook his head. "You're making a mistake, Tom. You're a natural-born killer. There's nothing else for you."

"Perhaps now," Blaine said. "I have to find out."

"Well, good luck," Sammy Jones said. "And take care of that body of yours. You picked a good one."

Blaine blinked involuntarily. "Is it so obvious?"

Jones grinned. "I been around, Tom. I can tell when a man is wearing a host. If your mind had been *born* in that body, you'd be away and hunting with me. And if your mind had been born in a different body—"

"Yes?"

"You wouldn't have gone hunting in the first place. It's a bad splice, Tom. You'd better figure out which way you're going."

"Thanks," Blaine said. They shook hands and Blaine left for his hotel.

He reached his room and flung himself, fully dressed, upon the bed. When he awoke he would call Marie. But first, he had to sleep. All plans, thoughts, problems, decisions, even dreams, would have to wait. He was tired down to the very bone.

He snapped off the lights. Within seconds he was asleep.

Several hours later he awoke with a sensation of something wrong. The room was dark. Everything was still, more silent and expectant than New York had any right to be.

He sat upright in bed and heard a faint movement on the other side of the room, near the washbasin.

Blaine reached out and snapped on the light. There was no one in the room. But as he watched, his enamelled washbasin rose in the air. Slowly it lifted, hovering impossibly without support. And at the same time he heard a thin shattering laugh.

He knew at once he was being haunted, and by a poltergeist.

Carefully he eased out of bed and moved towards the door. The suspended basin dipped suddenly and plunged towards his head. He ducked, and the basin shattered against the wall.

His water pitcher levitated now, followed by two heavy tumblers. Twisting and turning erratically, they edged towards him.

Blaine picked up a pillow as a shield and rushed to the door. He turned the lock as a tumbler shattered above his head. The door wouldn't open. The poltergeist was holding it shut.

The pitcher struck him violently in the ribs. The remaining tumbler buzzed in an ominous circle around his head, and he was forced to retreat from the door.

He remembered the fire escape outside his window. But the poltergeist thought of it as he started to move. The curtains suddenly burst into flame. At the same instant the pillow he was holding caught fire, and Blaine threw it from him.

"Help!" he shouted. "Help!"

He was being forced into a corner of the room. With a rumble the bed slid forward, blocking his retreat. A chair rose slowly into the air and poised itself for a blow at his head.

And continually there was a thin and shattering laughter that Blaine could almost recognize.

Part Three

As the bed crept towards him Blaine shouted for help in a voice that made the window rattle. His only answer was the poltergeist's high-pitched laugh.

Were they all deaf in the hotel? Why didn't someone answer?

Then he realized that, by the very nature of things, no one would even consider helping him. Violence was a commonplace in this world, and a man's death was entirely his own business. There would be no inquiry. The janitor would simply clean up the mess in the morning, and the room would be marked vacant.

His door was impassable. The only chance he could see was to jump over the bed and through the closed window. If he made the leap properly, he would fall against the waist-high fire escape railing outside. If he jumped too hard he would go right over the railing, and fall three storeys to the street.

The chair beat him over the shoulders, and the bed rumbled forward to pin him against the wall. Blaine made a quick calculation of angles and distances, drew himself together and flung himself at the window.

He hit squarely; but he had reckoned without the advances of modern science. The window bent outward like a sheet of rubber, and snapped back into place. He was thrown against a wall, and fell dazed to the floor. Looking up, he saw a heavy bureau wobble towards him and slowly tilt.

As the poltergeist threw his lunatic strength against the bureau, the unwatched door swung open. Smith entered the room, his thick-featured zombie face impassive, and deflected the falling bureau with his shoulder.

"Come on," he said.

Blaine asked no questions. He scrambled to his feet and grabbed the edge of the closing door. With Smith's help he pulled it open again, and the two men slipped out. From within the room he heard a shriek of baffled rage.

Smith hurried down the hall, one cold hand clasped around Blaine's wrist. They went downstairs, through the hotel lobby and into the street. The zombie's face was leaden white except for the purple bruise where Blaine had struck him. The bruise had spread across nearly half his face, piebalding it into a Harlequin's grotesque mask.

"Where are we going?" Blaine asked.

"To a safe place."

They reached an ancient unused subway entrance, and descended. One flight down they came to a small iron door set in the cracked concrete floor. Smith opened the door and beckoned Blaine to follow him.

Blaine hesitated, and caught the hint of high-pitched laughter. The poltergeist was pursuing him, as the Eumenides had once pursued their victims through the streets of ancient Athens. He could stay in the lighted upper world if he wished, hag-ridden by an insane spirit. Or he could descend with Smith, through the iron door and into the darkness beyond it, to some uncertain destiny in the underworld.

The shrill laughter increased. Blaine hesitated no longer. He followed Smith through the iron door and closed it behind him.

For the moment, the poltergeist had not chosen to pursue. They walked down a tunnel lighted by an occasional naked light bulb, past cracked masonry pipes and the looming grey corpse of a subway train, past rusted iron cables lying in giant serpent coils. The air was moist and rank, and a thin slime underfoot made walking treacherous.

"Where are we going?" Blaine asked.

"To where I can protect you," Smith said.

"Can you?"

"Spirits aren't invulnerable. Exorcism is possible if the true identity of the ghost is known."

"Then you know who is haunting me?"

"I think so. There's only one person it logically could be."

"Who?"

Smith shook his head. "I'd rather not say his name yet. No sense calling him if he's not here."

They descended a series of crumbling shale steps into a wider chamber, and circled the edge of a small black pond whose surface looked as hard and still as jet. On the other side of the pond was a passageway. A man stood in front of it, blocking the way.

He was a tall husky Negro, dressed in rags, armed with a length of iron pipe. From his look Blaine knew he was a zombie.

"This is my friend," Smith said. "May I bring him through?"

"You sure he's no inspector?"

"Absolutely sure."

"Wait here," the Negro said. He disappeared into the passageway.

"Where are we?" Blaine asked.

"Underneath New York, in a series of unused subway tunnels, old sewer conduits, and some passageways we've fashioned for ourselves."

"But why did we come here?" Blaine asked.

"Where else would we go?" Smith asked, surprised. "This is my home. Didn't you know? You're in New York's zombie colony."

Blaine didn't consider a zombie colony much improvement over a ghost; but he didn't have time to think about it. The Negro returned. With him was a very old man who walked with the aid of a stick. The man's face was broken into a network of a thousand lines and wrinkles. His eyes barely showed through the fine scrollwork of sagging flesh, and even his lips were wrinkled.

"This is the man you told me about?" he asked.

"Yes sir," said Smith. "This is the man. Blaine, let me introduce you to Mr. Kean, the leader of our colony. May I take him through, sir?"

"You may," the old man said. "And I will accompany you for a while."

They started down the passageway, Mr. Kean supporting himself heavily on the Negro's arm.

"In the usual course of events," Mr. Kean said, "only zombies are allowed in the colony. All others are barred. But it has been years since I spoke with a normal, and I thought the experience might be valuable. Therefore, at Smith's earnest request, I made an exception in your case."

"I'm very grateful," Blaine said, hoping he had reason to be.

"Don't misunderstand me. I am not averse to helping you. But first and foremost I am responsible for the safety of the eleven hundred zombies living beneath New York. For their sake, normals must be kept out. Exclusivity is our only hope in an ignorant world." Mr. Kean paused. "But perhaps you can help us, Blaine."

"How?"

"By listening and understanding, and passing on what you have learned. Education is our only hope. Tell me, what do you know about the problems of a zombie?"

"Very little."

"I will instruct you. Zombieism, Mr. Blaine, is a disease which has long had a powerful aura of superstition surrounding it, comparable to the aura generated by such diseases as epilepsy, leprosy, or St. Vitus' Dance. The spiritualizing tendency is a common one. Schizophrenia, you know, was once thought to mean possession by devils, and hydrocephalic idiots were considered peculiarly blessed. Similar fantasies attach to zombies."

They walked in silence for a few moments. Mr. Kean said, "The superstition of the zombie is essentially Haitian; the disease of the zombie is worldwide, although rare. But the superstition and the disease have become hopelessly confused in the public mind. The zombie of superstition is an element of the Haitian vodun cult; a human being whose soul has been stolen by magic. The zombie's body could be used as the magician wished, could even be slaughtered and sold for meat in the marketplace. If the zombie ate salt or beheld the sea, he realized that he was dead and returned to his grave. For all this, there is no basis in fact.

"The superstition arose from the descriptically similar disease. Once it was exceedingly rare. But today, with the increase in mind-switching and reincarnation techniques, zombieism has become more common. The *disease* of the zombie occurs when a mind occupies a body that has been untenanted too long. Mind and body are not then one, as yours are, Mr. Blaine. They exist, instead, as quasi-independent entities engaged in an uneasy co-operation. Take our friend Smith as typical. He can control his body's gross physical actions, but fine co-ordination is impossible for him. His voice is incapable of discrete modulation, and his ears do not receive subtle differences in tone. His face is expressionless, for he has little or no control over surface musculature. He drives his body, but is not truly a part of it."

"And can't anything be done?" Blaine asked.

"At the present time, nothing."

"I'm very sorry," Blaine said uncomfortably.

"This is not a plea for your sympathy," Kean told him. "It is a request only for the most elementary understanding. I simply want you and everyone to know that zombieism is not a visitation of sins, but a *disease*, like mumps or cancer, and nothing more."

Mr. Kean leaned against the wall of the passageway to catch his breath. "To be sure, the zombie's appearance is unpleasant. He shambles, his wounds never heal, his body deteriorates rapidly. He mumbles like an idiot, staggers like a drunk, stares like a pervert. But is this any reason to make him the repository of all guilt and shame upon Earth, the leper of the 22nd century? They say that zombies attack people; yet his body is fragile in the extreme, and the average zombie couldn't resist a child's determined assault. They believe the disease is communicable; and this is obviously not so. They say that zombies are sexually perverted, and the truth is that a zombie experiences no sexual feelings whatsoever. But people refuse to learn, and zombies are outcasts fit only for the hangman's noose or the lyncher's burning stake."

"What about the authorities?" Blaine asked.

Mr. Kean smiled bitterly. "They used to lock us up, as a kindness, in mental institutions. You see, they didn't want us hurt. Yet zombies are rarely insane, and the authorities knew it! So now, with their tacit approval, we occupy these abandoned subway tunnels and sewer lines."

"Couldn't you find a better place?" Blaine asked.

"Frankly, the underground suits us. Sunlight is bad for unre-generative skins."

They began walking again. Blaine said, "What can I do?"

"You can tell someone what you learned here. Write about it, perhaps. Widening ripples..."

"I'll do what I can."

"Thank you," Mr. Kean said gravely. "Education is our only hope. Education and the future. Surely people will be more enlightened in the future."

The future? Blaine felt suddenly dizzy. For *this* was the future, to which he had travelled from the idealistic and hopeful 20th century. *Now* was the future! But the promised enlightenment still had not come, and people were much the same as ever. For a second Blaine's centuries pressed heavily on him. He felt disoriented and old, older than Kean, older than the human race—a creature in a borrowed body standing in a place it did not know.

"And now," Mr. Kean said, "we have reached your destination."

Blaine blinked rapidly, and life came back into focus. The dim passageway had ended. In front of him was a rusted iron ladder fastened to the tunnel wall, leading upward into darkness.

"Good luck," Mr. Kean said. He left, supporting himself heavily on the Negro's arm. Blaine watched the old man go, then turned to Smith.

"Where are we going?"

"Up the ladder."

"But where does it lead?"

Smith had already begun climbing. He stopped and looked down, his lead-coloured lips drawn back into a grin. "We're going to visit a friend of yours, Blaine. We're going into his tomb, up to his coffin, and ask him to stop haunting you. Force him, maybe."

"Who is he?" Blaine asked.

Smith only grinned and continued climbing. Blaine mounted the ladder behind him.

20

Above the passageway was a ventilation shaft, which led to another passageway. They came at last to a door, and entered.

They were in a large, brilliantly lighted room. Upon the arched ceiling was a mural depicting a handsome, clear-eyed man entering a gauzy blue heaven in the company of angels. Blaine knew at once who had modelled for the painting.

"Reilly!"

Smith nodded. "We're inside his Palace of Death."

"How did you know Reilly was haunting me?"

"You should have thought of it yourself. Only two people connected with you have died recently. The ghost certainly was not Ray Melhill. It had to be Reilly."

"But why?"

"I don't know," Smith said. "Perhaps Reilly will tell you himself."

Blaine looked at the walls. They were inlaid with crosses, crescent moons, stars and swastikas, as well as Indian, African, Arabian, Chinese and Polynesian good-luck signs. On pedestals around the room were statues of ancient deities. Among the dozens Blaine recognized Zeus, Apollo, Dagon, Odin and Astarte. In front of each pedestal was an altar, and on each altar was a cut and polished jewel.

"What's that for?" Blaine asked.

"Propitiation."

"But life after death is a scientific fact."

"Mr. Kean told me that science has little effect upon superstition," Smith said. "Reilly was fairly sure he'd survive after death; but he saw no reason to take chances. Also, Mr. Kean says that the very rich, like the very religious, wouldn't enjoy a hereafter filled with just *anybody*. They think that, by suitable rites and symbols, they can get into a more exclusive part of the hereafter."

"Is there a more exclusive part?" Blaine asked.

"No one knows. It's just a belief."

Smith led him across the room to an ornate door covered with Egyptian hieroglyphics and Chinese ideographs.

"Reilly's body is inside here," Smith said.

"And we're going in?"

"Yes, we have to."

Smith pushed the door open. Blaine saw a vast marble-pillared room. In its very centre was a bronze and gold coffin inlaid with jewels. Surrounding the coffin was a great and bewildering quantity of goods; paintings and sculptures, musical instruments, carvings, objects like washing machines, stoves, refrigerators, even a complete helicopter. There was clothing and books, and a lavish banquet had been laid out.

"What's all this stuff for?" Blaine asked.

"The essence of these goods is intended to accompany the owner into the hereafter. It's an old belief."

Blaine's first reaction was one of pity. The scientific hereafter hadn't freed men from the fear of death, as it should have done. On the contrary, it had intensified their uncertainties and stimulated

their competitive drive. Given the surety of an afterlife, man wanted
to improve upon it, to enjoy a better heaven than anyone else.
Equality was all very well; but individual initiative came first. A
perfect and passionless levelling was no more palatable an idea in
the hereafter than it was on Earth. The desire to surpass caused a
man like Reilly to build a tomb like the Pharaohs of ancient Egypt,
to brood all his life about death, to live continually trying to find
ways of preserving his property and status in the grey uncertainties
ahead.

A shame. And yet, Blaine thought, wasn't his pity based upon a
lack of belief in the efficacy of Reilly's measures? Suppose you *could*
improve your situation in the hereafter? In that case, what better
way to spend one's time on Earth than working for a better
eternity?

The proposition seemed reasonable, but Blaine refused to believe
it. *That* couldn't be the only reason for existence on Earth! Good or
bad, fair or foul, the thing had to be lived for its own sake.

Smith walked slowly into the coffin room, and Blaine stopped his
speculations. The zombie stood, contemplating a small table covered
with ornaments. Dispassionately he kicked the table over. Then
slowly, one by one, he ground the delicate ornaments into the
polished marble floor.

"What are you doing?" Blaine asked.

"You want the poltergeist to leave you alone?"

"Of course."

"Then he must have some *reason* for leaving you alone," Smith
said, kicking over an elaborate ebony sculpture.

It seemed reasonable enough to Blaine. Even a ghost must know
he will eventually leave the Threshold and enter the hereafter.
When he does, he wants his goods waiting for him, intact. Therefore
fight fire with fire, persecution with persecution.

Still, he felt like a vandal when he picked up an oil painting and
prepared to shove his fist through it.

"Don't," said a voice above his head.

Blaine and Smith looked up. Above them there seemed to be a
faint silvery mist. From the mist an attenuated voice said, "Please
put down the painting."

Blaine held on to it, his fist poised. "Are you Reilly?"

"Yes."

"Why are you haunting me?"

"Because you're responsible! Everything's your fault! You killed
me with your evil murdering mind! Yes *you*, you hideous thing
from the past, you damned monster!"

"I didn't!" Blaine cried.

"You did! You aren't human! You aren't natural! Everything

shuns you except your friend the dead man! Why aren't *you* dead, murderer!"

Blaine's fist moved towards the painting. The thin voice screamed, "Don't!"

"Will you leave me alone?" Blaine asked.

"Put down the painting," Reilly begged.

Blaine put it carefully down.

"I'll leave you alone," Reilly said. "Why shouldn't I? There are things you can't see, Blaine, but *I* see them. Your time on Earth will be short, very short, painfully short. Those you trust will betray you, those you hate will conquer you. You will die, Blaine, not in years but soon, sooner than you could believe. You'll be betrayed, and you'll die by your own hand."

"You're crazy!" Blaine shouted.

"Am I?" Reilly cackled. "Am I? *Am I?*"

The silvery mist vanished. Reilly was gone.

Smith led him back through narrow winding passageways to the street level. Outside the air was chilly, and dawn had touched the tall buildings with red and grey.

Blaine started to thank him, but Smith shook his head. "No reason for thanks! After all, I need you, Blaine. Where would I be if the poltergeist killed you? Take care of yourself, be careful. Nothing is possible for me without you."

The zombie gazed anxiously at him for a moment, then hurried away. Blaine watched him go, wondering if it wouldn't be better to have a dozen enemies than Smith for a friend.

21

Half an hour later he was at Marie Thorne's apartment. Marie, without make-up, dressed in a housecoat, blinked sleepily and led him to the kitchen, where she dialled coffee, toast and scrambled eggs.

"I wish," she said, "you'd make your dramatic appearances at a decent hour. It's six-thirty in the morning."

"I'll try to do better in the future," Blaine said cheerfully.

"You said you'd call. What happened to you?"

"Did you worry?"

"Not in the slightest. What happened?"

Between bites of toast Blaine told her about the hunt, the haunting, and the exorcism. She listened to it all, then said, "So you're obviously very proud of yourself, and I guess you should be. But you still don't know what Smith wants from you, or even who he is."

"Haven't the slightest idea," Blaine said. "Smith doesn't, either. Frankly, I couldn't care less."

"What happens when he finds out?"

"I'll worry about that when it happens."

Marie raised both eyebrows but made no comment. "Tom, what are your plans now?"

"I'm going to get a job."

"As a hunter?"

"No. Logical or not, I'm going to try the yacht design agencies. Then I'm going to come around here and bother you at reasonable hours. How does that sound?"

"Impractical. Do you want some good advice?"

"No."

"I'm giving it to you anyhow. Tom, get out of New York. Go as far away as you can. Go to Fiji or Samoa."

"Why should I?"

Marie began to pace restlessly up and down the kitchen. "You simply don't understand this world."

"I think I do."

"No! Tom, you've had a few typical experiences, that's all. But that doesn't mean you've assimilated our culture. You've been snatched, haunted, and you've gone on a hunt. But it adds up to not much more than a guided tour. Reilly was right, you're as lost and helpless as a caveman would be in your own 1958."

"That's ridiculous, and I object to the comparison."

"All right, let's make it a 14th century Chinese. Suppose this hypothetical Chinaman had met a gangster, gone on a bus ride and seen Coney Island. Would you say he understood 20th century America?"

"Of course not. But what's the point?"

"The point," she said, "is that you aren't safe here, and you can't even sense what or where or how urgent the dangers are. For one, that damned Smith is after you. Next, Reilly's heirs might not take kindly to you desecrating his tomb; they might find it necessary to do something about it. And the directors at Rex are still arguing about what *they* should do about you. You've altered things, changed things, disrupted things. Can't you *feel* it?"

"I can handle Smith," Blaine said. "To hell with Reilly's heirs. As for the directors, what can they do to me?"

She came over to him and put her arms around his neck. "Tom," she said earnestly, "any man born here who found himself in your shoes would run as fast as he could!"

Blaine held her close for a moment and stroked her sleek dark hair. She cared for him, she wanted him to be safe. But he was in no mood for warnings. He had survived the dangers of the hunt, had passed through the iron door into the underworld and won through again to the light. Now, sitting in Marie's sunny kitchen, he felt elated and at peace with the world. Danger seemed an academic problem not worthy of discussion at the moment, and the idea of running away from New York was absurd.

"Tell me," Blaine said lightly, "among the things I've disrupted— is one of them you?"

"I'm probably going to lose my job, if that's what you mean."

"That's not what I mean."

"Then you should know the answer ... Tom, will you please get out of New York?"

"No. And please stop sounding so panicky."

"Oh Lord," she sighed, "we talk the same language but I'm not getting through. You don't understand. Let me try an example." She thought for a moment. "Suppose a man owned a sailboat—"

"Do you sail?" Blaine asked.

"Yes, I love sailing. Tom, listen to me! Suppose a man owned a sailboat in which he was planning an ocean voyage—"

"Across the sea of life," Blaine filled in.

"You're not funny," she said, looking very pretty and serious. "This man doesn't know anything about boats. He sees it floating, nicely painted, everything in place. He can't imagine any danger. Then _you_ look the boat over. You see that the frames are cracked, teredos have got into the rudder post, there's dry rot in the mast step, the sails are mildewed, the keel bolts are rusted, and the fastenings are ready to let go."

"Where'd you learn so much about boats?" Blaine asked.

"I've been sailing since I was a kid. Will you please pay attention? You tell that man his boat is not seaworthy, the first gale is likely to sink him."

"We'll have to go sailing sometime," Blaine said.

"But this man," Marie continued doggedly, "doesn't know anything about boats. The thing _looks_ all right. And the hell of it is, you can't tell him exactly what is going to happen, or when. Maybe the boat will hold together for a month, or a year, or maybe only a week. Maybe the keel bolts will go first, or perhaps it'll be the mast. You just don't know. And that's the situation here. I can't tell you what's going to happen, or when. I just know you're unseaworthy. You _must_ get out of here!"

She looked at him hopefully. Blaine nodded and said, "You'll make one hell of a crew."

"So you're not going?"

"No. I've been up all night. The only place I'm going now is to bed. Would you care to join me?"

"Go to hell!"

"Darling, please! Where's your pity for a homeless wanderer from the past?"

"I'm going out," she said. "Help yourself to the bedroom. You'd better think about what I told you."

"Sure," Blaine said. "But why should I worry when I have you looking out for me?"

"Smith's looking for you, too," she reminded him. She kissed him quickly and left the room.

Blaine finished his breakfast and turned in. He awoke in the early afternoon. Marie still hadn't returned, so before leaving he wrote her a cheerful note with the address of his hotel.

During the next few days he visited most of the yacht design agencies in New York, without success. His old firm, Mattison & Peters, was long defunct. The other firms weren't interested. Finally, at Jaakobsen Yachts, Ltd., the head designer questioned him closely about the now-extinct Chesapeake Bay and Bahamas work boats. Blaine demonstrated his considerable knowledge of the types, as well as his out-of date draftsmanship.

"We got a few calls for antique hulls," the head designer said. "Tell you what. We'll hire you as office boy. You can do classic hulls on a commission basis and study up on your designing, which, frankly, is old-fashioned. When you're ready, we'll upgrade you. What do you say?"

It was an inferior position; but it was a job, a legitimate job, with a fine chance for advancement. It meant that at last he had a real place in the world of 2110.

"I'll take it," Blaine said, "with thanks."

That evening, by way of celebrating, he went to a Sensory Shop to buy a player and a few recordings. He was entitled, he thought, to a little basic luxury.

The sensories were an inescapable part of 2110, as omnipresent and popular as television had been in Blaine's day. Larger and more elaborate versions of the sensories were used for theatre productions, and variations were employed for advertising and propaganda. They were to date the purest and most powerful form of the ready-made dream, tailored to fit anyone.

But they had their extremely vocal opponents, who deplored the ominous trend towards complete passivity in the spectator. These critics were disturbed by the excessive ease with which a person could assimilate a sensory; and in truth, many a housewife walked blank-eyed through her days, a modern-day mystic plugged into a continual bright vision.

In reading a book or watching television, the critics pointed out, the viewer had to exert himself, to participate. But the sensories merely swept over you, vivid, brilliant, insidious, and left behind the damaging schizophrenic impression that dreams were better and more desirable than life. Such an impression could not be allowed, even if it were true. Sensories were dangerous! To be sure, some valid artistic work was done in the sensory form. (One could not discount Verreho, Johnston or Telkin; and Mikkelsen showed promise.) But there was not *much* good work. And weighed against the damaging psychic effects, the lowering of popular taste, the drift towards complete passivity...

In another generation, the critics thundered, people will be incapable of reading, thinking or acting!

It was a strong argument. But Blaine, with his 152 years of perspective, remembered much the same sort of arguments hurled at radio, movies, comic books, television and paperbacks. Even the revered novel had once been bitterly chastised for its deviation from the standards of pure poetry. Every innovation seemed culturally destructive; and became, ultimately, a cultural staple, the embodiment of the good old days, the spirit of the Golden Age—to be threatened and finally destroyed by the next innovation.

The sensories, good or bad, were here. Blaine entered the store to partake of them.

After looking over various models he bought a medium-priced Bendix player. Then, with the clerk's aid, he chose three popular recordings and took them into a booth to play. Fastening the electrodes to his forehead, he turned the first one on.

It was a popular historical, a highly romantic rendition of the *Chanson de Roland*, done in a low-intensity non-identification technique that allowed large battle effects and massed movements. The dream began.

...and Blaine was in the pass of Roncesvalles on that hot and fateful August morning in 778, standing with Roland's rearguard, watching the main body of Charlemagne's army wind slowly on towards Frankland. The tired veterans slumped in their high-cantled saddles, leather creaked, spurs jingled against bronze stirrup-guards. There was a smell of pine and sweat in the air, a hint of smoke from razed Pampelona, a taste of oiled steel and dry summer grass...

Blaine decided to buy it. The next was a high-intensity chase on Venus, in which the viewer identified fully with the hunted but innocent man. The last was a variable-intensity recording of "War and Peace", with occasional identification sections.

As he paid for his purchases, the clerk winked at him and said, "Interested in the real stuff?"

"Maybe," Blaine said.

"I got great party records," the clerk told him. "Full identification with switches yet. No? Got a genuine horror piece—man dying in quicksand. The murderers recorded his death for the specialty trade."

"Perhaps some other time," Blaine said, moving towards the door.

"And also," the clerk told him, "I got a special recording, legitimately made but withheld from the public. A few copies are being bootlegged around. Man reborn from the past. Absolutely genuine."

"Really?"

"Yes, it's perfectly unique. The emotions come through clear as a bell, sharp as a knife. A collector's item. I predict it'll become a classic."

"That I'd like to hear," Blaine said grimly.

He took the unlabelled record back to the booth. In ten minutes he came out again, somewhat shaken, and purchased it for an exorbitant price. It was like buying a piece of himself.

The clerk and the Rex technicians were right. It was a real collector's item, and would probably become a classic.

Unfortunately, all names had been carefully wiped to prevent the police from tracing its source. He was famous—but in a completely anonymous fashion.

22

Blaine went to his job every day, swept the floor, emptied the wastepaper basket, addressed envelopes, and did a few antique hulls on commission. In the evenings he studied the complex science of 22nd century yacht design. After a while he was given a few small assignments writing publicity releases. He proved talented at this, and was soon promoted to the position of junior yacht designer. He began handling much of the liaison between Jaakobsen Yachts, Ltd., and the various yards building to their design.

He continued to study, but there were few requests for classic hulls. The Jaakobsen brothers handled most of the stock boats, while old Ed Richter, known as the Marvel of Salem, drew up the unusual racers and multi-hulls. Blaine took over publicity and advertising, and had no time for anything else.

It was responsible, necessary work. But it was *not* yacht designing. Irrevocably his life in 2110 was falling into much the same pattern it had assumed in 1958.

Blaine pondered this carefully. On the one hand, he was happy about it. It seemed to settle, once and for all, the conflict between his mind and his borrowed body. Obviously his mind was boss.

On the other hand, the situation didn't speak too well for the quality of that mind. Here was a man who had travelled 152 years into the future, had passed through wonders and horrors, and was working again, with a weary and terrible inevitability, as a junior yacht designer who did everything but design yachts. Was there some fatal flaw in his character, some hidden defect which doomed him to inferiority no matter what his environment?

Moodily he pictured himself flung back a million or so years, to a caveman era. Doubtless, after a period of initial adjustment, he would become a junior designer of dugouts. Only not *really* a designer. His job would be to count the wampum, check the quality of the tree trunks and contract for outriggers, while some other fellow (probably a Neanderthal genius) did the actual running of the lines.

That was disheartening. But fortunately it was not the only way of viewing the matter. His inevitable return could also be taken as a fine example of internal solidarity, of human steadfastness. He was a man who knew what he was. No matter how his environment changed, he remained true to his function.

Viewed this way, he could be very proud of being eternally and forever a junior yacht designer.

He continued working, fluctuating between these two basic views of himself. Once or twice he saw Marie, but she was usually busy in the high councils of the Rex Corporation. He moved out of his hotel and into a small, tastefully furnished apartment. New York was beginning to feel normal to him.

And, he reminded himself, if he had gained nothing else, he had at least settled his mind-body problem.

But his body was not to be disposed of so lightly. Blaine had overlooked one of the problems likely to exist with the ownership of a strong, handsome, and highly idiosyncratic body such as his.

One day the conflict flared again, more aggravated than ever.

He had left work at the usual time, and was waiting at a corner for his bus. He noticed a woman staring intently at him. She was perhaps twenty-five years old, a buxom, attractive redhead. She was commonly dressed. Her features were bold, yet they had a certain wistful quality.

Blaine realized that he had seen her before but never really noticed her. Now that he thought about it, she had once ridden a helibus with him. Once she had entered a store nearly on his footsteps. And several times she had been passing his building when he left work.

She had been watching him, probably for weeks. But why?

He waited, staring back at her. The woman hesitated a moment, then said, "Could I talk to you a moment?" Her voice was husky, pleasant, but very nervous. "Please, Mr. Blaine, it's very important."

So she knew his name. "Sure," Blaine said. "What is it?"

"Not here. Could we—uh—go somewhere?"

Blaine grinned and shook his head. She seemed harmless enough; but Orc had seemed so, too. Trusting strangers in this world was a good way of losing your mind, your body, or both.

"I don't know you," Blaine said, "and I don't know where you learned my name. Whatever you want, you'd better tell me here."

"I really shouldn't be bothering you," the woman said in a discouraged voice. "But I couldn't stop myself, I had to talk to you. I get so lonely sometimes, you know how it is?"

"Lonely? Sure, but why do you want to talk to me?"

She looked at him sadly. "That's right, you don't know."

"No, I don't," Blaine said patiently. "Why?"

"Can't we go somewhere? I don't like to say it in public like this."

"You'll have to," Blaine said, beginning to think that this was a very complicated game indeed.

"Oh, all right," the woman said, obviously embarrassed. "I've been following you around for a long time, Mr. Blaine. I found out your name and where you worked. I had to talk to you. It's all on account of that body of yours."

"What?"

"Your body," she said, not looking at him. "You see, it used to be my husband's body before he sold it to the Rex Corporation."

Blaine's mouth opened, but he could find no adequate words.

23

Blaine had always known that his body had lived its own life in the world before it had been given to him. It had acted, decided, loved, hated, made its own individual imprint upon society and woven its own complex and lasting web of relationships. He could even have assumed that it had been married; most bodies were. But he had preferred not thinking about it. He had let himself believe that everything concerning the previous owner had conveniently disappeared.

His own meeting with Ray Melhill's snatched body should have shown him how naïve that attitude was. Now, like it or not, he had to think about it.

They went to Blaine's apartment. The woman, Alice Kranch, sat dejectedly on one side of the couch and accepted a cigarette.

"The way it was," she said, "Frank—that was my husband's name, Frank Kranch—he was never satisfied with things, you know? He had a good job as a hunter, but he was never satisfied."

"A hunter?"

"Yes, he was a spearman in the China game."

"Hmm," Blaine said, wondering again what had induced him to go on that hunt. His own needs or Kranch's dormant reflexes? It was annoying to have this mind-body problem come up again just when it had seemed so nicely settled.

"But he wasn't ever satisfied," Alice Kranch said. "And it used to make him sore, those fancy rich guys getting themselves killed and going to the hereafter. He always hated the idea of dying like a dog, Frank did."

"I don't blame him," Blaine said.

She shrugged her shoulders. "What can you do? Frank didn't have a chance of making enough money for hereafter insurance. It bothered him. And then he got that big wound on the shoulder that nearly put him under. I suppose you still got the scar?"

Blaine nodded.

"Well, he wasn't ever the same after that. Hunters usually don't think much about death, but Frank started to. He started thinking about it all the time. And then he met this skinny dame from Rex."

"Marie Thorne?"

"That's the one," Alice said. "She was a skinny dame, hard as nails and cold as a fish. I couldn't understand what Frank saw in her. Oh, he played around some, most hunters do. It's on account of the danger. But there's playing around and playing around. He and this fancy Rex dame were thick as thieves. I just couldn't see what Frank saw in her. I mean she was so *skinny*, and so tight-faced. She was pretty in a pinched sort of way, but she looked like she'd wear her clothes to bed, if you know what I mean."

Blaine nodded, a little painfully. "Go on."

"Well, there's no accounting for some tastes, but I thought I knew Frank's. And I guess I did because it turned out he *wasn't* going with her. It was strictly business. He turned up one day and said to me, 'Baby, I'm leaving you. I'm taking that big fat trip into the hereafter. There's a nice piece of change in it for you, too.'"

Alice sighed and wiped her eyes. "That big idiot had sold his body! Rex had given him hereafter insurance and an annuity for me, and he was so damned proud of himself! Well, I talked myself blue in the face trying to get him to change his mind. No chance, he was going to eat pie in the sky. To his way of thinking his number was up anyhow, and the next hunt would do him. So off he went. He talked to me once from the Threshold."

"Is he still there?" Blaine asked, with a prickling sensation at the back of his neck.

"I haven't heard from him in over a year," Alice said, "so I guess he's gone on to the hereafter. The bastard!"

She cried for a few moments, then wiped her eyes with a tiny handkerchief and looked mournfully at Blaine. "I wasn't going to bother you. After all, it was Frank's body to sell and it's yours now. I don't have any claims on it or you. But I got so blue, so lonely."

"I can imagine," Blaine murmured, thinking that she was definitely not his type. Objectively speaking, she was pretty enough. Comely but overblown. Her features were well formed, bold, and vividly coloured. Her hair, although obviously not a natural red, was shoulder length and of a smooth texture. She was the sort of woman he could picture, hands on hips, arguing with a policeman; hauling in a fishnet; dancing to a flamenco guitar; or herding goats on a mountain path with a full skirt swishing around ample hips, and peasant blouse distended.

But she was not in good taste.

However, he reminded himself, Frank Kranch had found her very much to *his* taste. And he was wearing Kranch's body.

"Most of our friends," Alice was saying, "were hunters in the China game. Oh, they dropped around sometimes after Frank left. But you know hunters, they've got just one thing on their minds."

"Is that a fact?" Blaine asked.

"Yes. And so I moved out of Peking and came back to New York, where I was born. And then one day I saw Frank—I mean you. I could have fainted on the spot. I mean I might have expected it and all, but still it gives you a turn to see your husband's body walking around."

"I should think so," Blaine said.

"So I followed you and all. I wasn't ever going to bother you or anything, but it just kept bothering me all the time. And I sort of got to wondering what kind of a man was ... I mean, Frank was so —well, he and I got along very well, if you know what I mean."

"Certainly," Blaine said.

"I'll bet you think I'm terrible!"

"Not at all!" said Blaine. She looked him full in the face, her expression mournful and coquettish. Blaine felt Kranch's old scar throb.

But remember, he told himself, Kranch is gone. Everything is *Blaine* now, Blaine's will, Blaine's way, Blaine's taste...

Isn't it?

This problem must be settled, he thought, as he seized the willing Alice and kissed her with an unBlainelike fervour...

In the morning Alice made breakfast. Blaine sat, staring out of the window, thinking dismal thoughts.

Last night had proven to him conclusively that Kranch was still king of the Kranch-Blaine body-mind. For last night he had been completely unlike himself. He had been fierce, violent, rough, angry and exultant. He had been all the things he had always deplored, had acted with an abandon that must have bordered on madness.

That was not Blaine. That was *Kranch*, the Body Triumphant.

Blaine had always prized delicacy, subtlety, and the grasp of nuance. Too much, perhaps. Yet those had been his virtues, the expressions of his own individual personality. With them, he was Thomas Blaine. Without them he was less than nothing—a shadow cast by the eternally triumphant Kranch.

Gloomily he contemplated the future. He would give up the struggle, become what his body demanded; a fighter, a brawler, a lusty vagabond. Perhaps in time he would grow used to it, even enjoy it...

"Breakfast's ready," Alice announced.

They ate in silence, and Alice mournfully fingered a bruise on her forearm. At last Blaine could stand it no longer.

"Look," he said, "I'm sorry."

"What for?"

"Everything."

She smiled wanly. "That's all right. It was my fault, really."

"I doubt that. Pass the butter please," Blaine said.

She passed the butter. They ate in silence for a few minutes. Then Alice said, "I was very, very stupid."

"Why?"

"I guess I was chasing a dream," she said. "I thought I could find Frank all over again. I'm not really that way, Mr. Blaine. But I thought it would be like with Frank."

"And wasn't it?"

She shook her head. "No, of course not."

Blaine put down his coffee cup carefully. He said, "I suppose Kranch was rougher. I suppose he batted you from wall to wall. I suppose—"

"Oh, no!" she cried. "Never! Mr. Blaine, Frank was a hunter and he lived a hard life. But with me he was always a perfect gentleman. He had manners, Frank had."

"He had?"

"He certainly had! Frank was always gentle with me, Mr. Blaine. He was—delicate, if you know what I mean. Nice. Gentle. He was never, *never* rough. To tell the truth, he was the very opposite from you, Mr. Blaine."

"Uh," said Blaine.

"Not that there's anything wrong with you," she said with hasty kindness. "You *are* a little rough, but I guess it takes all kinds."

"I guess it does," Blaine said. "Yes, I guess it sure does."

They finished their breakfast in embarrassed silence. Alice, freed of her obsessive dream, left immediately afterwards, with no suggestion that they meet again. Blaine sat in his big chair, staring out of the window, thinking.

So he wasn't like Kranch!

The sad truth was, he told himself, he had acted as he *imagined* Kranch would have acted in similar circumstances. It had been pure auto-suggestion. Hysterically he had convinced himself that a strong, active, hearty outdoors man would necessarily treat a woman like a wrestling bear.

He had acted out a stereotype. He would feel even sillier if he weren't so relieved at regaining his threatened Blaineism.

He frowned as he remembered Alice's description of Marie: Skinny, hard as nails, cold as a fish. *More* stereotyping.

But under the circumstances, he could hardly blame Alice.

24

A few days later, Blaine received word that a communication was waiting for him at the Spiritual Switchboard. He went there after work, and was sent to the booth he had used previously.

Melhill's amplified voice said, "Hello, Tom."

"Hello, Ray. I was wondering where you were."

"I'm still in the Threshold," Melhill told him, "but I won't be much longer. I gotta go on and see what the hereafter is like. It pulls at me. But I wanted to talk to you again, Tom. I think you should watch out for Marie Thorne."

"Now Ray—"

"I mean it. She's been spending all her time at Rex. I don't know what's going on there, they got the conference rooms shielded against psychic invasion. But something's brewing over you, and she's in the middle of it."

"I'll keep my eyes open," Blaine said.

"Tom, please take my advice. Get out of New York. Get out fast, while you still have a body and a mind to run it with."

"I'm staying," Blaine said.

"You stubborn bastard," Melhill said, with deep feeling. "What's the use of having a protective spirit if you don't ever take his advice?"

"I appreciate your help," Blaine said. "I really do. But tell me truthfully, how much better off would I be if I ran?"

"You might be able to stay alive a little longer."

"Only a little? Is it that bad?"

"Bad enough. Tom, remember not to trust *anybody*. I gotta go now."

"Will I speak to you again, Ray?"

"Maybe," Melhill said. "Maybe not. Good luck, kid."

The interview was ended, Blaine returned to his apartment.

The next day was Saturday. Blaine lounged in bed late, made himself breakfast and called Marie. She was out. He decided to spend the day relaxing and playing his sensory recordings.

That afternoon he had two callers.

The first was a gentle, hunchbacked old woman dressed in a dark, severe uniform. Across her army-style cap were the words, "Old Church".

"Sir," she said in a slightly wheezy voice, "I am soliciting contributions for the old Church, an organization which seeks to promote faith in these dissolute and Godless times."

"Sorry," Blaine said, and started to close the door.

But the old woman must have had many doors closed on her. She wedged herself between door and jamb and continued talking.

"This, young sir, is the age of the Babylonian Beast, and the time of the soul's destruction. This is Satan's age, and the time of his seeming triumph. But be not deceived! The Lord Almighty has allowed this to come about for a trial and a testing, and a winnowing of grain from chaff. Beware the temptation! Beware the path of evil which lies splendid and glittering before you!"

Blaine gave her a dollar just to shut her up. The old woman thanked him but continued talking.

"Beware, young sir, that ultimate lure of Satan—the false heaven which men call the hereafter! For what better snare could Satan the Deceiver devise for the world of men than this, his greatest illusion! The illusion that hell is heaven! And men are deceived by the cunning deceit, and willingly go down into it!"

"Thank you," Blaine said, trying to shut the door.

"Remember my words!" the old woman cried, fixing him with a glassy blue eye. "The hereafter is evil! Beware the prophets of the hellish afterlife!"

"Thank you!" Blaine cried, and managed to close the door.

He relaxed in his armchair again and turned on the player. For nearly an hour he was absorbed in "Flight on Venus". Then there was a knock on his door.

Blaine opened it, and saw a short, well-dressed, chubby-faced, earnest-looking young man.

"Mr. Thomas Blaine?" the man asked.

"That's me."

"Mr. Blaine, I am Charles Farrell, from the Hereafter Corporation. Might I speak to you? If it is inconvenient now, perhaps we could make an appointment for some other—"

"Come in," Blaine said, opening the door wide for the prophet of the hellish afterlife.

Farrell was a mild, businesslike, soft-spoken prophet. His first move was to give Blaine a letter written on Hereafter, Inc. stationery, stating that Charles Farrell was a fully authorized representative of the Hereafter Corporation. Included in the letter was a meticulous description of Farrell, his signature, three stamped photographs and a set of fingerprints.

"And here are my identity proofs," Farrell said, opening his wallet and showing his heli licence, library card, voter's registration certificate and government clearance card. On a separate piece of treated paper Farrell impressed the fingerprints of his right hand and gave them to Blaine for comparison with those on the letter.

"Is all this necessary," Blaine asked.

"Absolutely," Farrell told him. "We've had some unhappy occurrences in the past. Unscrupulous operators frequently try to pass themselves as Hereafter representatives among the gullible and the poor. They offer salvation at a cut rate, take what they can get and skip town. Too many people have been cheated out of everything they own, and get nothing in return. For the illegal operators, even when they represent some little fly-by-night salvation company, have none of the expensive equipment and trained technicians that are needed for this sort of thing."

"I didn't know," Blaine said. "Won't you sit down?"

Farrell took a chair. "The Better Business Bureaus are trying to do something about it. But the fly-by-nights move too fast to be easily caught. Only Hereafter, Inc. and two other companies with government-approved techniques are able to deliver what they promise—a life after death."

"What about the various mental disciplines?" Blaine asked.

"I was purposely excluding them," Farrell said. "They're a completely different category. If you have the patience and determination necessary for twenty years or so of concentrated study, more power to you. If you don't, then you need scientific aid and implementation. And that's where we come in."

"I'd like to hear about it," Blaine said.

Mr. Farrell settled himself more comfortably in his chair. "If you're like most people, you probably want to know what is life? What is death? What is a mind? Where is the interaction point between mind and body? Is the mind also soul? Is the soul also mind? Are they independent of each other, or interdependent, or intermixed? Or is there any such thing as a soul?" Farrell smiled. "Are those some of the questions you want me to answer?"

Blaine nodded. Farrell said, "Well, I can't. We simply don't know, haven't the slightest idea. As far as we're concerned those are religio-philosophical questions which Hereafter, Inc. has no intention of even *trying* to answer. We're interested in results, not speculation. Our orientation is medical. Our approach is pragmatic. We don't care how or why we get our results, or how strange they seem. *Do they work?* That's the only question we ask, and that's our basic position."

"I think you've made it clear," Blaine said.

"It's important for me to do so at the start. So let me make one more thing clear. Don't make the mistake of thinking that we are offering heaven."

"No?"

"Not at all! Heaven is a religious concept, and we have nothing to do with religion. Our hereafter is a survival of the *mind* after the body's death. That's all. We don't claim the hereafter is heaven any more than early scientists claimed that the bones of the first cavemen were the remains of Adam and Eve."

"An old woman called here earlier," Blaine said. "She told me that the hereafter is hell."

"She's a fanatic," Farrell said, grinning. "She follows me around. And for all I know, she's perfectly right."

"What *do* you know about the hereafter?"

"Not very much," Farrell told him. "All we know for sure is this! After the body's death, the mind moves to a region we call the Threshold, which exists between Earth and the hereafter. It is, we believe, a sort of preparatory state to the hereafter itself. Once the mind is there, it can move at will into the hereafter."

"But what is the hereafter like?"

"We don't know. We're fairly sure it's non-physical. Past that, everything is conjecture. Some think that the mind is the essence of the body, and therefore the essences of a man's worldly goods can be brought into the hereafter with him. It could be so. Others disagree. Some feel that the hereafter is a place where souls await their turn for rebirth on other planets as part of a vast reincarnation cycle. Perhaps that's true, too. Some feel that the hereafter is only the first stage of post-Earth existence, and that there are six others, increasingly difficult to attain, culminating in a sort of nirvana. Could be. It's been said that the hereafter is a vast, misty region where you wander alone, forever searching, never finding. I've read theories that prove people must be grouped in the hereafter according to family; others say you're grouped there according to race, or religion, or skin coloration, or social position. Some people, as you've observed, say it's hell itself you're entering. There are advocates of a theory of illusion, who claim that the mind vanishes completely when it leaves the Threshold. And there are people who accuse us at the corporation of faking all our effects. A recent learned work states that you'll find whatever you want in the hereafter—heaven, paradise, valhalla, green pastures, take your choice. A claim is made that the old gods rule in the hereafter—the gods of Haiti, Scandinavia or the Belgian Congo, depending on whose theory you're following. Naturally a counter-theory shows that there can't be any gods at all. I've seen an English book proving that English spirits rule the hereafter, and a Russian book claiming that the Russians rule, and several American books that prove the Americans rule. A book came out last year stating that the government of the hereafter is anarchy. A leading philosopher insists that competition is a law of nature, and must be so in the hereafter, too. And so on. You can take your pick of any of those theories, Mr. Blaine, or you can make up one of your own."

"What do you think?" Blaine asked.

"Me? I'm keeping an open mind," Farrell said. "When the time comes, I'll go there and find out."

"That's good enough for me," Blaine said. "Unfortunately, I won't have a chance. I don't have the kind of money you people charge."

"I know," Farrell said. "I checked into your finances before I called."

"Then why—"

"Every year," Farrell said, "a number of free hereafter grants are made, some by philanthropists, some by corporations and trusts, a few on a lottery basis. I am happy to say, Mr. Blaine, that you have been selected for one of these grants."

"Me?"

"Let me offer my congratulations," Farrell said. "You're a very lucky man."

"But who gave me the grant?"

"The Main-Farbenger Textile Corporation."

"I never heard of them."

"Well, they heard of you. The grant is in recognition of your trip here from the year 1958. Do you accept it?"

Blaine stared hard at the hereafter representative. Farrell seemed genuine enough; anyhow, his story could be checked at the Hereafter Building. Blaine had his suspicions of the splendid gift thrust so unexpectedly into his hands. But the thought of an assured life after death outweighed any possible doubts, thrust aside any possible fears. Caution was all very well; but not when the gates of the hereafter were opening before you.

"What do I have to do?" he asked.

"Simply accompany me to the Hereafter Building," Farrell said. "We can have the necessary work done in a few hours."

Survival! Life after death!

"All right," Blaine said. "I accept the grant. Let's go!"
They left Blaine's apartment at once.

25

A helicab brought them directly to the Hereafter Building. Farrell
led the way to the Admissions Office, and gave a photostatic copy
of Blaine's grant to the woman in charge. Blaine made a set of
fingerprints, and produced his Hunter's Licence for further identity.
The woman checked all the data carefully against her master list
of acceptances. Finally she was satisfied with its validity, and signed
the admission papers.

Farrell then took Blaine to the Testing Room, wished him luck,
and left him.

In the Testing Room, a squad of young technicians took over
and ran Blaine through a gamut of examinations. Banks of calcu-
lators clicked and rattled, and spewed forth yards of paper and
showers of punched cards. Ominous machines bubbled and
squeaked at him, glared with giant red eyes, winked and turned
amber. Automatic pens squiggled across pieces of graph paper. And
through it all, the technicians kept up a lively shop talk.

"Interesting beta reaction. Think we can fair that curve?"

"Sure, sure, just lower his drive coefficient."

"Hate to do that. It weakens the web."

"You don't have to weaken it *that* much. He'll still take the
trauma."

"Maybe ... What about this Henliger factor? It's off."

"That's because he's in a host body. It'll come around."

"That one didn't last week. The guy went up like a rocket."

"He was a little unstable to begin with."

Blaine said, "Hey! Is there any chance of this not working?"

The technicians turned as though seeing him for the first time.

"Every case is different, pal," a technician told him.

"Each one has to be worked out on an individual basis."

"It's just problems, problems all the time."

Blaine said, "I thought the treatment was all worked out. I heard
it was infallible."

"Sure, that's what they tell the customers," one of the technicians
said scornfully.

"That's advertising crap."

"Things go wrong here every day. We still got a long way to go."

Blaine said, "But can you tell if the treatment takes?"

"Of course. If it takes, you're still alive."

"If it doesn't you never walk out of here."

"It *usually* takes," a technician said consolingly. "On everybody but a K3."

"It's that damned K3 factor that throws us. Come on, Jamiesen, is he a K3 or not?"

"I'm not sure," Jamiesen said, hunched over a flashing instrument. "The testing machine is all screwed up again."

Blaine said, "What is a K3?"

"I wish *we* knew," Jamiesen said moodily. "All we know for certain, guys with a K3 factor can't survive after death."

"Not under any circumstances."

"Old Fitzroy thinks it's a built-in limiting factor that nature included so the species wouldn't run wild."

"But K3s don't transmit the factor to their children."

"There's still a chance it lies dormant and skips a few generations."

"Am I a K3?" Blaine asked, trying to keep his voice steady.

"Probably not," Jamiesen said easily. "It's sort of rare. Let me check."

Blaine waited while the technicians went over their data, and Jamiesen tried to determine from his faulty machine whether or not Blaine had a K3 factor.

After a while, Jamiesen looked up. "Well, I guess he's not K3. Though who knows, really? Anyhow, let's get on with it."

"What comes next?" Blaine asked.

A hypodermic bit deeply into his arm.

"Don't worry," a technician told him, "everything's going to be just fine."

"Are you *sure* I'm not K3?" Blaine asked. The technician nodded in a perfunctory manner. Blaine wanted to ask more questions, but a wave of dizziness overcame him. The technicians were lifting him, putting him on a white operating table.

When he recovered consciousness he was lying on a comfortable couch listening to soothing music. A nurse handed him a glass of sherry, and Mr. Farrell was standing by, beaming.

"Feel OK?" Farrel asked. "You should. Everything went off perfectly."

"It did?"

"No possibility of error. Mr. Blaine, the hereafter is yours."

Blaine finished his sherry and stood up, a little shakily. "Life after death is mine? Whenever I die? Whatever I die of?"

"That's right. No matter how or when you die, your mind will survive after death. How do you feel?"

"I don't know," Blaine said.

It was only half an hour later, as he was returning to his apartment, that he began to react.

The hereafter was his!

He was filled with a sudden wild elation. Nothing mattered now, nothing whatsoever! He was immortal! He could be killed on the spot and yet live on!

He felt superbly drunk. Gaily he contemplated throwing himself under the wheels of a passing truck. What did it matter? Nothing could really hurt him! He could berserk now, slash merrily through the crowds. Why not? The only thing the flathats could really kill was his body!

The feeling was indescribable. Now, for the first time, Blaine realized what men had lived with before the discovery of the scientific hereafter. He remembered the heavy, sodden, constant, unconscious fear of death that subtly weighed every action and permeated every movement. The ancient enemy death, the shadow that crept down the corridors of a man's mind like some grisly tapeworm, the ghost that haunted nights and days, the croucher behind corners, the shape behind doors, the unseen guest at every banquet, the unidentified figure in every landscape, always present, always waiting—

No more.

For now a tremendous weight had been lifted from his mind. The fear of death was gone, intoxicatingly gone, and he felt light as air. Death, that ancient enemy, was defeated!

He returned to his apartment in a state of high euphoria. The telephone was ringing as he unlocked the door.

"Blaine speaking!"

"Tom!" It was Marie Thorne. "Where have you been? I've been trying to reach you all afternoon."

"I've been out, darling," Blaine said. "Where in the hell have you been?"

"At Rex," she said. "I've been trying to find out what they're up to. Now listen carefully, I have some important news for you."

"I've got some news for you, sweetheart," Blaine said.

"Listen to me! A man will call at your apartment today. He'll be a salesman from Hereafter, Inc., and he will offer you free hereafter insurance. Don't take it."

"Why not? Is he a fake?"

"No, he's perfectly genuine, and so is the offer. But you mustn't take it."

"I already did," Blaine said.

"You what?"

"He was here a few hours ago. I accepted it."

"Have they treated you yet?"

"Yes. Was that a fake?"

"No," Marie said, "of course it wasn't. Oh Tom, when will you learn not to accept gifts from strangers? There was time for here-after insurance later ... Oh, Tom!"

"What's wrong?" Blaine asked. "It was a grant from the Main-Farbenger Textile Corporation."

"They are owned completely by the Rex Corporation," Marie told him.

"Oh ... But so what?"

"Tom, the directors of Rex gave you that grant. They used Main-Farbenger as a front, but *Rex* gave you that grant! Can't you see what it means?"

"No. Will you please stop screaming and explain?"

"Tom, it's the Permitted Murder section of the Suicide Act. They're going to invoke it."

"What are you talking about?"

"I'm talking about the section of the Suicide Act that makes host-taking legal. Rex has guaranteed the survival of your mind after death, and you've accepted it. Now they can legally take your body for any purpose they desire. They own it. They can *kill* your body, Tom!"

"Kill me?"

"Yes. And of course they're going to. The government is planning action against them for illegally transporting you from the past. If you're not around, there's no case. Now listen. You *must* get out of New York, then out of the country. Maybe they'll leave you alone then. I'll help. I think that you should—"

The telephone went dead.

Blaine clicked the receiver several times, but got no dial tone. Apparently the line had been cut.

The elation he had been filled with a few seconds ago drained out of him. The intoxicating sense of freedom from death vanished. How could he have contemplated berserking? He wanted to *live*. He wanted to live in the flesh, upon the Earth he knew and loved. Spiritual existence was fine, but he didn't want it yet. Not for a long time. He wanted to live among solid objects, breathe air, eat bread and drink water, feel flesh surrounding him, touch other flesh.

When would they try to kill him? Any time at all. His apartment was like a trap. Quickly Blaine scooped all his money into a pocket and hurried to the door. He opened it, and looked up and down the hall. It was empty.

He hurried out, ran down the corridor, and stopped.

A man had just come around the corner. The man was standing

in the centre of the hall. He was carrying a large projector, which was levelled at Blaine's stomach.

The man was Sammy Jones.

"Ah, Tom, Tom," Jones sighed. "Believe me, I'm damned sorry it's you. But business is business."

Blaine stood, frozen, as the projector lifted to level on his chest.

"Why you?" Blaine managed to ask.

"Who else?" Sammy Jones said. "Aren't I the best hunter in the Western Hemisphere, and probably Europe, too? Rex hired every one of us in the New York area. But with beam and projectile weapons this time. I'm sorry it's you, Tom."

"But I'm a hunter, too," Blaine said.

"You won't be the first that got gunned. It's the breaks of the game, lad. Don't flinch. I'll make it quick and clean."

"I don't want to die!" Blaine gasped.

"Why not?" Jones asked. "You've got your hereafter insurance."

"I was tricked! I want to live! Sammy, don't do it!"

Sammy Jones' face hardened. He took careful aim, then lowered the gun.

"I'm growing too soft-hearted for this game," Jones said. "All right, Tom, start moving. I guess every Quarry should have a little head start. Makes it more sporting. But I'm only giving you a little."

"Thanks, Sammy," Blaine said, and hurried down the hall.

"But Tom—watch your step if you really want to live. I'm telling you, there's more hunters than citizens in New York right now. And every means of transportation is guarded."

"Thanks," Blaine called, as he hurried down the stairs.

He was in the street, but he didn't know where to go. Still, he had no time for indecision. It was late afternoon, hours before darkness could help him. He picked a direction and began walking.

Almost instinctively, his steps were leading him towards the slums of the city.

26

He walked past the rickety tenements and ancient apartment houses, past the cheap saloons and night clubs, hands thrust in his pockets, trying to think. He would have to come up with a plan. The hunters would get him in the next hour or two if he couldn't work out some plan, some way of getting out of New York.

Jones had told him that the transportation services were being watched. What hope had he, then? He was unarmed, defenceless—

Well, perhaps he could change that. With a gun in his hand, things would be a little different. In fact, things might be very different indeed. As Hull had pointed out, a hunter could legally shoot a Quarry; but if a Quarry shot a hunter he was liable for arrest and severe penalties.

If he did shoot a hunter, the police would have to arrest him! It would all get very involved, but it would save him from the immediate danger.

He walked until he came to a pawnshop. In the window was a glittering array of projectile and beam weapons, hunting rifles, knives and machetes. Blaine went in.

"I want a gun," he said to the moustached man behind the counter.

"A gun. So. And what kind of a gun?" the man asked.

"Have you got any beamers?"

The man nodded and went to a drawer. He took out a gleaming handgun with a bright copper finish.

"Now this," he said, "is a special buy. It's a genuine Sailes-Byrn needlebeam, used for hunting big Venusian game. At five hundred yards you can cut through anything that walks, crawls or flies. On the side is the aperture selector. You can fan wide for close-range work, or extend to a needle point for distance shooting."

"Fine, fine," Blaine said, pulling bills from his pocket.

"This button here," the pawnbroker said, "controls length of blast. Set as is, you get a standard fractional jolt. One click extends time to a quarter second. Put it on automatic and it'll cut like a scythe. It has a power supply of over four hours, and there's more than three hours still left in the original pack. What's more, you can use this weapon in your home workshop. With a special mounting and a baffle to cut down the power, you can slice plastic with this better than with a saw. A different baffle converts it into a blowtorch. The baffles can be purchased—"

"I'll buy it," Blaine broke in.

The pawnbroker nodded. "May I see your permit, please?"

Blaine took out his Hunter's licence and showed it to the man. The pawnbroker nodded, and, with maddening slowness, filled out a receipt.

"Don't bother. I'll take it as it is."

The pawnbroker said, "That'll be seventy-five dollars." As Blaine pushed the money across the counter, the pawnbroker consulted a list on the wall behind him.

"Hold it!" he said suddenly.

"Eh?"

"I can't sell you that weapon."

"Why not?" Blaine asked. "You saw my Hunter's Licence."

"But you didn't tell me you were a registered Quarry. You know a Quarry can't have weapons. Your name was flashed here half an hour ago. You can't buy a legal weapon anywhere in New York, Mr. Blaine."

The pawnbroker pushed the bills back across the counter. Blaine grabbed for the needlebeam. The pawnbroker scooped it up first and levelled it at him.

"I ought to save them the trouble," he said. "You've got your damned hereafter. What else do you want?"

Blaine stood perfectly still. The pawnbroker lowered the gun.

"But that's not my job," he said. "The hunters will get you soon enough."

He reached under the counter and pressed a button. Blaine turned and ran out of the store. It was growing dark. But his location had been revealed. The hunters would be closing in now.

He thought he heard someone calling his name. He pushed through the crowds, not looking back, trying to think of something to do. He couldn't die like this, could he? He couldn't have come 152 years through time to be shot before a million people! It just wasn't fair!

He noticed a man following close behind him, grinning. It was Theseus, gun out, waiting for a clear shot.

Blaine put on a burst of speed, dodged through the crowds and turned quickly into a side street. He sprinted down it, then came to a sudden stop.

At the far end of the street, silhouetted against the light, a man was standing. The man had one hand on his hip, the other raised in a shooting position. Blaine hesitated, and glanced back at Theseus.

The little hunter fired, scorching Blaine's sleeve. Blaine ran towards an open door, which was suddenly slammed in his face. A second shot charred his coat.

With dreamlike clarity he watched the hunters advance, Theseus close behind him, the other hunter in the distance, blocking the way out. Blaine ran on leaden feet, towards the more distant man, over manhole covers and subway gratings, past shuttered stores and locked buildings.

"Back off, Theseus!" the hunter called. "I got him!"

"Take him, Hendrick!" Theseus called back, and flattened himself against a wall, out of the way of the blast.

The gunman, fifty feet away, took aim and fired. Blaine fell flat and the beam missed him. He rolled, trying to make the inadequate shelter of a doorway. The beam probed after him, scoring the concrete and turning the puddles of sewer water into steam.

Then a subway grating gave way beneath him.

As he fell, he knew that the grating must have been weakened by the lancing beam. Blind luck! But he had to land on his feet. He had to stay conscious, drag himself away from the opening, use his luck. If he went unconscious, his body would be lying in full view of the opening, an easy target for hunters standing on the edge.

He tried to twist in mid-air, too late. He landed heavily on his shoulders, and his head slammed against an iron stanchion. But the need to stay conscious was so great that he pulled himself to his feet.

He had to drag himself out of the way, deep into the subway passage, far enough so they couldn't find him.

But even the first step was too much. Sickeningly, his legs buckled under him. He fell on his face, rolled over and stared at the gaping hole above him.

Then he passed out.

Part Four

27

When he revived, Blaine decided that he didn't like the hereafter. It was dark, lumpy, and it smelled of oil and slime. Also, his head ached, and his back felt as though it had been broken in three places.

Could a spirit ache? Blaine moved, and discovered that he still had a body. As a matter of fact, he felt all body. Apparently he wasn't in the hereafter.

"Just rest a minute," a voice said.

"Who is it?" Blaine asked into the impenetrable darkness.

"Smith."

"Oh. You." Blaine sat up and held his throbbing head. "How did you do it, Smith?"

"I nearly didn't," the zombie told him. "As soon as you were declared Quarry, I came for you. Some of my friends down here volunteered to help, but you were moving too fast. I shouted to you when you came out of the pawnshop."

"I thought I heard a voice," Blaine said.

"If you'd turned around, we could have taken you in there and then. But you didn't so we followed. A few times we opened subway grates and manhole covers for you, but it was hard to gauge it right. We were a little late each time."

"But not the last time," Blaine said.

"At last I had to open a grate right under you. I'm sorry you hit your head."

"Where am I?"

"I pulled you out of the main line," Smith said. "You're in a side passageway. The hunters can't find you here."

Blaine once again could find no adequate words for thanking Smith. And Smith once again wanted no thanks.

"I'm not doing it for you, Blaine. It's for me. I need you."

"Have you found out why yet?"

"Not yet," Smith said.

Blaine's eyes, adjusting to the gloom, could make out the outline of the zombie's head and shoulders. "What now?" he asked.

"Now you're safe. We can bring you underground as far as New Jersey. From there you're on your own. But I don't think you should have much trouble then."

"What are we waiting for now?"

"Mr. Kean. I need his permission to take you through the passageways."

They waited. In a few minutes, Blaine was able to make out Mr. Kean's thin shape, leaning on the big Negro's arm, coming towards him.

"I'm sorry about your troubles," Kean said, sitting down beside Blaine. "It's a great pity."

"Mr. Kean," Smith said, "if I could just be allowed to take him through the old Holland Tunnel, into New Jersey—"

"I'm truly sorry," Kean said, "but I cannot allow it."

Blaine looked around and saw that he was surrounded by a dozen ragged zombies.

"I've spoken to the hunters," Kean said, "and I have given them my guarantee that you will be back on the surface streets within half an hour. You must leave now, Blaine."

"But why?"

"We simply can't afford to help you," Kean said. "I was taking an unusual risk the first time, allowing you to defile Reilly's tomb. But I did it for Smith, because his destiny seems linked with yours in some way. And Smith is one of my people. But this is too much. You know we are allowed to live underground upon sufferance only."

"I know," Blaine said.

"Smith should have considered the consequences. When he opened that grating for you, the hunters poured in. They didn't find you, but they knew you were down here somewhere. So they searched, Blaine, they searched! Dozens of them, exploring our passageways, pushing our people around, threatening, shouting, talking on their little radios. Reporters came too, and even idle spectators. Some of the younger hunters became nervous and started shooting at the zombies."

"I'm very sorry about that," Blaine said.

"It wasn't your fault. But Smith should have known better. The world of the underground is not a sovereign kingdom. We exist on sufferance only on a toleration which might be wiped out at any time. So I spoke to the hunters and the reporters."

"What did you tell them?" Blaine asked.

"I told them that a faulty grate had given way beneath you. I said you had fallen in by accident and had crawled into hiding. I assured them that no zombie had been involved in this; that we found you and would place you back on the surface streets within half an hour. They accepted my word and left. I wish I could have done otherwise."

"I don't blame you," Blaine said, getting slowly to his feet.

"I didn't specify where you would emerge," Kean said. "At the very least, you'll have a better chance than before. I wish I could do more, but I cannot allow the underground to become a stage for hunts. We must stay neutral, annoy no one, frighten no one. Only in that way will we survive until an age of understanding is reached."

"Where am I going to come out?" Blaine asked.

"I have chosen an unused subway exit at West 79th Street," Mr. Kean said. "You should have a good chance from there. And I have done one more thing which I probably shouldn't have done."

"What's that?"

"I have contacted a friend of yours, who will be waiting at the exit. But please don't tell anyone about it. Let's hurry now!"

Mr. Kean led the procession through the winding underground maze, and Blaine brought up the rear, his headache slowly subsiding. Soon they stopped beside a concrete staircase.

"Here is the exit," Kean said. "Good luck, Blaine."

"Thanks," Blaine said. "And Smith—thanks."

"I've tried my best for you," Smith said. "If you die, I'll probably die. If you live, I'll keep on trying to remember."

"And if you do remember?"

"Then I'll come and visit you," Smith said.

Blaine nodded and walked up the staircase.

It was full night outside, and 79th Street seemed deserted. Blaine stood beside the exit, looking around, wondering what to do.

"Blaine!"

Someone was calling him. But it was not Marie, as he had expected. It was a man's voice, someone he knew—Sammy Jones, perhaps, or Theseus.

He turned quickly back to the subway exit. It was closed and fastened securely.

28

"Tom, Tom, it's me!"

"Ray?"

"Of course! Keep your voice down. There's hunters not far away. Wait now."

Blaine waited, crouched beside the barred subway exit, peering around. He could see no sign of Melhill. There was no ectoplasmic vapour, nothing except a whispering voice.

"OK," Melhill said. "Walk west now. Quickly."

Blaine walked, sensing Melhill's invisible presence hovering near him. He said, "Ray, how come?"

"It's about time I was some help," Melhill said. "That old Kean contacted your girl friend and she got in touch with me through the Spiritual Switchboard. Wait! Stop right here."

Blaine ducked back against the corner of a building. A heli cruised slowly by at housetop level.

"Hunters," Melhill said. "There's a field day on you, kid. Reward posted. Even a reward for information leading to. Tom, I told Marie I'd try to help. Don't know how long I can. Drains me. It's hereafter for me after this."

"Ray, I don't know how—"

"Cut it out. Look Tom, I can't talk much. Marie has fixed a deal with some friends of hers. They've got a plan, if I can get you to them. Stop!"

Blaine stopped and found shelter behind a mailbox. Long seconds passed. Then three hunters hurried by, sidearms ready. After they turned a corner, Blaine was able to start walking again.

"Some eyes you have," he said to Melhill.

"The vision's pretty good up here," Melhill said. "Cross this street fast."

Blaine sprinted across. For the next fifteen minutes, at Melhill's instructions, he wound in and out of streets, advancing and retreating across the battleground of the city.

"This is it," Melhill said at last. "That door over there, number 341. You made it! I'll see you, Tom. Watch—"

At that moment, two men rounded a corner, stopped, and stared hard at Blaine. One said, "Hey, that's the guy!"

"What guy?"

"The guy they got the reward out for. Hey *you*!"

They ran forward. Blaine, his fists swinging, quickly chopped the first man into unconsciousness. He whirled, looking for the second, but Melhill had the situation well in control.

The second man had his hands over his head, trying to guard himself. A garbage can cover, levitating mysteriously, was clanging angrily around his ears. Blaine stepped forward and finished the job.

"Damn good," Melhill said, his voice very weak. "Always wanted to try ghosting. But it drains ... Luck, Tom!"

"Ray!" Blaine waited, but there was no answer, and the sense of Melhill's presence was gone.

Blaine waited no longer. He went to number 341, opened the door and stepped in.

He was in a narrow hallway. At the end of it was a door. Blaine knocked.

"Come in," he was told.

He opened the door and walked into a small, dingy, heavily curtained room.

Blaine had thought he was proof against any further surprises. But it gave him a start all the same to see, grinning at him, Carl Orc, the body snatcher. And sitting beside him, also grinning, was Joe, the little Transplant pedlar.

29

Blaine made an automatic move backwards towards the door, but Orc beckoned him in. The body snatcher was unchanged, still very tall and thin, his tanned face long and mournful, his eyes narrow, direct and honest. His clothes still hung awkwardly on him, as though he were more used to levis than to tailored slacks.

"We were expecting you," Orc said. "Of course you remember Joe."

Blaine nodded, remembering very well the furtive-eyed little man who had distracted his attention so that Orc could drug his drink.

"Happy to see you again," Joe said.

"I'll bet," Blaine said, not moving from the door.

"Come in and sit down," Orc said. "We ain't planning to eat you, Tom. Truly not. Let's let bygones be bygones."

"You tried to kill me."

"That was business," Orc said in his straightforward fashion. "We're on the same side now."

"How can I be sure of that?"

"No man," Orc stated, "has ever questioned my honesty. Not when I'm really being honest, which I am now. Miss Thorne hired us to get you safe out of the country, and we intend to do same. Sit down and let's discuss it. Are you hungry?"

Reluctantly Blaine sat down. There were sandwiches on a table, and a bottle of red wine. He realized that he hadn't eaten all day. He started wolfing down sandwiches while Orc lighted a thin brown cigar, and Joe appeared to be dozing.

"You know," Orc said, exhaling blue smoke, "I very nearly didn't take this job. Not that the money wasn't right; I think Miss Thorne was more than generous. But Tom, this is one of the biggest manhunts our fair city's seen for a while. Ever see anything like it, Joe?"

"Never," Joe said, shaking his head rapidly. "Town's covered like flypaper."

"Rex really wants you," Orc said. "They've set their little hearts on nailing your corpus where they can see it. Makes a man nervous, bucking an organization that size. But it's a challenge, a real man-sized challenge."

"Carl likes a big challenge," Joe said.

"I admit that," Orc said. "Particularly if there's a big profit to be made from it."

"But where can I go?" Blaine asked. "Where won't Rex find me?"

"Just about nowhere," Orc said sadly.

"Off the Earth? Mars? Venus?"

"Even worse. The planets have just a few towns and small cities. Everybody knows everybody else. The news would be all over in a week. Also, you wouldn't fit in. Aside from the Chinese on Mars, the planets are still populated mostly with scientific types and their families, and a few youth-training programmes. You wouldn't like it."

"Where, then?"

"That's what I asked Miss Thorne," Orc said. "We discussed several possibilities. First, there's a zombie-making operation. I could perform it. Rex would never search for you underground."

"I'd rather die," Blaine said.

"I would too," Orc agreed. "So we ruled it out. We thought about finding you a little farm in the Atlantic Abyss. Pretty lonely territory out there. But it takes a special mentality to live undersea and like it, and we didn't figure you had it. You'd probably crack up. So, after due consideration, we decided the best place for you was in the Marquesas."

"The what?"

"The Marquesas. They're a scattered group of small islands, originally Polynesian, out towards the middle of the Pacific Ocean. They're not too far from Tahiti."

"The South Seas," Blaine said.

"Right. We figured you should feel more at home there than anywhere else on Earth. It's just like the 20th century, I'm told. And even more important, Rex might leave you alone."

"Why would they?"

"For obvious reasons, Tom. Why do they want to kill you in the first place? Because they snatched you illegally from the past and they're worried about what the government's going to do about it. But your going to the Marquesas removes you from the jurisdiction of the U.S. government. Without you, there's no case. And your going so far is a sign to Rex of your good faith. It certainly isn't the act of a man who's going to blab to Uncle Sam. Also, the Marquesas are an independent little nation since the French gave them up, so Rex would have to get special permission to hunt you there. On the whole, it *should* be just too much trouble for everyone concerned. The U.S. government will undoubtedly drop the matter, and I think Rex will leave you alone."

"Is that certain?" Blaine asked.

"Of course not. It's conjecture. But it's reasonable."

"Couldn't we make a deal with Rex beforehand?"

Orc shook his head. "In order to bargain, Tom, you have to have something to bargain with. As long as you're in New York it's easier and safer for them to kill you."

"I guess you're right," Blaine said. "How are you going to get me out?"

Orc and Joe looked at each other uncomfortably. Orc said, "Well, that was our big problem. There just didn't seem to be any way of getting you out alive."

"Heli or jet?"

"They have to stop at the air tolls, and hunters are waiting at all of them. Surface vehicle is equally out of the question."

"Disguise?"

"Maybe it would have worked during the first hour of the hunt. Now it's impossible, even if we could get you a complete plastic surgery job. By now the hunters are equipped with identity scanners. They'd see through you in a moment."

"Then there's no way out?" Blaine asked.

Orc and Joe exchanged another uneasy glance. "There is," Orc said. "Just one way. But you probably won't like it."

"I like to stay alive. What is it?"

Orc paused and lighted another cigar. "We plan to quick-freeze you near absolute zero, like for spaceship travel. Then we'll ship your carcass out in a crate of frozen beef. Your body will be in the centre of the load, so most likely it won't be detected."

"Sounds risky," Blaine said.

"Not too risky," Orc said.

Blaine frowned, sensing something wrong. "I'll be unconscious through it, won't I?"

After a long pause, Orc said, "No."

"I won't?"

"It can't be done that way," Orc told him. "The fact is, you and your body will have to separate. That's the part I'm afraid you won't like."

"What in hell are you talking about?" Blaine asked, getting to his feet.

"Take it easy," Orc said. "Sit down, smoke a cigarette, have some more wine. It's like this, Tom. We can't ship out a quick-frozen body with a mind in it. The hunters are waiting for something like that. Can you imagine what happens when they run a quick scan over that shipment of beef and detect a dormant mind in it? Up goes the kite! *Adieu la musique!* I'm not trying to con you, Tom. It just can't be done like that."

"Then what happens to my mind?" Blaine asked, sitting down again.

"That," Orc said, "is where Joe comes in. Tell him, Joe."

Joe nodded rapidly. "Transplant, my friend, is the answer."

"Transplant?"

"I told you about it," Joe said, "on that inauspicious evening when we first met. Remember? Transplant, the great pastime, the game any number can play, the jolt for jaded minds, the tonic for tired bodies. We've got a worldwide network of Transplantees, Mr Blaine. Folks who like to switch around, men and women who get tired of wearing the same old body. We're going to key you into the organization."

"You're going to ship my *mind* across the country?" Blaine asked.

"That's it! From body to body," Joe told him. "Believe me, it's instructive as well as entertaining."

Blaine got to his feet so quickly that he knocked over his chair. "Like hell!" he said. "I told you then and I'm telling you now, I'm not playing your lousy little game. I'll take my chances on the street."

He started towards the door.

Joe said, "I know it's a little frightening, but—"

"No!"

Orc shouted, "Damn it, Blaine, will you at least let the man speak?"

"All right," Blaine said. "Speak."

Joe poured himself half a glass of wine and threw it down. He said, "Mr Blaine, it's going to be difficult explaining this to you, a guy from the past. But try to understand what I'm saying."

Blaine nodded warily.

"Now then. Transplant is used as a sex game these days, and that's how I peddle it. Why? Because people are ignorant of its better uses, and because a reactionary government insists on banning it. But Transplant is a lot more than a game. It's an entire new way of life! And whether you or the government like it or not, Transplant represents the world of the future."

The little pusher's eyes glowed. Blaine sat down again.

"There are two basic elements in human affairs," Joe said sententiously. "One of them is man's eternal struggle for freedom: Freedom of worship, freedom of press and assembly, freedom to select government—freedom! And the other basic element in human affairs is the efforts of government to withhold freedom from the people."

Blaine considered this a somewhat simplified view of human affairs. But he continued listening.

"Government," Joe said, "withholds freedom for many reasons. For security, for personal profit, for power, or because they feel the people are unready for it. But whatever the reason, the basic facts remain: Man strives for freedom, and government strives to withhold freedom. Transplant is simply one more in a long series of freedoms that man has aspired to, and that his government feels is not good for him."

"Sexual freedom?" Blaine asked mockingly.

"No!" Joe cried. "Not that there's anything wrong with sexual freedom. But Transplant isn't primarily that. Sure, that's how we're pushing it—for propaganda purposes. Because people don't want abstract ideas, Mr. Blaine, and they don't go for cold theory. They want to know what a freedom will *do* for them. We show them a small part of it, and they learn a lot more themselves."

"What will Transplant do?" Blaine asked.

"Transplant," Joe said fervently, "gives man the ability to transcend the limits imposed by his heredity and his environment!"

"Huh?"

"Yes! Transplant lets you exchange knowledge, bodies, talents and skills with anyone who wishes to exchange with you. And plenty do. Most men don't want to perform a single set of skills all their life, no matter how satisfying those skills are. Man is too restless a creature. Musicians want to be engineers, advertising men want to be hunters, sailors want to be writers. But there usually isn't time to acquire and exploit more than one set of skills in a lifetime. And even if there were time, the blind factor of talent is an insurmountable stumbling block. With Transplant, you can get the inborn talents, the skills, the knowledge that you want. Think about it, Mr. Blaine. Why should a man be forced to live out his lifetime in a body he had no part in selecting? It's like telling him he must live with the diseases he's inherited, and mustn't try to cure them. Man must have the freedom to choose the body and talents best suited to his personality needs."

"If your plan went through," Blaine said, "you'd simply have a bunch of neurotics changing bodies every day."

"The same general argument was raised against the passage of every freedom," Joe said, his eyes glittering. "Throughout history it was argued that man didn't have the sense to choose his own religion, or that women didn't have the intelligence to use the vote, or that people couldn't be allowed to elect their own representatives because of the stupid choices they'd make. And of course there are plenty of neurotics around, people who'd louse up heaven itself. But you have a much greater number of people who'd use their freedoms well."

Joe lowered his voice to a persuasive whisper. "You must realize, Mr. Blaine, that a man is not his body, for he receives his body accidentally. He is not his skills, for those are frequently born of necessity. He is not his talents, which are produced by heredity and by early environmental factors. He is not the sicknesses to which he may be predisposed, and he is not the environment that shapes him. A man *contains* all these things, but he is greater than their total. He has the power to change his environment, cure his diseases, advance his skills—and, at last, to choose his body and talents! *That* is the next freedom, Mr. Blaine. It's historically inevitable, whether you or I or the government like it or not. For man must have every possible freedom!"

Joe finished his fierce and somewhat incoherent oration red-faced and out of breath. Blaine stared at the little man with new respect. He was looking, he realized, at a genuine revolutionary of the year 2110.

Orc said, "He's got a point, Tom. Transplant is legal in Sweden and Ceylon, and it doesn't seem to have hurt the moral fibre much."

"In time," Joe said, pouring himself a glass of wine, "the whole world will go Transplant. It's inevitable."

"Maybe," Orc said. "Or maybe they'll invent some new freedom to take its place. Anyhow, Tom, you can see that Transplant has some moral justifications. And it's the only way of saving that body of yours. What do you say?"

"Are you a revolutionary, too?" Blaine asked.

Orc grinned. "Could be. I guess I'm like the blockade runners during the American Civil War, or the guys who sold guns to Central American revolutionaries. They worked for a profit, but they weren't against social change."

"Well, well," Blaine said sardonically. "And up to now I thought you were just a common criminal."

"Skip it," Orc said pleasantly. "Are you willing to try?"

"Certainly. I'm overwhelmed," Blaine said. "I never thought I'd find myself in the advance guard of a social revolution."

Orc smiled and said, "Good. Hope it works out for you, Tom. Roll up your sleeve. We'd better get started."

Blaine rolled up his left sleeve while Orc took a hypodermic from a drawer.

"This is just to knock you out," Orc explained. "The Yoga Machine is in the next room. It does the real work. When you come to, you'll be a guest in someone else's mind, and your body will be travelling cross country in deep freeze. They'll be brought together as soon as it's safe."

"How many minds will I occupy?" Blaine asked. "And for how long?"

"I don't know how many we'll have to use. As for how long in each, a few seconds, minutes, maybe half an hour. We'll move you along as fast as we can. This isn't a full Transplant, you know. You won't be taking over the body. You'll just be occupying a small portion of its consciousness, as an observer. So stay quiet and act natural. Got that?"

Blaine nodded. "But how does this Yoga Machine work?"

"It works like Yoga," Orc said. "The machine simply does what you could do yourself if you were thoroughly trained in Yoga exercises. It relaxes every muscle and nerve in your body, focuses and calms your mind, helps build up your concentration. When you've reached potential, you're ready to make an astral projection. The machine does that for you, too. It helps you release your hold on the body, which a Yoga adept could do without mechanical assistance. It projects you to the person we've selected, who yields room. Attraction takes care of the rest. You slip in like a stranded fish going back into water."

"Sounds risky," Blaine said. "Suppose I can't get in?"

"Man, you can't *help* but get in! Look, you've heard of demoniac possession, haven't you? Guys under the control of so-called demons? The idea runs through most of the world's folklore. Some of the possessed were schizophrenic, of course, and some were downright frauds. But there was a lot of cases of real spiritual invasion, minds taken over by others who had learned the trick of breaking out of their own body and casting into another. The invaders took over with no mechanical help, and against an all-out battle on the part of their victims. In your case you've got the Yoga Machine, and the people are willing to have you in. So why worry?"

"All right," Blaine said. "What are the Marquesas like?"

"Beautiful," Orc said, sliding the needle into Blaine's arm. "You'll like it there."

Blaine drifted slowly into unconsciousness, thinking of palm trees, of white surf breaking against a coral reef, and of dark-eyed maidens worshipping a god of stone.

30

There was no sense of awakening, no feeling of transition. Abruptly, like a brilliantly coloured slide projected upon a white screen, he was conscious. Suddenly, like a marionette jerked into violent life, he was acting and moving.

He was not completely Thomas Blaine. He was Edgar Dyersen as well. Or he was Blaine within Dyersen, an integral part of Dyersen's body, a segment of Dyersen's mind, viewing the world through Dyersen's rheumy eyes, thinking Dyersen's thoughts, experiencing all the shadowy half-conscious fragments of Dyersen's memories, hopes, fears and desires. And yet he was still Blaine.

Dyersen-Blaine came out of the ploughed field and rested against his wooden fence. He was a farmer, an old-fashioned South Jersey truck farmer, with a minimum of machines which he distrusted anyhow. He was close to seventy and in damn good health. There was still a touch of arthritis in his joints, which the smart young medico in the village had mostly fixed; and his back sometimes gave him trouble before rain. But he considered himself healthy, healthier than most, and good for another twenty years.

Dyersen-Blaine started towards his cottage. His grey workshirt was drenched in acrid sweat, and sweat stained his shapeless levis.

In the distance he heard a dog barking and saw, blurrily, a yellow and brown shape come bounding towards him. (Eye-glasses? No thank you. Doing pretty well with what I got.)

"Hey, Champ! Hey there, boy!"

The dog ran a circle around him, then trotted along beside him. He had something grey in his jaws, a rat or perhaps a piece of meat. Dyersen-Blaine couldn't quite make it out.

He bent down to pat Champ's head...

Again there was no sense of transition or of the passage of time. A new slide was simply projected on to the screen, and a new marionette was jerked into life.

Now he was Thompson-Blaine, nineteen years old, lying on his back half dozing on the rough planks of a sailing skiff, the mainsheet and tiller held loosely in one brown hand. To starboard lay the low Eastern Shore, and to his port he could see a bit of Baltimore Harbour. The skiff moved easily on the light summer breeze, and water gurgled merrily beneath the forefoot.

Thompson-Blaine rearranged his lanky, tanned body on the planks, squirming around until he had succeeded in propping his feet against the mast. He had been home just a week, after a two-year work and study programme on Mars. It had sure been interesting, especially the archaeology and speleology. The sand-farming had got dull sometimes, but he had enjoyed driving the harvesting machines.

Now he was home for a two-year accelerated college course. Then he was supposed to return to Mars as a farm manager. That's the way his scholarship read. But they couldn't make him go back if he didn't want to.

Maybe he would. And maybe not.

The girls on Mars were such dedicated types. Tough, capable, and always a little bossy. When he went back—*if* he went back—he'd bring his own wife, not look for one there. Of course there had been Marcia, and she'd really been something. But her whole kibbutz had moved to the South Polar Cap, and she hadn't answered his last three letters. Maybe she hadn't been so much, anyhow.

"Hey, Sandy!"

Thompson-Blaine looked up and saw Eddie Duelitle, sailing his Thistle, waving at him. Languidly Thompson-Blaine waved back. Eddie was only seventeen, had never been off Earth, and wanted to be a spaceliner captain. Huh! Fat chance!

The sun was dipping towards the horizon, and Thompson-Blaine was glad to see it go down. He had a date tonight with Jennifer Hunt. They were going dancing at Starsling in Baltimore, and Dad was letting him use the heli. Man, how Jennifer had grown in two years! And she had a way of looking at a guy, sort of coy and bold at the same time. No telling what might happen after the dance, in the back seat of the heli. Maybe nothing. But maybe, maybe...

Thompson-Blaine sat up and put the tiller over. The skiff came into the wind and tacked over. It was time to return to the yacht basin, then home for dinner, then...

The blacksnake whip flicked across his back.

"Get working there, you!"

Piggot-Blaine redoubled his efforts, lifting the heavy pick high in the air and swinging it down into the dusty roadbed. The guard stood nearby, shotgun under his left arm, whip in his right, its lash trailing in the dust. Piggot-Blaine knew every line and pore of that guard's thin, stupid face, knew the downward twist of the tight little mouth, knew the squint of the faded eyes just like he knew his own face.

Just wait, buzzard meat, he silently told the guard. Your time's a-coming. Just wait, wait just a bit.

The guard moved away, walking slowly up and down the line of prisoners labouring under the white Mississippi sun. Piggot-Blaine tried to spit, but couldn't work up enough saliva. He thought, you talk about your fine modern world? Talk about your big old space-ships, your automatic farms, your big fine fat old hereafter? Think that's how it is? Then ask 'em how they build the roads in Quilleg County, Northern Mississippi. They won't tell you, so you better look for yourself and find out. 'Cause that's the kind of world it *really* is!

Arny, working on front of him, whispered, "You ready, Otis? You ready for it?"

"I'm a-ready," Piggot-Blaine whispered, his broad fingers clench-ing and unclenching on the pick's plastic handle. "I'm *past* ready, Arny."

"In a second, then. Watch Jeff."

Piggot-Blaine's hairy chest swelled expectantly. He brushed lank brown hair from his eyes and watched Jeff, five men ahead on the chain. Piggot-Blaine waited, his shoulders aching from sunburn. There were calloused scars on his ankles from the hoofcuffs, and old seams on his back from earlier whippings. He had a raging thirst in his gut. But no dipperful of water could ever cut that thirst, nothing could, that crazy thirst that brought him in here after he'd dismembered Gainsville's single saloon and killed that stinking old Indian.

Jeff's hand moved. The chained line of prisoners sprang forward. Piggot-Blaine jumped towards the thin-faced guard, his pick swung high, as the guard dropped his whip and fumbled to bring up the shotgun.

"Buzzard meat!" Piggot-Blaine screamed, and brought the pick down fair in the guard's forehead.

"Get the keys!"

Piggot-Blaine grabbed the keys from the dead guard's belt. He heard a shotgun go off, heard a high scream of agony. Anxiously he looked up...

Ramirez-Blaine was piloting his heli above the flat Texas plains, heading for El Paso. He was a serious young man and he paid strict attention to his work, coaxing the last knot of speed out of the old heli so he could reach El Paso before Johnson's Hardware Store closed.

He handled the balky rattletrap with care, and only an occasional thought came through his concentration, quick thoughts about the altitude and compass readings, a dance in Guanajuato next week, the price of hides in Ciudad Juarez.

The plain was mottled green and yellow below him. He glanced at his watch, then at the airspeed indicator.

Yes, Ramirez-Blaine thought, he *would* make El Paso before the store closed! He might even have time for a little...

Tyler-Blaine wiped his mouth on his sleeve and sopped up the last of the grease gravy on a piece of corn bread. He belched, pushed his chair back from the kitchen table and stood up. With elaborate unconcern he took a cracked bowl from the pantry and filled it with scraps of pork, a few greens, and a big piece of corn bread.

"Ed," his wife said, "what are you doing?"

He glanced at her. She was gaunt, tangle-haired, and faded past her years. He looked away, not answering.

"Ed! Tell me, Ed!"

Tyler-Blaine looked at her in annoyance, feeling his ulcer stir at the sound of that sharp, worried voice. Sharpest voice in all California, he told himself, and he'd married it. Sharp voice, sharp nose, sharp elbows and knees, breastless and barren to boot. Legs to support a body, but not for a second's delight. A belly for filling, not for touching. Of all the girls in California he'd doubtless picked the sorriest, just like the damn fool his Uncle Rafe always said he was.

"Where you taking that bowl of food?" she asked.

"Out to feed the dog," Tyler-Blaine said, moving towards the door.

"We ain't *got* no dog! Oh Ed, don't do it, not tonight!"

"I'm doin' it," he said, glad of her discomfort.

"Please, not tonight. Let him shift for himself somewhere else. Ed, listen to me! What if the town found out?"

"It's past sundown," Tyler-Blaine said, standing beside the door with his bowl of food.

"People spy," she said. "Ed, if they find out they'll lynch us, you know they will."

"You'd look mighty spry from the end of a rope," Tyler-Blaine remarked, opening the door.

"You do it just to spite me!" she cried.

He closed the door behind him. Outside, it was deep twilight. Tyler-Blaine stood in his yard near the unused chicken coop, looking around. The only house near his was the Flannagan's, a hundred yards away. But they minded their own business. He waited to make sure none of the town kids were snooping around. Then he walked forward, carefully holding the bowl of food.

He reached the edge of the scraggly woods and set the bowl down. "It's all right," he called softly. "Come out, Uncle Rafe."

A man crawled out of the woods on all fours. His face was leaden-white, his lips bloodless, his eyes blank and staring, his features coarse and unfinished, like iron before tempering or clay before firing. A long cut across his neck had festered, and his right leg, where the townsfolk had broken it, hung limp and useless.

"Thanks, boy," said Rafe, Tyler-Blaine's zombie uncle.

The zombie quickly gulped down the contents of the bowl. When he had finished, Tyler-Blaine asked, "How you feeling, Uncle Rafe?"

"Ain't feeling nothing. This old body's about through. Another couple days, maybe a week, and I'll be off your hands."

"I'll take care of you," Tyler-Blaine said, "just as long as you can stay alive, Uncle Rafe. I wish I could bring you into the house."

"No," the zombie said, "they'd find out. This is risky enough ... Boy, how's that skinny wife of yours?"

"Just as mean as ever," Tyler-Blaine sighed.

The zombie made a sound like laughter. "I warned you, boy, ten years ago I warned you not to marry that gal. Didn't I?"

"You sure did, Uncle Rafe. You was the only one had sense. Sure wish I'd listened to you."

"Better you had, boy. Well, I'm going back to my shelter."

"You feel confident, Uncle?" Tyler-Blaine asked anxiously.

"That I do."

"And you'll try to *die* confident?"

"I will, boy. And I'll get me into that Threshold, never you fear. And when I do, I'll keep my promise. I truly will."

"Thank you, Uncle Rafe."

"I'm a man of my word. I'll haunt her, boy, if the good Lord grants me Threshold. First comes that fat doctor that made me this. But then I'll haunt her. I'll haunt her crazy. I'll haunt her 'til she runs the length of the state of California away from you!"

"Thanks, Uncle Rafe."

The zombie made a sound like laughter and crawled back into the scraggly woods. Tyler-Blaine shivered uncontrollably for a moment, then picked up the empty bowl and walked back to the sagging washboard house...

Mariner-Blaine adjusted the strap of her bathing suit so that it clung more snugly to her slim, supple young body. She slipped the air tank over her back, picked up her respirator and walked towards the pressure lock.

"Janice?"

"Yes mother?" she said, turning, her face smooth and expressionless.

"Where are you going, dear?"

"Just out for a swim, Mom. I thought maybe I'd look at the new gardens on Level 12."

"You aren't by any chance planning to see Tom Leuwin, are you?"

Had her mother *guessed*? Mariner-Blaine smoothed her black hair and said, "Certainly not."

"All right," her mother said, half smiling and obviously not believing her. "Try to be home early, dear. You know how worried your father gets."

She stooped and gave her mother a quick kiss, then hurried into the pressure lock. Mother *knew*, she was sure of it! And wasn't stopping her! But then, why should she? After all, she was seventeen, plenty old enough to do anything she wanted. Kids grew up faster these days than they did in Mom's time, though parents didn't seem to realize it. Parents didn't realize very much. They just wanted to sit around and plan out new acres for the farm. Their idea of fun was to listen to some old classic recording, a Bop piece or a Rock 'n' Roll. And follow it with scores and talk about how free and expressionistic their ancestors had been. And sometimes they'd go through big, glossy art books filled with reproductions of 20th Century Comic Strips, and talk about the lost art of satire. Their idea of a really Big Night was to go down to the gallery and stare reverently at the collection of *Saturday Evening Post* Covers from the Great Period. But all that longhair stuff bored her. Nuts to art, she liked the sensories.

Mariner-Blaine adjusted her face mask and respirator, put on her flippers and turned the valve. In a few seconds the lock was filled with water. Impatiently she waited until the pressure had equalized with the water outside. Then the lock opened automatically and she shot out.

Her dad's pressure farm was at the hundred foot level, not far from the mammoth underwater bulk of Hawaii. She turned downward, descending into the green bloom with quick, powerful strokes. Tom would be waiting for her at the coral caves.

The darkness grew as Mariner-Blaine descended. She switched on her headlamp and took a firmer bite on her respirator. Was it true, she wondered, that soon the undersea farmers would be able to grow their own gills? That's what her science teacher said, and maybe it would happen in her own lifetime. How would she look with gills? Mysterious, probably, sleek and strange, a fish goddess.

Besides, she could always cover them with her hair if they weren't becoming.

In the yellow glow of her lamp she saw the coral caves ahead, a red and pink branched labyrinth with cozy, airlocked places deep within, where you could be sure of privacy. And she saw Tom.

Uncertainty flooded her. Gosh, what if she had a baby? Tom had assured her it would be all right, but he was only nineteen. Was she right in doing this? They had talked about it often enough, and she had shocked him with her frankness. But talking and doing were very different things. What would Tom think of her if she said no? Could she make a joke out of it, pretend she'd just been teasing him?

Long and golden, Tom swam beside her towards the caves. He flashed hello in finger talk. A trigger fish swam by, and then a small shark.

What was she going to do? The caves were very near, looming dark and suggestive before them. Tom smiled at her, and she could feel her heart melting...

Elgin-Blaine sat upright, realizing that he must have dozed off. He was aboard a small motor vessel, sitting in a deck chair with blankets tucked around him. The little ship rolled and pitched in the cross-sea, but overhead the sun was brilliant, and the trade wind carried the diesel smoke away in a wide dark plume.

"You feeling better, Mr. Elgin?"

Elgin-Blaine looked up at a small, bearded man wearing a captain's cap. "Fine, just fine," he said.

"We're almost there," the captain said.

Elgin-Blaine nodded, disoriented, trying to take stock of himself. He thought hard and remembered that he was shorter than average, heavily muscled, barrel chested, broad shouldered, with legs a little short for such a herculean torso, with large and calloused hands. There was an old, jagged scar on his shoulder, souvenir of a hunting accident...

Elgin and Blaine merged.

Then he realized that he was back at last in his own body. Blaine was his name, and Elgin was the pseudonym under which Carl Orc and Joe must have shipped him.

The long flight was over! His mind and his body were together again!

"We were told you weren't well, sir," the captain said. "But you've been in this coma for so long—"

"I'm fine now," Blaine told him. "Are we far from the Marquesas?"

"Not far. The island of Nuku Hiva is just a few hours away."

The captain returned to his wheelhouse. And Blaine thought about the many personalities he had met and mingled with.

He respected the staunch and independent old Dyersen walking slowly back to his cottage, hoped young Sandy Thompson would return to Mars, felt regret for the warped and murderous Piggot, enjoyed his meeting with the serious and upright Juan Ramirez, felt mingled sorrow and contempt for the sly and ineffectual Ed Tyler, prayed for the best for pretty Janice Mariner.

They were with him still. Good or bad, he wished them all well. They were his family now. Distant relatives, cousins and uncles he would never meet again, nieces and nephews upon whose destiny he would brood.

Like all families they were a mixed lot; but they were *his*, and he could never forget them.

"Nuku Hiva in sight!" the captain called.

Blaine saw, on the edge of the horizon, a tiny black dot capped by a white cumulus cloud. He rubbed his forehead vigorously, determined to think no more about his adopted family. There were present realities to deal with. Soon he would be coming to his new home; and that required a little serious thinking.

31

The ship steamed slowly into Taio Hae Bay. The captain, a proud native son, volunteered to Blaine the principal facts about his new home.

The Marquesas Islands, he explained, were composed of two fairly distinct island groups, all of them rugged and mountainous. Once the group had been called the Cannibal Islands, and the Marquesans had been noted for their ability at cutting out a trading ship or massacring a blackbirding schooner. The French had acquired the islands in 1842, and granted them autonomy in 1993. Nuku Hiva was the main island and capital for the group. Its highest peak, Temetiu, was nearly four thousand feet high. Its port city, Taiohae, boasted a population of almost five thousand souls. It was a quiet, easy-going place, the captain said, and it was considered a sort of shrine all over the hurried, bustling South Seas. For here was the last refuge of unspoiled 20th century Polynesia.

Blaine nodded, absorbing little of the captain's lecture, more impressed by the sight of the great dark mountain ahead laced with silver waterfalls, and by the sound of the ocean pounding against the island's granite face.

He decided he was going to like it here.

Soon the ship was docked at the town wharf, and Blaine stepped off to view the town of Taiohae.

He saw a supermarket and three movie theatres, rows of ranch-style houses, many palm trees, some low white stores with plate glass windows, numerous cocktail lounges, dozens of automobiles, a gas station and a traffic light. The sidewalks were filled with people wearing colourful shirts and pressed slacks. All had on sunglasses.

So this was the last refuge of unspoiled 20th century Polynesia, Blaine thought. A Florida town set in the South Seas!

Still, what more could he expect in the year 2110? Ancient Polynesia was as dead as Merrie England or Bourbon France. And 20th century Florida, he remembered, could be very pleasant indeed.

He walked down Main Street, and saw a notice on a building stating that Postmaster Alfred Gray had been appointed Hereafter, Inc. representative for the Marquesas Group. And further on, he came to a small black building with a sign on it that said *Public Suicide Booth.*

Ah, Blaine thought sardonically, modern civilization is encroaching even here! Next thing you know they'll be setting up a Spiritual Switchboard. And where will we be then?

He had reached the end of town. As he started back, a stout, red-faced man hurried up to him.

"Mr. Elgin? Mr. Thomas Elgin?"

"That's me," Blaine said, with a certain apprehension.

"Terribly sorry I missed you at the dock," said the red-faced man, mopping his wide and gleaming forehead with a bandanna. "No excuse, of course. Sheer oversight on my part. The languor of the islands. Inevitable after a while. Oh, I'm Davis, owner of the Point Boatyard. Welcome to Taiohae, Mr. Elgin."

"Thank you, Mr Davis," Blaine said.

"On the contrary. I want to thank *you* again for answering my advertisement," Davis said. "I've been needing a Master Boatwright for months. You have no idea! And frankly, I didn't expect to attract a man of your qualifications."

"Ummm," Blaine said, surprised and pleased at the thoroughness of Carl Orc's preparations.

"Not many men around with a grounding in 20th Century boat-building methods," Davis said sadly. "Lost art. Have you had a look around the island?"

"Just very briefly," Blaine said.

"Think you'll want to stay?" Davis asked anxiously. "You have no idea how hard it is getting a good boatwright to settle down in a quiet little backwater like this. No sooner do they get here, they want to go charging off to the big booming cities like Papeete or Apia. I know wages are higher in places like that, and there's more amusements, and society and things. But Taiohae has a charm of its own."

"I've had my fill of the cities," Blaine said, smiling. "I'm not likely to go charging off, Mr. Davis."

"Good, good!" Davis said. "Don't bother coming to work for a few days, Mr. Elgin. Rest, take it easy, look around our island. It's the last refuge of primitive Polynesia, you know. Here are the keys to your house. Number one Temetiu Road, straight up the mountain there. Shall I show you the way?"

"I'll find it," Blaine said. "Thanks very much, Mr. Davis."

"Thank *you*, Mr. Elgin. I'll drop in on you tomorrow after you're a bit more settled. Then you can meet some of our townsfolk. In fact, the mayor's wife is giving a party Thursday. Or is it Friday? Anyhow, I'll find out and let you know."

They shook hands and Blaine started up Temetiu Road, to his new home.

It was a small, freshly painted bungalow with a spectacular view of Nuku Hiva's three southern bays. Blaine admired the sight for a few minutes, then tried the door. It was unlocked, and he walked in.

"It's about time you got here."

Blaine just stared, not able to believe what he saw.

"Marie!"

She appeared as slim, lovely and cool as ever. But she was nervous. She talked rapidly and avoided meeting his eyes.

"I thought it would be best if I made the final arrangements on the spot," she said. "I've been here for two days, waiting for you. You've met Mr. Davis, haven't you? He seems like a very nice little man."

"Marie—"

"I told him I was your fiancée," she said. "I hope you don't mind, Tom. I had to have some excuse for being here. I said I had come out early to surprise you. Mr. Davis was delighted of course, he wants his Master Boatwright to settle here so badly. Do you mind, Tom? We can always say we broke off the engagement and—"

Blaine took her in his arms and said, "I don't want to break off the engagement. I love you, Marie."

"Oh Tom, Tom, I love you!" She clung to him fiercely for a moment, then stepped back. "We better arrange for a marriage ceremony soon, if you don't mind. They're *very* stuffy and small-townish here; very 20th century, if you know what I mean."

"I think I know what you mean," Blaine said.

They looked at each other and burst out laughing.

32

Marie insisted upon staying at the South Seas Motel until a wedding could be arranged. Blaine suggested a quiet ceremony before a justice of the peace; but Marie surprised him by wanting as large a wedding as Taiohae could produce. It was held on Sunday, at the Mayor's house.

Mr. Davis loaned them a little cutter from the boatyard. They set sail at sunrise for a honeymoon cruise to Tahiti.

For Blaine, it had the sensation of a delicious and fleeting dream. They sailed across a sea carved of green jade, and saw the moon, yellow and swollen, quartered by the cutter's shrouds and tangled in its stays. The sun rose out of a long black cloud, reached its zenith and declined, scouring the sea into a gleaming bowl of brass. They anchored in the lagoon at Papeete and saw the mountains of Moorea flaming in the sunset, more fantastic than the mountains of the Moon. And Blaine remembered a day on the Chesapeake when he had dreamed, *Ah, Raiatea, the mountains of Moorea, the fresh trade wind* ...

A continent and an ocean had separated him from Tahiti, and other obstacles besides. But that had been in another century.

They went to Moorea, rode horses up the slopes and picked the white tiare of Tahiti. They returned to their boat anchored in the bay below, and set sail for the Tuamotos.

At last they returned to Taiohae. Marie started housekeeping, and Blaine began to work at the boatyard.

They waited anxiously through the first weeks, scanning the New York papers, wondering what Rex would do. But no word or sign came from the corporation, and they decided that the danger must be past. Still, they read with relief two months later that the Blaine hunt had been called off.

Blaine's job at the boatyard was interesting and varied. The island cutters and ketches limped in with bent shafts or nicked propellers, with planks that had been splintered against a hidden coral head, with sails blown out by a sudden gale. There were underwater craft to be serviced, boats belonging to the nearby undersea pressure farms that used Taiohae as a supply base. And there were dinghies to build, and an occasional schooner.

Blaine handled all practical details with skill and dispatch. As time went by, he started to write a few publicity releases about the yard for the *South Seas Courier*. This brought in more business, which involved more paper work and a greater need for liaison between the Point Boatyard and the small yards to which it farmed out work. Blaine handled this, and took over advertising as well.

His job as Master Boatwright came to bear an uncanny resemblance to his past jobs as junior yacht designer.

But this no longer bothered him. It seemed obvious to him now that nature had intended him to be a junior yacht designer, nothing more nor less. This was his destiny, and he accepted it.

His life fell into a pleasant routine built around the boatyard and the white bungalow, filled with Saturday night movies and the microfilm *Sunday Times*, quick visits to the undersea farms and to other islands in the Marquesas Group, parties at the Mayor's house and poker at the yacht club, brisk sails across Comptroller Bay and moonlight swimming on Temuoa Beach. Blaine began to think that his life had taken its final and definitive form.

Then, nearly four months after he had come to Taiohae, the pattern changed again.

One morning like any other morning Blaine woke up, ate his breakfast, kissed his wife good-bye and went down to the boatyard. There was a fat, round-bilged ketch on the ways, a Tuamotan boat that had gauged wrong trying to shoot a narrow pass under sail, and had been tide-set against a foam-splattered granite wall before the crew could start the engine. Six frames needed sistering, and a few planks had to be replaced. Perhaps they could finish it in a week.

Blaine was looking over the ketch when Mr. Davis came over.

"Say Tom," the owner said, "there was a fellow around here just a little while ago looking for you. Did you see him?"

"No," Blaine said. "Who was it?"

"A mainlander," Davis said, frowning. "Just off the steamer this morning. I told him you weren't here yet and he said he'd see you at your house."

"What did he look like?" Blaine asked, feeling his stomach muscles tighten.

Davis frowned more deeply. "Well, that's the funny part of it. He was about your height, thin, and very tanned. Had a full beard and sideburns. You don't see that much any more. And he stank of shaving lotion."

"Sounds peculiar," Blaine said.

"Very peculiar. I'll swear his beard wasn't real."

"No?"

"It looked like a fake. Everything about him looked fake. And he limped pretty bad."

"Did he leave a name?"

"Said his name was Smith. Tom, where are you going?"

"I have to go home right now," Blaine said. "I'll try to explain later."

He hurried away. Smith must have found out who he was and what the connection was between them. And, exactly as he had promised, the zombie had come visiting.

33

When he told Marie, she went at once to a closet and took down their suitcases. She carried them into the bedroom and began flinging clothes into them.

"What are you doing?" Blaine asked.

"Packing."

"So I see. But why?"

"Because we're getting out of here."

"What are you talking about? We live here!"

"Not any more," she said. "Not with that damned Smith around. Tom, he means trouble."

"I'm sure he does," Blaine said. "But that's no reason to run. Stop packing a minute and listen! What do you think he can do to me?"

"We're not going to stay and find out," she said.

She continued to shove clothes into the suitcase until Blaine grabbed her wrists.

"Calm down," he told her. "I'm not going to run from Smith."

"But it's the only sensible thing to do," Marie said. "He's trouble, but he can't live much longer. Just a few more months, weeks maybe, and he'll be dead. He should have died long before now, that horrible zombie! Tom, let's go!"

"Have you gone crazy or something?" Blaine asked. "Whatever he wants, I can handle it."

"I've heard you say that before," Marie said.

"Things were different then."

"They're different now! Tom, we could borrow the cutter again, Mr. Davis would understand, and we could go to—"

"No! I'm damned if I'll run from him! Maybe you've forgotten, Marie, Smith saved my life."

"But what did he save it *for*?" she wailed. "Tom, I'm warning you! You mustn't see him, not if he remembers!"

"Wait a minute," Blaine said slowly. "Is there something you know? Something I don't?"

She grew immediately calm. "Of course not."

"Marie, are you telling me the truth?"

"Yes, darling. But I'm frightened of Smith. Please Tom, humour me this once, let's go away."

"I won't run another step from anyone," Blaine said. "I live here. And that's the end of it."

Marie sat down, looking suddenly exhausted. "All right, dear. Do what you think is best."

"That's better," Blaine said. "It'll turn out all right."

"Of course it will," Marie said.

Blaine put the suitcases back and hung up the clothes. Then he sat down to wait. He was physically calm. But in memory he had returned to the underground, had passed again through the ornate door covered with Egyptian hieroglyphics and Chinese ideograms, into the vast marble-pillared Palace of Death with its gold and bronze coffin. And heard again Reilly's screaming voice speak through a silvery mist:

"There are things you can't see, Blaine, but *I* see them. Your time on Earth will be short, very short, painfully short. Those you trust will betray you, those you hate will conquer you. You will die, Blaine, not in years but soon, sooner than you could believe. You'll be betrayed, and you'll die by your own hand."

That mad old man! Blaine shivered slightly and looked at Marie. She sat with downcast eyes, waiting. So he waited, too.

After a while there was a soft knock at the door.

"Come in," Blaine said to whoever was outside.

34

Blaine recognized Smith immediately, even with false beard, sideburns and tan stage make-up. The zombie came in, limping, bringing with him a faint odour of decay imperfectly masked by a powerful shaving lotion.

"Excuse the disguise," Smith said. "It isn't intended to deceive you, or anyone. I wear it because my face is no longer presentable."

"You've come a long way," Blaine said.

"Yes, quite far," Smith agreed, "and through difficulties I won't bore you by relating. But I got here, that's the important thing."

"Why did you come?"

"Because I know who I am," Smith said.

"And you think it concerns me?"

"Yes."

"I can't imagine how," Blaine said grimly. "But let's hear it."

Marie said, "Wait a minute. Smith, you've been after him since he came into this world. He's never had a moment's peace. Can't you just accept things as they are? Can't you just go and die quietly somewhere?"

"Not without telling him first," Smith said.

"Come on, let's hear it," Blaine said.

Smith said, "My name is James Olin Robinson."

"Never heard of you," Blaine said after a moment's thought.

"Of course not."

"Have we ever met before that time in the Rex building?"

"Not formally."

"But we met?"

"Briefly."

"All right, James Olin Robinson, tell me about it. When did we meet?"

"It was quite brief," Robinson said. "We glimpsed each other for a fraction of a second, then saw no more. It happened late one night in 1958, on a lonely highway, you in your car and me in mine."

"You were driving the car I had the accident with?"

"Yes. If you can call it an accident."

"But it was! It was completely accidental!"

"If that's true, I have no further business here," Robinson said. "But Blaine, I *know* it was not an accident. It was murder. Ask your wife."

Blaine looked at his wife sitting in a corner of the couch. Her face was waxen. She seemed drained of vitality. Her gaze seemed to turn inward and not enjoy what it saw there. Blaine wondered if she was staring at the ghost of some ancient guilt, long buried, long quickening, now come to terms with the appearance of the bearded Robinson.

Watching her, he slowly began piecing things together.

"Marie," he said, "what about that night in 1958? How did you know I was going to smash up my car?"

She said, "There are statistical prediction methods we use, valence factors..." Her voice trailed away.

"Or did you *make* me smash up my car?" Blaine asked. "Did you produce the accident when you wanted it, in order to snatch me into the future for your advertising campaign?"

Marie didn't answer. And Blaine thought hard about the manner of his dying.

He had been driving over a straight, empty highway, his head-lights probing ahead, the darkness receding endlessly before him ... His car swerved freakishly, violently, towards the oncoming head-

lights ... He twisted hard on the steering wheel. It wouldn't turn ...
The steering wheel came free and spun in his hands, and the engine
wailed ...

"By God, you made me have that accident!" Blaine shouted at his
wife. "You and Rex Power Systems, you forced my car into a swerve!
Look at me and answer! Isn't it true?"

"All right!" she said. "But we didn't mean to kill *him*. Robinson
just happened to be in the way. I'm sorry about that."

Blaine said, "You've known all along who he was."

"I've suspected."

"And never told me." Blaine paced up and down the room.
"Marie! Damn you, you killed me!"

"I didn't, Tom! Not really. I took you from 1958 into our time. I
gave you a different body. But I didn't really kill you."

"You simply killed *me*," Robinson said.

With an effort Marie turned from her inner gaze and looked at
him. "I'm afraid I was responsible for your death, Mr. Robinson,
although not intentionally. Your body must have died at the same
time as Tom's. The Rex Power System that snatched him into the
future pulled you along, too. Then you took over Reilly's host."

"A very poor exchange for my former body," Robinson said.

"I'm sure it was. But what do you want? What can I do? The
hereafter—"

"I don't want it," Robinson said. "I haven't had a chance on the
Earth yet."

"How old were you at the time of the accident?" Blaine asked.

"Nineteen."

Blaine nodded sadly.

"I'm not ready for the hereafter," Robinson said. "I want to travel,
do things, see things. I want to find out what kind of a man I am. I
want to live! Do you know, I've never really known a woman! I'd
exchange immortality for ten good years on Earth."

Robinson hesitated a moment, then said, "I want a body. I want
a man's good body that I can live in. Not this dead thing which I
wear. Blaine, your wife killed my former body."

Blaine said, "You want mine?"

"If you think it's fair," Robinson said.

"Now wait just a minute!" Marie cried. Colour had returned to her
face. With her confession, she seemed to have freed herself from the
grip of the ancient evil in her mind, to have come back to wrestle
again with life.

"Robinson," she said, "you can't ask that from him. He didn't
have anything to do with your death. It was my fault, and I'm sorry.
You don't want a woman's body, do you? I wouldn't give you mine,
anyhow. What's done is done! Get out of here!"

Robinson ignored her and looked at Blaine. "I always knew it was you, Blaine. When I knew nothing else, I knew it was you. I watched over you, Blaine, I saved your life."

"Yes, you did," Blaine said quietly.

"*So what!*" Marie screamed. "So he saved your life. That doesn't mean he owns it! One doesn't save a life and expect it to be forfeited upon request. Tom, don't listen to him!"

Robinson said, "I have no means or intention of forcing you, Blaine. You will decide what you think is right, and I will abide by it. And you will remember *everything.*"

Blaine looked at the zombie almost with affection. "So there's more to it. Much more. Isn't there, Robinson?"

Robinson nodded, his eyes fixed on Blaine's face.

"But how did you know?" Blaine asked. "How could you possibly know?"

"Because I understand you. I've made you my lifetime work. My life has revolved around you. I've thought, about nothing but you. And the better I know you, Blaine, the more certain I was about this."

"Perhaps," Blaine said.

Marie said, "What on earth are you talking about? What more? What more could there be?"

"I have to think about this," Blaine said. "I have to remember. Robinson, please wait outside for a little while."

"Certainly," the zombie said, and left immediately.

Blaine waved Marie into silence. He sat down and buried his head in his hands. Now he had to remember something he would rather not think about. Now, once and for all, he had to trace it back and understand it.

Etched sharp in his mind still were the words Reilly had screamed at him in the Palace of Death: "You're responsible! You killed me with your evil murdering mind! Yes *you*, you hideous thing from the past, you damned monster! Everything shuns you except your friend the dead man! Why aren't *you* dead, murderer!"

Had Reilly known?

He remembered Sammy Jones saying to him after the hunt: "Tom, you're a natural-born killer. There's nothing else for you."

Had Sammy guessed?

And now the most important thing of all. That most significant moment of his life—the time of his death on a night in 1958. Vividly he remembered:

The steering wheel was working again, but Blaine ignored it, filled with a sudden fierce exultancy, a lightning switch of mood that welcomed the smash, lusted for it, and for pain and cruelty and death ...

Blaine shuddered convulsively as he relived the moment he had wanted to forget—the moment when he might have avoided catastrophe, but had preferred to kill.

He lifted his head and looked at his wife. He said, "I killed him. That's what Robinson knew. And now I know it, too."

35

Carefully he explained it all to Marie. She refused at first to believe him.

"It was so far back, Tom! How can you be sure of what happened?"

"I'm sure," Blaine said. "I don't think anyone could forget the way they died. I remember mine very well. *That* was how I died."

"Still, you can't call yourself a murderer because of one moment, one fraction of a second—"

"How long does it take to shoot a bullet or to drive in a knife?" Blaine asked. "A fraction of a second! That's how long it takes to become a murderer."

"But Tom, you had no motive!"

Blaine shook his head. "It's true that I didn't kill for gain or revenge. But then, I'm not that kind of murderer. That kind is relatively rare. I'm the grass-roots variety, the ordinary average guy with a little of everything in his make-up, including murder. I killed because, in that moment, I had the *opportunity*. My special opportunity, a unique interlocking of events, moods, train of thought, humidity, temperature, and lord knows what else, which might not have come up again in two lifetimes."

"But you're not to blame!" Marie said. "It would never have happened if Rex Power Systems and I hadn't created that special opportunity for you."

"Yes. But I seized the opportunity," Blaine said, "seized it and performed a cold-blooded murder just for fun, because I knew I could never be caught at it. *My* murder."

"Well ... Our murder," she said.

"Yes."

"All right, we're murderers," Marie said calmly. "Accept it, Tom. Don't get mushy-minded about it. We've killed once, we can kill again."

"Never," Blaine said.

"He's almost finished! I swear to you, Tom, there's not a month of life in him. He's almost played out. One blow and he's done for. One push."

"I'm not that kind of murderer," Blaine said.

"Will you let me do it?"

"I'm not that kind, either."

"You idiot! Then just do nothing! Wait. A month, no more than
that, and he's finished. You can wait a month, Tom—"

"More murder," Blaine said wearily.

"Tom! You're not going to give him your body! What about our
life together?"

"Do you think we could go on after this?" Blaine asked. "I couldn't.
Now stop arguing with me. I don't know if I'd do this if there weren't
a hereafter. Quite probably I wouldn't. But there *is* a hereafter. I'd
like to go there with my accounts as straight as possible, all bills paid
in full, all restitutions made. If this were my only existence, I'd cling
to it with everything I've got. But it isn't! Can you understand that?"

"Yes, of course," Marie said unhappily.

"Frankly, I'm getting pretty curious about this afterlife. I want to
see it. And there's one thing more."

"What that?"

Marie's shoulders were trembling, so Blaine put his arm around
her. He was thinking back to the conversation he had had with
Hull, the elegant and aristocratic Quarry.

Hull had said: "We follow Nietzsche's dictum—to die at the right
time! Intelligent people don't clutch at the last shreds of life like
drowning men clinging to a bit of board. They know that the body's
life is only an infinitesimal portion of man's total existence. Why
shouldn't those bright pupils skip a grade or two of school?"

Blaine remembered how strange, dark, atavistic and noble Hull's
lordly selection of death had seemed. Pretentious, of course; but
then, life itself was a pretension in the vast universe of unliving
matter. Hull had seemed like an ancient Japanese nobleman kneeling to perform the ceremonial act of hara-kiri, and emphasizing the
importance of life in the very selection of death.

And Hull had said: "The deed of dying transcends class and
breeding. It is every man's patent of nobility, his summons from the
king, his knightly adventure. And how he acquits himself in that
lonely and perilous enterprise is his true measure as a man."

Marie broke into his reverie, asking, "What was that one thing
more?"

"Oh." Blaine thought for a moment. "I just wanted to say that I
guess some of the attitudes of the 22nd century have rubbed off on
me. Especially the aristocratic ones." He grinned and kissed her. "But
of course, I always had good taste."

36

Blaine opened the door of the cottage. "Robinson," he said, "come with me to the Suicide Booth. I'm giving you my body."

"I expected no less of you, Tom," the zombie said.

"Then let's go."

Together they went slowly down the mountainside. Marie watched them from a window for a few seconds, then started down after them.

They stopped at the door to the Suicide Booth. Blaine said, "Do you think you can take over all right?"

"I'm sure of it," Robinson said. "Tom, I'm grateful for this. I'll use your body well."

"It's not mine, really," Blaine said. "Belonged to a fellow named Kranch. But I've grown fond of it. You'll get used to its habits. Just remind it once in a while who's boss. Sometimes it wants to go hunting."

"I think I'll like that," Robinson said.

"Yes, I suppose you would. Well, good luck."

"Good luck to you, Tom."

Marie came up and kissed Blaine good-bye with icy lips. Blaine said, "What will you do?"

She shrugged her shoulders. "I don't know. I feel so numb ... Tom, must you?"

"I must," Blaine said.

He looked around once more at the palm trees whispering under the sun, the blue expanse of the sea, and the great dark mountain above him cut with silver waterfalls. Then he turned and entered the Suicide Booth, and closed the door behind him.

There were no windows, no furniture except a single chair. The instructions posted on one wall were very simple. You just sat down, and, at your leisure, closed the switch upon the right arm. You would then die, quickly and painlessly, and your body would be left intact for the next inhabitant.

Blaine sat down, made sure of the location of the switch and leaned back, his eyes closed.

He thought again about the first time he died, and wished it had been more interesting. By rights he should have rectified the error this time, and gone down like Hull, hunted fiercely across a mountain ledge at sundown. Why couldn't it have been like that? Why couldn't death have come while he was battling a typhoon, meeting a tiger's charge, or climbing Mount Everest? Why, again, would his death be so tame, so commonplace, so ordinary?

But then, why had he never really designed yachts?

An enterprising death, he realized again, would be out of character for him. Undoubtedly he was meant to die in just this quick, commonplace, painless way. And all his life in the future must have gone into the forming and shaping of this death—a vague indication when Reilly died, a fair certainty in the Palace of Death, an implacable destiny when he settled in Taiohae.

Still, no matter how ordinary, one's death is the most interesting event of one's life. Blaine looked forward eagerly to his.

He had no complaint to make. Although he had lived in the future little over a year, he had gained its greatest prize—the hereafter! He felt again what he had experienced after leaving the Hereafter Building—release from the heavy, sodden, constant, unconscious fear of death that subtly weighed every action and permeated every movement. No man of his own age could live without the shadow that crept down the corridors of his mind like some grisly tapeworm, the ghost that haunted nights and days, the croucher behind corners, the shape behind doors, the unseen guest at every banquet, the unidentified figure in every landscape, always present, always waiting—

No more!

For now the ancient enemy was defeated. And men no longer died; they *moved on*!

But he had gained even more than an afterlife. He had managed to squeeze and compress an entire lifetime into that year.

He had been born in a white room with dazzling lights and a doctor's bearded face above him, and a motherly nurse to feed him while he listened, alarmed, to the babble of strange tongues. He had ventured early into the world, raw and uneducated, and had stared at the oriental marvel of New York, and allowed a straight-eyed fast-talking stranger to make a fool and nearly a corpse of him, until wiser heads rescued him from his folly and soothed his pain. Clothed in his fine, strong, mysterious body he had ventured out again, wiser this time, and had moved as an equal among men equipped with glittering weapons in the pursuit of danger and honour. And he had lived through that folly, too, and still older, had chosen an honourable occupation. But certain dark omens present at his birth finally reached fruition, and he had to flee his homeland and run to the furthest corner of the Earth. Yet he still managed to acquire a family on the way; a family with certain skeletons in the closet, but his all the same. In the fullness of manhood he had come to a land he loved, taken a wife, and, on his honeymoon, seen the mountains of Moorea flaming in the sunset. He had settled down to spend his declining months in peace and useful labour, and in fond recollection of the wonders he had seen. And so he had spent them, honoured and respected by all.

It was sufficient. Blaine turned the switch.

37

"Where am I? Who am I? What am I?"

No answer.

"I remember. I am Thomas Blaine, and I have just died. I am now in the Threshold, a very real and completely indescribable place. I sense Earth. And ahead, I sense the hereafter."

"Tom—"

"Marie!"

"Yes."

"But how could you— I didn't think—"

"Well, perhaps in some ways I wasn't a very good wife, Tom. But I was always a faithful one, and I did what I did for you. I love you, Tom. Of course I would follow."

"Marie, this makes me very happy."

"I'm glad."

"Shall we go on?"

"Where, Tom?"

"Into the hereafter."

"Tom, I'm frightened. Couldn't we just stay right here for a while?"

"It'll be all right. Come with me."

"Oh, Tom! What if they separate us? What will it be like? I don't think I'm going to like it. I'm afraid it's going to be terribly strange and ghostly and horrible."

"Marie, don't worry. I've been a junior yacht designer three times in two lifetimes. It's my destiny! Surely it can't end here!"

"All right. I'm ready now, Tom. Let's go."

SPECIALIST

THE PHOTON STORM struck without warning, pouncing upon the Ship from behind a bank of giant red stars. Eye barely had time to flash a last-second warning through Talker before it was upon them.

It was Talker's third journey into deep space, and his first light-pressure storm. He felt a sudden pang of fear as the Ship yawed violently, caught the force of the wave-front and careened end for end. Then the fear was gone, replaced by a strong pulse of excitement.

Why should he be afraid, he asked himself—hadn't he been trained for just this sort of emergency?

He had been talking to Feeder when the storm hit, but he cut off the conversation abruptly. He hoped Feeder would be all right. It was the youngster's first deep-space trip.

The wire-like filaments that made up most of Talker's body were extended throughout the Ship. Quickly he withdrew all except the ones linking him to Eye, Engine, and the Walls. This was strictly their job now. The rest of the Crew would have to shift for themselves until the storm was over.

Eye had flattened his disc-like body against a Wall, and had one seeing organ extended outside the Ship. For greater concentration, the rest of his seeing organs were collapsed, clustered against his body.

Through Eye's seeing organ, Talker watched the storm. He translated Eye's purely visual image into a direction for Engine, who shoved the Ship around to meet the waves. At appreciably the same time, Talker translated direction into velocity for the Walls who stiffened to meet the shocks.

The co-ordination was swift and sure—Eye measuring the waves, Talker relaying the messages to Engine and Walls, Engine driving the Ship nose-first into the waves, and Walls bracing to meet the shock.

Talker forgot any fear he might have had in the swiftly functioning teamwork. He had no time to think. As the Ship's communication system, he had to translate and flash his messages at top speed, co-ordinating information and directing action.

In a matter of minutes, the storm was over.

"All right," Talker said. "Let's see if there was any damage!" His filaments had become tangled during the storm, but he untwisted and extended them through the Ship, plugging everyone into circuit. "Engine?"

"I'm fine," Engine said. The tremendous old fellow had dampened his plates during the storm, easing down the atomic explosions in his stomach. No storm could catch an experienced spacer like Engine unaware.

"Walls?"

The Walls reported one by one, and this took a long time. There were almost a thousand of them, thin, rectangular fellows making up the entire skin of the Ship. Naturally, they had reinforced their edges during the storm, giving the whole Ship resiliency. But one or two were dented badly.

Doctor announced that he was all right. He removed Talker's filament from his head, taking himself out of circuit, and went to work on the dented Walls. Made mostly of hands, Doctor had clung to an Accumulator during the storm.

"Let's go a little faster now!" Talker said, remembering that there still was the problem of determining where they were. He opened the circuit to the four Accumulators. "How are you?" he asked.

There was no answer. The Accumulators were asleep. They had had their receptors open during the storm and were bloated on energy. Talker twitched his filaments around them, but they didn't stir.

"Let me!" Feeder said. Feeder had taken quite a beating before planting his suction cups to a Wall, but his cockiness was intact. He was the only member of the Crew who never needed Doctor's attention; his body was quite capable of repairing itself.

He scuttled across the floor on a dozen or so tentacles, and booted the nearest Accumulator. The big, conical storage unit opened one eye, then closed it again. Feeder kicked him again, getting no response. He reached for the Accumulator's safety valve and drained off some energy.

"Stop that!" the Accumulator said.

"Then wake up and report!" Talker told him.

The Accumulators said testily that they were all right, as any fool could see. They had been anchored to the floor during the storm.

The rest of the inspection went quickly. Thinker was fine, and Eye was ecstatic over the beauty of the storm. There was only one casualty.

Pusher was dead. Bipedal, he didn't have the stability of the rest of the Crew. The storm had caught him in the middle of a floor, thrown him against a stiffened Wall, and broken several of his important bones. He was beyond Doctor's skill to repair.

They were silent for a while. It was always serious when a part of the Ship died. The Ship was a co-operative unit, composed entirely of the Crew. The loss of any member was a blow to all the rest.

It was especially serious now. They had just delivered a cargo to a port several thousand light-years from Galactic Centre. There was no telling where they might be.

Eye crawled to a Wall and extended a seeing organ outside. The Walls let it through, then sealed around it. Eye's organ pushed out, far enough from the Ship so he could view the entire sphere of stars. The picture travelled through Talker, who gave it to Thinker.

Thinker lay in one corner of the room, a great shapeless blob of protoplasm. Within him were all the memories of his space-going ancestors. He considered the picture, compared it rapidly with others stored in his cells, and said, "No galactic planets within reach."

Talker automatically translated for everyone. It was what they had feared.

Eye, with Thinker's help, calculated that they were several hundred light-years off their course, on the galactic periphery.

Every Crew member knew what that meant. Without a Pusher to boost the Ship to a multiple of the speed of light, they would never get home. The trip back, without a Pusher, would take longer than most of their lifetimes.

"What would you suggest?" Talker asked Thinker.

This was too vague a question for the literal-minded Thinker. He asked to have it rephrased.

"What would be our best line of action," Talker asked, "to get back to a galactic planet?"

Thinker needed several minutes to go through all the possibilities stored in his cells. In the meantime, Doctor had patched the Walls and was asking to be given something to eat.

"In a little while we'll all eat," Talker said, twitching his tendrils nervously. Even though he was the second youngest Crew member —only Feeder was younger—the responsibility was largely on him. This was still an emergency; he had to co-ordinate information and direct action.

One of the Walls suggested that they get good and drunk. This unrealistic solution was vetoed at once. It was typical of the Walls' attitude, however. They were fine workers and good shipmates, but happy-go-lucky fellows at best. When they returned to their home planets, they would probably blow all their wages on a spree.

"Loss of the Ship's Pusher cripples the Ship for sustained faster-than-light speeds," Thinker began without preamble. "The nearest galactic planet is four hundred and five light-years off."

Talker translated all this instantly along his wave-packet body.

"Two courses of action are open. First, the Ship can proceed to the nearest galactic planet under atomic power from Engine. This will take approximately two hundred years. Engine might still be alive at this time, although no one else will.

"Second, locate a primitive planet in this region, upon which are latent Pushers. Find one and train him. Have him push the Ship back to galactic territory."

Thinker was silent, having given all the possibilities he could find in the memories of his ancestors.

They held a quick vote and decided upon Thinker's second alternative. There was no choice, really. It was the only one which offered them any hope of getting back to their homes.

"All right," Talker said. "Let's eat! I think we all deserve it."

The body of the dead Pusher was shoved into the mouth of Engine, who consumed it at once, breaking down the atoms to energy. Engine was the only member of the Crew who lived on atomic energy.

For the rest, Feeder dashed up and loaded himself from the nearest Accumulator. Then he transformed the food within him into the substances each member ate. His body chemistry changed, altered, adapted, making the different foods for the Crew.

Eye lived entirely on a complex chlorophyll chain. Feeder reproduced this for him, then went over to give Talker his hydrocarbons, and the Walls their chlorine compound. For Doctor he made a fascimile of a silicate fruit that grew on Doctor's native planet.

Finally, feeding was over and the Ship back in order. The Accumulators were stacked in a corner, blissfully sleeping again. Eye was extending his vision as far as he could, shaping his main seeing organ for high-powered telescopic reception. Even in this emergency, Eye couldn't resist making verses. He announced that he was at work on a new narrative poem, called *Peripheral Glow*. No one wanted to hear it, so Eye fed it to Thinker, who stored everything, good or bad, right or wrong.

Engine never slept. Filled to the brim on Pusher, he shoved the Ship along at several times the speed of light.

The Walls were arguing among themselves about who had been the drunkest during their last leave.

Talker decided to make himself comfortable. He released his hold on the Walls and swung in the air, his small round body suspended by his criss-crossed network of filaments.

He thought briefly about Pusher. It was strange. Pusher had been everyone's friend and now he was forgotten. That wasn't because of indifference; it was because the Ship was a unit. The loss of a member was regretted, but the important thing was for the unit to go on.

The Ship raced through the suns of the periphery.

Thinker laid out a search spiral, calculating their odds on finding a Pusher planet at roughly four to one. In a week they found a planet

of primitive Walls. Dropping low, they could see the leathery, rectangular fellows basking in the sun, crawling over rocks, stretching
themselves thin in order to float in the breeze.

All the Ship's Walls heaved a sigh of nostalgia. It was just like
home.

These Walls on the planet hadn't been contacted by a galactic
team yet, and were still unaware of their great destiny—to join in
the vast Co-operation of the Galaxy.

There were plenty of dead worlds in the spiral, and worlds too
young to bear life. They found a planet of Talkers. The Talkers had
extended their spidery communication lines across half a continent.

Talker looked at them eagerly, through Eye. A wave of self-pity
washed over him. He remembered home, his family, his friends. He
thought of the tree he was going to buy when he got back.

For a moment, Talker wondered what he was doing here, part of a
Ship in a far corner of the Galaxy.

He shrugged off the mood. They were bound to find a Pusher
planet, if they looked long enough.

At least, he hoped so.

There was a long stretch of arid worlds as the Ship sped through
the unexplored periphery. Then a planetful of primeval Engines,
swimming in a radio-active ocean.

"This is rich territory," Feeder said to Talker. "Galactic should
send a Contact party here."

"They probably will, after we get back," Talker said.

They were good friends, above and beyond the all-enveloping
friendship of the Crew. It wasn't only because they were the youngest Crew members, although that had something to do with it. They
both had the same kind of functions and that made for a certain
rapport. Talker translated languages; Feeder transformed foods.
Also, they looked somewhat alike. Talker was a central core with
radiating filaments; Feeder was a central core with radiating tentacles.

Talker thought that Feeder was the next most aware being on
the Ship. He was never really able to understand how some of the
others carried on the processes of consciousness.

More suns, more planets! Engine started to overheat. Usually,
Engine was used only for taking off and landing, and for fine
manoeuvring in a planetary group. Now he had been running continuously for weeks, both over and under the speed of light. The
strain was telling on him.

Feeder, with Doctor's help, rigged a cooling system for him. It was
crude, but it had to suffice. Feeder rearranged nitrogen, oxygen and
hydrogen atoms to make a coolant for the system. Doctor diagnosed
a long rest for Engine. He said that the gallant old fellow couldn't

stand the strain for more than a week.

The search continued, with the Crew's spirits gradually dropping. They all realized that Pushers were rather rare in the Galaxy, as compared to the fertile Walls and Engines.

The Walls were getting pock-marked from interstellar dust. They complained that they would need a full beauty treatment when they got home. Talker assured them that the company would pay for it.

Even Eye was getting bloodshot from staring into space so continuously.

They dipped over another planet. Its characteristics were flashed to Thinker, who mulled over them.

Closer, and they could make out the forms.

Pushers! Primitive Pushers!

They zoomed back into space to make plans. Feeder produced twenty-three different kinds of intoxicants for a celebration.

The Ship wasn't fit to function for three days.

"Everyone ready now?" Talker asked, a bit fuzzily. He had a hangover that burned all along his nerve ends. What a drunk he had thrown! He had a vague recollection of embracing Engine, and inviting him to share his tree when they got home.

He shuddered at the idea.

The rest of the Crew were pretty shaky, too. The Walls were letting air leak into space; they were just too wobbly to seal their edges properly. Doctor had passed out.

But the worst off was Feeder. Since his system could adapt to any type of fuel except atomic, he had been sampling every batch he made, whether it was an unbalanced iodine, pure oxygen or a supercharged ester. He was really miserable. His tentacles, usually a healthy aqua, were shot through with orange streaks. His system was working furiously, purging itself of everything, and Feeder was suffering the effects of the purge.

The only sober ones were Thinker and Engine. Thinker didn't drink, which was unusual for a spacer, though typical of Thinker, and Engine couldn't.

They listened while Thinker reeled off some astounding facts. From Eye's pictures of the planet's surface, Thinker had detected the presence of metallic construction. He put forth the alarming suggestion that these Pushers had constructed a mechanical civilization.

"That's impossible," three of the Walls said flatly, and most of the Crew were inclined to agree with them. All the metal they had ever seen had been buried in the ground or lying around in worthless oxidized chunks.

"Do you mean that they make things out of metal?" Talker demanded. "Out of just plain dead metal? What could they make?"

"They couldn't make anything," Feeder said positively. "It would break down constantly. I mean metal doesn't *know* when it's weakening."

But it seemed to be true. Eye magnified his pictures, and everyone could see that the Pushers had made vast shelters, vehicles, and other articles from inanimate material.

The reason for this was not readily apparent, but it wasn't a good sign. However, the really hard part was over. The Pusher planet had been found. All that remained was the relatively easy job of convincing a native Pusher.

That shouldn't be too difficult. Talker knew that co-operation was the keystone of the Galaxy, even among primitive peoples.

The Crew decided not to land in a populated region. Of course, there was no reason not to expect a friendly greeting, but it was the job of a Contact Team to get in touch with them as a race. All they wanted was an individual.

Accordingly, they picked out a sparsely populated landmass, drifting in while that side of the planet was dark.

They were able to locate a solitary Pusher almost at once.

Eye adapted his vision to see in the dark, and they followed the Pusher's movements. He lay down, after a while, beside a small fire. Thinker told them that this was a well-known resting habit of Pushers.

Just before dawn, the Walls opened, and Feeder, Talker and Doctor came out.

Feeder dashed forward and tapped the creature on the shoulder. Talker followed with a communication tendril.

The Pusher opened his seeing organs, blinked them, and made a movement with his eating organ. Then he leaped to his feet and started to run.

The three Crew members were amazed. The Pusher hadn't even waited to find out what the three of them wanted!

Talker extended a filament rapidly, and caught the Pusher, fifty feet away, by a limb. The Pusher fell.

"Treat him gently!" Feeder said. "He might be startled by our appearance." He twitched his tendrils at the idea of a Pusher—one of the strangest sights in the Galaxy, with his multiple organs— being startled at someone else's appearance.

Feeder and Doctor scurried to the fallen Pusher, picked him up and carried him back to the Ship.

The Walls sealed again. They released the Pusher and prepared to talk.

As soon as he was free, the Pusher sprang to his limbs and ran at the place where the Walls had sealed. He pounded against them frantically, his eating organ open and vibrating.

"Stop that!" the Wall said. He bulged, and the Pusher tumbled
to the floor. Instantly, he jumped up and started to run forward.
"Stop him!" Talker said. "He might hurt himself."
One of the Accumulators woke up enough to roll into the Pusher's
path. The Pusher fell, got up again, and ran on.
Talker had his filaments in the front of the Ship also, and he
caught the Pusher in the bow. The Pusher started to tear at his
tendrils, and Talker let go hastily.
"Plug him into the communication system!" Feeder shouted.
"Maybe we can reason with him."
Talker advanced a filament towards the Pusher's head, waving it
in the universal sign of communication. But the Pusher continued
his amazing behaviour, jumping out of the way. He had a piece of
metal in his hand and he was waving it frantically.
"What do you think he's going to do with that?" Feeder asked.
The Pusher started to attack the side of the Ship, pounding at one
of the Walls. The Wall stiffened instinctively and the metal snapped.
"Leave him alone," Talker said. "Give him a chance to calm down."
Talker consulted with Thinker, but they couldn't decide what to
do about the Pusher. He wouldn't accept communication. Every time
Talker extended a filament, the Pusher showed all the signs of
violent panic. Temporarily, it was an impasse.
Thinker vetoed the plan of finding another Pusher on the planet.
He considered this Pusher's behaviour typical; nothing would be
gained by approaching another. Also, a planet was supposed to be
contacted only by a Contact Team.
If they couldn't communicate with this Pusher, they never would
with another on the planet.
"I think I know what the trouble is," Eye said. He crawled up on
an Accumulator. "These Pushers have evolved a mechanical civilization. Consider for a minute how they went about it. They developed the use of their fingers, like Doctor, to shape metal. They
utilized their seeing organs, like myself. And probably countless
other organs." He paused for effect.
"These Pushers have become unspecialized."
They argued over it for several hours. The Walls maintained that
no intelligent creature could be unspecialized. It was unknown in
the Galaxy. But the evidence was before them—The Pusher cities,
their vehicles— This Pusher, exemplifying the rest, seemed capable
of a multitude of things.
He was able to do everything except Push.
Thinker supplied a partial explanation. "This is not a primitive
planet. It is relatively old and should have been in the Co-operation
thousands of years ago. Since it was not, the Pushers upon it were
robbed of their birthright. Their ability, their specialty was to Push,

but there was nothing *to* Push. Naturally, they have developed a deviant culture.

"Exactly what this culture is, we can only guess. But on the basis of the evidence, there is reason to believe that these Pushers are— unco-operative."

Thinker had a habit of uttering the most shattering statement in the quietest possible way.

"It is entirely possible," Thinker went on inexorably, "that these Pushers will have nothing to do with us. In which case, our chances are approximately two hundred and eighty-three to one against finding another Pusher planet."

"We can't be sure he won't co-operate," Talker said, "until we get him into communication." He found it almost impossible to believe that any intelligent creature would refuse to co-operate willingly.

"But how?" Feeder asked. They decided upon a course of action. Doctor walked slowly up to the Pusher, who backed away from him. In the meantime, Talker extended a filament outside the Ship, around, and in again, behind the Pusher.

The Pusher backed against a Wall—and Talker shoved the filament through the Pusher's head, into the communication socket in the centre of his brain.

The Pusher collapsed.

When he came to, Feeder and Doctor had to hold the Pusher's limbs, or he would have ripped out the communication line. Talker exercised his skill in learning the Pusher's language.

It wasn't too hard. All Pusher languages were of the same family, and this was no exception. Talker was able to catch enough surface thoughts to form a pattern.

He tried to communicate with the Pusher.

The Pusher was silent.

"I think he needs food," Feeder said. They remembered that it had been almost two days since they had taken the Pusher on board. Feeder worked up some standard Pusher food and offered it.

"My God! A steak!" the Pusher said.

The Crew cheered along Talker's communication circuits. The Pusher had said his first words.

Talker examined the words and searched his memory. He knew about two hundred Pusher languages and many more simple variations. He found that this Pusher was speaking a cross between two Pusher tongues.

After the Pusher had eaten, he looked around. Talker caught his thoughts and broadcast them to the Crew.

The Pusher had a queer way of looking at the Ship. He saw it as a riot of colours. The walls undulated. In front of him was something resembling a gigantic spider, coloured black and green, with his web running all over the Ship and into the heads of all the creatures. He saw Eye as a strange, naked little animal, something between a skinned rabbit and an egg yolk—whatever those things were.

Talker was fascinated by the new perspective the Pusher's mind gave him. He had never seen things that way before. But now that the Pusher was pointing it out, Eye *was* a pretty funny-looking creature.

They settled down to communication.

"What in hell *are* you things?" the Pusher asked, much calmer now than he had been during the two days. "Why did you grab me? Have I gone nuts?"

"No," Talker said, "you are not psychotic. We are a galactic trading ship. We were blown off our course by a storm and our Pusher was killed."

"Well, what does that have to do with me?"

"We would like you to join our crew," Talker said, "to be our new Pusher."

The Pusher thought it over after the situation was explained to him. Talker could catch the feeling of conflict in the Pusher's thoughts. He hadn't decided whether to accept this as a real situation or not. Finally, the Pusher decided that he wasn't crazy.

"Look, boys," he said, "I don't know what you are or how this makes sense. I have to get out of here. I'm on a furlough, and if I don't get back soon, the U.S. Army's going to be very interested."

Talker asked the Pusher to give him more information about "army", and he fed it to Thinker.

"These Pushers engage in personal combat," was Thinker's conclusion.

"But *why*?" Talker asked. Sadly he admitted to himself that Thinker might have been right; the Pusher didn't show many signs of willingness to co-operate.

"I'd like to help you lads out," Pusher said, "but I don't know where you get the idea that I could push anything this size. You'd need a whole division of tanks just to budge it."

"Do you approve of these wars?" Talker asked, getting a suggestion from Thinker.

"Nobody likes war—not those who have to do the dying at least."

"Then why do you fight them?"

The Pusher made a gesture with his eating organ, which Eye picked up and sent to Thinker. "It's kill or be killed. You guys know what war is, don't you?"

"We don't have any wars," Talker said.

"You're lucky," the Pusher said bitterly. "We do. Plenty of them."

"Of course," Talker said. He had the full explanation from Thinker now. "Would you like to end them?"

"Of course I would."

"Then come with us! Be our Pusher!"

The Pusher stood up and walked up to an Accumulator. He sat down on it and doubled the ends of his upper limbs.

"How the hell can I stop all wars?" the Pusher demanded. "Even if I went to the big shots and told them—"

"You won't have to," Talker said. "All you have to do is come with us. Push us to our base. Galactic will send a Contact Team to your planet. That will end your wars."

"The hell you say," the Pusher replied. "You boys are stranded here, huh? Good enough! No monsters are going to take over Earth."

Bewildered, Talker tried to understand the reasoning. Had he said something wrong? Was it possible that the Pusher didn't understand him?

"I thought you wanted to end wars," Talker said.

"Sure I do. But I don't want anyone *making* us stop. I'm no traitor. I'd rather fight."

"No one will make you stop. You will just stop because there will be no further need for fighting."

"Do you know why we're fighting?"

"It's obvious."

"Yeah? What's your explanation?"

"You Pushers have been separated from the main stream of the Galaxy," Talker explained. "You have your speciality—pushing—but nothing to push. Accordingly, you have no real jobs. You play with things—metal, inanimate objects—but find no real satisfaction. Robbed of your true vocation, you fight from sheer frustration.

"Once you find your place in the galactic Co-operation—and I assure you that it is an important place—your fighting will stop. Why should you fight, which is an unnatural occupation, when you can push? Also, your mechanical civilization will end, since there will be no need for it."

The Pusher shook his head in what Talker guessed was a gesture of confusion. "What is this pushing?"

Talker told him as best he could. Since the job was out of his scope, he had only a general idea of what a Pusher did.

"You mean to say that *that* is what every Earthman should be doing?"

"Of course," Talker said. "It is your great specialty."

The Pusher thought about it for several minutes. "I think you want a physicist or a mentalist or something. I could never do anything like that. I'm a junior architect. And besides—well, it's difficult to explain."

But Talker had already caught Pusher's objection. He saw a Pusher female in his thoughts. No, two, three. And he caught a feeling of loneliness, strangeness. The Pusher was filled with doubts. He was afraid.

"When we reach galactic," Talker said, hoping it was the right thing, "you can meet other Pushers. Pusher females, too. All you Pushers look alike, so you should become friends with them. As far as loneliness in the Ship goes—it just doesn't exist. You don't understand the Co-operation yet. No one is lonely in the Co-operation."

The Pusher was still considering the idea of there being other Pushers. Talker couldn't understand why he was so startled at that. The Galaxy was filled with Pushers, Feeders, Talkers, and many other species, endlessly duplicated.

"I can't believe that anybody could end all war," Pusher said. "How do I know you're not lying?"

Talker felt as if he had been struck in the core. Thinker must have been right when he said these Pushers would be unco-operative. Was this going to be the end of Talker's career? Were he and the rest of the Crew going to spend the rest of their lives in space, because of the stupidity of a bunch of Pushers?

Even thinking this, Talker was able to feel sorry for the Pusher. It must be terrible, he thought. Doubting, uncertain, never trusting anyone. If these Pushers didn't find their place in the Galaxy, they would exterminate themselves. Their place in the Co-operation was long overdue.

"What can I do to convince you?" Talker asked.

In despair, he opened all the circuits to the Pusher. He let the Pusher see Engine's good-natured gruffness, the devil-may-care humour of the Walls; he showed him Eye's poetic attempts, and Feeder's cocky good nature. He opened his own mind and showed the Pusher a picture of his home planet, his family, the tree he was planning to buy when he got home.

The pictures told the story of all of them, from different planets, representing different ethics, united by a common bond—the galactic Co-operation.

The Pusher watched it all in silence.

After a while, he shook his head. The thought accompanying the gesture was uncertain, weak—but negative.

Talker told the Walls to open. They did, and the Pusher stared in amazement.

"You may leave," Talker said. "Just remove the communication line and go."

"What will you do?"

"We will look for another Pusher planet."

"Where? Mars? Venus?"

"We don't know. All we can do is hope there is another in this region."

The Pusher looked at the opening, then back at the Crew. He hesitated and his face screwed up in a grimace of indecision.

"All that you showed me was true?"

No answer was necessary.

"All right," the Pusher said suddenly. "I'll go. I'm a damned fool, but I'll go. If this means what you say—it *must* mean what you say!"

Talker saw that the agony of the Pusher's decision had forced him out of contact with reality. He believed that he was in a dream, where decisions are easy and unimportant.

"There's just one little trouble," Pusher said with the lightness of hysteria. "Boys, I'll be damned if I know how to push. You said something about faster-than-light? I can't even run the mile in an hour."

"Of course you can push," Talker assured him, hoping he was right. He knew what a Pusher's abilities were; but this one—

"Just try it."

"Sure," Pusher agreed. "I'll probably wake up out of this, anyhow."

They sealed the ship for take-off while Pusher talked to himself.

"Funny," Pusher said. "I thought a camping trip would be a nice way to spend a furlough and all I do is get nightmares!"

Engine boosted the Ship into the air. The Walls were sealed and Eye was guiding them away from the planet.

"We're in open space now," Talker said. Listening to Pusher, he hoped his mind hadn't cracked. "Eye and Thinker will give a direction, I'll transmit it to you, and you push along it."

"You're crazy," Pusher mumbled. "You must have the wrong planet. I wish you nightmares would go away."

"You're in the Co-operation now," Talker said desperately. "There's the direction. Push!"

The Pusher didn't do anything for a moment. He was slowly emerging from his fantasy, realizing that he wasn't in a dream, after all. He felt the Co-operation. Eye to Thinker, Thinker to Talker, Talker to Pusher, all inter-co-ordinated with Walls, and with each other.

"What is this?" Pusher asked. He felt the oneness of the Ship, the great warmth, the closeness achieved only in the Co-operation.

He pushed.

Nothing happened.

"Try again," Talker begged.

Pusher searched his mind. He found a deep well of doubt and

fear. Staring into it, he saw his own tortured face.

Thinker illuminated it for him.

Pushers had lived with this doubt and fear for centuries. Pushers had fought through fear, killed through doubt.

That was where the Pusher organ was!

Human—specialist—Pusher—he entered fully into the Crew, merged with them, threw mental arms around the shoulders of Thinker and Talker.

Suddenly, the Ship shot forward at eight times the speed of light. It continued to accelerate.

BAD MEDICINE

On May 2, 2103, Elwood Caswell walked rapidly down Broadway with a loaded revolver hidden in his coat pocket. He didn't want to use the weapon, but feared he might anyhow. This was a justifiable assumption, for Caswell was a homicidal maniac.

It was a gentle, misty spring day and the air held the smell of rain and blossoming dogwood. Caswell gripped the revolver in his sweaty right hand and tried to think of a single valid reason why he should not kill a man named Magnessen, who, the other day, had commented on how well Caswell looked.

What business was it of Magnessen's how he looked? Damned busybodies, always spoiling things for everybody . . .

Caswell was a choleric little man with fierce red eyes, bulldog jowls and ginger-red hair. He was the sort you would expect to find perched on a detergent box, orating to a crowd of lunching businessmen and amused students, shouting, "Mars for the Martians, Venus for the Venusians!"

But in truth, Caswell was uninterested in the deplorable social conditions of extraterrestrials. He was a jetbus conductor for the New York Rapid Transit Corporation. He minded his own business. And he was quite mad.

Fortunately, he knew this at least part of the time, with at least half of his mind.

Perspiring freely, Caswell continued down Broadway towards the 43rd Street branch of Home Therapy Appliances, Inc. His friend Magnessen would be finishing work soon, returning to his little apartment less than a block from Caswell's. How easy it would be, how pleasant, to saunter in, exchange a few words and . . .

No! Caswell took a deep gulp of air and reminded himself that he didn't *really* want to kill anyone. It was not right to kill people. The authorities would lock him up, his friends wouldn't understand, his mother would never have approved.

But these arguments seemed pallid, over-intellectual and entirely without force. The simple fact remained—he wanted to kill Magnessen.

Could so strong a desire be wrong? Or even unhealthy?

Yes, it could! With an agonized groan, Caswell sprinted the last few steps into the Home Therapy Appliances Store.

Just being within such a place gave him an immediate sense of relief. The lighting was discreet, the draperies were neutral, the displays of glittering therapy machines were neither too bland nor obstreperous. It was the kind of place where a man could happily lie down on the carpet in the shadow of the therapy machines, secure in the knowledge that help for any sort of trouble was at hand.

A clerk with fair hair and a long, supercilious nose glided up softly, but not too softly, and murmured, "May one help?"

"Therapy!" said Caswell.

"Of course, sir," the clerk answered, smoothing his lapels and smiling winningly. "That is what we are here for." He gave Caswell a searching look, performed an instant mental diagnosis, and tapped a gleaming white-and-copper machine.

"Now this," the clerk said, "is the new Alcoholic Reliever, built by IBM and advertised in the leading magazines. A handsome piece of furniture, I think you will agree, and not out of place in any home. It opens into a television set."

With a flick of his narrow wrist, the clerk opened the Alcoholic Reliever, revealing a 52-inch screen.

"I need—" Caswell began.

"Therapy," the clerk finished for him. "Of course. I just wanted to point out that this model need never cause embarrassment for yourself, your friends or loved ones. Notice, if you will, the recessed dial which controls the desired degree of drinking. See? If you do not wish total abstinence, you can set it to heavy, moderate, social or light. That is a new feature, unique in mechanotherapy."

"I am not an alcoholic," Caswell said, with considerable dignity. "The New York Rapid Transit Corporation does not hire alcoholics."

"Oh," said the clerk, glancing distrustfully at Caswell's bloodshot eyes. "You seem a little nervous. Perhaps the portable Bendix Anxiety Reducer—"

"Anxiety's not my ticket, either. What have you got for homicidal mania?"

The clerk pursed his lips. "Schizophrenic or manic-depressive origins?"

"I don't know," Caswell admitted, somewhat taken aback.

"It really doesn't matter," the clerk told him. "Just a private theory of my own. From my experience in the store, redheads and blonds are prone to schizophrenia, while brunettes incline towards the manic-depressive."

"That's interesting. Have you worked here long?"

"A week. Now then, here is just what you need, sir." He put his hand affectionately on a squat black machine with chrome trim.

"What's that?"

"That, sir, is the Rex Regenerator, built by General Motors. Isn't it handsome? It can go with any décor and opens up into a well-stocked bar. Your friends, family, loved ones need never know—"

"Will it cure a homicidal urge?" Caswell asked. "A *strong* one?"

"Absolutely. Don't confuse this with the little ten amp neurosis models. This is a hefty, heavy-duty, twenty-five amp machine for a really deep-rooted major condition."

"That's what I've got," said Caswell, with pardonable pride.

"This baby'll jolt it out of you. Big, heavy-duty thrust bearings! Oversize heat absorbers! Completely insulated! Sensitivity range of over—"

"I'll take it," Caswell said. "Right now. I'll pay cash."

"Fine! I'll just telephone Storage and—"

"This one'll do," Caswell said, pulling out his billfold. "I'm in a hurry to use it. I want to kill my friend Magnessen, you know."

The clerk clucked sympathetically. "You wouldn't want to do that.... Plus five per cent sales tax. Thank you, sir. Full instructions are inside."

Caswell thanked him, lifted the Regenerator in both arms and hurried out.

After figuring his commission, the clerk smiled to himself and lighted a cigarette. His enjoyment was spoiled when the manager, a large man impressively equipped with pince-nez, marched out of his office.

"Haskins," the manager said, "I thought I asked you to rid yourself of that filthy habit."

"Yes, Mr. Follansby, sorry, sir," Haskins apologized, snubbing out the cigarette. "I'll use the display Denicotinizer at once. Made rather a good sale, Mr. Follansby. One of the big Rex Regenerators."

"Really?" said the manager, impressed. "It isn't often we—wait a minute! You didn't sell the *floor model*, did you?"

"Why—why, I'm afraid I did, Mr. Follansby. The customer was in such a terrible hurry. Was there any reason—"

Mr. Follansby gripped his prominent white forehead in both hands, as though he wished to rip it off. "Haskins, I told you. I *must* have told you! That display Regenerator was a *Martian* model. For giving mechanotherapy to *Martians*."

"Oh," Haskins said. He thought for a moment. "Oh."

Mr. Follansby stared at his clerk in grim silence.

"But does it really matter?" Haskins asked quickly. "Surely the machine won't discriminate. I should think it would treat a homicidal tendency even if the patient were not a Martian."

"The Martian race has never had the slightest tendency towards homicide. A Martian Regenerator doesn't even possess the concept. Of course the Regenerator will treat him. It has to. *But what will it treat?*"

"Oh," said Haskins.

"That poor devil must be stopped before—you say he was *homicidal?* I don't know what will happen! Quick, what is his address?"

"Well, Mr. Follansby, he was in such a terrible hurry—"

The manager gave him a long, unbelieving look. "Get the police! Call the General Motors Security Division! Find him!"

Haskins raced for the door.

"Wait!" yelled the manager, struggling into a raincoat. "I'm coming, too!"

Elwood Caswell returned to his apartment by taxicopter. He lugged the Regenerator into his living-room, put it down near the couch and studied it thoughtfully.

"That clerk was right," he said after a while. "It *does* go with the room."

Aesthetically, the Regenerator was a success.

Caswell admired it for a few more moments, then went into the kitchen and fixed himself a chicken sandwich. He ate slowly, staring fixedly at a point just above and to the left of his kitchen clock.

Damn you, Magnessen! Dirty no-good lying shifty-eyed enemy of all that's decent and clean in the world...

Taking the revolver from his pocket, he laid it on the table. With a stiffened forefinger, he poked it into different positions.

It was time to begin therapy.

Except that...

Caswell realized worriedly that he didn't want to lose the desire to kill Magnessen. What would become of him if he lost that urge? His life would lose all purpose, all coherence, all flavour and zest. It would be quite dull, really.

Moreover, he had a great and genuine grievance against Magnessen, one he didn't like to think about.

Irene!

His poor sister, debauched by the subtle and insidious Magnessen, ruined by him and cast aside. What better reason could a man have to take his revolver and...

Caswell finally remembered that he did not have a sister.

Now was *really* the time to begin therapy.

He went into the living-room and found the operating instructions tucked into a ventilation louvre of the machine. He opened them and read:

To Operate All Rex Model Regenerators:
1. Place the Regenerator near a comfortable couch. (A comfortable couch can be purchased as an additional accessory from any General Motors dealer.)
2. Plug in the machine.
3. Affix the adjustable contact-band to the forehead. And that's all! Your Regenerator will do the rest! There will be no language bar or dialect problem, since the Regenerator communicates by Direct Sense Contact (Patent Pending). All you must do is co-operate.

Try not to feel any embarrassment or shame. Everyone has problems and many are worse than yours! Your Regenerator has no interest in your morals or ethical standards, so don't feel it is "judging" you. It desires only to aid you in becoming well and happy.

As soon as it has collected and processed enough data, your Regenerator will begin treatment. You make the sessions as short or as long as you like. You are the boss! And of course you can end a session at any time.

That's all there is to it! Simple, isn't it? Now plug in your General Motors Regenerator and GET SANE!

"Nothing hard about that," Casswell said to himself. He pushed the Regenerator closer to the couch and plugged it in. He lifted the headband, started to slip it on, stopped.

"I feel so silly!" he giggled.

Abruptly he closed his mouth and stared pugnaciously at the black-and-chrome machine.

"So you think you can make me sane, huh?"

The Regenerator didn't answer.

"Oh, well, go ahead and try." He slipped the headband over his forehead, crossed his arms on his chest and leaned back.

Nothing happened. Caswell settled himself more comfortably on the couch. He scratched his shoulder and put the headband at a more comfortable angle. Still nothing. His thoughts began to wander.

Magnessen! You noisy, overbearing oaf, you disgusting—

"Good afternoon," a voice murmured in his head. "I am your mechanotherapist."

Caswell twitched guiltily. "Hello. I was just—you know, just sort of—"

"Of course," the machine said soothingly. "Don't we all? I am now scanning the material in your preconscious with the intent of synthesis, diagnosis, prognosis and treatment. I find . . ."

"Yes?"

"Just one moment." The Regenerator was silent for several minutes. Then, hesitantly, it said, "This is beyond doubt a most unusual case."

"Really?" Cassidy asked, pleased.

"Yes. The coefficients seem—I'm not sure . . ." The machine's robotic voice grew feeble. The pilot light began to flicker and fade.

"Hey, what's the matter?"

"Confusion," said the machine. "Of course," it went on in a stronger voice, "the unusual nature of the symptoms need not prove entirely baffling to a competent therapeutic machine. A symptom, no matter how bizarre, is no more than a signpost, an indication of inner difficulty. And *all* symptoms can be related to the broad mainstream of proven theory. Since the theory is effective, the symptoms must relate. We will proceed on that assumption."

"Are you sure you know what you're doing?" asked Caswell, feeling light-headed.

The machine snapped back, its pilot-light blazing, "Mechanotherapy today is an exact science and admits no significant errors. We will proceed with a word-association test."

"Fire away," said Caswell.

"House?"

"Home."

"Dog?"

"Cat."

"Fleefl?"

Caswell hesitated, trying to figure out the word. It sounded vaguely Martian, but it might be Venusian or even—

"Fleefl?" the Regenerator repeated.

"Marfoosh," Caswell replied, making up the word on the spur of the moment.

"Loud?"

"Sweet."

"Green?"

"Mother."

"Thanagoyes?"

"Patamathonga."

"Arrides?"

"Nexothesmodrastica."

"Chtheesnohelgnopteces?"

"Rigamaroo latasentricpropatria!" Caswell shot back. It was a collection of sounds he was particularly proud of. The average man would not have been able to pronounce them.

"Hmm," said the Regenerator. "The pattern fits. It always does."

"What pattern?"

"You have," the machine informed him, "a classic case of feem desire, complicated by strong dwarkish intentions."

"I do? I thought I was homicidal."

"That term has no referent," the machine said severely. "Therefore I must reject it as nonsense syllabification. Now consider these points: The feem desire is perfectly normal. Never forget that. But it is usually replaced at an early age by the hovendish revulsion. Individuals lacking in this basic environmental reponse—"

"I'm not absolutely sure I know what you're talking about," Caswell confessed.

"Please, sir! We must establish one thing at once. *You* are the patient. *I* am the mechanotherapist. You have brought your troubles to me for treatment. But you cannot expect help unless you co-operate."

"All right," Caswell said. "I'll try."

Up to now, he had been bathed in a warm glow of superiority. Everything the machine said had seemed mildly humorous. As a matter of fact, he had felt capable of pointing out a few things wrong with the mechanotherapist.

Now that sense of well-being evaporated, as it always did, and Caswell was alone, terribly alone and lost, a creature of his compulsions, in search of a little peace and contentment.

He would undergo anything to find them. Sternly he reminded himself that he had no right to comment on the mechanotherapist. These machines knew what they were doing and had been doing it for a long time. He would co-operate, no matter how outlandish the treatment seemed from his layman's viewpoint.

But it was obvious, Caswell thought, settling himself grimly on the couch, that mechanotherapy was going to be far more difficult than he had imagined.

The search for the missing customer had been brief and useless. He was nowhere to be found on the teeming New York streets and no one could remember seeing a red-haired, red-eyed little man lugging a black therapeutic machine.

It was all too common a sight.

In answer to an urgent telephone call, the police came immediately, four of them, led by a harassed young lieutenant of detectives named Smith.

Smith just had time to ask, "Say, why don't you people put tags on things?" when there was an interruption.

A man pushed his way past the policeman at the door. He was tall and gnarled and ugly, and his eyes were deep-set and bleakly blue.

His clothes, unpressed and uncaring, hung on him like corrugated iron.

"What do you want?" Lieutenant Smith asked.

The ugly man flipped back his lapel, showing a small silver badge beneath. "I'm John Rath, General Motors Security Division."

"Oh ... Sorry, sir," Lieutenant Smith said, saluting. "I didn't think you people would move in so fast."

Rath made a non-committal noise. "Have you checked for prints, Lieutenant? The customer might have touched some other therapy machine."

"I'll get right on it, sir," Smith said. It wasn't often that one of the operatives from GM, GE or IBM came down to take a personal hand. If a local cop showed he was really clicking, there just might be the possibility of an Industrial Transfer ...

Rath turned to Follansby and Haskins, and transfixed them with a gaze as piercing and as impersonal as a radar beam. "Let's have the full story," he said, taking a notebook and pencil from a shapeless pocket.

He listened to the tale in ominous silence. Finally he closed his notebook, thrust it back into his pocket and said, "The therapeutic machines are a sacred trust. To give a customer the wrong machine is a betrayal of that trust, a violation of the Public Interest, and a defamation of the Company's good reputation."

The manager nodded in agreement, glaring at his unhappy clerk.

"A Martian model," Rath continued, "should never have been on the floor in the first place."

"I can explain that," Follansby said hastily. "We needed a demonstrator model and I wrote to the Company, telling them—"

"This might," Rath broke in inexorably, "be considered a case of gross criminal negligence."

Both the manager and the clerk exchanged horrified looks. They were thinking of the General Motors Reformatory outside of Detroit, where Company offenders passed their days in sullen silence, monotonously drawing micro-circuits for pocket television sets.

"However, that is out of my jurisdiction," Rath said. He turned his baleful gaze full upon Haskins. "You are certain that the customer never mentioned his name?"

"No, sir. I mean yes, I'm sure," Haskins replied rattledly.

"Did he mention any names at all?"

Haskins plunged his face into his hands. He looked up and said eagerly, "Yes! He wanted to kill someone! A friend of his!"

"Who?" Rath asked, with terrible patience.

"The friend's name was—let me think—Magneton! That was it! Magneton! Or was it Morrison? Oh, dear ..."

Mr. Rath's iron face registered a rather corrugated disgust. People were useless as witnesses. Worse than useless, since they were frequently misleading. For reliability, give him a robot every time.

"Didn't he mention *anything* significant?"

"Let me *think*!" Haskins said, his face twisting into a fit of concentration.

Rath waited.

Mr. Follansby cleared his throat. "I was just thinking, Mr. Rath. About that Martian machine. It won't treat a Terran homicidal case as homicidal, will it?"

"Of course not. Homicide is unknown on Mars."

"Yes. But what will it do? Might it not reject the entire case as unsuitable? Then the customer would merely return the Regenerator with a complaint and we would—"

Mr. Rath shook his head. "The Rex Regenerator must treat if it finds evidence of psychosis. By Martian standards, the customer is a very sick man, a psychotic—*no matter what is wrong with him.*"

Follansby removed his pince-nez and polished them rapidly. "What will the machine do, then?"

"It will treat him for the Martian illness most analogous to his case. Feem desire, I should imagine, with various complications. As for what will happen once treatment begins, I don't know. I doubt whether anyone knows, since it has never happened before. Offhand, I would say there are two major alternatives: The patient may reject the therapy out of hand, in which case he is left with his homicidal mania unabated. Or he may accept the Martian therapy and reach a cure."

Mr. Follansby's face brightened. "Ah! A cure is possible!"

"You don't understand," Rath said. "He may effect a cure—*of his non-existent Martian psychosis.* But to cure something that is not there is, in effect, to erect a gratuitous delusional system. You might say that the machine would work in reverse, producing psychosis instead of removing it."

Mr. Follansby groaned and leaned against a Bell Psychosomatica.

"The result," Rath summed up, "would be to convince the customer that he was a Martian. A *sane* Martian, naturally."

Haskins suddenly shouted, "I remember! I remember now! He said he worked for the New York Rapid Transit Corporation! I remember distinctly!"

"That's a break," Rath said, reaching for the telephone.

Haskins wiped his perspiring face in relief. "And I just remembered something else that should make it easier still."

"What?"

"The customer said he had been an alcoholic at one time. I'm sure of it, because he was interested at first in the IBM Alcoholic Reliever, until I talked him out of it. He had red hair, you know,

and I've had a theory for some time about red-headedness and alcoholism. It seems—"

"Excellent," Rath said. "Alcoholism will be on his records. It
narrows the search considerably."

As he dialled the NYRT Corporation, the expression on his crag-
like face was almost pleasant.

It was good, for a change, to find that a human *could* retain some
significant facts.

"But surely you remember your goricae?" the Regenerator was
saying.

"No," Caswell answered wearily.

"Tell me, then, about your juvenile experiences with the
thorastrian fleep."

"Never had any."

"Hmm. Blockage," muttered the machine. "Resentment. Repres-
sion. Are you sure you don't remember your goricae and what it
meant to you? The experience is universal."

"Not for me," Caswell said, swallowing a yawn.

He had been undergoing mechanotherapy for close to four hours
and it struck him as futile. For a while, he had talked voluntarily
about his childhood, his mother and father, his older brother. But
the Regenerator had asked him to put aside those fantasies. The
patient's relationships to an imaginary parent or sibling, it explained,
were unworkable and of minor importance psychologically. The important thing was the patient's feelings—both revealed and repressed
—towards his goricae.

"Aw, look," Caswell complained, "I don't even know what a goricae
is."

"Of course you do. You just won't *let* yourself know."

"I don't know. Tell me."

"It would be better if you told me."

"How can I?" Caswell raged. "I don't know!"

"What do you *imagine* a goricae would be?"

"A forest fire," Caswell said. "A salt tablet. A jar of de-natured
alcohol. A small screwdriver. Am I getting warm? A notebook. A
revolver—"

"These associations are meaningful," the Regenerator assured
him. "Your attempt at randomness shows a clearly underlying pattern. Do you begin to recognize it?"

"What in hell is a goricae?" Caswell roared.

"The tree that nourished you during infancy, and well into
puberty, if my theory about you is correct. Inadvertently, the goricae
stifled your necessary rejection of the feem desire. This in turn gave
rise to your present urge to dwark someone in a vlendish manner."

"No tree nourished *me*."

"You cannot recall the experience?"

"Of course not. It never happened."

"You are sure of that?"

"Positive."

"Not even the tiniest bit of doubt?"

"No! No goricae ever nourished me. Look, I can break off these sessions at any time, right?"

"Of course," the Regenerator said. "But it would not be advisable at this moment. You are expressing anger, resentment, fear. By your rigidly summary rejection—"

"Nuts," said Caswell, and pulled off the headband.

The silence was wonderful. Caswell stood up, yawned, stretched and massaged the back of his neck. He stood in front of the humming black machine and gave it a long leer.

"You couldn't cure me of a common cold," he told it.

Stiffly he walked the length of the living-room and returned to the Regenerator.

"Lousy fake!" he shouted.

Caswell went into the kitchen and opened a bottle of beer. His revolver was still on the table, gleaming dully.

Magnessen! You unspeakable treacherous filth! You fiend incarnate! You inhuman, hideous monster! Someone must destroy you, Magnessen! Someone...

Someone? He himself would have to do it. Only he knew the bottomless depths of Magnessen's depravity, his viciousness, his disgusting lust for power.

Yes, it was his duty, Caswell thought. But strangely, the knowledge brought him no pleasure.

After all, Magnessen was his friend.

He stood up, ready for action. He tucked the revolver into his right-hand coat pocket and glanced at the kitchen clock. Nearly six-thirty. Magnessen would be home now, gulping his dinner, grinning over his plans.

This was the perfect time to take him.

Caswell strode to the door, opened it, started through, and stopped.

A thought had crossed his mind, a thought so tremendously involved, so meaningful, so far-reaching in its implications that he was stirred to his depths. Caswell tried desperately to shake off the knowledge it brought. But the thought, permanently etched upon his memory, would not depart.

Under the circumstances, he could do only one thing.

He returned to the living-room, sat down on the couch and slipped on the headband.

The Regenerator said, "Yes?"

"It's the damnedest thing," Caswell said, "but do you know, I think I *do* remember my goricae!"

John Rath contacted the New York Rapid Transit Corporation by televideo and was put into immediate contact with Mr. Bemis, a plump, tanned man with watchful eyes.

"Alcoholism?" Mr. Bemis repeated, after the problem was explained. Unobtrusively, he turned on his tape recorder. "Among *our* employees?" Pressing a button beneath his foot, Bemis alerted Transit Security, Publicity, Inter-company Relations and the Psychoanalysis Division. This done, he looked earnestly at Rath. "Not a chance of it, my dear sir. Just between us, why does General Motors *really* want to know?"

Rath smiled bitterly. He should have anticipated this. NYRT and GM had had their differences in the past. Officially, there was cooperation between the two giant corporations. But for all practical purposes—

"The question is in terms of the Public Interest," Rath said.

"Oh, certainly," Mr. Bemis replied, with a subtle smile. Glancing at his tattle board, he noticed that several company executives had tapped in on his line. This might mean a promotion, if handled properly.

"The Public Interest of GM," Mr. Bemis added with polite nastiness. "The insinuation is, I suppose, that drunken conductors are operating our jetbuses and helis?"

"Of course not. I was searching for a single alcoholic predilection, an individual latency—"

"There's no possibility of it. We at Rapid Transit do not hire people with even the merest tendency in that direction. And may I suggest, sir, that you clean your own house before making implications about others?"

And with that, Mr. Bemis broke the connection.

No one was going to put anything over on *him*.

"Dead end," Rath said heavily. He turned and shouted, "Smith! Did you find any prints?"

Lieutenant Smith, his coat off and sleeves rolled up, bounded over. "Nothing usable, sir."

Rath's thin lips tightened. It had been close to seven hours since the customer had taken the Martian machine. There was no telling what harm had been done by now. The customer would be justified in bringing suit against the Company. Not that the money mattered much; it was the bad publicity that was to be avoided at all cost.

"Beg pardon, sir," Haskins said.

Rath ignored him. What next? Rapid Transit was not going to cooperate. Would the Armed Services make their records available for scansion by somatotype and pigmentation?

"Sir," Haskins said again.

"What is it?"

"I just remembered the customer's friend's name. It was Magnessen."

"Are you sure of that?"

"Absolutely," Haskins said, with the first confidence he had shown in hours. "I've taken the liberty of looking him up in the telephone book, sir. There's only one Manhattan listing under that name."

Rath glowered at him from under shaggy eyebrows. "Haskins, I hope you are not wrong about this. I sincerely hope that."

"I do too, sir," Haskins admitted, feeling his knees begin to shake.

"Because if you are," Rath said, "I will ... Never mind. Let's go!"

By police escort, they arrived at the address in fifteen minutes. It was an ancient brownstone and Magnessen's name was on a second-floor door. They knocked.

The door opened and a stocky, crop-headed, shirt-sleeved man in his thirties stood before them. He turned slightly pale at the sight of so many uniforms, but held his ground.

"What is this?" he demanded.

"You Magnessen?" Lieutenant Smith barked.

"Yeah. What's the beef? If it's about my hi-fi playing too loud, I can tell you that old hag downstairs—"

"May we come in?" Rath asked. "It's important."

Magnessen seemed about to refuse, so Rath pushed past him, followed by Smith, Follansby, Haskins and a small army of policemen. Magnessen turned to face them, bewildered, defiant and more than a little awed.

"Mr. Magnessen," Rath said, in the pleasantest voice he could muster, "I hope you'll forgive the intrusion. Let me assure you, it is in the Public Interest, as well as your own. Do you know a short, angry-looking, red-haired, red-eyed man?"

"Yes," Magnessen said slowly and warily.

Haskins let out a sigh of relief.

"Would you tell us his name and address?" asked Rath.

"I suppose you mean—hold it! What's he done?"

"Nothing."

"Then what you want him for?"

"There's no time for explanations," Rath said. "Believe me, it's in his own best interest, too. What is his name?"

Magnessen studied Rath's ugly, honest face, trying to make up his mind.

Lieutenant Smith said, "Come on, talk, Magnessen, if you know what's good for you. We want the name and we want it quick."

It was the wrong approach. Magnessen lighted a cigarette, blew smoke in Smith's direction and inquired, "You got a warrant, buddy?"

"You bet I have," Smith said, striding forward. "I'll warrant you, wise guy."

"Stop it!" Rath ordered. "Lieutenant Smith, thank you for your assistance. I won't need you any longer."

Smith left sulkily, taking his platoon with him.

Rath said, "I apologize for Smith's over-eagerness. You had better hear the problem." Briefly but fully, he told the story of the customer and the Martian therapeutic machine.

When he was finished, Magnessen looked more suspicious than ever. "You say he wants to kill *me*?"

"Definitely."

"That's a lie! I don't know what your game is, mister, but you'll never make me believe that. Elwood's my best friend. We been best friends since we was kids. We been in service together. Elwood would cut off his arm for me. And I'd do the same for him."

"Yes, yes," Rath said impatiently, "in a sane frame of mind, he would. But your friend Elwood—is that his first name or last?"

"First," Magnessen said tauntingly.

"Your friend Elwood is psychotic."

"You don't know him. That guy loves me like a brother. Look, what's Elwood really done? Defaulted on some payments or something? I can help out."

"You thick-headed imbecile!" Rath shouted. "I'm trying to save your life, and the life and sanity of your friend!"

"But how do I know?" Magnessen pleaded. "You guys come busting in here—"

"You must trust me," Rath said.

Magnessen studied Rath's face and nodded sourly. "His name's Elwood Caswell. He lives just down the block at number 341."

The man who came to the door was short, with red hair and red-rimmed eyes. His right hand was thrust into his coat pocket. He seemed very calm.

"Are you Elwood Caswell?" Rath asked. "The Elwood Caswell who bought a Regenerator early this afternoon at the Home Therapy Appliances Store?"

"Yes," said Caswell. "Won't you come in?"

Inside Caswell's small living-room, they saw the Regenerator, glistening black and chrome, standing near the couch. It was unplugged.

"Have you used it?" Rath asked anxiously.

"Yes."

Follansby stepped foward. "Mr. Caswell, I don't know how to explain this, but we made a terrible mistake. The Regenerator you took was a Martian model—for giving therapy to Martians."

"I know," said Caswell.

"You do?"

"Of course. It became pretty obvious after a while."

"It was a dangerous situation," Rath said. "Especially for a man with your—ah—troubles." He studied Caswell covertly. The man seemed fine, but appearances were frequently deceiving, especially with psychotics. Caswell had been homicidal; there was no reason why he should not still be.

And Rath began to wish he had not dismissed Smith and his policemen so summarily. Sometimes an armed squad was a comforting thing to have around.

Caswell walked across the room to the therapeutic machine. One hand was still in his jacket pocket; the other he laid affectionately upon the Regenerator.

"The poor thing tried its best," he said. "Of course, it couldn't cure what wasn't there." He laughed. "But it came very near succeeding!"

Rath studied Caswell's face and said, in a trained, casual tone, "Glad there was no harm, sir. The Company will, of course, reimburse you for your lost time and for your mental anguish—"

"Naturally," Caswell said.

"—and we will substitute a proper Terran Regenerator at once."

"That won't be necessary."

"It *won't?*"

"No." Caswell's voice was decisive. "The machine's attempt at therapy forced me into a complete self-appraisal. There was a moment of absolute insight, during which I was able to evaluate and discard my homicidal intentions towards poor Magnessen."

Rath nodded dubiously. "You feel no such urge now?"

"Not in the slightest."

Rath frowned deeply, started to say something, and stopped. He turned to Follansby and Haskins. "Get that machine out of here. I'll have a few things to say to you at the store."

The manager and the clerk lifted the Regenerator and left.

Rath took a deep breath. "Mr. Caswell, I would strongly advise that you accept a new Regenerator from the Company, gratis. Unless a cure is effected in a proper mechanotherapeutic manner, there is always the danger of a setback."

"No danger with me," Caswell said, airily but with deep conviction. "Thank you for your consideration, sir. And good night."

Rath shrugged and walked to the door.

"Wait!" Caswell called.

Rath turned. Caswell had taken his hand out of his pocket. In it was a revolver. Rath felt sweat trickle down his arms. He calculated the distance between himself and Caswell. Too far.

"Here," Caswell said, extending the revolver butt-first. "I won't need this any longer."

Rath managed to keep his face expressionless as he accepted the revolver and stuck it into a shapeless pocket.

"Good night," Caswell said. He closed the door behind Rath and bolted it.

At last he was alone.

Caswell walked into the kitchen. He opened a bottle of beer, took a deep swallow and sat down at the kitchen table. He stared fixedly at a point just above and to the left of the clock.

He had to form his plans now. There was no time to lose.

Magnessen! That inhuman monster who cut down the Caswell goricae! Magnessen! The man who, even now, was secretly planning to infect New York with the abhorrent feem desire! Oh, Magnessen, I wish you a long, long life, filled with the torture I can inflict on you. And to start with . . .

Caswell smiled to himself as he planned exactly how he would dwark Magnessen in a vlendish manner.

PILGRIMAGE TO EARTH

ALFRED SIMON WAS born on Kazanga IV, a small agricultural planet near Arcturus, and there he drove a combine through the wheat fields, and in the long hushed evenings listened to the recorded love songs of Earth.

Life was pleasant enough on Kazanga, and the girls were buxom, jolly, frank and acquiescent, good companions for a hike through the hills or a swim in the brook, staunch mates for life. But romantic—never! There was good fun to be had on Kazanga, in a cheerful open manner. But there was no more than fun.

Simon felt that something was missing in this bland existence. One day, he discovered what it was.

A vendor came to Kazanga in a battered spaceship loaded with books. He was gaunt, white-haired, and a little mad. A celebration was held for him, for novelty was appreciated on the outer worlds.

The vendor told them all the latest gossip; of the price war between Detroit II and III, and how fishing fared on Alana, and what the president's wife on Moracia wore, and how oddly the men of Doran V talked. And at last someone said, "Tell us of Earth."

"Ah!" said the vendor, raising his eyebrows. "You want to hear of the mother planet? Well, friends, there's no place like old Earth, no place at all. On Earth, friends, everything is possible, and nothing is denied."

"Nothing?" Simon asked.

"They've got a law against denial," the vendor explained, grinning. "No one has ever been known to break it. Earth is *different*, friends. You folks specialize in farming? Well, Earth specializes in impracticalities such as madness, beauty, war, intoxication, purity, horror, and the like, and people come from light-years away to sample these wares."

"And love?" a woman asked.

"Why girl," the vendor said gently, "Earth is the only place in the galaxy that still has love! Detroit II and III tried it and found it too expensive, you know, and Alana decided it was unsettling, and there was no time to import it on Moracia or Doran V. But as I said, Earth specializes in the impractical, and makes it pay."

"Pay?" a bulky farmer asked.

"Of course! Earth is old, her minerals are gone and her fields are barren. Her colonies are independent now, and filled with sober folk such as yourselves, who want value for their goods. So what else can old Earth deal in, except the non-essentials that make life worth living?"

"Were you in love on Earth?" Simon asked.

"That I was," the vendor answered, with a certain grimness. "I was in love, and now I travel. Friends, these books…"

For an exorbitant price, Simon bought an ancient poetry book, and reading, dreamed of passion beneath the lunatic moon, of dawn glimmering whitely upon lovers' parched lips, of locked bodies on a dark sea-beach, desperate with love and deafened by the booming surf.

And only on Earth was this possible! For, as the vendor told, Earth's scattered children were too hard at work wrestling a living from alien soil. The wheat and corn grew on Kazanga, and the factories increased on Detroit II and III. The fisheries of Alana were the talk of the Southern star belt, and there were dangerous beasts on Moracia, and a whole wilderness to be won on Doran V. And this was well, and exactly as it should be.

But the new worlds were austere, carefully planned, sterile in their perfections. Something had been lost in the dead reaches of space, and only Earth knew love.

Therefore, Simon worked and saved and dreamed. And in his twenty-ninth year he sold his farm, packed all his clean shirts into a serviceable handbag, put on his best suit and a pair of stout walking shoes, and boarded the Kazanga-Metropole Flyer.

At last he came to Earth, where dreams *must* come true, for there is a law against their failure.

He passed quickly through Customs at Spaceport New York, and was shuttled underground to Times Square. There he emerged blinking into daylight, tightly clutching his handbag, for he had been warned about pickpockets, cut-purses, and other denizens of the city.

Breathless with wonder, he looked around.

The first thing that struck him was the endless array of theatres, with attractions in two dimensions, three or four, depending upon your preference. And what attractions!

To the right of him a beetling marquee proclaimed: LUST ON VENUS! A DOCUMENTARY ACCOUNT OF SEX PRACTICES AMONG THE INHABITANTS OF THE GREEN HELL! SHOCKING! REVEALING!

He wanted to go in. But across the street was a war film. The billboard shouted, THE SUN BUSTERS! DEDICATED TO THE DARE-DEVILS

OF THE SPACE MARINES! And further down was a picture called TARZAN BATTLES THE SATURNIAN GHOULS!

Tarzan, he recalled from his reading, was an ancient ethnic hero of Earth.

It was all wonderful, but there was so much more! He saw little open shops where one could buy food of all worlds, and especially such native Terran dishes as pizza, hotdogs, spaghetti and knishes. And there were stores which sold surplus clothing from the Terran spacefleets, and other stores which sold nothing but beverages.

Simon didn't know what to do first. Then he heard a staccato burst of gunfire behind him, and whirled.

It was only a shooting gallery, a long, narrow, brightly painted place with a waist-high counter. The manager, a swarthy fat man with a mole on his chin, sat on a high stool and smiled at Simon.

"Try your luck?"

Simon walked over and saw that, instead of the usual targets, there were four scantily dressed women at the end of the gallery, seated upon bullet-scored chairs. They had tiny bulls-eyes painted on their foreheads and above each breast.

"But do you fire real bullets?" Simon asked.

"Of course!" the manager said. "There's a law against false advertising on Earth. Real bullets and real gals! Step up and knock one off!"

One of the women called out, "Come on, sport! Bet you miss me!"

Another screamed, "He couldn't hit the broad side of a space-ship!"

"Sure he can!" another shouted. "Come on, sport!"

Simon rubbed his forehead and tried not to act surprised. After all, this was Earth, where anything was allowed as long as it was commercially feasible.

He asked, "Are there galleries where you shoot men, too?"

"Of course," the manager said. "But you ain't no pervert, are you?"

"Certainly not!"

"You an outworlder?"

"Yes. How did you know?"

"The suit. Always tell by the suit." The fat man closed his eyes and chanted, "Step up, step up and kill a woman! Get rid of a load of repressions! Squeeze the trigger and feel the old anger ooze out of you! Better than a massage! Better than getting drunk! Step up, step up and kill a woman!"

Simon asked one of the girls, "Do you stay dead when they kill you?"

"Don't be stupid," the girl said.

"But the shock—"

She shrugged her shoulders. "I could do worse."

Simon was about to ask how she could do worse, when the manager leaned over the counter, speaking confidentially.

"Look, buddy. Look what I got here."

Simon glanced over the counter and saw a compact submachine-gun.

"For a ridiculously low price," the manager said, "I'll let you use the tommy. You can spray the whole place, shoot down the fixtures, rip up the walls. This drives a .45 slug, buddy, and it kicks like a mule. You really know you're firing when you fire the tommy."

"I am not interested," Simon said sternly.

"I've got a grenade or two," the manager said. "Fragmentation, of course. You could really—"

"No!"

"For a price," the manager said, "you can shoot *me*, too, if that's how your tastes run, although I wouldn't have guessed it. What do you say?"

"No! Never! This is horrible!"

The manager looked at him blankly. "Not in the mood now? OK. I'm open twenty-four hours a day. See you later, sport."

"Never!" Simon said, walking away.

"Be expecting you, lover!" one of the women called after him.

Simon went to a refreshment stand and ordered a small glass of cola-cola. He found that his hands were shaking. With an effort he steadied them, and sipped his drink. He reminded himself that he must not judge Earth by his own standards. If people on Earth enjoyed killing people, and the victims didn't mind being killed, why should anyone object?

Or should they?

He was pondering this when a voice at his elbow said, "Hey, bub."

Simon turned and saw a wizened, furtive-faced little man in an oversize raincoat standing beside him.

"Out-of-towner?" the little man asked.

"I am," Simon said. "How did you know?"

"The shoes. I always look at the shoes. How do you like our little planet?"

"It's—confusing," Simon said carefully. "I mean I didn't expect—well—"

"Of course," the little man said. "You're an idealist. One look at your honest face tells me that, my friend. You've come to Earth for a definite purpose. Am I right?"

Simon nodded. The little man said, "I know your purpose, my friend. You're looking for a war that will make the world safe for something, and you've come to the right place. We have six major wars running at all times, and there's never any waiting for an important position in any of them."

"Sorry, but—"

"Right at this moment," the little man said impressively, "the downtrodden workers of Peru are engaged in a desperate struggle against a corrupt and decadent monarchy. One more man could swing the contest! *You*, my friend, could be that man! *You* could guarantee the socialist victory!"

Observing the expression on Simon's face, the little man said quickly, "But there's a lot to be said for an enlightened aristocracy. The wise old king of Peru (a philosopher-king in the deepest Platonic sense of the word) sorely needs your help. His tiny corps of scientists, humanitarians, Swiss guards, knights of the realm and royal peasants is sorely pressed by the foreign-inspired socialist conspiracy. A single man, now—"

"I'm not interested," Simon said.

"In China, the Anarchists—"

"No."

"Perhaps you'd prefer the Communists in Wales? Or the Capitalists in Japan? Or if your affinities lie with a splinter group such as Feminists, Prohibitionists, Free Silverists, or the like, we could probably arrange—"

"I don't want a war," Simon said.

"Who could blame you?" the little man said, nodding rapidly. "War is hell. In that case, you've come to Earth for love."

"How did you know?" Simon asked.

The little man smiled modestly. "Love and war," he said, "are Earth's two staple commodities. We've been turning them both out in bumper crops since the beginning of time."

"Is love very difficult to find?" Simon asked.

"Walk uptown two blocks," the little man said briskly. "Can't miss it. Tell 'em Joe sent you."

"But that's impossible! You can't just walk out and—"

"What do you know about love?" Joe asked.

"Nothing."

"Well, we're experts on it."

"I know what the books say," Simon said. "Passion beneath the lunatic moon—"

"Sure, and bodies on a dark sea-beach desperate with love and deafened by the booming surf."

"You've read that book?"

"It's the standard advertising brochure. I must be going. Two blocks uptown. Can't miss it."

And with a pleasant nod, Joe moved into the crowd.

Simon finished his cola-cola and walked slowly up Broadway, his brow knotted in thought, but determined not to form any premature judgments.

When he reached 44th Street he saw a tremendous neon sign flashing brightly. It said LOVE, INC.

Smaller neon letters read, *Open 24 Hours a Day!*

Beneath that it read, *Up One Flight.*

Simon frowned, for a terrible suspicion had just crossed his mind. Still, he climbed the stairs and entered a small, tastefully furnished reception room. From there he was sent down a long corridor to a numbered room.

Within the room was a handsome grey-haired man who rose from behind an impressive desk and shook his hand, saying, "Well! How are things on Kazanga?"

"How did you know I was from Kazanga?"

"That shirt. I always look at the shirt. I'm Mr. Tate, and I'm here to serve you to the best of my ability. You are—"

"Simon, Alfred Simon."

"Please be seated, Mr. Simon. Cigarette? Drink? You won't regret coming to us, sir. We're the oldest love-dispensing firm in the business, and much larger than our closest competitor, Passion Unlimited. Moreover, our fees are far more reasonable, and bring you an improved product. Might I ask how you heard of us? Did you see our full page ad in the *Times*? Or—"

"Joe sent me," Simon said.

"Ah, he's an active one," Mr. Tate said, shaking his head playfully. "Well sir, there's no reason to delay. You've come a long way for love, and love you shall have." He reached for a button on his desk, but Simon stopped him.

Simon said, "I don't want to be rude or anything, but..."

"Yes?" Mr. Tate said, with an encouraging smile.

"I don't understand this," Simon blurted out, flushing deeply, beads of perspiration standing out on his forehead. "I think I'm in the wrong place. I didn't come all the way to Earth just for ... I mean, you can't really sell *love*, can you? Not *love*! I mean, then it isn't really *love*, is it?"

"But of course!" Mr. Tate said, half rising from his chair in astonishment. "That's the whole point! Anyone can buy sex. Good lord, it's the cheapest thing in the universe, next to human life. But *love* is rare, *love* is special, *love* is found only on Earth. Have you read our brochure?"

"Bodies on a dark sea-beach?" Simon asked.

"Yes, that one. I wrote it. Gives something of the feeling, doesn't it? You can't get that feeling from just *anyone*, Mr. Simon. You can get that feeling only from someone who loves you."

Simon said dubiously, "It's not genuine love though, is it?"

"Of course it is! If we were selling simulated love, we'd label it as such. The advertising laws on Earth are strict, I can assure you. Anything can be sold, but it must be labelled properly. That's ethics, Mr. Simon!"

Tate caught his breath, and continued in a calmer tone. "No sir, make no mistake. Our product is not a substitute. It is the exact selfsame feeling that poets and writers have raved about for thousands of years. Through the wonders of modern science we can bring this feeling to you at your convenience, attractively packaged, completely disposable, and for a ridiculously low price."

Simon said, "I pictured something more—spontaneous."

"Spontaneity has its charm," Mr. Tate agreed. "Our research labs are working on it. Believe me, there's nothing science can't produce, as long as there's a market for it."

"I don't like any of this," Simon said, getting to his feet. "I think I'll just go see a movie."

"Wait!" Mr. Tate cried. "You think we're trying to put something over on you. You think we'll introduce you to a girl who will *act* as though she loved you, but who in reality will not. Is that it?"

"I guess so," Simon said.

"But it just isn't so! It would be too costly for one thing. For another, the wear and tear on the girl would be tremendous. And it would be psychologically unsound for her to attempt living a lie of such depth and scope."

"Then how do you do it?"

"By utilizing our understanding of science and the human mind."

To Simon, this sounded like double-talk. He moved towards the door.

"Tell me something," Mr. Tate said. "You're a bright looking young fellow. Don't you think you could tell real love from a counterfeit item?"

"Certainly."

"There's your safeguard! *You* must be satisfied, or don't pay us a cent."

"I'll think about it," Simon said.

"Why delay? Leading psychologists say that *real* love is a fortifier and a restorer of sanity, a balm for damaged egos, a restorer of hormone balance, and an improver of the complexion. The love we supply you has everything: deep and abiding affection, unrestrained passion, complete faithfulness, an almost mystic affection for your defects as well as your virtues, a pitiful desire to please, *and*, as a plus that only Love Inc., can supply: that uncontrollable first spark, that blinding moment of love at first sight!"

Mr. Tate pressed a button. Simon frowned undecisively. The door opened, a girl stepped in, and Simon stopped thinking.

She was tall and slender, and her hair was brown with a sheen of red. Simon could have told you nothing about her face, except that it brought tears to his eyes. And if you asked him about her figure, he might have killed you.

"Miss Penny Bright," said Tate, "meet Mr. Alfred Simon."

The girl tried to speak but no words came, and Simon was equally dumbstruck. He looked at her and *knew*. Nothing else mattered. To the depths of his heart he knew that he was truly and completely loved.

They left at once, hand in hand, and were taken by jet to a small white cottage in a pine grove, overlooking the sea, and there they talked and laughed and loved, and later Simon saw his beloved wrapped in the sunset flame like a goddess of fire. And in blue twilight she looked at him with eyes enormous and dark, her known body mysterious again. The moon came up, bright and lunatic, changing flesh to shadow, and she wept and beat his chest with her small fists, and Simon wept too, although he did not know why. And at last dawn came, faint and disturbed, glimmering upon their parched lips and locked bodies, and nearby the booming surf deafened, inflamed, and maddened them.

At noon they were back in the offices of Love, Inc. Penny clutched his hand for a moment, then disappeared through an inner door.

"Was it real love?" Mr. Tate asked.

"Yes!"

"And was everything satisfactory?"

"Yes! It was love, it was the real thing! But why did she insist on returning?"

"Post-hypnotic command," Mr. Tate said.

"What?"

"What did you expect? Everyone wants love, but few wish to pay for it. Here is your bill, sir."

Simon paid, fuming. "This wasn't necessary," he said. "Of course I would pay you for bringing us together. Where is she now? What have you done with her?"

"Please," Mr. Tate said soothingly. "Try to calm yourself."

"I don't want to be calm!" Simon shouted. "I want Penny!"

"That will be impossible," Mr. Tate said, with the barest hint of frost in his voice. "Kindly stop making a spectacle of yourself."

"Are you trying to get more money out of me?" Simon shrieked. "All right, I'll pay. How much do I have to pay to get her out of your clutches?" And Simon yanked out his wallet and slammed it on the desk.

Mr. Tate poked the wallet with a stiffened forefinger. "Put that back in your pocket," he said. "We are an old and respectable firm. If you raise your voice again, I shall be forced to have you ejected."

Simon calmed himself with an effort, put the wallet back in his pocket and sat down. He took a deep breath and said, very quietly, "I'm sorry."

"That's better," Mr. Tate said. "I will not be shouted at. However, if you are reasonable, I can be reasonable too. Now, what's the trouble?"

"The trouble?" Simon's voice started to lift. He controlled it and said, "She loves me."

"Of course."

"Then how can you separate us?"

"What has the one thing got to do with the other?" Mr. Tate asked. "Love is a delightful interlude, a relaxation, good for the intellect, for the ego, for the hormone balance, and for the skin tone. But one would hardly wish to *continue* loving, would one?"

"I would," Simon said. "This love was special, unique—"

"They all are," Mr. Tate said. "But as you know, they are all produced in the same way."

"What?"

"Surely you know something about the mechanics of love production?"

"No," Simon said. "I thought it was—natural."

Mr. Tate shook his head. "We gave up natural selection centuries ago, shortly after the Mechanical Revolution. It was too slow, and commercially unfeasible. Why bother with it, when we can produce any feeling at will by conditioning and proper stimulation of certain brain centres? The result? Penny, completely in love with you! Your own bias, which we calculated, in favour of her particular somato-type, made it complete. We always throw in the dark sea-beach, the lunatic moon, the pallid dawn—"

"Then she could have been made to love anyone," Simon said slowly.

"Could have been *brought* to love anyone," Mr. Tate corrected.

"Oh, lord, how did she get into this horrible work?" Simon asked.

"She came in and signed a contract in the usual way," Tate said. "It pays very well. And at the termination of the lease, we return her original personality—untouched! But why do you call the work horrible? There's nothing reprehensible about love."

"It wasn't love!" Simon cried.

"But it was! The genuine article! Unbiassed scientific firms have made qualitative tests of it, in comparison with the natural thing. In every case, *our* love tested out to more depth, passion, fervour and scope."

Simon shut his eyes tightly, opened them and said, "Listen to me.

I don't care about your scientific tests. I love her, she loves me, that's all that counts. Let me speak to her! I want to marry her!"

Mr. Tate wrinkled his nose in distaste. "Come, come, man! You wouldn't want to *marry* a girl like that! But if it's marriage you're after, we deal in that, too. I can arrange an idyllic and nearly spontaneous love-match for you with a guaranteed government-inspected virgin—"

"No! I love Penny! At least let me speak to her!"

"That will be quite impossible," Mr. Tate said.

"Why?"

Mr. Tate pushed a button on his desk. "Why do you think? We've wiped out the previous indoctrination. Penny is now in love with someone else."

And then Simon understood. He had realized that even now Penny was looking at another man with that passion he had known, feeling for another man that complete and bottomless love that un-biassed scientific firms had shown to be so much greater than the old-fashioned, commercially unfeasible natural selection, and that upon that same dark sea-beach mentioned in the advertising brochure—

He lunged for Tate's throat. Two attendants, who had entered the office a few moments earlier, caught him and led him to the door.

"Remember!" Tate called. "This in no way invalidates your own experience."

Hellishly enough, Simon knew that what Tate said was true.

And then he found himself on the street.

At first, all he desired was to escape from Earth, where the commercial impracticalities were more than a normal man could afford. He walked very quickly, and his Penny walked beside him, her face glorified with love for him, and him, and him, and you, and you.

And of course he came to the shooting gallery.

"Try your luck?" the manager asked.

"Set 'em up," said Alfred Simon.

ASK A FOOLISH QUESTION

ANSWERER WAS BUILT to last as long as was necessary—which was quite long, as some races judge time, and not long at all, according to others. But to Answerer, it was just long enough.

As to size, Answerer was large to some and small to others. He could be viewed as complex, although some believed that he was really very simple.

Answerer knew that he was as he should be. Above and beyond all else, he was The Answerer. He Knew.

Of the race that built him, the less said the better. They also Knew, and never said whether they found the knowledge pleasant.

They built Answerer as a service to less-sophisticated races, and departed in a unique manner. Where they went only Answerer knows.

Because Answerer knows everything.

Upon his planet, circling his sun, Answerer sat. Duration continued, long, as some judge duration, short as others judge it. But as it should be, to Answerer.

Within him were the Answers. He knew the nature of things, and why things are as they are, and what they are, and what it all means.

Answerer could answer anything, provided it was a legitimate question. And he wanted to! He was eager to!

How else should an Answerer be?

What else should an Answerer do?

So he waited for creatures to come and ask.

"How do you feel, sir?" Morran asked, floating gently over to the old man.

"Better," Lingman said, trying to smile. No-weight was a vast relief. Even though Morran had expended an enormous amount of fuel, getting into space under minimum acceleration, Lingman's feeble heart hadn't liked it. Lingman's heart had balked and sulked, pounded angrily against the brittle rib-case, hesitated and sped up. It seemed for a time as though Lingman's heart was going to stop, out of sheer pique.

But no-weight was a vast relief, and the feeble heart was going again.

Morran had no such problems. His strong body was built for strain and stress. He wouldn't experience them on this trip, not if he expected old Lingman to live.

"I'm going to live," Lingman muttered, in answer to the unspoken question. "Long enough to find out." Morran touched the controls, and the ship slipped into sub-space like an eel into oil.

"We'll find out," Morran murmured. He helped the old man unstrap himself. "We're going to find the Answerer!"

Lingman nodded at his young partner. They had been reassuring themselves for years. Originally it had been Lingman's project. Then Morran, graduating from Cal Tech, had joined him. Together they had traced the rumours across the solar system. The legends of an ancient humanoid race who had known the answer to all things, and who had built Answerer and departed.

"Think of it," Morran said. "The answer to everything!" A physicist, Morran had many questions to ask Answerer. The expanding universe; the binding force of atomic nuclei; novae and super-novae; planetary formation; red shift, relativity and a thousand others.

"Yes," Lingman said. He pulled himself to the vision plate and looked out on the bleak prairie of the illusory sub-space. He was a biologist and an old man. He had two questions.

What is life?

What is death?

After a particularly-long period of hunting purple, Lek and his friends gathered to talk. Purple always ran thin in the neighbourhood of multiple-cluster stars—why, no one knew—so talk was definitely in order.

"Do you know," Lek said, "I think I'll hunt up this Answerer." Lek spoke the Ollgrat language now, the language of imminent decision.

"Why?" Ilm asked him, in the Hvest tongue of light banter. "Why do you want to know things? Isn't the job of gathering purple enough for you?"

"No," Lek said, still speaking the language of imminent decision. "It is not." The great job of Lek and his kind was the gathering of purple. They found purple imbedded in many parts of the fabric of space, minute quantities of it. Slowly, they were building a huge mound of it. What the mound was for, no one knew.

"I suppose you'll ask him what purple is?" Ilm asked, pushing a star out of his way and lying down.

"I will," Lek said. "We have continued in ignorance too long. We must know the true nature of purple, and its meaning in the scheme of things. We must know why it governs our lives." For this speech Lek switched to Ilgret, the language of incipient knowledge.

Ilm and the others didn't try to argue, even in the tongue of arguments. They knew that the knowledge was important. Ever since the dawn of time, Lek, Ilm and the others had gathered purple. Now it was time to know the ultimate answers to the universe—what purple was, and what the mound was for.

And of course, there was the Answerer to tell them. Everyone had heard of the Answerer, built by a race not unlike themselves, now long departed.

"Will you ask him anything else?" Ilm asked Lek.

"I don't know," Lek said. "Perhaps I'll ask about the stars. There's really nothing else important." Since Lek and his brothers had lived since the dawn of time, they didn't consider death. And since their numbers were always the same, they didn't consider the question of life.

But purple? And the mound?

"I go!" Lek shouted, in the vernacular of decision-to-fact.

"Good fortune!" his brothers shouted back, in the jargon of greatest-friendship.

Lek strode off, leaping from star to star.

Alone on his little planet, Answerer sat, waiting for the Questioners. Occasionally he mumbled the answers to himself. This was his privilege. He Knew.

But he waited, and the time was neither too long nor too short, for any of the creatures of space to come and ask.

There were eighteen of them, gathered in one place.

"I invoke the rule of eighteen," cried one. And another appeared, who had never before been, born by the rule of eighteen.

"We must go to the Answerer," one cried. "Our lives are governed by the rule of eighteen. Where there are eighteen, there will be nineteen. Why is this so?"

No one could answer.

"Where am I?" asked the newborn nineteenth. One took him aside for instruction.

That left seventeen. A stable number.

"And we must find out," cried another. "Why all places are different, although there is no distance."

That was the problem. One is here. Then one is there. Just like that, no movement, no reason. And yet, without moving, one is in another place.

"The stars are cold," one cried.

194 THE ROBERT SHECKLEY OMNIBUS

"Why?"

"We must go to the Answerer."

For they had heard the legends, knew the tales. "Once there was a race, a good deal like us, and they Knew—and they told Answerer. Then they departed to where there is no place, but much distance."

"How do we get there?" the newborn nineteenth cried, filled now with knowledge.

"We go." And eighteen of them vanished. One was left. Moodily he stared at the tremendous spread of an icy star, then he too vanished.

"Those old legends are true," Morran gasped. "There it is."

They had come out of sub-space at the place the legends told of, and before them was a star unlike any other star. Morran invented a classification for it, but it didn't matter. There was no other like it.

Swinging around the star was a planet, and this too was unlike any other planet. Morran invented reasons, but they didn't matter. This planet was the only one.

"Strap yourself in, sir," Morran said. "I'll land as gently as I can."

Lek came to Answerer, striding swiftly from star to star. He lifted Answerer in his hand and looked at him.

"So you are Answerer," he said.

"Yes," Answerer said.

"Then tell me," Lek said, settling himself comfortably in a gap between the stars, "tell me what I am."

"A partiality," Answerer said. "An indication."

"Come now," Lek muttered, his pride hurt. "You can do better than that. Now then. The purpose of my kind is to gather purple, and to build a mound of it. Can you tell me the real meaning of this?"

"Your question is without meaning," Answerer said. He knew what purple actually was, and what the mound was for. But the explanation was concealed in a greater explanation. Without this, Lek's question was inexplicable, and Lek had failed to ask the real question.

Lek asked other questions, and Answerer was unable to answer them. Lek viewed things through his specialized eyes, extracted a part of the truth and refused to see more. How to tell a blind man the sensation of green?

Answerer didn't try. He wasn't supposed to.

Finally, Lek emitted a scornful laugh. One of his little stepping-stones flared at the sound, then faded back to its usual intensity.

Lek departed, striding swiftly across the stars.

* * *

Answerer knew. But he had to be asked the proper questions first. He pondered this limitation, gazing at the stars which were neither large nor small, but exactly the right size.

The proper questions. The race which built Answerer should have taken that into account, Answerer thought. They should have made some allowance for semantic nonsense, allowed him to attempt an unravelling.

Answerer contented himself with muttering the answers to himself.

Eighteen creatures came to Answerer, neither walking nor flying, but simply appearing. Shivering in the cold glare of the stars, they gazed up at the massiveness of Answerer.

"If there is no distance," one asked, "then how can things be in other places?"

Answerer knew what distance was, and what places were. But he couldn't answer the question. There was distance, but not as these creatures saw it. And there were places, but in a different fashion from that which the creatures expected.

"Rephrase the question," Answerer said hopefully.

"Why are we short here," one asked, "and long over there? Why are we fat over there, and thin here? Why are the stars cold?"

Answerer knew all things. He knew why stars were cold, but he couldn't explain it in terms of stars or coldness.

"Why," another asked, "is there a rule of eighteen? Why, when eighteen gather, is another produced?"

But of course the answer was part of another, greater question, which hadn't been asked.

Another was produced by the rule of eighteen, and the nineteen creatures vanished.

Answerer mumbled the right questions to himself, and answered them.

"We made it," Morran said. "Well, well." He patted Lingman on the shoulder—lightly, because Lingman might fall apart.

The old biologist was tired. His face was sunken, yellow, lined. Already the mark of the skull was showing in his prominent yellow teeth, his small, flat nose, his exposed cheekbones. The matrix was showing through.

"Let's get on," Lingman said. He didn't want to waste any time. He didn't have any time to waste.

Helmeted, they walked along the little path.

"Not so fast," Lingman murmured.

"Right," Morran said. They walked together, along the dark

path of the planet that was different from all other planets, soaring alone around a sun different from all other suns.

"Up here," Morran said. The legends were explicit. A path, leading to stone steps. Stone steps to a courtyard. And then—the Answerer!

To them, Answerer looked like a white screen set in a wall. To their eyes, Answerer was very simple.

Lingman clasped his shaking hands together. This was the culmination of a lifetime's work, financing, arguing, ferreting bits of legend, ending here, now.

"Remember," he said to Morran, "we will be shocked. The truth will be like nothing we have imagined."

"I'm ready," Morran said, his eyes rapturous.

"Very well. Answerer," Lingman said, in his thin little voice, "what is life?"

A voice spoke in their heads. "The question has no meaning. By 'life', the Questioner is referring to a partial phenomenon, inexplicable except in terms of its whole."

"Of what is life a part?" Lingman asked.

"This question, in its present form, admits of no answer. Questioner is still considering 'life', from his personal, limited bias."

"Answer it in your own terms, then," Morran said.

"The Answerer can only answer questions." Answerer thought again of the sad limitation imposed by his builders.

Silence.

"Is the universe expanding?" Morran asked confidently.

" 'Expansion' is a term inapplicable to the situation. Universe, as the Questioner views it, is an illusory concept."

"Can you tell us *anything*?" Morran asked.

"I can answer any valid question concerning the nature of things."

The two men looked at each other.

"I think I know what he means," Lingman said sadly. "Our basic assumptions are wrong. All of them."

"They can't be," Morran said. "Physics, biology—"

"Partial truths," Lingman said, with a great weariness in his voice. "At least we've determined that much. We've found out that our inferences concerning observed phenomena are wrong."

"But the rule of the simplest hypothesis—"

"It's only a theory," Lingman said.

"But life—he certainly could answer what life is?"

"Look at it this way," Lingman said. "Suppose you were to ask, 'Why was I born under the constellation Scorpio, in conjunction with Saturn?' I would be unable to answer your question *in terms of the zodiac*, because the zodiac has nothing to do with it."

"I see," Morran said slowly. "He can't answer questions in terms of our assumptions."

"That seems to be the case. And he can't alter our assumptions. He is limited to valid questions—which imply, it would seem, a knowledge we just don't have."

"We can't even ask a valid question?" Morran asked. "I don't believe that. We must know *some* basics." He turned to Answerer. "What is death?"

"I cannot explain an anthropomorphism."

"Death an anthropomorphism" Morran said, and Lingman turned quickly. "Now we're getting somewhere!"

"Are anthropomorphisms unreal?" he asked.

"Anthropomorphisms may be classified, tentatively, as, A, false truths, or B, partial truths in terms of a partial situation."

"Which is applicable here?"

"Both."

That was the closest they got. Morran was unable to draw any more from Answerer. For hours the two men tried, but truth was slipping farther and farther away.

"It's maddening," Morran said, after a while. "This thing has the answer to the whole universe, and he can't tell us unless we ask the right question. But how are we supposed to know the right question?"

Lingman sat down on the ground, leaning against a stone wall. He closed his eyes.

"Savages, that's what we are," Morran said, pacing up and down in front of Answerer. "Imagine a bushman walking up to a physicist and asking him why he can't shoot his arrow into the sun. The scientist can explain it only in his own terms. What would happen?"

"The scientist wouldn't even attempt it," Lingman said, in a dim voice; "he would know the limitations of the questioner."

"It's fine," Morran said angrily. "How do you explain the earth's rotation to a bushman? Or better, how do you explain relativity to him—maintaining scientific rigour in your explanation at all times, of course."

Lingman, eyes closed, didn't answer.

"We're bushmen. But the gap is much greater here. Worm and superman, perhaps. The worm desires to know the nature of dirt, and why there's so much of it. Oh, well."

"Shall we go, sir?" Morran asked. Lingman's eyes remained closed. His taloned fingers were clenched, his cheeks sunk further in. The skull was emerging.

"Sir! Sir!"

And Answerer knew that that was not the answer.

*　　*　　*

Alone on his planet, which is neither large nor small, but exactly the right size, Answerer waits. He cannot help the people who come to him, for even Answerer has restrictions.

He can answer only valid questions.

Universe? Life? Death? Purple? Eighteen?

Partial truths, half-truths, little bits of the great question.

But Answerer, alone, mumbles the questions to himself, the true questions, which no one can understand.

How could they understand the true answers?

The questions will never be asked, and Answerer remembers something his builders knew and forgot.

In order to ask a question you must already know most of the answer.

A TICKET TO TRANAI

ONE FINE DAY in June, a tall, thin, intent, soberly dressed young man walked into the offices of the Transstellar Travel Agency. Without a glance, he marched past the gaudy travel poster depicting the Harvest Feast on Mars. The enormous photomural of dancing forests on Triganium didn't catch his eye. He ignored the somewhat suggestive painting of dawn-rites on Opiuchus II, and arrived at the desk of the booking agent.

"I would like to book passage to Tranai," the young man said.

"It is not," the young man said. "Tranai is a planet, revolving "Tranai? Tranai? Is that one of the moons of Kent IV?"

"It is not," the young man said ."Tranai is a planet, revolving around a sun of the same name. I want to book passage there."

"Never heard of it." The agent pulled down a star catalogue, a simplified star chart, and a copy of *Lesser Space Routes*.

"Well, now," he said finally. "You learn something new every day. You want to book passage to Tranai, Mister—"

"Goodman. Marvin Goodman."

"Goodman. Well, it seems that Tranai is about as far from Earth as one can get and still be in the Milky Way. *Nobody* goes there."

"I know. Can you arrange passage for me?" Goodman asked, with a hint of suppressed excitement in his voice.

The agent shook his head. "Not a chance. Even the non-skeds don't go that far."

"How close can you get me?"

The agent gave him a winning smile. "Why bother? I can send you to a world that'll have everything this Tranai place has, with the additional advantages of proximity, bargain rates, decent hotels, tours—"

"I'm going to Tranai," Goodman said grimly.

"But there's no way of getting there," the agent explained patiently. "What is it you expected to find? Perhaps I could help."

"You can help by booking me as far as—"

"Is it adventure?" the agent asked, quickly sizing up Goodman's unathletic build and scholary stoop. "Let me suggest Africanus II, a dawn-age world filled with savage tribes, sabre-tooths, man-eating ferns, quicksand, active volcanoes, pterodactyls and all the rest. Expeditions leave New York every five days and they combine the utmost in danger with absolute safety. A dinosaur head guaranteed or your money refunded."

"Tranai," Goodman said.

"Hmm." The clerk looked appraisingly at Goodman's set lips and uncompromising eyes. "Perhaps you are tired of the puritanical restrictions of Earth? Then let me suggest a trip to Almagordo III, the Pearl of the Southern Ridge Belt. Our ten day all-expense plan includes a trip through the mysterious Almagordian Casbah, visits to eight nightclubs (first drink on us), a trip to a zintal factory, where you can buy genuine zintal belts, shoes and pocket-books at phenomenal savings, and a tour through two distilleries. The girls of Almagordo are beautiful, vivacious and refreshingly naïve. They consider the Tourist the highest and most desirable type of human being. Also—"

"Tranai," Goodman said. "How close can you get me?"

Sullenly the clerk extracted a strip of tickets. "You can take the *Constellation Queen* as far as Legis II and transfer to the *Galactic Splendor*, which will take you to Oumé. Then you'll have to board a local, which, after stopping at Machang, Inchang, Pankang, Lekung and Oyster, will leave you at Tung-Bradar IV, if it doesn't break down en route. Then a non-sked will transport you past the Galactic Whirl (if it gets past) to Aloomsridgia, from which the mail ship will take you to Bellismoranti. I believe the mail ship is still functioning. That brings you about half-way. After that, you're on your own."

"Fine," Goodman said. "Can you have my forms made out by this afternoon?"

The clerk nodded. "Mr. Goodman," he asked in despair, "just what sort of place is this Tranai supposed to be?"

Goodman smiled a beatific smile. "A utopia," he said.

Marvin Goodman had lived most of his life in Seakirk, New Jersey, a town controlled by one political boss or another for close to fifty years. Most of Seakirk's inhabitants were indifferent to the spectacle of corruption in high places and low, the gambling, the gang wars, the teenage drinking. They were used to the sight of their roads crumbling, their ancient water mains bursting, their power plants breaking down, their decrepit old buildings falling apart, while the bosses built bigger homes, longer swimming pools and warmer stables. People were used to it. But not Goodman.

A natural-born crusader, he wrote exposé articles that were never published, sent letters to Congress that were never read, stumped for honest candidates who were never elected, and organized the League for Civic Improvement, the People Against Gangsterism, the Citizen's Union for an Honest Police Force, the Association Against Gambling, the Committee for Equal Job Opportunities for Women, and a dozen others.

Nothing came of his efforts. The people were too apathetic to care. The politicoes simply laughed at him, and Goodman couldn't stand being laughed at. Then, to add to his troubles, his fiancée jilted him for a noisy young man in a loud sports jacket who had no re-deeming feature other than a controlling interest in the Seakirk Construction Corporation.

It was a shattering blow. The girl seemed unaffected by the fact that the SCC used disproportionate amounts of sand in their concrete and shaved whole inches from the width of their steel girders. As she put it, "Gee whiz, Marvie, so what? That's how things are. You gotta be realistic."

Goodman had no intention of being realistic. He immediately repaired to Eddie's Moonlight Bar, where, between drinks, he began to contemplate the attractions of a grass shack in the green hell of Venus.

An erect, hawk-faced old man entered the bar. Goodman could tell he was a spacer by his gravity-bound gait, his pallor, his radiation scars and his far-piercing grey eyes.

"A Tranai Special, Sam," the old spacer told the bartender.

"Coming right up, Captain Savage, sir," the bartender said.

"Tranai?" Goodman murmured involuntarily.

"Tranai," the captain said. "Never heard of it, did you sonny?"

"No, sir," Goodman confessed.

"Well, sonny," Captain Savage said, "I'm feeling a mite wordy tonight, so I'll tell you a tale of Tranai the Blessed, out past the Galactic Whirl."

The captain's eyes grew misty and a smile softened the grim line of his lips.

"We were iron men in steel ships in those days. Me and Johnny Cavanaugh and Frog Larsen would have blasted to hell itself for half a load of terganium. Aye, and shanghaied Beelzebub for a wiper if we were short of men. Those were the days when space scurvy took every third man, and the ghost of Big Dan McClintock haunted the spaceways. Moll Gann still operated the Red Rooster Inn out on Asteroid 342-AA, asking five hundred Earth dollars for a glass of beer, and getting it too, there being no other place within ten billion miles. In those days, the Scarbies were still cutting up along Star Ridge and ships bound for Prodengum had to run the Swayback Gantlet. So you can imagine how I felt, sonny, when one fine day I came upon Tranai."

*   *   *

Goodman listened as the old captain limned a picture of the great days, of frail ships against an iron sky, ships outward bound, forever outward, to the far limits of the Galaxy.

And there, at the edge of the Great Nothing, was Tranai.

Tranai, where The Way had been found and men were no longer bound to The Wheel! Tranai the Bountiful, a peaceful, creative, happy society, not saints or ascetics, not intellectuals, but ordinary people who had achieved utopia.

For an hour, Captain Savage spoke of the multiform marvels of Tranai. After finishing his story, he complained of a dry throat. Space throat, he called it, and Goodman ordered him another Tranai Special and one for himself. Sipping the exotic, green-grey mixture, Goodman too was lost in the dream.

Finally, very gently, he asked, "Why don't you go back, Captain?"

The old man shook his head. "Space gout. I'm grounded for good. We didn't know much about modern medicine in those days. All I'm good for now is a landsman's job."

"What job do you have?"

"I'm a foreman for the Seakirk Construction Corporation," the old man sighed. "Me, that once commanded a fifty-tube clipper. The way those people make concrete.... Shall we have another short one in honour of beautiful Tranai?"

They had several short ones. When Goodman left the bar, his mind was made up. Somewhere in the Universe, the *modus vivendi* had been found, the working solution to Man's old dream of perfection.

He could settle for nothing less.

The next day, he quit his job as designer at the East Coast Robot Works and drew his life savings out of the bank.

He was going to Tranai.

He boarded the *Constellation Queen* for Legis II and took the *Galactic Splendor* to Oumé. After stopping at Machang, Inchang, Pankang, Lekung and Oyster—dreary little places—he reached Tung-Bradar IV. Without incident, he passed the Galactic Whirl and finally reached Bellismoranti, where the influence of Terra ended.

For an exorbitant fee, a local spaceline took him to Dvasta II. From there, a freighter transported him past Seves, Olgo and Mi, to the double planet Mvanti. There he was bogged down for three months and used the time to take a hypnopedic course in the Tranaian language. At last he hired a bush pilot to take him to Ding.

On Ding, he was arrested as a Higastomeritreian spy, but managed to escape in the cargo of an ore rocket bound for g'Moree. At g'Moree, he was treated for frostbite, heat poisoning and superficial radiation burns, and at last arranged passage to Tranai.

He could hardly believe it when the ship slipped past the moons Doé and Ri, to land at Port Tranai.

After the airlocks opened, Goodman found himself in a state of profound depression. Part of it was plain letdown, inevitable after a journey such as his. But more than that, he was suddenly terrified that Tranai might turn out to be a fraud.

He had crossed the Galaxy on the basis of an old spaceman's yarn. But now it all seemed less likely. Eldorado was a more probable place than the Tranai he expected to find.

He disembarked. Port Tranai seemed a pleasant enough town. The streets were filled with people and the shops were piled high with goods. The men he passed looked much like humans anywhere. The women were quite attractive.

But there was something strange here, something subtly yet definitely wrong, something *alien*. It took a moment before he could puzzle it out.

Then he realized that there were at least ten men for every woman in sight. And stranger still, practically all the women he saw apparently were under eighteen or over thirty-five.

What had happened to the nineteen-to-thirty-five age group? Was there a taboo on their appearing in public? Had a plague struck them?

He would just have to wait and find out.

He went to the Idrig Building, where all Tranai's governmental functions were carried out, and presented himself at the office of the Extraterrestrials Minister. He was admitted at once.

The office was small and cluttered, with strange blue blotches on the wallpaper. What struck Goodman at once was a high-powered rifle complete with silencer and telescopic sight, hanging ominously from one wall. He had no time to speculate on this, for the minister bounded out of his chair and vigorously shook Goodman's hand.

The minister was a stout, jolly man of about fifty. Around his neck he wore a small medallion stamped with the Tranaian seal— a bolt of lightning splitting an ear of corn. Goodman assumed, correctly, that this was an official seal of office.

"Welcome to Tranai," the minister said heartily. He pushed a pile of papers from a chair and motioned Goodman to sit down.

"Mister Minister—" Goodman began, in formal Tranaian.

"Den Melith is the name. Call me Den. We're all quite informal around here. Put your feet up on the desk and make yourself at home. Cigar?"

"No, thank you," Goodman said, somewhat taken back. "Mister— ah—Den, I have come from Terra, a planet you may have heard of."

"Sure I have," said Melith. "Nervous, hustling sort of place, isn't it? No offence intended, of course."

"Of course. That's exactly how I feel about it. The reason I came here—" Goodman hesitated, hoping he wouldn't sound too ridiculous. "Well, I heard certain stories about Tranai. Thinking them over now, they seem preposterous. But if you don't mind, I'd like to ask you—"

"Ask anything," Melith said expansively. "You'll get a straight answer."

"Thank you. I heard that there has been no war of any sort on Tranai for four hundred years."

"Six hundred," Melith corrected. "And none in sight."

"Someone told me that there is no crime on Tranai."

"None whatsoever."

"And therefore no police force or courts, no judges, sheriffs, marshals, executioners, truant officers or government investigators. No prisons, reformatories, or other places of detention."

"We have no need of them," Melith explained, "since we have no crime."

"I have heard," said Goodman, "that there is no poverty on Tranai."

"None that I ever heard of," Melith said cheerfully. "Are you sure you won't have a cigar?"

"No, thank you," Goodman was leaning forward eagerly now. "I understand that you have achieved a stable economy without resorting to socialistic, communistic, fascistic or bureaucratic practices."

"Certainly," Melith said.

"That yours is, in fact, a free enterprise society, where individual initiative flourishes and governmental functions are kept to an absolute minimum."

Melith nodded. "By and large, the government concerns itself with minor regulatory matters, care of the aged and beautifying the landscape."

"Is it true that you have discovered a method of wealth distribution without resorting to governmental intervention, without even taxation, based entirely upon individual choice?" Goodman challenged.

"Oh, yes, absolutely."

"Is it true that there is no corruption in any phase of the Tranaian government?"

"None," Melith said. "I suppose that's why we have a hard time finding men to hold public office."

"Then Captain Savage was right!" Goodman cried, unable to control himself any longer. "This is utopia!"

"We like it," Melith said.

Goodman took a deep breath and asked, "May I stay here?"

"Why not?" Melith pulled out a form. "We've had no restrictions on immigration. Tell me, what is your occupation?"

"On Earth, I was a robot designer."

"Plenty of openings in that." Melith started to fill in the form. His pen emitted a blob of ink. Casually, the minister threw the pen against the wall, where it shattered, adding another blue blotch to the wallpaper.

"We'll make out the paper some other time," he said. "I'm not in the mood now." He leaned back in his chair. "Let me give you a word of advice. Here on Tranai, we feel that we have come pretty close to utopia, as you call it. But ours is not a highly organized state. We have no complicated set of laws. We live by observance of a number of unwritten laws, or customs, as you might call them. You will discover what they are. You would be advised—although certainly not ordered—to follow them."

"Of course I will," Goodman exclaimed. "I can assure you, sir, I have no intention of endangering any phase of your paradise."

"Oh, I wasn't worried about *us*," Melith said with an amused smile. "It was your own safety I was considering. Perhaps my wife has some further advice for you."

He pushed a large red button on his desk. Immediately there was a bluish haze. The haze solidified, and in a moment Goodman saw a handsome young woman standing before him.

"Good morning, my dear," she said to Melith.

"It's afternoon," Melith informed her. "My dear, this young man came all the way from Earth to live on Tranai. I gave him the usual advice. Is there anything else we can do for him?"

Mrs. Melith thought for a moment, then asked Goodman, "Are you married?"

"No, ma'am," Goodman answered.

"In that case, he should meet a nice girl," Mrs. Melith told her husband. "Bachelordom is not encouraged on Tranai, although certainly not prohibited. Let me see ... How about that cute Driganti girl?"

"She's engaged," Melith said.

"Really? Have I been in stasis *that* long? My dear, it's not too thoughtful of you."

"I was busy," Melith said apologetically.

"How about Mihna Vensis?"

"Not his type."

"Janna Vley?"

"Perfect!" Melith winked at Goodman. "A most attractive little lady." He found a new pen in his desk, scribbled an address and handed it to Goodman. "My wife will telephone her to be expecting you tomorrow evening."

"And do come around for dinner some night," said Mrs. Melith.

"Delighted," Goodman replied, in a complete daze.

"It's been nice meeting you," Mrs. Melith said. Her husband pushed the red button. The blue haze formed and Mrs. Melith vanished.

"Have to close up now," said Melith, glancing at his watch. "Can't work overtime—people might start talking. Drop in some day and we'll make out those forms. You really should call on Supreme President Borg, too, at the National Mansion. Or possibly he'll call on you. Don't let the old fox put anything over on you. And don't forget about Janna." He winked roguishly and escorted Goodman to the door.

In a few moments, Goodman found himself alone on the sidewalk. He had reached utopia, he told himself, a real, genuine, sure-enough utopia.

But there were some very puzzling things about it.

Goodman ate dinner at a small restaurant and checked in at a nearby hotel. A cheerful bellhop showed him to his room, where Goodman stretched out immediately on the bed. Wearily he rubbed his eyes, trying to sort out his impressions.

So much had happened to him, all in one day! And so much was bothering him. The ratio of men to women, for example. He had meant to ask Melith about that.

But Melith might not be the man to ask, for there were some curious things about him. Like throwing his pen against the wall. Was that the act of a mature, responsible official? And Melith's wife...

Goodman knew that Mrs. Melith had come out of a derrsin stasis field; he had recognized the characteristic blue haze. The derrsin was used on Terra, too. Sometimes there were good medical reasons for suspending all activity, all growth, all decay. Suppose a patient had a desperate need for a certain serum, procurable only on Mars. Simply project the person into stasis until the serum could arrive.

But on Terra, only a licensed doctor could operate the field. There were strict penalties for its misuse.

He had never heard of keeping one's wife in one.

Still, if all the wives on Tranai *were* kept in stasis, that would explain the absence of the nineteen-to-thirty-five age group and would account for the ten-to-one ratio of men to women.

But what was the reason for this technological purdah?

And something else was on Goodman's mind, something quite

insignificant, but bothersome all the same.

That rifle on Melith's wall.

Did he hunt game with it? Pretty big game, then. Target practice? Not with a telescopic sight. Why the silencer? Why did he keep it in his office?

But these were minor matters, Goodman decided, little local idiosyncrasies which would become clear when he had lived a while on Tranai. He couldn't expect immediate and complete comprehension of what was, after all, an alien planet.

He was just beginning to doze off when he heard a knock at his door.

"Come in," he called.

A small, furtive, grey-faced man hurried in and closed the door behind him. "You're the man from Terra, aren't you?"

"That's right."

"I figured you'd come here," the little man said, with a pleased smile. "Hit it right the first time. Going to stay on Tranai?"

"I'm here for good."

"Fine," the man said. "How would you like to become Supreme President?"

"Huh?"

"Good pay, easy hours, only a one-year term. You look like a public-spirited type," the man said sunnily. "How about it?"

Goodman hardly knew what to answer. "Do you mean," he asked incredulously, "that you offer the highest office in the land so casually?"

"What do you mean, *casually*?" the little man spluttered. "Do you think we offer the Supreme Presidency to just anybody? It's a great honour to be asked."

"I didn't mean—"

"And you, as a Terran, are uniquely suited."

"Why?"

"Well, it's common knowledge that Terrans derive pleasure from ruling. We Tranaians don't, that's all. Too much trouble."

As simple as that. The reformer blood in Goodman began to boil. Ideal as Tranai was, there was undoubtedly room for improvement. He had a sudden vision of himself as ruler of utopia, doing the great task of making perfection even better. But caution stopped him from agreeing at once. Perhaps the man was a crackpot.

"Thank you for asking me," Goodman said. "I'll have to think it over. Perhaps I should talk with the present incumbent and find out something about the nature of the work."

"Well, why do you think I'm here?" the little man demanded. "I'm Supreme President Borg."

Only then did Goodman notice the official medallion around the little man's neck.

"Let me know your decision. I'll be at the National Mansion." He shook Goodman's hand, and left.

Goodman waited five minutes, then rang for the bellhop. "Who was that man?"

"That was Supreme President Borg," the bellhop told him. "Did you take the job?"

Goodman shook his head slowly. He suddenly realized that he had a *great* deal to learn about Tranai.

The next morning, Goodman listed the various robot factories of Port Tranai in alphabetical order and went out in search of a job. To his amazement, he found one with no trouble at all, at the very first place he looked. The great Abbag Home Robot Works signed him on after only a cursory glance at his credentials.

His new employer, Mr. Abbag, was short and fierce-looking, with a great mane of white hair and an air of tremendous personal energy.

"Glad to have a Terran on board," Abbag said. "I understand you're an ingenious people and we certainly need some ingenuity around here. I'll be honest with you, Goodman—I'm hoping to profit by your alien viewpoint. We've reached an impasse."

"Is it a production problem?" Goodman asked.

"I'll show you." Abbag led Goodman through the factory, around the Stamping Room, Heat-Treat, X-ray Analysis, Final Assembly and to the Testing Room. This room was laid out like a combination kitchen–living-room. A dozen robots were lined up against one wall.

"Try one out," Abbag said.

Goodman walked up to the nearest robot and looked at its controls. They were simple enough; self-explanatory, in fact. He put the machine through a standard repertoire: picking up objects, washing pots and pans, setting a table. The robot's responses were correct enough, but maddeningly slow. On Earth, such sluggishness had been ironed out a hundred years ago. Apparently they were behind the times here on Tranai.

"Seems pretty slow," Goodman commented cautiously.

"You're right," Abbag said. "Damned slow. Personally, I think it's about right. But Consumer Research indicates that our customers want it slower still."

"Huh?"

"Ridiculous, isn't it?" Abbag asked moodily. "We'll lose money if we slow it down any more. Take a look at its guts."

Goodman opened the back panel and blinked at the maze of wiring

within. After a moment, he was able to figure it out. The robot was
built like a modern Earth machine, with the usual inexpensive high-
speed circuits. But special signal-delay relays, impulse-rejection units
and step-down gears had been installed.

"Just tell me," Abbag demanded angrily, "how can we slow it
down any more without building the thing a third bigger and twice
as expensive? I don't know what kind of a disimprovement they'll
be asking for next."

Goodman was trying to adjust his thinking to the concept of
disimproving a machine.

On Earth, the plants were always trying to build robots with
faster, smoother, more accurate responses. He had never found any
reason to question the wisdom of this. He still didn't.

"And as if that weren't enough," Abbag complained, "the new
plastic we developed for this particular model has catalysed or some
damned thing. Watch."

He drew back his foot and kicked the robot in the middle. The
plastic bent like a sheet of tin. He kicked again. The plastic bent still
further and the robot began to click and flash pathetically. A third
kick shattered the case. The robot's innards exploded in spectacular fashion, scattering over the floor.

"Pretty flimsy," Goodman said.

"Not flimsy enough. It's supposed to fly apart on the first kick. Our
customers won't get any satisfaction out of stubbing their toes on its
stomach all day. But tell me, how am I supposed to produce a plastic
that'll take normal wear and tear—we don't want these things falling
apart accidentally—and still go to pieces when a customer wants it
to?"

"Wait a minute," Goodman protested. "Let me get this straight.
You purposely slow these robots down so they will irritate people
enough to destroy them?"

Abbag raised both eyebrows. "Of course!"

"Why?"

"You *are* new here," Abbag said. "Any child knows that. It's
fundamental."

"I'd appreciate it if you'd explain."

Abbag sighed. "Well, first of all, you are undoubtedly aware that
any mechanical contrivance is a source of irritation. Human-kind
has a deep and abiding distrust of machines. Psychologists call it the
instinctive reaction of life to pseudo-life. Will you go along with me
on that?"

Marvin Goodman remembered all the anxious literature he had
read about machines revolting, cybernetic brains taking over the
world, androids on the march, and the like. He thought of humorous
little newspaper items about a man shooting his television set, smash-

ing his toaster against the wall, "getting even" with his car. He remembered all the robot jokes, with their undertone of deep hostility.

"I guess I can go along on that," said Goodman.

"Then allow me to restate the proposition," Abbag said pedantically. "Any machine is a source of irritation. The better a machine operates, the stronger the irritation. So, by extension, a *perfectly operating* machine is a focal point for frustration, loss of self-esteem, undirected resentment—"

"Hold on there!" Goodman objected. "I won't go *that* far!"

"—and schizophrenic fantasies," Abbag continued inexorably. "But machines are necessary to an advanced economy. Therefore the best *human* solution is to have malfunctioning ones."

"I don't see that at all."

"It's obvious. On Terra, your gadgets work close to the optimum, producing inferiority feelings in their operators. But unfortunately you have a masochistic tribal tabu against destroying them. Result? Generalized anxiety in the presence of the sacrosanct and un-humanly efficient Machine, and a search for an aggression-object, usually a wife or friend. A very poor state of affairs. Oh, it's efficient, I suppose, in terms of robot-hour production, but very inefficient in terms of long-range health and well-being."

"I'm not sure—"

"The human is an anxious beast. Here on Tranai, we direct anxiety towards this particular point and let it serve as an outlet for a lot of other frustrations as well. A man's had enough—blam! He kicks hell out of his robot. There's an immediate and therapeutic discharge of feeling, a valuable—and valid—sense of superiority over mere machinery, a lessening of general tension, a healthy flow of adrenalin into the bloodstream, and a boost to the industrial economy of Tranai, since he'll go right out and buy another robot. And what, after all, has he done? He hasn't beaten his wife, suicided, declared a war, invented a new weapon, or indulged in any of the other more common modes of aggression-resolution. He has simply smashed an inexpensive robot which he can replace immediately."

"I guess it'll take me a little time to understand," Goodman admitted.

"Of course it will. I'm sure you're going to be a valuable man here, Goodman. Think over what I've said and try to figure out some inexpensive way of disimproving this robot."

Goodman pondered the problem for the rest of the day, but he couldn't immediately adjust his thinking to the idea of producing an inferior machine. It seemed vaguely blasphemous. He knocked off work at five-thirty, dissatisfied with himself, but determined to do better—or worse, depending on viewpoint and conditioning.

After a quick and lonely supper, Goodman decided to call on Janna Vley. He didn't want to spend the evening alone with his thoughts and he was in desperate need of finding something pleasant, simple and uncomplicated in this complex utopia. Perhaps this Janna would be the answer.

The Vley home was only a dozen blocks away and he decided to walk.

The basic trouble was that he had had his own idea of what utopia would be like and it was difficult adjusting his thinking to the real thing. He had imagined a pastoral setting, a planetful of people in small, quaint villages, walking around in flowing robes and being very wise and gentle and understanding. Children who played in the golden sunlight, young folk danced in the village square . . .

Ridiculous! He had pictured a tableau rather than a scene, a series of stylized postures instead of the ceaseless movement of life. Humans could never live that way, even assuming they wanted to. If they could, they would no longer be humans.

He reached the Vley house and paused irresolutely outside. What was he getting himself into now? What alien—although indubitably utopian—customs would he run into?

He almost turned away. But the prospect of a long night alone in his hotel room was singularly unappealing. Gritting his teeth, he rang the bell.

A red-haired, middle-aged man of medium height opened the door. "Oh, you must be that Terran fellow. Janna's getting ready. Come in and meet the wife."

He escorted Goodman into a pleasantly furnished living-room and pushed a red button on the wall. Goodman wasn't startled this time by the bluish derrsin haze. After all, the manner in which Tranaians treated their women was their own business.

A handsome woman of about twenty-eight appeared from the haze.

"My dear," Vley said, "this is the Terran, Mr. Goodman."

"So pleased to meet you," Mrs. Vley said. "Can I get you a drink?" Goodman nodded. Vley pointed out a comfortable chair. In a moment, Mrs. Vley brought in a tray of frosted drinks and sat down.

"So you're from Terra," said Mr. Vley. "Nervous, hustling sort of place, isn't it? People always on the go?"

"Yes, I suppose it is," Goodman replied.

"Well, you'll like it here. We know how to live. It's all a matter of—"

There was a rustle of skirts on the stairs. Goodman got to his feet.

"Mr. Goodman, this is our daughter Janna," Mrs. Vley said.

Goodman noted at once that Janna's hair was the exact colour of the supernova in Circe, her eyes were that deep, unbelievable blue of the autumn sky over Algo II, her lips were the tender pink of a Scarsclott-Turner jet stream, her nose—

But he had run out of astronomical comparisons, which weren't suitable anyhow. Janna was a slender and amazingly pretty blonde girl and Goodman was suddenly very glad he had crossed the Galaxy and come to Tranai.

"Have a good time, children," Mrs. Vley said.

"Don't come in too late," Mr. Vley told Janna.

Exactly as parents said on Earth to their children.

There was nothing exotic about the date. They went to an inexpensive night club, danced, drank a little, talked a lot. Goodman was amazed at their immediate *rapport*. Janna agreed with everything he said. It was refreshing to find intelligence in so pretty a girl.

She was impressed, almost overwhelmed, by the dangers he had faced in crossing the Galaxy. She had always known that Terrans were adventurous (though nervous) types, but the risks Goodman had taken passed all understanding.

She shuddered when he spoke of the deadly Galactic Whirl and listened wide-eyed to his tales of running the notorious Swayback Gantlet, past the bloodthirsty Scarbies who were still cutting up along Star Ridge and infesting the hell holes of Prodengum. As Goodman put it, Terrans were iron men in steel ships, exploring the edges of the Great Nothing.

Janna didn't even speak until Goodman told of paying five hundred Terran dollars for a glass of beer at Moll Gann's Red Rooster Inn on Asteroid 342-AA.

"You must have been very thirsty," she said thoughtfully.

"Not particularly," Goodman said. "Money just didn't mean much out there."

"Oh. But wouldn't it have been better to have saved it? I mean someday you might have a wife and children—" She blushed.

Goodman said coolly, "Well, that part of my life is over. I'm going to marry and settle down right here on Tranai."

"How *nice!*" she cried.

It was a most successful evening.

Goodman returned Janna to her home at a respectable hour and arranged a date for the following evening. Made bold by his own tales, he kissed her on the cheek. She didn't really seem to mind, but Goodman didn't try to press his advantage.

"Till tomorrow then," she said, smiled at him, and closed the door.

He walked away feeling light-headed. Janna! Janna! Was it conceivable that he was in love already? Why not? Love at first sight was a proven psycho-physiological possibility and, as such, was perfectly respectable. Love in utopia! How wonderful it was that here, upon a perfect planet, he had found the perfect girl!

A man stepped out of the shadows and blocked his path. Goodman noted that he was wearing a black silk mask which covered everything except his eyes. He was carrying a large and powerful-looking blaster, and it was pointed steadily at Goodman's stomach.

"Okay, buddy," the man said, "gimme all your money."

"What?" Goodman gasped.

"You heard me. Your money. Hand it over."

"You can't do this," Goodman said, too startled to think coherently. "There's no crime on Tranai!"

"Who said there was?" the man asked quietly. "I'm merely asking you for your money. Are you going to hand it over peacefully or do I have to club it out of you?"

"You can't get away with this! Crime does not pay!"

"Don't be ridiculous," the man said. He hefted the heavy blaster.

"All right. Don't get excited." Goodman pulled out his billfold, which contained all he had in the world, and gave its contents to the masked man.

The man counted it, and he seemed impressed. "Better than I expected. Thanks, buddy. Take it easy now."

He hurried away down a dark street.

Goodman looked wildly around for a policeman, until he remembered that there were no police on Tranai. He saw a small cocktail lounge on the corner with a neon sign saying Kitty Kat Bar. He hurried into it.

Inside, there was only a bartender, sombrely wiping glasses.

"I've been robbed!" Goodman shouted at him.

"So?" the bartender said, not even looking up.

"But I thought there wasn't any crime on Tranai."

"There isn't."

"But I was *robbed*."

"You must be new here," the bartender said, finally looking at him.

"I just came in from Terra."

"Terra? Nervous, hustling sort of—"

"Yes, yes," Goodman said. He was getting a little tired of that stereotype. "But how can there be no crime on Tranai if I was robbed?"

"That should be obvious. On Tranai, robbery is no crime."

"But robbery is *always* a crime!"

"What colour mask was he wearing?"

Goodman thought for a moment. "Black. Black silk."

The bartender nodded. "Then he was a government tax collector."

"That's a ridiculous way to collect taxes," Goodman snapped.

The bartender set a Tranai Special in front of Goodman. "Try to see this in terms of the general welfare. The government has to have *some* money. By collecting it this way, we can avoid the necessity of an income tax, with all its complicated legal and legislative apparatus. And in terms of mental health, it's far better to extract money in a short, quick, painless operation than to permit the citizen to worry all year long about paying at a specific date."

Goodman downed his drink and the bartender set up another.

"But," Goodman said, "I thought this was a society based upon the concepts of free will and individual initiative."

"It is," the bartender told him. "Then surely the government, what little there is of it, has the same right to free will as any private citizen, hasn't it?"

Goodman couldn't quite figure that out, so he finished his second drink. "Could I have another of those? I'll pay you as soon as I can."

"Sure, sure," the bartender said good-naturedly, pouring another drink and one for himself.

Goodman said, "You asked me what colour his mask was. Why?"

"Black is the government mask colour. Private citizens wear white masks."

"You mean that private citizens commit robbery also?"

"Well, certainly! That's our method of wealth distribution. Money is equalized without government intervention, without even taxation, entirely in terms of individual initiative." The bartender nodded emphatically. "And it works perfectly, too. Robbery is a great leveller, you know."

"I suppose it is," Goodman admitted, finishing his third drink. "If I understand correctly, then, any citizen can pack a blaster, put on a mask, and go out and rob."

"Exactly," the bartender said. "Within limits, of course."

Goodman snorted. "If that's how it works, I can play that way. Could you loan me a mask? And a gun?"

The bartender reached under the bar. "Be sure to return them, though. Family heirlooms."

"I'll return them," Goodman promised. "And when I come back, I'll pay for my drinks."

He slipped the blaster into his belt, donned the mask and left the bar. If this was how things worked on Tranai, he could adjust all right. Rob him, would they? He'd rob them right back and then some!

He found a suitably dark street corner and huddled in the shadows, waiting. Presently he heard footsteps and, peering around the corner, saw a portly, well-dressed Tranaian hurrying down the street. Goodman stepped in front of him, snarling, "Hold it, buddy."

The Tranaian stopped and looked at Goodman's blaster. "Hmmm. Using a wide-aperture Drog 3, eh? Rather an old-fashioned weapon. How do you like it?"

"It's fine," Goodman said. "Hand over your—"

"Slow trigger action, though," the Tranaian mused. "Personally, I recommend a Mils-Sleeven needler. As it happens, I'm a sales representative for Sleeven Arms. I could get you a very good price on a trade-in—"

"Hand over your money," Goodman barked.

The portly Tranaian smiled. "The basic defect of your Drog 3 is the fact that it won't fire at all unless you release the safety lock." He reached out and slapped the gun out of Goodman's hand. "You see? You couldn't have done a thing about it." He started to walk away.

Goodman scooped up the blaster, found the safety lock, released it and hurried after the Tranaian.

"Stick up your hands," Goodman ordered, beginning to feel slightly desperate.

"No, no, my good man," the Tranaian said, not even looking back. "Only one try to a customer. Mustn't break the unwritten law, you know."

Goodman stood and watched until the man turned a corner and was gone. He checked the Drog 3 carefully and made sure that all safeties were off. Then he resumed his post.

After an hour's wait, he heard footsteps again. He tightened his grip on the blaster. This time he was going to rob and nothing was going to stop him.

"Okay, buddy," he said, "hands up!"

The victim this time was a short, stocky Tranaian, dressed in old workman's clothes. He gaped at the gun in Goodman's hand.

"Don't shoot, mister," the Tranaian pleaded.

That was more like it! Goodman felt a glow of deep satisfaction.

"Just don't move," he warned. "I've got all safeties off."

"I can see that," the stocky man said cringing. "Be careful with that cannon, mister. I ain't moving a hair."

"You'd better not. Hand over your money."

"Money?"

"Yes, your money, and be quick about it."

"I don't have any money," the man whined. "Mister, I'm a poor man. I'm poverty-stricken."

"There is no poverty on Tranai," Goodman said sententiously.

"I know. But you can get so close to it, you wouldn't know the difference. Give me a break, mister."

"Haven't you any initiative?" Goodman asked. "If you're poor, why don't you go out and rob like everybody else?"

"I just haven't had a chance. First the kid got the whooping cough and I was up every night with her. Then the derrsin broke down, so I had the wife yakking at me all day long. I say there oughta be a spare derrsin in every house! So she decided to clean the place while the derrsin generator was being fixed and she put my blaster somewhere and she can't remember where. So I was all set to borrow a friend's blaster when—"

"That's enough," Goodman said. "This is a robbery and I'm going to rob you of *something*. Hand over your wallet."

The man snuffled miserably and gave Goodman a worn billfold. Inside it, Goodman found one deeglo, the equivalent of a Terran dollar.

"It's all I got," the man snuffled miserably, "but you're welcome to it. I know how it is, standing on a drafty street corner all night—"

"Keep it," Goodman said, handing the billfold back to the man and walking off.

"Gee, thanks, mister!"

Goodman didn't answer. Disconsolately, he returned to the Kitty Kat Bar and gave back the bartender's blaster and mask. When he explained what had happened, the bartender burst into rude laughter.

"Didn't have any money! Man, that's the oldest trick in the books. Everybody carries a fake wallet for robberies—sometimes two or even three. Did you search him?"

"No," Goodman confessed.

"Brother, are you a greenhorn!"

"I guess I am. Look, I really will pay you for those drinks as soon as I can make some money."

"Sure, sure," the bartender said. "You better go home and get some sleep. You had a busy night."

Goodman agreed. Wearily he returned to his hotel room and was asleep as soon as his head hit the pillow.

He reported at the Abbag Home Robot Works and manfully grappled with the problem of disimproving automata. Even in unhuman work such as this, Terran ingenuity began to tell.

Goodman began to develop a new plastic for the robot's case. It was a silicone, a relative of the "silly putty" that had appeared on Earth a long while back. It had the desired properties of toughness, resiliency and long wear; it would stand a lot of abuse, too. But the case would shatter immediately and with spectacular effect upon receiving a kick delivered with an impact of thirty pounds or more.

His employer praised him for this development, gave him a

bonus (which he sorely needed), and told him to keep working on the idea and, if possible, to bring the needed impact down to twenty-three pounds. This, the research department told them, was the average frustration kick.

He was kept so busy that he had practically no time to explore further the mores and folkways of Tranai. He did manage to see the Citizen's Booth. This uniquely Tranaian institution was housed in a small building on a quiet back street.

Upon entering, he was confronted by a large board, upon which was listed the names of the present officeholders of Tranai, and their titles. Beside each name was a button. The attendant told Goodman that, by pressing a button, a citizen expressed his disapproval of that official's acts. The pressed button was automatically registered in History Hall and was a permanent mark against the officeholder.

No minors were allowed to press the buttons, of course.

Goodman considered this somewhat ineffectual; but perhaps, he told himself, officials on Tranai were differently motivated from those on Earth.

He saw Janna almost every evening and together they explored the many cultural aspects of Tranai: the cocktail lounges and movies, the concert halls, the art exhibitions, the science museum, the fairs and festivals. Goodman carried a blaster and, after several unsuccessful attempts, robbed a merchant of nearly five hundred deeglo.

Janna was ecstatic over the achievement, as any sensible Tranaian girl would be, and they celebrated at the Kitty Kat Bar. Janna's parents agreed that Goodman seemed to be a good provider.

The following night, the five hundred deeglo—plus some of Goodman's bonus money—was robbed back, by a man of approximately the size and build of the bartender at the Kitty Kat, carrying an ancient Drog 3 blaster.

Goodman consoled himself with the thought that the money was circulating freely, as the system had intended.

Then he had another triumph. One day at the Abbag Home Robot Works, he discovered a completely new process for making a robot's case. It was a special plastic, impervious even to serious bumps and falls. The robot owner had to wear special shoes, with a catalytic agent imbedded in the heels. When he kicked the robot, the catalyst came in contact with the plastic case, with immediate and gratifying effect.

Abbag was a little uncertain at first; it seemed too gimmicky. But the thing caught on like wildfire and the Home Robot Works went into the shoe business as a subsidiary, selling at least one pair with every robot.

This horizontal industrial development was very gratifying to the plant's stockholders and was really more important than the original catalyst-plastic discovery. Goodman received a substantial raise in pay and a generous bonus.

On the crest of his triumphant wave, he proposed to Janna and was instantly accepted. Her parents favoured the match; all that remained was to obtain official sanction from the government, since Goodman was still technically an alien.

Accordingly, he took a day off from work and walked down to the Idrig Building to see Melith. It was a glorious spring day of the sort that Tranai has for ten months out of the year, and Goodman walked with a light and springy step. He was in love, a success in business, and soon to become a citizen of utopia.

Of course, utopia could use some changes, for even Tranai wasn't quite perfect. Possibly he should accept the Supreme Presidency, in order to make the needed reforms. But there was no rush...

"Hey, mister," a voice said, "can you spare a deeglo?"

Goodman looked down and saw, squatting on the pavement, an unwashed old man, dressed in rags, holding out a tin cup.

"What?" Goodman asked.

"Can you spare a deeglo, brother?" the man repeated in a wheedling voice. "Help a poor man buy a cup of oglo? Haven't eaten in two days, mister."

"This is disgraceful! Why don't you get a blaster and go out and rob someone?"

"I'm too old," the man whimpered. "My victims just laugh at me."

"Are you sure you aren't just lazy?" Goodman asked sternly.

"I'm not, sir!" the beggar said. "Just look how my hands shake!"

He held out both dirty paws; they trembled.

Goodman took out his billfold and gave the old man a deeglo. "I thought there was no poverty on Tranai. I understood that the government took care of the aged."

"The government does," said the old man. "Look." He held out his cup. Engraved on its side was: GOVERNMENT AUTHORIZED BEGGAR, NUMBER DR-43241-3.

"You mean the government makes you do this?"

"The government lets me do it," the old man told him. "Begging is a government job and is reserved for the aged and infirm."

"Why, that's disgraceful!"

"You must be a stranger here."

"I'm a Terran."

"Aha! Nervous, hustling sort of people, aren't you?"

"Our government does not let people beg," Goodman said.

"No? What do the old people do? Live off their children? Or sit in some home for the aged and wait for death by boredom? Not here, young man. On Tranai, every old man is assured of a government job, and one for which he needs no particular skill, although skill helps. Some apply for indoor work, within the churches and theatres. Others like the excitement of fairs and carnivals. Personally, I like it outdoors. My job keeps me out in the sunlight and fresh air, gives me mild exercise, and helps me meet many strange and interesting people, such as yourself."

"But *begging!*"

"What other work would I be suited for?"

"I don't know. But—but look at you! Dirty, unwashed, in filthy clothes—"

"These are my working clothes," the government beggar said. "You should see me on Sunday."

"You have other clothes?"

"I certainly do, and a pleasant little apartment, and a season box at the opera, and two Home Robots, and probably more money in the bank than you've seen in your life. It's been pleasant talking to you, young man, and thanks for your contribution. But now I must return to work and suggest you do likewise."

Goodman walked away, glancing over his shoulder at the government beggar. He observed that the old man seemed to be doing a thriving business.

But *begging!*

Really, that sort of thing should be stopped. If he ever assumed the Presidency—and quite obviously he should—he would look into the whole matter more carefully.

It seemed to him that there had to be a more dignified answer.

At the Idrig Building, Goodman told Melith about his marriage plans.

The immigrations minister was enthusiastic.

"Wonderful, absolutely wonderful," he said. "I've known the Vley family for a long time. They're splendid people. And Janna is a girl any man would be proud of."

"Aren't there some formalities I should go through?" Goodman asked. "I mean being an alien and all—"

"None whatsoever. I've decided to dispense with the formalities. You can become a citizen of Tranai, if you wish, by merely stating your intention verbally. Or you can retain Terran citizenship, with no hard feelings. Or you can do both—be a citizen of Terra *and* Tranai. If Terra doesn't mind, we certainly don't."

"I think I'd like to become a citizen of Tranai," Goodman said.

"It's entirely up to you. But if you're thinking about the Presidency, you can retain Terran status and still hold office. We aren't at all stuffy about that sort of thing. One of our most success-

ful Supreme Presidents was a lizard-evolved chap from Aquarella
XI."

"What an enlightened attitude!"

"Sure, give everybody a chance, that's our motto. Now as to your
marriage—any government employee can perform the ceremonies.
Supreme President Borg would be happy to do it, this afternoon if
you like." Melith winked. "The old codger likes to kiss the bride.
But I think he's genuinely fond of you."

"This afternoon?" Goodman said. "Yes, I *would* like to be married
this afternoon, if it's all right with Janna."

"It probably will be," Melith assured him. "Next, where are you
going to live after the honeymoon? A hotel room is hardly suitable." He thought for a moment. "Tell you what—I've got a little
house on the edge of town. Why don't you move in there, until you
find something better? Or stay permanently, if you like it."

"Really," Goodman protested, "you're too generous—"

"Think nothing of it. Have you ever thought of becoming the
next immigrations minister? You might like the work. No red tape,
short hours, good pay— No? Got your eye on the Supreme Presidency, eh? Can't blame you, I suppose."

Melith dug in his pockets and found two keys. "This is for the
front door and this is for the back. The address is stamped right
on them. The place is fully equipped, including a brand-new derrsin
field generator."

"A derrsin?"

"Certainly. No home on Tranai is complete without a derrsin
stasis field generator."

Clearing his throat, Goodman said carefully, "I've been meaning to ask you—exactly what is the stasis field used for?"

"Why, to keep one's wife in," Melith answered. "I thought you
knew."

"I did," said Goodman. "But *why*?"

"Why?" Melith frowned. Apparently the question had never
entered his head. "Why does one do anything? It's the custom, that's
all. And very logical, too. You wouldn't want a woman chattering
around you all the time, night and day."

Goodman blushed, because ever since he had met Janna, he had
been thinking how pleasant it would be to have her around him
all the time, night and day.

"It hardly seems fair to the women," Goodman pointed out.

Melith laughed. "My dear friend, are you preaching the doctrine
of equality of the sexes? Really, it's a completely disproved theory.
Men and women just aren't the same. They're different, no matter
what you've been told on Terra. What's good for men isn't
necessarily—or even usually—good for women."

"Therefore you treat them as inferiors," Goodman said, his reformer's blood beginning to boil.

"Not at all. We treat them in a *different* manner from men, but not in an *inferior* manner. Anyhow, they don't object."

"That's because they haven't been allowed to know any better. Is there any law that requires me to keep my wife in the derrsin field?"

"Of course not. The custom simply suggests that you keep her *out* of stasis for a certain minimum amount of time every week. Not fair incarcerating the little woman, you know."

"Of course not," Goodman said sarcastically. "Must let her live *some* of the time."

"Exactly," Melith said, seeing no sarcasm in what Goodman said. "You'll catch on."

Goodman stood up. "Is that all?"

"I guess that's about it. Good luck and all that."

"Thank you," Goodman said stiffly, turned sharply and left.

That afternoon, Supreme President Borg performed the simple Tranaian marriage rites at the National Mansion and afterward kissed the bride with zeal. It was a beautiful ceremony and was marred by only one thing.

Hanging on Borg's wall was a rifle, complete with telescopic sight and silencer. It was a twin to Melith's and just as inexplicable.

Borg took Goodman to one side and asked, "Have you given any further thought to the Supreme Presidency?"

"I'm still considering it," Goodman said. "I don't really want to hold public office—"

"No one does."

"But there are certain reforms that Tranai needs badly. I think it may be my duty to bring them to the attention of the people."

"That's the spirit," Borg said approvingly. "We haven't had a really enterprising Supreme President for some time. Why don't you take office right now? Then you could have your honeymoon in the National Mansion with complete privacy."

Goodman was tempted. But he didn't want to be bothered by affairs of state on his honeymoon, which was all arranged anyhow. Since Tranai had lasted so long in its present near-utopian condition, it would undoubtedly keep for a few weeks more.

"I'll consider it when I come back," Goodman said.

Borg shrugged. "Well, I guess I can bear the burden a while longer. Oh, here." He handed Goodman a sealed envelope.

"What's this?"

"Just the standard advice," Borg said. "Hurry, your bride's waiting for you!"

"Come on, Marvin!" Janna called. "We don't want to be late for the spaceship!"

Goodman hurried after her, into the spaceport limousine.

"Good luck!" her parents cried.

"Good luck!" Borg shouted.

"Good luck!" added Melith and his wife, and all the guests.

On the way to the spaceport, Goodman opened the envelope and read the printed sheet within:

ADVICE TO A NEW HUSBAND

You have just been married and you expect, quite naturally, a lifetime of connubial bliss. This is perfectly proper, for a happy marriage is the foundation of good government. But you must do more than merely wish for it. Good marriage is not yours by divine right. A good marriage must be worked for!

Remember that your wife is a human being. She should be allowed a certain measure of freedom as her inalienable right. We suggest you take her out of stasis at least once a week. Too long in stasis is bad for her orientation. Too much stasis is bad for her complexion and this will be your loss as well as hers.

At intervals, such as vacations and holidays, it's customary to let your wife remain out of stasis for an entire day at a time, or even two or three days. It will do no harm and the novelty will do wonders for her state of mind.

Keep in mind these few common-sense rules and you can be assured of a happy marriage.

—By the Government
Marriage Council

Goodman slowly tore the card into little bits, and let them drop to the floor of the limousine. His reforming spirit was now thoroughly aroused. He had known that Tranai was too good to be true. Someone had to pay for perfection. In this case, it was the women.

He had found the first serious flaw in paradise.

"What was that, dear?" Janna asked, looking at the bits of paper.

"That was some very foolish advice," Goodman said. "Dear, have you ever thought—really thought—about the marriage customs of this planet of yours?"

"I don't think I have. Aren't they all right?"

"They are wrong, completely wrong. They treat women like toys, like little dolls that one puts away when one is finished playing. Can't you see that?"

"I never thought about it."

"Well, you can think about it now," Goodman told her, "because some changes are going to be made and they're going to start in our home."

"Whatever you think best, darling," Janna said dutifully. She squeezed his arm. He kissed her.

And then the limousine reached the spaceport and they got aboard the ship.

Their honeymoon on Doé was like a brief sojourn in a flawless paradise. The wonders of Tranai's little moon had been built for lovers, and for lovers only. No businessman came to Doé for a quick rest; no predatory bachelor prowled the paths. The tired, the disillusioned, the lewdly hopeful all had to find other hunting grounds. The single rule on Doé, strictly enforced, was two by two, joyous and in love, and in no other state admitted.

This was one Tranaian custom that Goodman had no trouble appreciating.

On the little moon, there were meadows of tall grass and deep, green forests for walking and cool black lakes in the forests and jagged, spectacular mountains that begged to be climbed. Lovers were continually getting lost in the forests, to their great satisfaction; but not too lost, for one could circle the whole moon in a day. Thanks to the gentle gravity, no one could drown in the black lakes, and a fall from a mountaintop was frightening, but hardly dangerous.

There were, at strategic locations, little hotels with dimly lit cocktail lounges run by friendly, white-haired bartenders. There were gloomy caves which ran deep (but never too deep) into phosphorescent caverns glittering with ice, past sluggish underground rivers in which swam great luminous fish with fiery eyes.

The Government Marriage Council had considered these simple attractions sufficient and hadn't bothered putting in a golf course, swimming pool, horse track or shuffleboard court. It was felt that once a couple desired these things, the honeymoon was over.

Goodman and his bride spent an enchanted week on Doé and at last returned to Tranai.

After carrying his bride across the threshold of their new home, Goodman's first act was to unplug the derrsin generator.

"My dear," he said, "up to now, I have followed all the customs of Tranai, even when they seemed ridiculous to me. But this is one thing I will not saction. On Terra, I was the founder of the Committee for Equal Job Opportunities for Women. On Terra, we treat our women as equals, as companions, as partners in the adventure of life."

"What a strange concept," Janna said, a frown clouding her pretty face.

"Think about it," Goodman urged. "Our life will be far more satisfying in this companionable manner than if I shut you up in the purdah of the derrsin field. Don't you agree?"

"You know far more than I, dear. You've travelled all over the Galaxy, and I've never been out of Port Tranai. If you say it's the best way, then it must be."

Past a doubt, Goodman thought, she was the most perfect of women.

He returned to his work at the Abbag Home Robot Works and was soon deep in another disimprovement project. This time, he conceived the bright idea of making the robot's joints squeak and grind. The noise would increase the robot's irritation value, thereby making its destruction more pleasing and psychologically more valuable. Mr. Abbag was overjoyed with the idea, gave him another pay raise, and asked him to have the disimprovement ready for early production.

Goodman's first plan was simply to remove some of the lubrication ducts. But he found that friction would then wear out vital parts too soon. That naturally could not be sanctioned.

He began to draw up plans for a built-in squeak-and-grind unit. It had to be absolutely life-like and yet cause no real wear. It had to be inexpensive and it had to be small, because the robot's interior was already packed with disimprovements.

But Goodman found that small squeak-producing units sounded artificial. Larger units were too costly to manufacture or couldn't be fitted inside the robot's case. He began working several evenings a week, lost weight, and his temper grew edgy.

Janna became a good, dependable wife. His meals were always ready on time and she invariably had a cheerful word for him in the evenings and a sympathetic ear for his difficulties. During the day, she supervised the cleaning of the house by the Home Robots. This took less than an hour and afterward she read books, baked pies, knitted, and destroyed robots.

Goodman was a little alarmed at this, because Janna destroyed them at the rate of three or four a week. Still, everyone had to have a hobby. He could afford to indulge her, since he got the machines at cost.

Goodman had reached a complete impasse when another designer, a man named Dath Hergo, came up with a novel control. This was based upon a counter-gyroscopic principle and allowed a robot to enter a room at a ten-degree list. (Ten degrees, the research department said, was the most irritating angle of list a robot could assume.) Moreover, by employing a random-selection principle, the robot would *lurch*, drunkenly, annoyingly, at irregular intervals—never dropping anything, but always on the verge of it.

This development was, quite naturally, hailed as a great advance in disimprovement engineering. And Goodman found that he could centre his built-in squeak-and-grind unit right in the lurch control. His name was mentioned in the engineering journals next to that of Dath Hergo.

The new line of Abbag Home Robots was a sensation.

At this time, Goodman decided to take a leave of absence from his job and assume the Supreme Presidency of Tranai. He felt he owed it to the people. If Terran ingenuity and know-how could bring out improvements in disimprovements, they would do even better improving improvements. Tranai was a near-utopia. With his hand on the reins, they could go the rest of the way to perfection.

He went down to Melith's office to talk it over.

"I suppose there's always room for change," Melith said thoughtfully. The immigration chief was seated by the window, idly watching people pass by. "Of course, our present system has been working for quite some time and working very well. I don't know what you'd improve. There's no crime, for example—"

"Because you've legalized it," Goodman declared. "You've simply evaded the issue."

"We don't see it that way. There's no poverty—"

"Because everybody steals. And there's no trouble with old people because the government turns them into beggars. Really, there's plenty of room for change and improvement."

"Well, perhaps," Melith said. "But I think—" he stopped suddenly, rushed over to the wall and pulled down the rifle. "There he is!"

Goodman looked out of the window. A man, apparently no different from anyone else, was walking past. He heard a muffled click and saw the man stagger, then drop to the pavement.

Melith had shot him with the silenced rifle.

"What did you do that for?" Goodman gasped.

"Potential murderer," Melith said.

"What?"

"Of course. We don't have any out-and-out crime here, but, being human, we have to deal with the potentiality."

"What did he do to make him a potential murderer?"

"Killed five people," Melith stated.

"But—damn it, man, this isn't fair! You didn't arrest him, give him a trial, the benefit of counsel!—"

"How could I?'" Melith asked, slightly annoyed. "We don't have any police to arrest people with and we don't have any legal system. Good Lord, you didn't expect me to just let him go on, did you? Our definition of a murderer is a killer of ten and he was well on his way. I couldn't just sit idly by. It's my duty to protect the people. I can assure you, I made careful inquiries."

"It isn't just!" Goodman shouted.

"Who ever said it was?" Melith shouted back. "What has *justice* got to do with utopia?"

"Everything!" Goodman had calmed himself with an effort. "Justice is the basis of human dignity, human desire—"

"Now you're just using words," Melith said, with his usual good-natured smile. "Try to be realistic. We have created a utopia for *human beings*, not for saints who don't need one. We must accept the deficiencies of the human character, not pretend they don't exist. To our way of thinking, a police apparatus and a legal-judicial system all tend to create an atmosphere for crime and an acceptance of crime. It's better, believe me, not to accept the possibility of crime at all. The vast majority of the people will go along with you."

"But when crime does turn up as it inevitably does—"

"Only the potentiality turns up," Melith insisted stubbornly. "And even that is much rarer than you would think. When it shows up, we deal with it, quickly and simply."

"Suppose you get the wrong man?"

"We can't get the wrong man. Not a chance of it."

"Why not?"

"Because," Melith said, "anyone disposed of by a government official is, by definition and by unwritten law, a potential criminal."

Marvin Goodman was silent for a while. Then he said, "I see that the government has more power than I thought at first."

"It does," Melith said. "But not as much as you now imagine."

Goodman smiled ironically. "And is the Supreme Presidency still mine for the asking?"

"Of course. And with no strings attached. Do you want it?"

Goodman thought deeply for a moment. Did he really want it? Well, someone had to rule. Someone had to protect the people. Someone had to make a few reforms in this utopian madhouse.

"Yes, I want it," Goodman said.

The door burst open and Supreme President Borg rushed in. "Wonderful! Perfectly wonderful! You can move into the National Mansion today. I've been packed for a week, waiting for you to make up your mind."

"There must be certain formalities to go through—"

"No formalities," Borg said, his face shining with perspiration. "None whatsoever. All we do is hand over the Presidential Seal; then I'll go down and take my name off the rolls and put yours on."

Goodman looked at Melith. The immigration minister's round face was expressionless.

"All right," Goodman said.

Borg reached for the Presidential Seal, started to remove it from his neck—

It exploded suddenly and violently.

Goodman found himself staring in horror at Borg's red, ruined head. The Supreme President tottered for a moment, then slid to the floor.

Melith took off his jacket and threw it over Borg's head. Goodman backed to a chair and fell into it. His mouth opened, but no words came out.

"It's really a pity," Melith said. "He was so near the end of his term. I warned him against licensing that new spaceport. The citizens won't approve, I told him. But he was sure they would like to have two spaceports. Well, he was wrong."

"Do you mean—I mean—how—what—"

"All government officials," Melith explained, "wear the badge of office, which contains a traditional amount of tessium, an explosive you may have heard of. The charge is radio-controlled from the Citizen's Booth. Any citizen has access to the Booth, for the purpose of expressing his disapproval of the government." Melith sighed. "This will go down as a permanent black mark against poor Borg's record."

"You let the people express their disapproval by blowing up officials?" Goodman croaked, appalled.

"It's the only way that means anything," said Melith. "Check and balance. Just as the people are in our hands, so we are in the people's hands."

"And *that's* why he wanted me to take over his term. Why didn't anyone tell me?"

"You didn't ask," Melith said, with the suspicion of a smile. "Don't look so horrified. Assassination is always possible, you know, on any planet, under any government. We try to make it a constructive thing. Under this system, the people never lose touch with the government, and the government never tries to assume dictatorial powers. And, since everyone knows he can turn to the Citizen's Booth, you'd be surprised how sparingly it's used. Of course, there are always hot-heads."

Goodman got to his feet and started to the door, not looking at Borg's body.

"Don't you still want the Presidency?" asked Melith.

"No!"

"That's so like you Terrans," Melith remarked sadly. "You want responsibility only if it doesn't incur risk. That's the wrong attitude for running a government."

"You may be right," Goodman said. "I'm just glad I found out in time."

He hurried home.

His mind was in a complete turmoil when he entered his house. Was Tranai a utopia or a planet-wide insane asylum? Was there much difference? For the first time in his life, Goodman was wondering if utopia was worth having. Wasn't it better to strive for perfection than to possess it? To have ideals rather than to live by them? If justice was a fallacy, wasn't the fallacy better than the truth?

Or was it? Goodman was a sadly confused young man when he shuffled into his house and found his wife in the arms of another man.

The scene had a terrible slow-motion clarity in his eyes. It seemed to take Janna forever to rise to her feet, straighten her disarranged clothing and stare at him open-mouthed. The man—a tall, good-looking fellow whom Goodman had never before seen—appeared too startled to speak. He made small, aimless gestures, brushing the lapel of his jacket, pulling down his cuffs.

Then, tentatively, the man smiled.

"Well!" Goodman said. It was feeble enough, under the circumstances, but it had its effect. Janna started to cry.

"Terribly sorry," the man murmured. "Didn't expect you home for hours. This must come as a shock to you. I'm terribly sorry."

The one thing Goodman hadn't expected or wanted was sympathy from his wife's lover. He ignored the man and stared at the weeping Janna.

"Well, what did you expect?" Janna screamed at him suddenly. "I had to! You didn't love me!"

"Didn't love you! How can you say that?"

"Because of the way you treated me."

"I loved you very much, Janna," he said softly.

"You didn't!" she shrilled, throwing back her head. "Just look at the way you treated me. You kept me around all day, every day, doing *housework, cooking, sitting*. Marvin, I could *feel* myself ageing. Day after day, the same weary, stupid routine. And most of the time, when you came home, you were too tired to even notice me. All you could talk about was your stupid robots! I was being wasted, Marvin, *wasted*!"

It suddenly occurred to Goodman that his wife was unhinged. Very gently he said, "But, Janna, that's how life is. A husband and wife settle into a companionable situation. They age together side by side. It can't all be high spots—"

"But of course it can! Try to undersand, Marvin. It can, on
Tranai—for a woman!"

"It's impossible," Goodman said.

"On Tranai, a woman expects a life of enjoyment and pleasure.
It's her right, just as men have their rights. She expects to come
out of stasis and find a little party prepared, or a walk in the moonlight, or a swim, or a movie." She began to cry again. "But *you*
were so smart. *You* had to change it. I should have known better
than to trust a Terran."

The other man sighed and lighted a cigarette.

"I know you can't help being an alien, Marvin," Janna said. "But
I do want you to understand. Love isn't everything. A woman must
be practical, too. The way things were going, I would have been an
old woman while all my friends were still young."

"Still young?" Goodman repeated blankly.

"Of course," the man said. "A woman doesn't age in the derrsin
field."

"But the whole thing is ghastly," said Goodman. "My wife would
still be a young woman when I was old."

"That's just when you'd appreciate a young woman," Janna said.

"But how about you?" Goodman asked. "Would you appreciate an
old man?"

"He still doesn't understand," the man said.

"Marvin, *try*. Isn't it clear yet? Throughout your life, you would
have a young and beautiful woman whose only desire would be to
please you. And when you died—don't look shocked, dear; everybody dies—when you died, I would still be young, and by law I'd
inherit all your money."

"I'm beginning to see," Goodman said. "I suppose that's another
accepted phase of Tranaian life—the wealthy young widow who
can pursue her own pleasures."

"Naturally. In this way, everything is for the best for everybody.
The man has a young wife whom he sees only when he wishes. He
has his complete freedom and a nice home as well. The woman is
relieved of all the dullness of ordinary living and, while she can
still enjoy it, is well provided for."

"You should have told me," Goodman complained.

"I thought you knew," Janna said, "since you thought you had a
better way. But I can see that you would never have understood,
because you're so naïve—though I must admit it's one of your
charms." She smiled wistfully. "Besides, if I'd told you, I would
never have met Rondo."

The man bowed slightly. "I was leaving samples of Greah's Con-
fections. You can imagine my surprise when I found this lovely
young woman *out of stasis*. I mean it was like a storybook tale

come true. One never expects old legends to happen, so you must admit that there's a certain appeal when they do."

"Do you love him?" Goodman asked heavily.

"Yes," said Janna. "Rondo cares for me. He's going to keep me in stasis long enough to make up for the time I've lost. It's a sacrifice on his part, but Rondo has a generous nature."

"If that's how it is," Goodman said glumly, "I certainly won't stand in your way. I am a civilized being, after all. You may have a divorce."

He folded his arms across his chest, feeling quite noble. But he was dimly aware that his decision stemmed not so much from nobility as from a sudden, violent distaste for all things Tranaian.

"We have no divorce on Tranai," Rondo said.

"No?" Goodman felt a cold chill run down his spine.

A blaster appeared in Rondo's hand. "It would be too unsettling, you know, if people were always swapping around. There's only one way to change a marital status."

"But this is revolting!" Goodman blurted, backing away. "It's against all decency!"

"Not if the wife desires it. And that, by the by, is another excellent reason for keeping one's spouse in stasis. Have I your permission, my dear?"

"Forgive me, Marvin," Janna said. She closed her eyes. "Yes!"

Rondo levelled the blaster. Without a moment's hesitation, Goodman dived head-first out of the nearest window. Rondo's shot fanned right over him.

"See here!" Rondo called. "Show some spirit, man. Stand up to it!"

Goodman had landed heavily on his shoulder. He was up at once, sprinting, and Rondo's second shot scorched his arm. Then he ducked behind a house and was momentarily safe. He didn't stop to think about it. Running for all he was worth, he headed for the spaceport.

Fortunately, a ship was preparing for blast-off and took him to g'Moree. From there he wired to Tranai for his funds and bought passage to Higastomeritreia, where the authorities accused him of being a Ding spy. The charge couldn't stick, since the Dingans were an amphibious race, and Goodman almost drowned proving to everyone's satisfaction that he could breathe only air.

A drone transport took him to the double planet Mvanti, past Seves, Olgo and Mi. He hired a bush pilot to take him to Bellismoranti, where the influence of Terra began. From there, a local spaceline transported him past the Galactic Whirl and, after stopping at Oyster, Lekung, Pankang, Inchang and Machang, arrived at Tung-Bradar IV.

His money was now gone, but he was practically next door to Terra, as astronomical distances go. He was able to work his passage to Oumé, and from Oumé to Legis II. There the Interstellar Travellers Aid Society arranged a berth for him and at last he arrived back on Earth.

Goodman has settled down in Seakirk, New Jersey, where a man is perfectly safe as long as he pays his taxes. He holds the post of Chief Robotic Technician for the Seakirk Construction Corporation and has married a small, dark, quiet girl, who obviously adores him, although he rarely lets her out of the house.

He and old Captain Savage go frequently to Eddie's Moonlight Bar, drink Tranai Specials, and talk of Tranai the Blessed, where The Way has been found and Man is no longer bound to The Wheel. On such occasions, Goodman complains of a touch of space malaria—because of it, he can never go back into space, can never return to Tranai.

There is always an admiring audience on these nights.

Goodman has recently organized, with Captain Savage's help, the Seakirk League to Take the Vote from Women. They are its only members, but as Goodman puts it, when did that ever stop a crusader?

THE BATTLE

Supreme General Fetterer barked "At ease!" as he hurried into the command room. Obediently, his three generals stood at ease.

"We haven't much time," Fetterer said, glancing at his watch. "We'll go over the plan of battle again."

He walked to the wall and unrolled a gigantic map of the Sahara Desert.

"According to our best theological information, Satan is going to present his forces at these co-ordinates." He indicated the place with a blunt forefinger. "In the front rank there will be the devils, demons, succubi, incubi, and the rest of the ratings. Bael will command the right flank, Buer the left. His Satanic Majesty will hold the centre."

"Rather medieval," General Dell murmured.

General Fetterer's aide came in, his face shining and happy with the thought of the Coming.

"Sir," he said, "the priest is outside again."

"Stand to attention, soldier," Fetterer said sternly. "There's still a battle to be fought and won."

"Yes sir," the aide said, and stood rigidly, some of the joy fading from his face.

"The priest, eh?" Supreme General Fetterer rubbed his fingers together thoughtfully. Even since the Coming, since the knowledge of the imminent Last Battle, the religious workers of the world had made a complete nuisance of themselves. They had stopped their bickering, which was commendable. But now they were trying to run military business.

"Send him away," Fetterer said. "He knows we're planning Armageddon."

"Yes sir," the aide said. He saluted sharply, wheeled, and marched out.

"To go on," Supreme General Fetterer said. "Behind Satan's first line of defence will be the resurrected sinners, and various elemental forces of evil. The fallen angels will act as his bomber corps. Dell's robot interceptors will meet them."

General Dell smiled grimly.

"Upon contact, MacFee's automatic tank corps will proceed towards the centre of the line. MacFee's automatic tank corps will proceed towards the centre," Fetterer went on, "supported by General Ongin's robot infantry. Dell will command the H bombing of the rear, which should be tightly massed. I will thrust with the mechanized cavalry, here and here."

The aide came back, and stood rigidly at attention. "Sir," he said, "the priest refuses to go. He says he must speak with you."

Supreme General Fetterer hesitated before saying no. He remembered that this was the Last Battle, and that the religious workers *were* connected with it. He decided to give the man five minutes.

"Show him in," he said.

The priest wore a plain business suit, to show that he represented no particular religion. His face was tired but determined.

"General," he said, "I am a representative of all the religious workers of the world, the priests, rabbis, ministers, mullahs, and all the rest. We beg of you, General, to let us fight in the Lord's battle."

Supreme General Fetterer drummed his fingers nervously against his side. He wanted to stay on friendly terms with these men. Even he, the Supreme Commander, might need a good word, when all was said and done. . . .

"You can understand my position," Fetterer said unhappily. "I'm a general. I have a battle to fight."

"But it's the Last Battle," the priest said. "It should be the people's battle."

"It is," Fetterer said. "It's being fought by their representatives, the military."

The priest didn't look at all convinced.

Fetterer said, "You wouldn't want to lose this battle, would you? Have Satan win?"

"Of course not," the priest murmured.

"Then we can't take chances," Fetterer said. "All the governments agreed on that, didn't they? Oh, it would be very nice to fight Armageddon with the mass of humanity. Symbolic, you might say. But could we be certain of victory?"

The priest tried to say something, but Fetterer was talking rapidly.

"How do we know the strength of Satan's forces? We simply *must* put forth our best foot, militarily speaking. And that means the automatic armies, the robot interceptors and tanks, the H bombs."

The priest looked very unhappy. "But it isn't *right*," he said. "Certainly you can find some place in your plan for *people*?"

Fetterer thought about it, but the request was impossible. The plan of battle was fully developed, beautiful, irresistible. Any introduction of a gross human element would only throw it out of order. No living flesh could stand the noise of that mechanical attack, the energy potentials humming in the air, the all-enveloping fire power. A human being who came within a hundred miles of the front would not live to see the enemy.

"I'm afraid not," Fetterer said.

"There are some," the priest said sternly, "who feel that it was an error to put this in the hands of the military."

"Sorry," Fetterer said cheerfully. "That's defeatist talk. If you don't mind—" He gestured at the door. Wearily, the priest left.

"These civilians," Fetterer mused. "Well gentlemen, are your troops ready?"

"We're ready to fight for Him," General MacFee said enthusiastically. "I can vouch for every automatic in my command. Their metal is shining, all relays have been renewed, and the energy reservoirs are fully charged. Sir, they're positively itching for battle!"

General Ongin snapped fully out of his daze. "The ground troops are ready, sir!"

"Air arm ready," General Dell said.

"Excellent," General Fetterer said. "All other arrangements have been made. Television facilities are available for the total population of the world. No one, rich or poor, will miss the spectacle of the Last Battle."

"And after the battle—" General Ongin began, and stopped. He looked at Fetterer.

Fetterer frowned deeply. He didn't know what was supposed to happen after the Battle. That part of it was, presumably, in the hands of the religious agencies.

"I suppose there'll be a presentation or something," he said vaguely.

"You mean we will meet—Him?" General Dell asked.

"Don't really know," Fetterer said. "But I should think so. After all—I mean, you know what I mean."

"But what should we wear?" General MacFee asked, in a sudden panic. "I mean, what *does* one wear?"

"What do the angels wear?" Fetterer asked Ongin.

"I don't know," Ongin said.

"Robes, do you think?" General Dell offered.

"No," Fetterer said sternly. "We will wear dress uniform, without decorations."

The generals nodded. It was fitting.

And then it was time.

Gorgeous in their battle array, the legions of Hell advanced over the desert. Hellish pipes skirled, hollow drums pounded, and the great ghost moved forward.

In a blinding cloud of sand, General MacFee's automatic tanks hurled themselves against the satanic foe. Immediately, Dell's automatic bombers screeched overhead, hurling their bombs on the massed horde of the damned. Fetterer thrust valiantly with his automatic cavalry.

Into this mêlée advanced Ongin's automatic infantry, and metal did what metal could.

The hordes of the damned overflowed the front, ripping apart tanks and robots. Automatic mechanisms died, bravely defending a patch of sand. Dell's bombers were torn from the skies by the fallen angels, led by Marchocias, his griffin's wings beating the air into a tornado.

The thin, battered line of robots held, against gigantic presences that smashed and scattered them, and struck terror into the hearts of television viewers in homes around the world. Like men, like heroes the robots fought, trying to force back the forces of evil.

Astaroth shrieked a command, and Behemoth lumbered forward. Bael, with a wedge of devils behind him, threw a charge at General Fetterer's crumbling left flank. Metal screamed, electrons howled in agony at the impact.

Supreme General Fetterer sweated and trembled, a thousand miles behind the firing line. But steadily, nervelessly, he guided the pushing of buttons and the throwing of levers.

His superb corps didn't disappoint him. Mortally damaged robots swayed to their feet and fought. Smashed, trampled, destroyed by the howling fiends, the robots managed to hold their line. Then the veteran Fifth Corps threw in a counter-attack, and the enemy front was pierced.

A thousand miles behind the firing line, the generals guided the mopping up operations.

"The battle is won," Supreme General Fetterer whispered, turning away from the television screen. "I congratulate you, gentlemen."

The generals smiled wearily.

They looked at each other, then broke into a spontaneous shout. Armageddon was won, and the forces of Satan had been vanquished.

But something was happening on their screens.

"Is that—is that—" General MacFee began, and then couldn't speak.

For The Presence was upon the battlefield, walking among the piles of twisted, shattered metal.

The generals were silent.

The Presence touched a twisted robot.

Upon the smoking desert, the robots began to move. The twisted, scored, fused metals straightened.

The robots stood on their feet again.

"MacFee," Supreme General Fetterer whispered. "Try your controls. Make the robots kneel or something."

The general tried, but his controls were dead.

The bodies of the robots began to rise in the air. Around them were the angels of the Lord, and the robot tanks and soldiers and bombers floated upward, higher and higher.

"He's saving them!" Ongin cried hysterically. "He's saving the robots!"

"It's a mistake!" Fetterer said. "Quick. Send a messenger to—no! We will go in person!"

And quickly a ship was commanded, and quickly they sped to the field of battle. But by then it was too late, for Armageddon was over, and the robots gone, and the Lord and his host departed.

HANDS OFF

THE SHIP'S MASS detector flared pink, then red. Agee had been dozing at the controls, waiting for Victor to finish making dinner. Now he looked up quickly. "Planet coming," he called, over the hiss of escaping air.

Captain Barnett nodded. He finished shaping a hot patch, and slapped it on *Endeavor's* worn hull. The whistle of escaping air dropped to a low moan, but was not entirely stopped. It never was.

When Barnett came over, the planet was just visible beyond the rim of a little red sun. It glowed green against the black night of space and gave both men an identical thought.

Barnett put the thought into words. "Wonder if there's anything on it worth taking," he said, frowning.

Agee lifted a white eyebrow hopefully. They watched as the dials began to register.

They would never have spotted the planet if they had taken *Endeavor* along the South Galactic Trades. But the Confederacy police were becoming increasingly numerous along that route and Barnett preferred to give them a wide berth.

The *Endeavor* was listed as a trader—but the only cargo she carried consisted of several bottles of an extremely powerful acid used in opening safes, and three medium-sized atomic bombs. The authorities looked with disfavour upon such goods and they were always trying to haul in the crew on some old charge—a murder on Luna, larceny on Omega, breaking and entering on Samia II. Old, almost forgotten crimes that the police drearily insisted on raking up.

To make matters worse, *Endeavor* was outgunned by the newer police cruisers. So they had taken an outside route to New Athens, where a big uranium strike had opened.

"Don't look like much," Agee commented, inspecting the dials critically.

"Might as well pass it by," Barnett said.

The readings were uninteresting. They showed a planet smaller than Earth, uncharted, and with no commercial value other than oxygen atmosphere.

As they swung past, their heavy-metals detector came to life.

"There's stuff down there!" Agee said, quickly interpreting the multiple readings. "Pure. *Very* pure—and on the surface!"

He looked at Barnett, who nodded. The ship swung towards the planet.

Victor came from the rear, wearing a tiny wool cap crammed on his big shaven head. He stared over Barnett's shoulder as Agee brought the ship down in a tight spiral. Within half a mile of the surface, they saw their deposit of heavy metal.

It was a spaceship, resting on its tail in a natural clearing.

"Now *this* is interesting," Barnett said. He motioned Agee to make a closer approach.

Agee brought the ship down with deft skill. He was well past the compulsory retirement limit for master pilots, but it didn't affect his co-ordination. Barnett, who found him stranded and penniless, had signed him on. The captain was always glad to help another human, if it was convenient and likely to be profitable. The two men shared the same attitude towards private property, but sometimes disagreed on ways of acquiring it. Agee preferred a sure thing. Barnett, on the other hand, had more courage than was good for a member of a relatively frail species like *Homo sapiens*.

Near the surface of the planet, they saw that the strange ship was larger than *Endeavor* and bright, shining new. The hull shape was unfamiliar, as were the markings.

"Ever see anything like it?" Barnett asked.

Agee searched his capacious memory. "Looks a bit like a Cephean job, only they don't build 'em so squat. We're pretty far out, you know. That ship might not even be from the Confederacy."

Victor stared at the ship, his big lips parted in wonder. He sighed noisily. "We could sure use a ship like that, huh, Captain?"

Barnett's sudden smile was like a crack appearing in granite. "Victor," he said, "in your simplicity, you have gone to the heart of the matter. We *could* use a ship like that. Let's go down and talk with its skipper."

Before strapping in, Victor made sure the freeze-blasters were on full charge.

On the ground, they sent up an orange and green parley flare, but there was no answer from the alien ship. The planet's atmosphere tested breathable, with a temperature of 72 degrees Fahrenheit. After waiting a few minutes, they marched out, freeze-blasters ready under their jumpers.

All three men wore studiously pleasant smiles as they walked the fifty yards between ships.

Up close, the ship was magnificent. Its glistening silver-grey hide had hardly been touched by meteor strikes. The airlock was open and a low hum told them that the generators were recharging.

"Anyone home?" Victor shouted into the airlock. His voice echoed hollowly through the ship. There was no answer—only the soft hum of the generators and the rustle of grass on the plain.

"Where do you suppose they went?" Agee asked.

"For a breath of air, probably," Barnett said. "I don't suppose they'd expect any visitors."

Victor placidly sat down on the ground. Barnett and Agee prowled around the base of the ship, admiring its great drive ports.

"Think you can handle it?" Barnett asked.

"I don't see why not," Agee said. "For one thing, it's conventional drive. The servos don't matter—oxygen-breathers use similar drive control systems. It's just a matter of time until I figure it out."

"Someone coming," Victor called.

They hurried back to the airlock. Three hundred yards from the ship was a ragged forest. A figure had just emerged from among the trees, and was walking towards them.

Agee and Victor drew their blasters simultaneously.

Barnett's binoculars resolved the tiny figure into a rectangular shape, about two feet high by a foot wide. The alien was less than two inches thick and had no head.

Barnett frowned. He had never seen a rectangle floating above tall grass.

Adjusting the binoculars, he saw that the alien was roughly humanoid. That is, it had four limbs. Two, almost hidden by the grass, were being used for walking, and the other two jutted stiffly into the air. In its middle, Barnett could just make out two tiny eyes and a mouth. The creature was not wearing any sort of suit or helmet.

"Queer-looking," Agee muttered, adjusting the aperture of his blaster. "Suppose he's all there is?"

"Hope so," Barnett said, drawing his own blaster.

"Range about two hundred yards." Agee levelled his weapon, then looked up. "Did you want to talk to him first, Captain?"

"What's there to say?" Barnett asked, smiling lazily. "Let him get a little closer, though. We don't want to miss."

Agee nodded and kept the alien steadily in his sights.

Kalen had stopped at this deserted little world hoping to blast out a few tons of erol, a mineral highly prized by the Mabogian people. He had had no luck. The unused thetnite bomb was still lodged in his body pouch, next to a stray kerla nut. He would have to return to Mabog with ballast instead of cargo.

Well, he thought, emerging from the forest, better luck next—

He was shocked to see a thin, strangely tapered spaceship near his own. He had never expected to find anyone else on this deadly little world.

And the inhabitants were waiting in front of his own airlock! Kalen saw at once they were roughly Mabogian in form. There was a race much like them in the Mabogian Union, but their spaceships were completely different. Intuition suggested that these aliens might well be representative of that great civilization rumoured to be on the periphery of the Galaxy.

He advanced eagerly to meet them.

Strange, the aliens were not moving. Why didn't they come forward to meet him? He knew that they saw him, because all three were pointing at him.

He walked faster, realizing that he knew nothing of their customs. He only hoped that they didn't run to long-drawn out ceremonies. Even an hour on this inimical world had tired him. He was hungry, badly in need of a shower...

Something intensely cold jarred him backward. He looked around apprehensively. Was this some unknown property of the planet?

He moved forward again. Another bolt lanced into him, frosting the outer layer of his hide.

This was serious. Mabogians were among the toughest lifeforms in the Galaxy, but they had their limits. Kalen looked around for the source of the trouble.

The aliens were *shooting* at him!

For a moment, his thinking centres refused to accept the evidence of his senses. Kalen knew what murder was. He had observed this perversity with stunned horror among certain debased animal forms. And, of course, there were the abnormal psychology books, which documented every case of premeditated murder that had occurred in the history of Mabog.

But to have such a thing actually happen to *him*! Kalen was unable to believe it.

Another bolt lanced into him. Kalen stood still, trying to convince himself that this was really happening. He couldn't understand how creatures with sufficient sense of co-operation to run a spaceship could be capable of *murder*.

Besides, they didn't even know him!

Almost too late, Kalen whirled and ran towards the forest. All three aliens were firing now and the grass around him was crackling white with frost. His skin surface was completely frosted over. Cold was something the Mabogian constitution was not designed for and the chill was creeping into his internal organs.

But he could still hardly believe it.

Kalen reached the forest and a double blast caught him as he slid behind a tree. He could feel his internal system labouring desperately to restore warmth to his body and, with profound regret, he allowed the darkness to take him.

"Stupid kind of alien," Agee observed, holstering his blaster.

"Stupid and strong," Barnett said. "But no oxygen-breather can take much of that." He grinned proudly and slapped the silver-grey side of the ship. "We'll christen her *Endeavor II*."

"Three cheers for the captain!" Victor cried enthusiastically.

"Save your breath," Barnett said. "You'll need it." He glanced overhead. "We've got about four hours of light left. Victor, transfer the food, oxygen and tools from *Endeavor I* and disarm her piles. We'll come back and salvage the old girl some day. But I want to blast off by sundown."

Victor hurried off. Barnet and Agee entered the ship.

The rear half of *Endeavor II* was filled with generators, engines, converters, servos, fuel and air tanks. Past that was an enormous cargo hold, occupying almost another half of the ship. It was filled with nuts of all shapes and colours, ranging in size from two inches in diameter to some twice the size of a man's head. That left only two compartments in the bow of the ship.

The first should have been a crew room, since it was the only available living space. But it was completely bare. There were no deceleration cots, no tables or chairs—nothing but polished metal floor. In the walls and ceiling were several small openings, but their purpose was not readily apparent.

Connected to this room was the pilot's compartment. It was very small, barely large enough for one man, and the panel under the observation blister was packed solidly with instruments.

"It's all yours," Barnett said. "Let's see what you can do."

Agee nodded, looked for a chair, then squatted in front of the panel. He began to study the layout.

In several hours, Victor had transferred all their stores to *Endeavor II*. Agee still had not touched anything. He was trying to figure out what controlled what, from the size, colour, shape and location of the instruments. It wasn't easy, even accepting similar nervous systems and patterns of thought. Did the auxiliary set-up system run from left to right? If not, he would have to unlearn his previous flight co-ordination. Did red signify danger to the designers of this ship? If it did, that big switch could be for dumping fuel. But red could also mean hot fuel, in which case the switch might control coarse energy flow.

For all he knew, its purpose was to overload the piles in case of enemy attack.

Agee kept all this in mind as he studied the controls. He wasn't too worried. For one thing, spaceships were tough beasts, practically indestructible from the inside. For another, he believed he had caught on to the pattern.

Barnett stuck his head in the doorway, with Victor close behind him. "You ready?"

Agee looked over the panel. "Guess so." He touched a dial lightly. "This *should* control the airlocks."

He turned it. Victor and Barnett waited, perspiring, in the chilly room.

They heard the smooth flow of lubricated metal. The airlocks had closed.

Agee grinned and blew on his fingertips for luck. "Here's the air-control system." He closed a switch.

Out of the ceiling, a yellow smoke began to trickle.

"Impurities in the system," Agee muttered, adjusting a dial. Victor began to cough.

"Turn it off," Barnett said.

The smoke poured out in thick streams, filling the two rooms almost instantly.

"*Turn it off!*"

"I can't see it!" Agee thrust at the switch, missed and struck a button under it. Immediately the generators began to whine angrily. Blue sparks danced along the panel and jumped to the wall.

Agee staggered back from the panel and collapsed. Victor was already at the door to the cargo hold, trying to hammer it down with his fists. Barnett covered his mouth with one hand and rushed to the panel. He fumbled blindly for the switch, feeling the ship revolve giddily around him.

Victor fell to the deck, still beating feebly at the door.

Barnett jabbed blindly at the panel.

Instantly the generators stopped. Then Barnett felt a cold breeze on his face. He wiped his streaming eyes and looked up.

A lucky stab had closed the ceiling vents, cutting off the yellow gas. He had accidentally opened the locks, and the gas in the ship was being replaced by the cold night air of the planet. Soon the atmosphere was breathable.

Victor climbed shakily to his feet, but Agee didn't move. Barnett gave the old pilot artificial respiration, cursing softly as he did. Agee's eyelids finally fluttered and his chest began to rise and fall. A few minutes later, he sat up and shook his head.

"What *was* that stuff?" Victor asked.

"I'm afraid," Barnett said, "that our alien friend considered it a breathable atmosphere."

Agee shook his head. "Can't be, Captain. He was here on an oxygen world, walking around with no helmet—"

"Air requirements vary tremendously," Barnett pointed out. "Let's face it—our friend's physical make-up was quite different from ours."

"That's not so good," Agee said.

The three men looked at each other. In the silence that followed, they heard a faint, ominous sound.

"What was that?" Victor yelped, yanking out his blaster.

"Shut up!" Barnett shouted.

They listened. Barnett could feel the hairs lift on the back of his neck as he tried to identify the sound.

It came from a distance. It sounded like metal striking a hard non-metallic object.

The three men looked out of the port. In the last glow of sunset, they could see the main port of *Endeavor I* was open. The sound was coming from the ship.

"It's impossible," Agee said. "The freeze-blasters—"

"Didn't kill him," Barnett finished.

"That's bad," Agee grunted. "That's very bad."

Victor was still holding his blaster. "Captain, suppose I wander over that way—"

Barnett shook his head. "He wouldn't let you within ten feet of the lock. No, let me think. Was there anything on board he could use? The piles?"

"I've got the links, Captain," Victor said.

"Good. Then there's nothing that—"

"The acid," Agee interrupted. "It's powerful stuff. But I don't suppose he can do much with that stuff."

"Not a thing," Barnett said. "We're in this ship and we're staying here. But get it off the ground now."

Agee looked at the instrument panel. Half an hour ago, he had almost understood it. Now it was a cunningly rigged death trap— a booby trap, with invisible wires leading to destruction.

The trap was unintentional. But a spaceship was necessarily a machine for living as well as travelling. The controls would try to reproduce the alien's living conditions, supply his needs.

That might be fatal to them.

"I wish I knew what kind of planet he came from," Agee said unhappily. If they knew the alien's environment, they could anticipate what his ship would do.

All they knew was that he breathed a poisonous yellow gas.

"We're doing all right," Barnett said, without much confidence. "Just dope out the drive mechanism and we'll leave everything else alone."

Agee turned back to the controls.

Barnett wished he knew what the alien was up to. He stared

at the bulk of his old ship in the twilight and listened to the incomprehensible sound of metal striking non-metal.

Kalen was surprised to find that he was still alive. But there was a saying among his people—"Either a Mabogian is killed fast or he isn't killed at all." It was not at all—so far.

Groggily, he sat up and leaned against a tree. The single red sun of the planet was low on the horizon and breezes of poisonous oxygen swirled around him. He tested at once and found that his lungs were still securely sealed. His life-giving yellow air, although vitiated from long use, was still sustaining him.

But he couldn't seem to get oriented. A few hundred yards away, his ship was resting peacefully. The fading red light glistened from its hull and, for a moment, Kalen was convinced that there were no aliens. He had imagined the whole thing and now he would return to his ship...

He saw one of the aliens loaded down with goods, enter his vessel. In a little while, the airlocks closed.

It was true, all of it. He wrenched his mind back to grim realities.

He needed food and air badly. His outer skin was dry and cracked, and in need of nutritional cleaning. But food, air and cleansers were on his lost ship. All he had was a single red kerla nut and the thetnite bomb in his body pouch.

If he could open and eat the nut, he could regain a little strength. But how could he open it?

It was shocking, how complete his dependence on machinery had been! How he would have to find some way of doing the most simple, ordinary, everyday things—the sort of things his ship had done automatically, without the operator even thinking about them.

Kalen noticed that the aliens had apparently abandoned their own ship. Why? It didn't matter. Out on the plain, he would die before morning. His only chance for survival lay inside their ship.

He slid slowly through the grass, stopping only when a wave of dizziness swept over him. He tried to keep watch on his ship. If the aliens came after him now, all would be lost. But nothing happened. After an eternity of crawling, he reached the ship and slipped inside.

It was twilight. In the dimness, he could see that the vessel was old. The walls, too thin in the first place, had been patched and repatched. Everything spoke of long, hard use.

He could understand why they wanted his ship.

Another wave of dizziness swept over him. It was his body's way of demanding immediate attention.

Food seemed to be the first problem. He slipped the kerla nut out of his pouch. It was round, almost four inches in diameter, and its hide was two inches thick. Nuts of this sort were the main ingredient of a Mabogian spaceman's diet. They were energy-packed and would last almost forever, sealed.

He propped the nut against a wall, found a steel bar and smashed down on it. The bar, striking the nut, emitted a hollow, drum-like sound. The nut was undamaged.

Kalen wondered if the sound could be heard by the aliens. He would have to chance it. Setting himself firmly, he flailed away. In fifteen minutes, he was exhausted and the bar was bent almost in half.

The nut was undamaged.

He was unable to open the nut without a Cracker, a standard device on every Mabogian ship. No one ever thought of opening a nut in any other way.

It was terrifying evidence of his helplessness.

He lifted the bar for another whack and found that his limbs were stiffening. He dropped the bar and took stock.

His chilled outer hide was hampering his motions. The skin was hardening slowly into impervious horn. Once the hardening was completed, he would be immobilized. Frozen in position, he would sit or stand until he died of suffocation.

Kalen fought back a wave of despair and tried to think. He had to treat his skin without delay. That was more important than food. On board his own ship, he would wash and bathe it, soften it and eventually cure it. But it was doubtful whether the aliens carried the proper cleansers.

The only other course was to rip off his outer hide. The second layer would be tender for a few days, but at least he would be mobile.

He searched on stiffening limbs for a Changer. Then he realized that the aliens wouldn't have even this piece of basic apparatus. He was still on his own.

He took the steel bar, bent it into a hook and inserted the point under a fold of skin. He yanked upward with all his strength.

His skin refused to yield.

Next, he wedged himself between a generator and the wall and inserted the hook in a different way. But his arms weren't long enough to gain leverage, and the tough hide held stubbornly.

He tried a dozen different positions, unsuccessfully. Without mechanical assistance, he couldn't hold himself rigidly enough.

Wearily, he dropped the bar. He could do nothing, nothing at all.

Then he remembered the thetnite bomb in his pouch.

A primitive part of his mind which he had not previously known existed said that there was an easy way out of all this. He could slip the bomb under the hull of his ship, while the aliens weren't looking. The light charge would do no more than throw the ship twenty or thirty feet into the air, but would not really damage it. The aliens, however, would undoubtedly be killed.

Kalen was horrified. How could he think such a thing? The Mabogian ethic, ingrained in the fibre of his being, forbade the taking of intelligent life for any reason whatsoever. *Any* reason.

"But wouldn't this be justified?" that primitive portion of his mind whispered. "These aliens are diseased. You would be doing the Universe a favour by getting rid of them and only incidentally helping yourself. Don't think of it as murder. Consider it extermination."

He took the bomb out of his pouch and looked at it, then hastily put it away. "No!" he told himself, with less conviction.

He refused to think any more. On tired, almost rigid limbs, he began to search the alien ship, looking for something that would save his life.

Agee was crouched in the pilot's compartment, wearily marking switches with an indelible pencil. His lungs ached and he had been working all night. Now there was a bleak grey dawn outside and a chill wind was whipping around *Endeavor II*. The spaceship was lighted but cold, for Agee didn't want to touch the temperature controls.

Victor came into the crew room, staggering under the weight of a heavy packing case.

"Barnett?" Agee called out.

"He's coming," Victor said.

The captain wanted all their equipment up front, where they could get at it quickly. But the crew room was small and he had used most of the available space.

Looking around for a spot to put the case, Victor noticed a door in one wall. He pressed its stud and the door slid smartly into the ceiling revealing a room the size of a closet, Victor decided it would make an ideal storage space.

Ignoring the crushed red shells on the floor, he slid the case inside. Immediately, the ceiling of the little room began to descend.

Victor let out a yell that could be heard throughout the ship. He leaped up—and slammed his head against the ceiling. He fell on his face, stunned.

Agee rushed out of the pilot's compartment and Barnett sprinted into the room. Barnett grabbed Victor's legs and tried to drag him out, but Victor was heavy and the captain was unable to get a purchase on the smooth metal floor.

With rare presence of mind, Agee up-ended the packing case. The ceiling was momentarily stopped by it.

Together, Barnett and Agee tugged at Victor's legs. They managed to drag him out just in time. The heavy case splintered and, in another moment, was crushed like a piece of balsa wood.

The ceiling of the little room, descending on a greased shaft, compressed the packing case to a six-inch thickness. Then its gears clicked and it slid back into place without a sound.

Victor sat up and rubbed his head. "Captain," he said plaintively, "can't we get our own ship back?"

Agee was doubtful of the venture, too. He looked at the deadly little room, which again resembled a closet with crushed red shells on the floor.

"Sure seems like a jinx ship," he said worriedly. "Maybe Victor's right."

"You want to give her up?" Barnett asked.

Agee squirmed uncomfortably and nodded. "Trouble is," he said, not looking at Barnett, "we don't know what she'll do next. It's just too risky, Captain."

"Do you realize what you'd be giving up?" Barnett challenged. "Her hull alone is worth a fortune. Have you looked at her engines? There's nothing this side of Earth that could stop her. She could drill her way through a planet and come out the other side with all her paint on. And you want to give her up!"

"She won't be worth much if she kills us," Agee objected.

Victor nodded emphatically. Barnett stared at them.

"Now listen to me carefully," Barnett said. "We are *not* going to give up this ship. She is *not* jinxed. She's alien and filled with alien apparatus. All we have to do is keep our hands off things until we reach drydock. Understand?"

Agee wanted to say something about closets that turned into hydraulic presses. It didn't seem to him a promising sign for the future. But, looking at Barnett's face, he decided against it.

"Have you marked all the operating controls?" Barnett asked.

"Just a few more to go," Agee said.

"Right. Finish up and those are the only ones we'll touch. If we leave the rest of the ship alone, she'll leave us alone. There's no danger if we just keep *hands off*."

Barnett wiped perspiration from his face, leaned against a wall and unbuttoned his coat.

Immediately, two metal bands slid out of openings on either side of him and circled his waist and stomach.

Barnett stared at them for a moment, then threw himself forward with all his strength. The bands didn't give. There was a peculiar clicking sound in the walls and a slender wire filament slid out. It touched Barnett's coat appraisingly, then retreated into the wall.

Agee and Victor stared helplessly.

"Turn it off," Barnett said tensely.

Agee rushed into the control room. Victor continued staring. Out of the wall slid a metal limb, tipped with a glittering three-inch blade.

"*Stop it!*" Barnett screamed.

Victor unfroze. He ran up and tried to wrench the metal limb out of the wall. It twisted once and sent him reeling across the room.

With the precision of a surgeon, the knife slit Barnett's coat down the middle, not touching the shirt underneath. Then the limb slid out of sight.

Agee was punching controls now and the generators whined, the locks opened and closed, stabilizers twitched, lights flickered. The mechanism that held Barnett was unaffected.

The slender filament returned. It touched Barnett's shirt and paused an instant. The internal mechanism chittered alarmingly. The filament touched Barnett's shirt again, as if unsure of its function in this case.

Agee shouted from the control room, "I can't turn it off! It must be fully automatic!"

The filament slid into the wall. It disappeared and the knife-tipped limb slid out.

By this time, Victor had located a heavy wrench. He rushed over, swung it above his head and smashed it against the limb, narrowly missing Barnett's head.

The limb was not even dented. Serenely, it cut Barnett's shirt from his back, leaving him naked to the waist.

Barnett was not hurt, but his eyes rolled wildly as the filament came out. Victor put his fist in his mouth and backed away. Agee shut his eyes.

The filament touched Barnett's warm living flesh, clucked approvingly and slid back into the wall. The bands opened. Barnett tumbled to his knees.

For a while, no one spoke. There was nothing to say. Barnett stared moodily into space. Victor started to crack his knuckles over and over again, until Agee nudged him.

The old pilot was trying to figure out why the mechanism had slit Barnett's clothing and then stopped when it reached living flesh. Was this the way the alien undressed himself? It didn't make sense. But then, the press-closet didn't make sense, either.

In a way, he was glad it had happened. It must have taught Barnett something. Now they would leave this jinxed monstrosity and figure out a way of regaining their own ship.

"Get me a shirt," Barnett said. Victor hurriedly found one for him. Barnett slipped it on, staying clear of the walls. "How soon can you get this ship moving?" he asked Agee, a bit unsteadily.

"*What?*"

"You heard me."

"Haven't you had enough?" Agee gasped.

"No. How soon can we blast out?"

"About another hour," Agee grumbled. What else could he say? The captain was just too much. Wearily, Agee returned to the control room.

Barnett put a sweater over the shirt and a coat over that. It was chilly in the room and he had begun to shiver violently.

Kalen lay motionless on the deck of the alien ship. Foolishly, he had wasted most of his remaining strength in trying to rip off his stiff outer hide. But the hide grew progressively tougher as he grew weaker. Now it seemed hardly worthwhile to move. Better to rest and feel his internal fires burn lower...

Soon he was dreaming of the ridged hills of Mabog and the great port of Canthanope, where the interstellar traders swung down with their strange cargoes. He was there in twilight, looking over the flat roofs at the two great setting suns. But why were they setting together in the south, the blue sun and the yellow? How could they set together in the south? A physical impossibility.... Perhaps his father could explain it, for it was rapidly growing dark.

He shook himself out of the fantasy and stared at the grim light of morning. This was not the way for a Mabogian spaceman to die. He would try again.

After half an hour of slow, painful searching, he found a sealed metal box in the rear of the ship. The aliens had evidently overlooked it. He wrenched off the top. Inside were several bottles, carefully fastened and padded against shock. Kalen lifted one and examined it.

It was marked with a large white symbol. There was no reason why he should know the symbol, but it seemed faintly familiar. He searched his memory, trying to recall where he had seen it.

Then, hazily, he remembered. It was a representation of a humanoid skull. There was one humanoid race in the Mabogian Union and he had seen replicas of their skulls in a museum.

But why would anyone put such a thing on a bottle?

To Kalen, a skull conveyed an emotion of reverence. This must be what the manufacturers had intended. He opened the bottle and sniffed.

The odour was interesting. It reminded him of—

Skin-cleansing solution!

Without further delay, he poured the entire bottle over himself.

Hardly daring to hope, he waited. If he could put his skin back into working order...

Yes, the liquid in the skull-marked bottle *was* a mild cleanser! It was pleasantly scented, too.

He poured another bottle over his armoured hide and felt the nutritious fluid seep in. His body, starved for nourishment, called eagerly for more. He drained another bottle.

For a long time, Kalen just lay back and let the life-giving fluid soak in. His skin loosened and became pliable. He could feel a new surge of energy within him, a new will to live.

He *would* live!

After the bath, Kalen examined the spaceship's controls, hoping to pilot the old crate back to Mabog. There were immediate difficulties. For some reason, the piloting controls weren't sealed into a separate room. He wondered why not? Those strange creatures couldn't have turned their whole ship into a deceleration chamber. They couldn't! There wasn't enough tank space to hold the fluid.

It was perplexing, but everything about the aliens was perplexing. He could overcome that difficulty. But when Kalen inspected the engines, he saw that a vital link had been removed from the piles. They were useless.

That left only one alternative. He had to win back his own ship. But how?

He paced the deck restlessly. The Mabogian ethic forbade killing intelligent life, and there were no ifs or buts about it. Under no circumstances—not even to save your own life—were you allowed to kill. It was a wise rule and had served Mabog well. By strict adherence to it, the Mabogians had avoided war for three thousand years and had trained their people to a high degree of civilization. Which would have been impossible had they allowed exceptions to creep in. Ifs and buts could erode the soundest of principles.

He could not be a backslider.

But was he going to die here passively?

Looking down, Kalen was surprised to see that a puddle of cleaning solution had eaten a hole in the deck. How flimsily these ships were made—even a mild cleaning solution could damage one! The aliens themselves must be very weak.

One thetnite bomb could do it.

He walked to the port. No one seemed to be on guard. He supposed they were too busy preparing for take-off. It would be easy to slide through the grass, up to his ship...

And no one on Mabog would ever have to know about it.

Kalen found, to his surprise, that he had covered almost half the distance between ships without realizing it. Strange, how his body could do things without his mind being aware of it.

He took out the bomb and crawled another twenty feet.

Because after all—taking the long view—what difference would this killing make?

"Aren't you ready yet?" Barnett asked, at noon.

"I guess so," Agee said. He looked over the marked panel. "As ready as I'll ever be."

Barnett nodded. "Victor and I will strap down in the crew room. Take off under minimum acceleration."

Barnett returned to the crew room. Agee fastened the straps he had rigged and rubbed his hands together nervously. As far as he knew, all the essential controls were marked. Everything should go all right. He hoped.

For there were that closet and the knife. It was anyone's guess what this insane ship would do next.

"Ready out here," Barnett called from the crew room.

"All right. About ten seconds." He closed and sealed the airlocks. His door closed automatically, cutting him off from the crew room. Feeling a slight touch of claustrophobia, Agee activated the piles. Everything was fine so far.

There was a thin slick of oil on the deck. Agee decided it was from a loose joint and ignored it. The control surfaces worked beautifully. He punched a course into the ship's tape and activated the flight controls.

Then he felt something lapping against his foot. Looking down, he was amazed to see that thick, evil-smelling oil was almost three inches deep on the deck. It was quite a leak. He couldn't understand how a ship as well built as this could have such a flaw. Unstrapping himself, he groped for the source.

He found it. There were four small vents in the deck and each of them was feeding a smooth, even flow of oil.

Agee punched the stud that opened his door and found that it remained sealed. Refusing to grow panicky, he examined the door with care.

It *should* open.

It didn't.

The oil was almost up to his knees.

He grinned foolishly. Stupid of him! The pilot room was sealed from the control board. He pressed the release and went back to the door.

It still refused to open.

Agee tugged at it with all his strength, but it wouldn't budge. He waded back to the control panel. There had been no oil when they found the ship. That meant there had to be a drain somewhere.

The oil was waist-deep before he found it. Quickly the oil disappeared. Once it was gone, the door opened easily.

"What's the matter?" Barnett asked.

Agee told him.

"So that's how he does it," Barnett said quietly. "Glad I found out."

"Does what?" Agee asked, feeling that Barnett was taking the whole thing too lightly.

"How he stands the acceleration of take-off. It bothered me. He hadn't anything on board that resembled a bed or cot. No chairs, nothing to strap into. So he floats in the oil bath, which turned on automatically when the ship is prepared for flight."

"But why wouldn't the door open?" Agee asked.

"Isn't it obvious?" Barnett said, smiling patiently. "He wouldn't want oil all over the ship. And he wouldn't want it to drain out accidentally."

"We can't take off," Agee insisted.

"Why not?"

"Because I can't breathe very well under oil. It turns on automatically with the power and there's no way of turning it off."

"Use your head," Barnett told him. "Just tie down the drain switch. The oil will be carried away as fast as it comes in."

"Yeah, I hadn't thought of that," Agee admitted unhappily.

"Go ahead, then."

"I want to change my clothes first."

"No. Get this damned ship off the ground."

"But, Captain—"

"Get her moving," Barnett ordered. "For all we know, that alien is planning something."

Agee shrugged his shoulders, returned to the pilot room and strapped in.

"Ready?"

"Yes, get her moving."

He tied down the drain circuit and the oil flowed safely in and out, not rising higher than the tops of his shoes. He activated all the controls without further incident.

"Here goes." He set minimum acceleration and blew on his fingertips for luck.

Then he punched the blast-switch.

With profound regret, Kalen watched his ship depart. He was still holding the thetnite bomb in his hand.

He had reached his ship, had even stood under her for a few seconds. Then he had crept back to the alien vessel. He had been unable to set the bomb. Centuries of conditioning were too much to overcome in a few hours.

Conditioning—and something more.

Few individuals of any race murder for pleasure. There are perfectly adequate reasons to kill, though, reasons which might satisfy any philosopher.

But, once accepted, there are more reasons, and more and more. And murder, once accepted, is hard to stop. It leads irresistibly to war and, from there, to annihilation.

Kalen felt that this murder somehow involved the destiny of his race. His abstinence had been almost a matter of race-survival.

But it didn't make him feel any better.

He watched his ship dwindle to a dot in the sky. The aliens were leaving at a ridiculously slow speed. He could think of no reason for this, unless they were doing it for his benefit.

Undoubtedly they were sadistic enough for that.

Kalen returned to the ship. His will to live was as strong as ever. He had no intention of giving up. He would hang on to life as long as he could, hoping for the one chance in a million that would bring another ship to this planet.

Looking around, he thought that he might concoct an air substitute out of the skull-marked cleanser. It would sustain him for a day or two. Then, if he could open the kerla nut...

He thought he heard a noise outside and rushed to look. The sky was empty. His ship had vanished, and he was alone.

He returned to the alien ship and set about the serious business of staying alive.

As Agee recovered consciousness, he found that he had managed to cut the acceleration in half, just before passing out. This was the only thing that had saved his life.

And the acceleration, hovering just above zero on the dial, was still unbearably heavy! Agee unsealed the door and crawled out.

Barnett and Victor had burst their straps on the take-off. Victor was just returning to consciousness. Barnett picked himself out of a pile of smashed cases.

"Do you think you're flying in a circus?" he complained. "I told you *minimum acceleration*."

"I started *under* minimum acceleration," Agee said. "Go read the tape for yourself."

Barnett marched to the control room. He came out quickly.

"That's bad. Our alien friend operates this ship at three times our acceleration."

"That's the way it looks."

"I hadn't thought of that," Barnett said thoughtfully. "He must come from a heavy planet—a place where you have to blast out at high speed, if you expect to get out at all."

"What hit me?" Victor groaned, rubbing his head.

There was a clicking in the walls. The ship was fully awake now, and its servos turned on automatically.

"Getting warm, isn't it?" Victor asked.

"Yeah, and thick," Agee said. "Pressure build-up." He went back to the control room. Barnett and Victor stood anxiously in the doorway, waiting.

"I can't turn it off," Agee said, wiping perspiration from his streaming face. "The temperature and pressure are automatic. They must go to 'normal' as soon as the ship is in flight."

"You damn well better turn them off," Barnett told him. "We'll fry in here if you don't."

"There's no way."

"He must have some kind of heat regulation."

"Sure—there!" Agee said, pointing. "The control is already set at its lowest point."

"What do you suppose his normal temperature is?" Barnett asked.

"I'd hate to find out," Agee said. "This ship is built of extremely high melting-point alloys. It's constructed to withstand ten times the pressure of an Earth ship. Put those together . . ."

"You must be able to turn it off somewhere!" Barnett said. He peeled off his jacket and sweater. The heat was mounting rapidly and the deck was becoming too hot to stand on.

"Turn it *off!*" Victor howled.

"Wait a minute," Agee said. "*I* didn't build this ship, you know. How should I know—"

"*Off!*" Victor screamed, shaking Agee up and down like a rag doll. "*Off!*"

"Let go!" Agee half-drew his blaster. Then, in a burst of inspiration, he turned off the ship's engines.

The clicking in the walls stopped. The room began to cool.

"What happened?" Victor asked.

"The temperature and pressure fall when the power is off," Agee said. "We're safe—as long as we don't run the engines."

"How long will it take us to coast to a port?" Barnett asked.

Agee figured it out. "About three years," he said. "We're pretty far out."

"Isn't there any way we can rip out those servos? Disconnect them?"

"They're built into the guts of the ship," Agee said. "We'd need a full machine shop and skilled help. Even then, it wouldn't be easy."

Barnett was silent for a long time. Finally he said, "All right."

"All right what?"

"We're licked. We've got to go back to that planet and take our own ship."

Agee heaved a sigh of relief and punched a new course on the ship's tape.

"You think the alien'll give it back?" Victor asked.

"Sure he will," Barnett said, "if he's not dead. He'll be pretty anxious to get his own ship back. And he has to leave our ship to get in his."

"Sure. But once he gets back in this ship . . ."

"We'll gimmick the controls," Barnett said. "That'll slow him down."

"For a little while," Agee pointed out. "But he'll get into the air sooner or later, with blood in his eye. We'll never outrun him."

"We won't have to," Barnett said. "All we have to do is get into the air first. He's got a strong hull, but I don't think it'll take three atomic bombs."

"I hadn't thought of that," Agee said, smiling faintly.

"Only logical move," Barnett said complacently. "The alloys in the hull will still be worth something. Now, get us back without frying us, if you can."

Agee turned the engines on. He swung the ship around in a tight curve, piling on all the Gs they could stand. The servos clicked on, and the temperature shot rapidly up. Once the curve was rounded, Agee pointed *Endeavor II* in the right direction and shut off the engines.

They coasted most of the way. But when they reached the planet, Agee had to leave the engines on, to bring them around the deceleration spiral and into the landing.

They were barely able to get out of the ship. Their skins were blistered and their shoes burned through. There was no time to gimmick the controls.

They retreated to the woods and waited.

"Perhaps he's dead," Agee said hopefully.

They saw a small figure emerge from *Endeavor I*. The alien was moving slowly, but he was moving.

They watched. "Suppose," Victor said, "he's made a weapon of some kind. Suppose he comes after us."

"Suppose you shut up," Barnett said.

The alien walked directly to his own ship. He went inside and shut the locks.

"All right," Barnett said, standing up. "We'd better blast off in a hurry. Agee, you take the controls. I'll connect the piles. Victor, you secure the locks. Let's go!"

They sprinted across the plain and, in a matter of seconds, had reached the open airlock of *Endeavor I*.

Even if he had wanted to hurry, Kalen didn't have the necessary strength to pilot his ship. But he knew that he was safe, inside. No alien was going to walk through those sealed ports.

He found a spare air tank in the rear and opened it. His ship filled with rich, life-giving yellow air. For long minutes, Kalen just breathed it.

Then he lugged three of the biggest kerla nuts he could find to the galley and let the Cracker open them.

After eating, he felt much better. He let the Changer take off his outer hide. The second layer was dead, too, and the Changer cut that off him, but stopped at the third, living layer.

He was almost as good as new when he slipped into the pilot's room.

It was apparent to him now that the aliens had been temporarily insane. There was no other way to explain why they had come back and returned his ship.

Therefore, he would find their authorities and report the location of the planet. They could be found and cured, once and for all.

Kalen felt very happy. He had not deviated from the Mabogian ethic, and that was the important thing. He could so easily have left the thetnite bomb in their ship, all set and timed. He could have wrecked their engines. And there *had* been a temptation.

But he had not. He had done nothing at all.

All he had done was construct a few minimum essentials for the preservation of life.

Kalen activated his controls and found that everything was in perfect working order. The acceleration fluid poured in as he turned on the piles.

Victor reached the airlock first and dashed in. Instantly, he was hurled back.

"What happened?" Barnett asked.

"Something hit me," Victor said.

Cautiously, they looked inside.

It was a very neat death trap. Wires from the storage batteries had been hooked in series and rigged across the port. If Victor had been touching the side of the ship, he would have been electrocuted instantly.

They shorted out the system and entered the ship.

It was a mess. Everything movable had been ripped up and strewn around. There was a bent steel bar in a corner. Their high-potency acid had been spilled over the deck and had eaten through in several places. The *Endeavor*'s old hull was holed.

"I never thought *he'd* gimmick *us!*" Agee said.

They explored further. Towards the rear was another booby

trap! The cargo hold door had been cunningly rigged to the starter motor. If anyone touched it, the door would be slammed against the wall. A man caught between would be crushed.

There were other hook-ups that gave no hint of their purpose.

"Can we fix it?" Barnett asked.

Agee shrugged his shoulders. "Most of our tools are still on board *Endeavor II*. I suppose we can get her patched up inside of a year. But even then, I don't know if the hull will hold."

They walked outside. The alien ship blasted off.

"What a monster!" Barnett said, looking at the acid-eaten hull of his ship.

"You can never tell what an alien will do," Agee answered.

"The only good alien is a dead alien," Victor said.

Endeavor I was now as incomprehensible and dangerous as *Endeavor II*.

And *Endeavor II* was gone.

THE PRIZE OF PERIL

RAEDER LIFTED HIS head cautiously above the window sill. He saw the fire-escape, and below it a narrow alley. There was a weather-beaten baby carriage in the alley, and three garbage cans. As he watched, a black-sleeved arm moved from behind the furthest can, with something shiny in its fist. Raeder ducked down. A bullet smashed through the window above his head and punctured the ceiling, showering him with plaster.

Now he knew about the alley. It was guarded, just like the door.

He lay at full length on the cracked linoleum, staring at the bullet hole in the ceiling, listening to the sounds outside the door. He was a tall man with bloodshot eyes and a two-day stubble. Grime and fatigue had etched lines into his face. Fear had touched his features, tightening a muscle here and twitching a nerve there. The results were startling. His face had character now, for it was re-shaped by the expectation of death.

There was a gunman in the alley and two on the stairs. He was trapped. He was dead.

Sure, Raeder thought, he still moved and breathed; but that was only because of death's inefficiency. Death would take care of him in a few minutes. Death would poke holes in his face and body, artistically dab his clothes with blood, arrange his limbs in some grotesque position of the graveyard ballet...

Raeder bit his lip sharply. He wanted to live. There had to be a way.

He rolled on to his stomach and surveyed the dingy cold-water apartment into which the killers had driven him. It was a perfect little one-room coffin. It had a door, which was watched, and a fire-escape, which was watched. And it had a tiny windowless bathroom.

He crawled to the bathroom and stood up. There was a ragged hole in the ceiling, almost four inches wide. If he could enlarge it, crawl through into the apartment above...

He heard a muffled thud. The killers were impatient. They were beginning to break down the door.

He studied the hole in the ceiling. No use even considering it. He could never enlarge it in time.

They were smashing against the door, grunting each time they struck. Soon the lock would tear out, or the hinges would pull out of the rotting wood. The door would go down, and the two blank-faced men would enter, dusting off their jackets...

But surely someone would help him! He took the tiny television set from his pocket. The picture was blurred, and he didn't bother to adjust it. The audio was clear and precise.

He listened to the well-modulated voice of Mike Terry addressing his vast audience.

"... terrible spot," Terry was saying. "Yes folks, Jim Raeder is in a truly terrible predicament. He had been hiding, you'll remember, in a third-rate Broadway hotel under an assumed name. It seemed safe enough. But the bellhop recognized him, and gave that information to the Thompson gang."

The door creaked under repeated blows. Raeder clutched the little television set and listened.

"Jim Raeder just managed to escape from the hotel! Closely pursued, he entered a brownstone at one fifty-six West End Avenue. His intention was to go over the roofs. And it might have worked, folks, it just might have worked. But the roof door was locked. It looked like the end.... But Raeder found that apartment seven was unoccupied and unlocked. He entered..."

Terry paused for emphasis, then cried: "—and now he's trapped there, trapped like a rat in a cage! The Thompson gang is breaking down the door! The fire-escape is guarded! Our camera crew, situated in a nearby building, is giving you a close-up now. Look, folks, just look! Is there no hope for Jim Raeder?"

Is there no hope, Raeder silently echoed, perspiration pouring from him as he stood in the dark, stifling little bathroom, listening to the steady thud against the door.

"Wait a minute!" Mike Terry cried. "Hang on, Jim Raeder, hang on a little longer. Perhaps there is hope! I have an urgent call from one of our viewers, a call on the Good Samaritan Line! Here's someone who thinks he can help you, Jim. Are you listening, Jim Raeder?"

Raeder waited, and heard the hinges tearing out of rotten wood.

"Go right ahead, sir," said Mike Terry. "What is your name, sir?"

"Er—Felix Bartholemow."

"Don't be nervous, Mr. Bartholemow. Go right ahead."

"Well, OK. Mr. Raeder," said an old man's shaking voice, "I used to live at one five six West End Avenue. Same apartment you're trapped in, Mr. Raeder—fact! Look, that bathroom has got a window, Mr. Raeder. It's been painted over, but it has got a—"

Raeder pushed the television set into his pocket. He located the outlines of the window and kicked. Glass shattered, and daylight poured startling in. He cleared the jagged sill and quickly peered down.

Below was a long drop to a concrete courtyard.

The hinges tore free. He heard the door opening. Quickly Raeder climbed through the window, hung by his fingertips for a moment, and dropped.

The shock was stunning. Groggily he stood up. A face appeared at the bathroom window.

"Tough luck," said the man, leaning out and taking careful aim with a snub-nosed .38.

At that moment a smoke bomb exploded inside the bathroom.

The killer's shot went wide. He turned, cursing. More smoke bombs burst in the courtyard, obscuring Raeder's figure.

He could hear Mike Terry's frenzied voice over the TV set in his pocket. *"Now run for it!"* Terry was screaming. *"Run, Jim Raeder, run for your life. Run now, while the killers' eyes are filled with smoke. And thank Good Samaritan Sarah Winters, of three four one two Edgar Street, Brockton, Mass., for donating five smoke bombs and employing the services of a man to throw them!"*

In a quieter voice, Terry continued: *"You've saved a man's life today, Mrs. Winters. Would you tell our audience how it—"*

Raeder wasn't able to hear any more. He was running through the smoke-filled courtyard, past clothes lines, into the open street.

He walked down 63rd Street, slouching to minimize his height, staggering slightly from exertion, dizzy from lack of food and sleep.

"Hey you!"

Raeder turned. A middle-aged woman was sitting on the steps of a brownstone, frowning at him.

"You're Raeder, aren't you? The one they're trying to kill?"

Raeder started to walk away.

"Come inside here, Raeder," the woman said.

Perhaps it was a trap. But Raeder knew that he had to depend upon the generosity and good-heartedness of the people. He was their representative, a projection of themselves, an average guy in trouble. Without them, he was lost. With them, nothing could harm him.

Trust in the people, Mike Terry had told him. They'll never let you down.

He followed the woman into her parlour. She told him to sit down and left the room, returning almost immediately with a plate of stew. She stood watching him while he ate, as one would watch an ape in the zoo eat peanuts.

Two children came out of the kitchen and stared at him. Three overalled men came out of the bedroom and focused a television camera on him. There was a big television set in the parlour. As he gulped his food, Raeder watched the image of Mike Terry, and listened to the man's strong, sincere, worried voice.

"*There he is, folks,*" Terry was saying. "*There's Jim Raeder now, eating his first square meal in two days. Our camera crews have really been working to cover this for you! Thanks, boys.... Folks, Jim Raeder has been given a brief sanctuary by Mrs. Velma O'Dell, of three forty-three Sixty-Third Street. Thank you, Good Samaritan O'Dell! It's really wonderful, how people from all walks of life have taken Jim Raeder to their hearts!*"

"You better hurry," Mrs. O'Dell said.

"Yes ma'am," Raeder said.

"I don't want no gunplay in my apartment."

"I'm almost finished, ma'am."

One of the children asked, "Aren't they going to kill him?"

"Shut up," said Mrs. O'Dell.

"*Yes Jim,*" chanted Mike Terry, "*you'd better hurry. Your killers aren't far behind. They aren't stupid men, Jim. Vicious, warped, insane—yes! But not stupid. They're following a trail of blood—blood from your torn hand, Jim!*"

Raeder hadn't realized until now that he'd cut his hand on the window sill.

"Here, I'll bandage that," Mrs. O'Dell said. Raeder stood up and let her bandage his hand. Then she gave him a brown jacket and a grey slouch hat.

"My husband's stuff," she said.

"*He has a disguise, folks!*" Mike Terry cried delightedly. "*This is something new! A disguise! With seven hours to go until he's safe!*"

"Now get out of here," Mrs. O'Dell said.

"I'm going, ma'am," Raeder said. "Thanks."

"I think you're stupid," she said. "I think you're stupid to be involved in this."

"Yes ma'am."

"It just isn't worth it."

Raeder thanked her and left. He walked to Broadway, caught a subway to 59th Street, then an uptown local to 86th. There he bought a newspaper and changed for the Manhasset thru-express.

He glanced at his watch. He had six and a half hours to go.

The subway roared under Manhattan. Raeder dozed, his bandaged hand concealed under the newspaper, the hat pulled over his face. Had he been recognized yet? Had he shaken the Thompson gang?

Or was someone telephoning them now?

Dreamily he wondered if he had escaped death. Or was he still a cleverly animated corpse, moving around because of death's inefficiency? (My dear, death is so *laggard* these days! Jim Raeder walked about for hours after he died, and actually answered people's *questions* before he could be decently buried!)

Raeder's eyes snapped open. He had dreamed something ... unpleasant. He couldn't remember what.

He closed his eyes again and remembered, with mild astonishment, a time when he had been in no trouble.

That was two years ago. He had been a big pleasant young man working as a truck driver's helper. He had no talents. He was too modest to have dreams.

The tight-faced little truck driver had the dreams for him. "Why not try for a television show, Jim? I would if I had your looks. They like nice average guys with nothing much on the ball. As contestants. Everybody likes guys like that. Why not look into it?"

So he had looked into it. The owner of the local television store had explained it further.

"You see, Jim, the public is sick of highly trained athletes with their trick reflexes and their professional courage. Who can feel for guys like that? Who can identify? People want to watch exciting things, sure, but not when some joker is making it his business for fifty thousand a year. That's why organized sports are in a slump. That's why the thrill shows are booming."

"I see," said Raeder.

"Six years ago, Jim, Congress passed the Voluntary Suicide Act. Those old senators talked a lot about free will and self-determinism at the time. But that's all crap. You know what the Act really means? It means the amateurs can risk their lives for the big loot, not just professionals. In the old days you had to be a professional boxer or footballer or hockey player if you wanted your brains beaten out legally for money. But now that opportunity is open to ordinary people like you, Jim."

"I see," Raeder said again.

"It's a marvellous opportunity. Take you. You're no better than anyone, Jim. Anything you can do, anyone can do. You're *average*. I think the thrill shows would go for you."

Raeder permitted himself to dream. Television shows looked like a sure road to riches for a pleasant young fellow with no particular talent or training. He wrote a letter to a show called *Hazard* and enclosed a photograph of himself.

Hazard was interested in him. The JBC network investigated, and found that he was average enough to satisfy the wariest viewer.

His parentage and affiliations were checked. At last he was sum-
moned to New York, and interviewed by Mr. Moulian.

Moulian was dark and intense, and chewed gum as he talked.
"You'll do," he snapped. "But not for *Hazard*. You'll appear on
Spills. It's a half-hour daytime show on Channel Three."

"Gee," said Raeder.

"Don't thank me. There's a thousand dollars if you win or place
second, and a consolation prize of a hundred dollars if you lose. But
that's not important."

"No sir."

"*Spills* is a *little* show. The JBC network uses it as a testing
ground. First- and second-place winners on *Spills* move on to
Emergency. The prizes are much bigger on *Emergency*."

"I know they are, sir."

"And if you do well on *Emergency* there are the first-class thrill
shows, like *Hazard* and *Underwater Perils*, with their nationwide
coverage and enormous prizes. And then comes the really big time.
How far you go is up to you."

"I'll do my best, sir," Raeder said.

Moulian stopped chewing gum for a moment and said, almost
reverently, "You can do it, Jim. Just remember. You're *the people*,
and *the people* can do anything."

The way he said it made Raeder feel momentarily sorry for Mr.
Moulian, who was dark and frizzy-haired and pop-eyed, and was
obviously not *the people*.

They shook hands. Then Raeder signed a paper absolving the
JBC of all responsibility should he lose his life, limbs or reason
during the contest. And he signed another paper exercising his
rights under the Voluntary Suicide Act. The law required this, and
it was a mere formality.

In three weeks, he appeared on *Spills*.

The programme followed the classic form of the automobile race.
Untrained drivers climbed into powerful American and European
competition cars and raced over a murderous twenty-mile course.
Raeder was shaking with fear as he slid his big Maserati into the
wrong gear and took off.

The race was a screaming, tyre-burning nightmare. Raeder
stayed back, letting the early leaders smash themselves up on the
counterbanked hairpin turns. He crept into third place when a
Jaguar in front of him swerved against an Alfa-Romeo, and the two
cars roared into a ploughed field. Raeder gunned for second place
on the last three miles, but couldn't find passing room. An S-curve
almost took him, but he fought the car back on the road, still holding third. Then the lead driver broke a crankshaft in the final fifty
yards, and Jim ended in second place.

He was now a thousand dollars ahead. He received four fan letters, and a lady in Oshkosh sent him a pair of argyles. He was invited to appear on *Emergency*.

Unlike the others, *Emergency* was not a competition-type programme. It stressed individual initiative. For the show, Raeder was knocked out with a non-habit-forming narcotic. He awoke in the cockpit of a small aeroplane, cruising on autopilot at ten thousand feet. His fuel gauge showed nearly empty. He had no parachute. He was supposed to land the plane.

Of course, he had never flown before.

He experimented gingerly with the controls, remembering that last week's participant had recovered consciousness in a submarine, had opened the wrong valve, and had drowned.

Thousands of viewers watched spellbound as this average man, a man just like themselves, struggled with the situation just as they would do. Jim Raeder was *them*. Anything he could do, they could do. He was representative of *the people*.

Raeder managed to bring the ship down in some semblance of a landing. He flipped over a few times, but his seat belt held. And the engine, contrary to expectation, did not burst into flames.

He staggered out with two broken ribs, three thousand dollars, and a chance, when he healed, to appear on *Torero*.

At last, a first-class thrill show! *Torero* paid ten thousand dollars. All you had to do was kill a black Miura bull with a sword, just like a real trained matador.

The fight was held in Madrid, since bullfighting was still illegal in the United States. It was nationally televised.

Raeder had a good cuadrilla. They liked the big, slow-moving American. The picadors really leaned into their lances, trying to slow the bull for him. The banderilleros tried to run the beast off his feet before driving in their banderillas. And the second matador, a mournful man from Algiceras, almost broke the bull's neck with fancy capework.

But when all was said and done it was Jim Raeder on the sand, a red muleta clumsily gripped in his left hand, a sword in his right, facing a ton of black, blood-streaked, wide-horned bull.

Someone was shouting, "Try for the lung, *hombre*. Don't be a hero, stick him in the lung." But Jim only knew what the technical adviser in New York had told him: Aim with the sword and go in over the horns.

Over he went. The sword bounced off bone, and the bull tossed him over its back. He stood up, miraculously ungouged, took another sword and went over the horns again with his eyes closed. The god who protects children and fools must have been watching, for the sword slid in like a needle through butter, and the bull looked startled, stared at him unbelievingly, and dropped like a deflated balloon.

They paid him ten thousand dollars, and his broken collarbone healed in practically no time. He received twenty-three fan letters, including a passionate invitation from a girl in Atlantic City, which he ignored. And they asked him if he wanted to appear on another show.

He had lost some of his innocence. He was now fully aware that he had been almost killed for pocket money. The big loot lay ahead. Now he wanted to be almost killed for something worthwhile.

So he appeared on *Underwater Perils*, sponsored by Fairlady's Soap. In face mask, respirator, weighted belt, flippers and knife, he slipped into the warm waters of the Caribbean with four other contestants, followed by a cage-protected camera crew. The idea was to locate and bring up a treasure which the sponsor had hidden there.

Mask diving isn't especially hazardous. But the sponsor had added some frills for public interest. The area was sown with giant clams, moray eels, sharks of several species, giant octopuses, poison coral, and other dangers of the deep.

It was a stirring contest. A man from Florida found the treasure in a deep crevice, but a moray eel found him. Another diver took the treasure, and a shark took him. The brilliant blue-green water became cloudy with blood, which photographed well on colour TV. The treasure slipped to the bottom and Raeder plunged after it, popping an eardrum in the process. He plucked it from the coral, jettisoned his weighted belt and made for the surface. Thirty feet from the top he had to fight another diver for the treasure.

They feinted back and forth with their knives. The man struck, slashing Raeder across the chest. But Raeder, with the self-possession of an old contestant, dropped his knife and tore the man's respirator out of his mouth.

That did it. Raeder surfaced, and presented the treasure at the stand-by boat. It turned out to be a package of Fairlady's Soap—"The Greatest Treasure of All."

That netted him twenty-two thousand dollars in cash and prizes, and three hundred and eight fan letters, and an interesting proposition from a girl in Macon, which he seriously considered. He received free hospitalization for his knife slash and burst eardrum, and injections for coral infection.

But best of all, he was invited to appear on the biggest of the thrill shows. *The Prize of Peril.*

And that was when the real trouble began....

The subway came to a stop, jolting him out of his reverie. Raeder pushed back his hat and observed, across the aisle, a man staring at him and whispering to a stout woman. Had they recognized him? He stood up as soon as the doors opened, and glanced at his watch. He had five hours to go.

At the Manhasset station he stepped into a taxi and told the driver to take him to New Salem.

"New Salem?" the driver asked, looking at him in the rear vision mirror.

"That's right."

The driver snapped on his radio. "Fare to New Salem. Yep, that's right. *New Salem.*"

They drove off. Raeder frowned, wondering if it had been a signal. It was perfectly usual for taxi drivers to report to their dispatchers, of course. But something about the man's voice...

"Let me off here," Raeder said.

He paid the driver and began walking down a narrow country road that curved through sparse woods. The trees were too small and too widely separated for shelter. Raeder walked on, looking for a place to hide.

There was a heavy truck approaching. He kept on walking, pulling his hat low on his forehead. But as the truck drew near, he heard a voice from the television set in his pocket. It cried, *"Watch out!"*

He flung himself into the ditch. The truck careened past, narrowly missing him, and screeched to a stop. The driver was shouting, "There he goes! Shoot, Harry, shoot!"

Bullets clipped leaves from the trees as Raeder sprinted into the woods.

"It's happened again!" Mike Terry was saying, his voice high-pitched with excitement. *"I'm afraid Jim Raeder let himself be lulled into a false sense of security. You can't do that, Jim! Not with your life at stake! Not with killers pursuing you! Be careful, Jim, you still have four and a half hours to go!"*

The driver was saying, "Claude, Harry, go around with the truck. We got him boxed."

"They've got you boxed, Jim Raeder!" Mike Terry cried. *"But they haven't got you yet! And you can thank Good Samaritan Susy Peters of twelve Elm Street, South Orange, New Jersey, for that warning shout just when the truck was bearing down on you. We'll have little Susy on stage in just a moment.... Look, folks, our studio helicopter has arrived on the scene. Now you can see Jim Raeder running, and the killers pursuing, surrounding him..."*

Raeder ran through a hundred yards of woods and found himself on a concrete highway, with open woods beyond. One of the killers was trotting through the woods behind him. The truck had driven to a connecting road, and was now a mile away, coming towards him.

A car was approaching from the other direction. Raeder ran into the highway, waving frantically. The car came to a stop.

"Hurry!" cried the blonde young woman driving it.

Raeder dived in. The woman made a U-turn on the highway. A bullet smashed through the windshield. She stamped on the accelerator, almost running down the lone killer who stood in the way.

The car surged away before the truck was within firing range.

Raeder leaned back and shut his eyes tightly. The woman concentrated on her driving, watching for the truck in her rear-vision mirror.

"*It's happened again!*" cried Mike Terry, his voice ecstatic. "*Jim Raeder has been plucked again from the jaws of death, thanks to Good Samaritan Janice Morrow of four three three Lexington Avenue, New York City. Did you ever see anything like it, folks? The way Miss Morrow drove through a fusillade of bullets and plucked Jim Raeder from the mouth of doom! Later we'll interview Miss Morrow and get her reactions. Now, while Jim Raeder speeds away—perhaps to safety, perhaps to further peril—we'll have a short announcement from our sponsor. Don't go away! Jim's got four hours and ten minutes until he's safe, anything can happen!*"

"OK," the girl said. "We're off the air now. Raeder, what in the hell is the matter with you?"

"Eh?" Raeder asked. The girl was in her early twenties. She looked efficient, attractive, untouchable. Raeder noticed that she had good features, a trim figure. And he noticed that she seemed angry.

"Miss," he said, "I don't know how to thank you for—"

"Talk straight," Janice Morrow said. "I'm no Good Samaritan. I'm employed by the JBC network."

"So the programme had me rescued!"

"Cleverly reasoned," she said.

"But why?"

"Look, this is an expensive show, Raeder. We have to turn in a good performance. If our rating slips, we'll all be in the street selling candy apples. And you aren't co-operating."

"What? Why?"

"Because you're terrible," the girl said bitterly. "You're a flop, a fiasco. Are you trying to commit suicide? Haven't you learned *anything* about survival?"

"I'm doing the best I can."

"The Thompsons could have had you a dozen times by now. We told them to take it easy, stretch it out. But it's like shooting a clay pigeon six feet tall. The Thompsons are co-operating, but they can only fake so far. If I hadn't come along, they'd have had to kill you—air-time or not."

Raeder stared at her, wondering how such a pretty girl could talk that way. She glanced at him, then quickly looked back to the road.

"Don't give me that look!" she said. "*You* chose to risk your life for money, buster. And plenty of money! You knew the score. Don't act like some innocent little grocer who finds the nasty hoods are after him. That's a different plot."

"I know," Raeder said.

"If you can't live well, at least try to die well."

"You don't mean that," Raeder said.

"Don't be too sure.... You've got three hours and forty minutes until the end of the show. If you can stay alive, fine. The boodle's yours. But if you can't at least try to give them a run for the money."

Raeder nodded, staring intently at her.

"In a few moments we're back on the air. I develop engine trouble, let you off. The Thompsons go all out now. They kill you when and if they can, as soon as they can. Understand?"

"Yes," Raeder said. "If I make it, can I see you some time?"

She bit her lip angrily. "Are you trying to kid me?"

"No. I'd like to see you again. May I?"

She looked at him curiously. "I don't know. Forget it. We're almost on. I think your best bet is the woods to the right. Ready?"

"Yes. Where can I get in touch with you? Afterward, I mean."

"Oh, Raeder, you aren't paying attention. Go through the woods until you find a washed-out ravine. It isn't much, but it'll give you some cover."

"Where can I get in touch with you?" Raeder asked again.

"I'm in the Manhattan telephone book." She stopped the car. "OK, Raeder, start running."

He opened the door.

"Wait." She leaned over and kissed him on the lips. "Good luck, you idiot. Call me if you make it."

And then he was on foot, running into the woods.

He ran through birch and pine, past an occasional split-level house with staring faces at the big picture window. Some occupant of those houses must have called the gang, for they were close behind him when he reached the washed-out little ravine. Those quiet, mannerly, law-abiding people didn't want him to escape, Raeder thought sadly. They wanted to see a killing. Or perhaps they wanted to see him *narrowly escape* a killing.

It came to the same thing, really.

He entered the ravine, burrowed into the thick underbrush and lay still. The Thompsons appeared on both ridges, moving slowly, watching for any movement. Raeder held his breath as they came parallel to him.

He heard the quick explosion of a revolver. But the killer had only shot a squirrel. It squirmed for a moment, then lay still.

Lying in the underbrush, Raeder heard the studio helicopter overhead. He wondered if any cameras were focused on him. It was possible. And if someone were watching, perhaps some Good Samaritan would help.

So looking upward, towards the helicopter, Raeder arranged his face in a reverent expression, clasped his hands and prayed. He prayed silently, for the audience didn't like religious ostentation. But his lips moved. That was every man's privilege.

And a real prayer was on his lips. Once, a lipreader in the audience had detected a fugitive *pretending* to pray, but actually just reciting multiplication tables. No help for that man!

Raeder finished his prayer. Glancing at his watch, he saw that he had nearly two hours to go.

And he didn't want to die! It wasn't worth it, no matter how much they paid! He must have been crazy, absolutely insane to agree to such a thing....

But he knew that wasn't true. And he remembered just how sane he had been.

One week ago he had been on the *Prize of Peril* stage, blinking in the spotlight, and Mike Terry had shaken his hand.

"Now Mr. Raeder," Terry had said solemnly, "do you understand the rules of the game you are about to play?"

Raeder nodded.

"If you accept, Jim Raeder, you will be a *hunted man* for a week. *Killers* will follow you, Jim. *Trained* killers, men wanted by the law for other crimes, granted immunity for this single killing under the Voluntary Suicide Act. They will be trying to kill *you*, Jim. Do you understand?"

"I understand," Raeder said. He also understood the two hundred thousand dollars he would receive if he could live out the week.

"I ask you again, Jim Raeder. We force no man to play for stakes of death."

"I want to play," Raeder said.

Mike Terry turned to the audience. "Ladies and gentlemen, I have here a copy of an exhaustive psychological test which an impartial psychological testing firm made on Jim Raeder at our request. Copies will be sent to anyone who desires them for twenty-five cents to cover the cost of mailing. The test shows that

Jim Raeder is sane, well-balanced, and fully responsible in every way." He turned to Raeder.

"Do you still want to enter the contest, Jim?"

"Yes, I do."

"Very well!" cried Mike Terry. "Jim Raeder, meet your would-be killers!"

The Thompson gang moved on stage, booed by the audience.

"Look at them, folks," said Mike Terry, with undisguised contempt. "Just look at them! Anti-social, thoroughly vicious, completely amoral. These men have no code but the criminal's warped code, no honour but the honour of the cowardly hired killer. They are doomed men, doomed by our society which will not sanction their activities for long, fated to an early and unglamorous death."

The audience shouted enthusiastically.

"What have you to say, Claude Thompson?" Terry asked.

Claude, the spokesman of the Thompsons, stepped up to the microphone. He was a thin, clean-shaven man, conservatively dressed.

"I figure," Claude Thompson said hoarsely, "I figure we're no worse than anybody. I mean, like soldiers in a war, *they* kill. And look at the graft in government, and the unions. Everybody's got their graft."

That was Thompson's tenuous code. But how quickly, with what precision Mike Terry destroyed the killer's rationalizations! Terry's questions pierced straight to the filthy soul of the man.

At the end of the interview Claude Thompson was perspiring, mopping his face with a silk handkerchief and casting quick glances at his men.

Mike Terry put a hand on Raeder's shoulder. "Here is the man who has agreed to become your victim—if you can catch him."

"We'll catch him," Thompson said, his confidence returning.

"Don't be too sure," said Terry. "Jim Raeder has fought wild bulls—now he battles jackals. He's an average man. He's *the people*—who mean ultimate doom to you and your kind."

"We'll get him," Thompson said.

"And one thing more," Terry said, very softly. "Jim Raeder does not stand alone. The folks of America are for him. Good Samaritans from all corners of our great nation stand ready to assist him. Unarmed, defenceless, Jim Raeder can count on the aid and goodheartedness of *the people*, whose representative he is. So don't be too sure, Claude Thompson! The average men are for Jim Raeder—and there are a lot of average men!"

Raeder thought about it, lying motionless in the underbrush. Yes, *the people* had helped him. But they had helped the killers, too.

A tremor ran through him. He had chosen, he reminded himself. He alone was responsible. The psychological test had proved that.

And yet, how responsible were the psychologists who had given him the test? How responsible was Mike Terry for offering a poor man so much money? Society had woven the noose and put it around his neck, and he was hanging himself with it, and calling it free will.

Whose fault?

"Aha!" someone cried.

Raeder looked up and saw a portly man standing near him. The man wore a loud tweed jacket. He had binoculars around his neck, and a cane in his hand.

"Mister," Raeder whispered, "please don't tell!"

"Hi!" shouted the portly man, pointing at Raeder with his cane. "Here he is!"

A madman, thought Raeder. The damned fool must think he's playing Hare and Hounds.

"Right over here!" the man screamed.

Cursing, Raeder sprang to his feet and began running. He came out of the ravine and saw a white building in the distance. He turned towards it. Behind him he could still hear the man.

"That way, over there. Look, you fools, can't you see him yet?"

The killers were shooting again. Raeder ran, stumbling over uneven ground, past three children playing in a tree house.

"Here he is!" the children screamed. "Here he is!"

Raeder groaned and ran on. He reached the steps of the building, and saw that it was a church.

As he opened the door, a bullet struck him behind the right kneecap.

He fell, and crawled inside the church.

The television set in his pocket was saying, *"What a finish, folks, what a finish! Raeder's been hit! He's been hit, folks, he's crawling now, he's in pain, but he hasn't given up! NOT Jim Raeder!"*

Raeder lay in the aisle near the altar. He could hear a child's eager voice saying, "He went in there, Mr. Thompson. Hurry, you can still catch him!"

Wasn't a church considered a sanctuary, Raeder wondered.

Then the door was flung open, and Raeder realized that the custom was no longer observed. He gathered himself together and crawled past the altar, out of the back door of the church.

He was in an old graveyard. He crawled past crosses and stars, past slabs of marble and granite, past stone tombs and rude wooden markers. A bullet exploded on a tombstone near his head, showering him with fragments. He crawled to the edge of an open grave.

They had deceived him, he thought. All of those nice average normal people. Hadn't they said he was their representative? Hadn't they sworn to protect their own? But no, they loathed him. Why hadn't he seen it? Their hero was the cold, blank-eyed gunman, Thompson, Capone, Billy the Kid, Young Lochinvar, El Cid, Cuchulain, the man without human hopes or fears. They worshipped him, that dead, implacable robot gunman, and lusted to feel his foot in their face.

Raeder tried to move, and slid helplessly into the open grave.

He lay on his back, looking at the blue sky. Presently a black silhouette loomed above him, blotting out the sky. Metal twinkled. The silhouette slowly took aim.

And Raeder gave up all hope forever.

"*WAIT, THOMPSON!*" roared the amplified voice of Mike Terry. The revolver wavered.

"*It is one second past five o'clock! The week is up!* JIM RAEDER HAS WON!"

There was a pandemonium of cheering from the studio audience.

The Thompson gang, gathered around the grave, looked sullen.

"*He's won, friends, he's won!*" Mike Terry cried. "*Look, look on your screen! The police have arrived, they're taking the Thompsons away from their victim—the victim they could not kill. And all this is thanks to you, Good Samaritans of America. Look folks, tender hands are lifting Jim Raeder from the open grave that was his final refuge. Good Samaritan Janice Morrow is there. Could this be the beginning of a romance? Jim seems to have fainted, friends, they're giving him a stimulant. He's won two hundred thousand dollars! Now we'll have a few words from Jim Raeder!*"

There was a short silence.

"*That's odd,*" said Mike Terry. "*Folks, I'm afraid we can't hear from Jim just now. The doctors are examining him. Just one moment...*"

There was a silence. Mike Terry wiped his forehead and smiled.

"*It's the strain, folks, the terrible strain. The doctor tells me ... Well, folks, Jim Raeder is temporarily not himself. But it's only temporary! JBC is hiring the best psychiatrists and psychoanalysts in the country. We're going to do everything humanly possible for this gallant boy. And entirely at our own expense.*"

Mike Terry glanced at the studio clock. "*Well, it's about time to sign off, folks. Watch for the announcement of our next great thrill show. And don't worry, I'm sure that very soon we'll have Jim Raeder back with us.*"

Mike Terry smiled, and winked at the audience. "*He's bound to get well, friends. After all, we're all pulling for him!*"

HUNTING PROBLEM

It was the last troop meeting before the big Scouter Jamboree, and all the patrols had turned out. Patrol 22—the Soaring Falcon Patrol—was camped in a shady hollow, holding a tentacle pull. The Brave Bison Patrol, number 31, was moving around a little stream. The Bisons were practising their skill at drinking liquids, and laughing excitedly at the odd sensation.

And the Charging Mirash Patrol, number 19, was waiting for Scouter Drog, who was late as usual.

Drog hurtled down from the ten-thousand-foot level, went solid, and hastily crawled into the circle of scouters. "Gee," he said, "I'm sorry. I didn't realize what time—"

The Patrol Leader glared at him. "You're out of uniform, Drog."

"Sorry, sir," Drog said, hastily extruding a tentacle he had forgotten.

The others giggled. Drog blushed a dim orange. He wished he were invisible.

But it wouldn't be proper right now.

"I will open our meeting with the Scouter Creed," the Patrol Leader said. He cleared his throat. "We, the Young Scouters of planet Elbonai, pledge to perpetuate the skills and virtues of our pioneering ancestors. For that purpose, we Scouters adopt the shape our forebears were born to when they conquered the virgin wilderness of Elbonai. We hereby resolve—"

Scouter Drog adjusted his hearing receptors to amplify the Leader's soft voice. The Creed always thrilled him. It was hard to believe that his ancestors had once been earthbound. Today the Elbonai were aerial beings, maintaining only the minimum of body, fuelling by cosmic radiation at the twenty-thousand-foot level, sensing by direct perception, coming down only for sentimental or sacramental purposes. They had come a long way since the Age of Pioneering. The modern world had begun with the Age of Submolecular Control, which was followed by the present age of Direct Control.

"...honesty and fair play," the Leader was saying. "And we further resolve to drink liquids, as they did, and to eat solid food, and to increase our skill in their tools and methods."

The invocation completed the youngsters scattered around the plain. The Patrol Leader came up to Drog.

"This is the last meeting before the Jamboree," the Leader said.

"I know," Drog said.

"And you are the only second-class scouter in the Charging Mirash Patrol. All the others are first-class, or at least Junior Pioneers. What will people think about our patrol?"

Drog squirmed uncomfortably. "It isn't entirely my fault," he said. "I know I failed the tests in swimming and bomb making, but those just aren't my skills. It isn't fair to expect me to know everything. Even among the pioneers there were specialists. No one was expected to know all—"

"And just what are your skills?" the Leader interrupted.

"Forest and Mountain Lore," Drog answered eagerly. "Tracking and hunting."

The Leader studied him for a moment. Then he said slowly, "Drog, how would you like one last chance to make first-class, and win an achievement badge as well?"

"I'd do anything!" Drog cried.

"Very well," the Patrol Leader said. "What is the name of our patrol."

"The Charging Mirash Patrol."

"And what is a Mirash?"

"A large and ferocious animal," Drog answered promptly. "Once they inhabited large parts of Elbonai, and our ancestors fought many savage battles with them. Now they are extinct."

"Not quite," the Leader said. "A scouter was exploring the woods five hundred miles north of here, co-ordinates S-233 by 482-W, and he came upon a pride of three Mirash, all bulls, and therefore huntable. I want you, Drog, to track them down, to stalk them, using Forest and Mountain Lore. Then, utilizing only pioneering tools and methods, I want you to bring back the pelt of one Mirash. Do you think you can do it?"

"I know I can, sir!"

"Go at once," the Leader said. "We will fasten the pelt to our flagstaff. We will undoubtedly be commended at the Jamboree."

"Yes, sir!" Drog hastily gathered up his equipment, filled his canteen with liquid, packed a lunch of solid food, and set out.

A few minutes later, he had levitated himself to the general area of S-233 by 482-W. It was a wild and romantic country of jagged rocks and scrubby trees, thick underbrush in the valleys, snow on the peaks. Drog looked around, somewhat troubled.

He had told the Patrol Leader a slight untruth.

The fact of the matter was, he wasn't particularly skilled in Forest and Mountain Lore, hunting or tracking. He wasn't particularly skilled in anything except dreaming away long hours among the clouds at the five-thousand-foot level. What if he failed to find a Mirash? What if the Mirash found him first?

But that couldn't happen, he assured himself. In a pinch, he could always gestibulize. Who would ever know?

In another moment he picked up a faint trace of Mirash scent. And then he saw a slight movement about twenty yards away, near a curious T-shaped formation of rock.

Was it really going to be this easy? How nice! Quietly he adopted an appropriate camouflage and edged forward.

The mountain trail became steeper, and the sun beat harshly down. Paxton was sweating, even in his air-conditioned coverall. And he was heartily sick of being a good sport.

"Just when are we leaving this place?" he asked.

Herrera slapped him genially on the shoulder. "Don't you wanna get rich?"

"We're rich already," Paxton said.

"But not rich enough," Herrera told him, his long brown face creasing into a brilliant grin.

Stellman came up, puffing under the weight of his testing equipment. He set it carefully on the path and sat down. "You gentlemen interested in a short breather?" he asked.

"Why not?" Herrera said. "All the time in the world." He sat down with his back against a T-shaped formation of rock.

Stellman lighted a pipe and Herrera found a cigar in the zippered pocket of his coverall. Paxton watched them for a while. Then he asked, "Well, when *are* we getting off this planet? Or do we set up permanent residence?"

Herrera just grinned and scratched a light for his cigar.

"Well, how about it?" Paxton shouted.

"Relax, you're outvoted," Stellman said. "We formed this company as three equal partners."

"All using *my* money," Paxton said.

"Of course. That's why we took you in. Herrera had the practical mining experience. I had the theoretical knowledge and a pilot's licence. You had the money."

"But we've got plenty of stuff on board now," Paxton said. "The storage compartments are completely filled. Why can't we go to some civilized place now and start spending?"

"Herrera and I don't have your aristocratic attitude towards wealth," Stellman said with exaggerated patience. "Herrera and I have the childish desire to fill every nook and cranny with treasure. Gold nuggets in the fuel tanks, emeralds in the flour cans, diamonds a foot deep on deck. And this is just the place for it. All manner of costly baubles are lying around just begging to be picked up. We want to be disgustingly, abysmally rich, Paxton."

Paxton hadn't been listening. He was staring intently at a point near the edge of the trail. In a low voice, he said, "That tree just moved."

Herrera burst into laughter. "Monsters, I suppose," he sneered.

"Be calm," Stellman said mournfully. "My boy, I am a middle-aged man, overweight and easily frightened. Do you think I'd stay here if there were the slightest danger?"

"There! It moved again!"

"We surveyed this planet three months ago," Stellman said. "We found no intelligent beings, no dangerous animals, no poisonous plants, remember? All we found were woods and mountains and gold and lakes and emeralds and rivers and diamonds. If there were something here, wouldn't it have attacked us long before?"

"I'm telling you I saw it move," Paxton insisted.

Herrera stood up. "This tree?" he asked Paxton.

"Yes. See, it doesn't even look like the others. Different texture—"

In a single synchronized movement, Herrera pulled a Mark II blaster from a side holster and fired three charges into the tree. The tree and all underbrush for ten yards around burst into flame and crumpled.

"All gone now," Herrera said.

Paxton rubbed his jaw. "I heard a scream when you shot it."

"Sure. But it's dead now," Herrera said soothingly. "If anything else moves, you just tell me, I shoot it. Now we find some more little emeralds, huh?"

Paxton and Stellman lifted their packs and followed Herrera up the trail. Stellman said in a low, amused voice, "Direct sort of fellow, isn't he?"

Slowly Drog returned to consciousness. The Mirash's flaming weapon had caught him in camouflage, almost completely un-shielded. He still couldn't understand how it had happened. There had been no premonitory fear-scent, no snorting, no snarling, no warning whatsoever. The Mirash had attacked with blind sudden-ness, without waiting to see whether he was friend or foe.

At last Drog understood the nature of the beast he was up against.

He waited until the hoofbeats of the three bull Mirash had faded into the distance. Then, painfully, he tried to extrude a visual receptor. Nothing happened. He had a moment of utter panic. If his central nervous system was damaged, this was the end.

He tried again. This time, a piece of rock slid off him, and he was able to reconstruct.

Quickly he performed an internal scansion. He sighed with relief. It had been a close thing. Instinctively he had quondicated at the flash moment and it had saved his life.

He tried to think of another course of action, but the shock of that sudden, vicious, unpremeditated assault had driven all Hunting Lore out of his mind. He found that he had absolutely no desire to encounter the savage Mirash again.

Suppose he returned without the stupid hide? He could tell the Patrol Leader that the Mirash were all females, and therefore un-huntable. A Young Scouter's word was honoured, so no one would question him, or even check up.

But that would never do. How could he even consider it?

Well, he told himself gloomily, he could resign from the Scouters, put an end to the whole ridiculous business; the campfires, the singing, the games, the comradeship...

This would never do, Drog decided, taking himself firmly in hand. He was acting as though the Mirash were antagonists capable of planning against him. But the Mirash were not even intelligent beings. No creature without tentacles had ever developed true intelligence. That was Etlib's Law, and it had never been disputed.

In a battle between intelligence and instinctive cunning, intelligence always won. It had to. All he had to do was figure out how.

Drog began to track the Mirash again, following their odour. What colonial weapon should he use? A small atomic bomb? No, that would more than likely ruin the hide.

He stopped suddenly and laughed. It was really very simple, when one applied oneself. Why should he come into direct and dangerous contact with the Mirash? The time had come to use his brain, his understanding of animal psychology, his knowledge of Lures and Snares.

Instead of tracking the Mirash, he would go to their den.

And there he would set a trap.

Their temporary camp was in a cave, and by the time they arrived there it was sunset. Every crag and pinnacle of rock threw a precise and sharp-edged shadow. The ship lay five miles below them on the valley floor, its metallic hide glistening red and silver. In their packs were a dozen emeralds, small, but of an excellent colour.

At an hour like this, Paxton thought of a small Ohio town, a soda fountain, a girl with bright hair. Herrera smiled to himself, contemplating certain gaudy ways of spending a million dollars before settling down to the serious business of ranching. And Stellman was already phrasing his Ph.D. thesis on extraterrestrial mineral deposits.

They were all in a pleasant, relaxed mood. Paxton had recovered completely from his earlier attack of nerves. Now he wished an alien monster *would* show up—a green one, by preference—chasing a lovely, scantily clad woman.

"Home again," Stellman said as they approached the entrance of the cave. "Want beef stew tonight?" It was his turn to cook.

"With onions," Paxton said, starting into the cave. He jumped back abruptly. "What's that?"

A few feet from the mouth of the cave was a small roast beef, still steaming hot, four large diamonds, and a bottle of whiskey.

"That's odd," Stellman said. "And a trifle unnerving."

Paxton bent down to examine a diamond. Herrera pulled him back.

"Might be booby-trapped."

"There aren't any wires," Paxton said.

Herrera stared at the roast beef, the diamonds, the bottle of whiskey. He looked very unhappy.

"I don't trust this," he said.

"Maybe there *are* natives here," Stellman said. "Very timid ones. This might be their goodwill offering."

"Sure," Herrera said. "They sent to Terra for a bottle of Old Space Ranger just for us."

"What are we going to do?" Paxton asked.

"Stand clear," Herrera said. "Move 'way back." He broke off a long branch from a nearby tree and poked gingerly at the diamonds.

"Nothing's happening," Paxton said.

The long grass Herrera was standing on whipped tightly around his ankles. The ground beneath him surged, broke into a neat disc fifteen feet in diameter and, trailing root-ends, began to lift itself into the air. Herrera tried to jump free, but the grass held him like a thousand green tentacles.

"Hang on!" Paxton yelled idiotically, rushed forward and grabbed a corner of the rising disc of earth. It dipped steeply, stopped for a moment, and began to rise again. By then Herrera had his knife out, and was slashing the grass around his ankles. Stellman came unfrozen when he saw Paxton rising past his head.

Stellman seized him by the ankles, arresting the flight of the disc once more. Herrera wrenched one foot free and threw himself over the edge. The other ankle was held for a moment, then the tough grass parted under his weight. He dropped head-first to the ground, at the last moment ducking his head and landing on his shoulders.

Paxton let go of the disc and fell, landing on Stellman's stomach.

The disc of earth, with its cargo of roast beef, whiskey and diamonds, continued to rise until it was out of sight.

The sun had set. Without speaking, the three men entered their cave, blasters drawn. They built a roaring fire at the mouth and moved back into the cave's interior.

"We'll guard in shifts tonight," Herrera said.

Paxton and Stellman nodded.

Herrera said, "I think you're right, Paxton. We've stayed here long enough."

"Too long," Paxton said.

Herrera shrugged his shoulders. "As soon as it's light, we return to the ship and get out of here."

"If," Stellman said, "we are able to reach the ship."

Drog was quite discouraged. With a sinking heart he had watched the premature springing of his trap, the struggle, and the escape of the Mirash. It had been such a splendid Mirash, too. The biggest of the three!

He knew now what he had done wrong. In his eagerness, he had overbaited his trap. Just the minerals would have been sufficient, for Mirash were notoriously mineral-tropic. But no, he had to improve on pioneer methods, he had to use food stimuli as well. No wonder they had reacted suspiciously, with their senses so overburdened.

Now they were enraged, alert, and decidedly dangerous.

And a thoroughly aroused Mirash was one of the most fearsome sights in the Galaxy.

Drog felt very much alone as Elbonai's twin moons rose in the western sky. He could see the Mirash campfire blazing in the mouth of their cave. And by direct perception he could see the Mirash crouched within, every sense alert, weapons ready.

Was a Mirash hide really worth all this trouble?

Drog decided that he would much rather be floating at the five-thousand-foot level, sculpturing cloud formations and dreaming. He wanted to sop up radiation instead of eating nasty old solid food. And what use was all this hunting and trapping, anyhow? Worthless skills that his people had outgrown.

For a moment he almost had himself convinced. And then, in a flash of pure perception, he understood what it was all about.

True, the Elbonaians had outgrown their competition, developed past all danger of competition. But the Universe was wide, and capable of many surprises. Who could foresee what would come, what new dangers the race might have to face? And how could they meet them if the hunting instinct was lost?

No, the old ways had to be preserved, to serve as patterns; as reminders that peaceable, intelligent life was an unstable entity in an unfriendly Universe.

He was going to get that Mirash hide, or die trying!

The most important thing was to get them out of that cave. Now his hunting knowledge had returned to him.

Quickly, skilfully, he shaped a Mirash horn.

"Did you hear that?" Paxton asked.

"I thought I heard something," Stellman said, and they all listened intently.

The sound came again. It was a voice crying, "Oh, help, help me!"

"It's a girl!" Paxton jumped to his feet.

"It *sounds* like a girl," Stellman said.

"Please, help me," the girl's voice wailed. "I can't hold out much longer. Is there anyone who can help me?"

Blood rushed to Paxton's face. In a flash he saw her, small, exquisite, standing beside her wrecked sports-spacer (what a foolhardly trip it had been!) with monsters, green and slimy, closing in on her. And then *he* arrived, a foul alien beast.

Paxton picked up a spare blaster. "I'm going out there," he said coolly.

"Sit down, you moron!" Herrera ordered.

"But you heard her, didn't you?"

"That can't be a girl," Herrera said. "What would a girl be doing on this planet?"

"I'm going to find out," Paxton said, brandishing two blasters. "Maybe a spaceliner crashed, or she could have been out joyriding, and—"

"Siddown!" Herrera yelled.

"He's right," Stellman tried to reason with Paxton. "Even if a girl is out there, which I doubt, there's nothing we can do."

"Oh, help, help, it's coming after me!" the girl's voice screamed.

"Get out of my way," Paxton said, his voice low and dangerous.

"You're really going?" Herrera asked incredulously.

"Yes! Are you going to stop me?"

"Go ahead." Herrera gestured at the entrance of the cave.

"We can't let him!" Stellman gasped.

"Why not? His funeral," Herrera said lazily.

"Don't worry about me," Paxton said. "I'll be back in fifteen minutes—with her!" He turned on his heel and started towards the entrance. Herrera leaned forward and, with considerable precision, clubbed Paxton behind the ear with a stick of firewood. Stellman caught him as he fell.

They stretched Paxton out in the rear of the cave and returned to their vigil. The lady in distress moaned and pleaded for the next

five hours. Much too long, as Paxton had to agree, even for a movie
serial.

A gloomy, rain-splattered daybreak found Drog still camped a
hundred yards from the cave. He saw the Mirash emerge in a tight
group, weapons ready, eyes watching warily for any movement.

Why had the Mirash horn failed? The Scouter Manual said it was
an infallible means of attracting the bull Mirash. But perhaps this
wasn't mating season.

They were moving in the direction of a metallic ovoid which
Drog recognized as a primitive spatial conveyance. It was crude,
but once inside it the Mirash were safe from him.

He could simply trevest them, and that would end it. But it
wouldn't be very humane. Above all, the ancient Elbonaians had
been gentle and merciful, and a Young Scouter tried to be like
them. Besides, trevestment wasn't a true pioneering method.

That left ilitrocy. It was the oldest trick in the book, and he'd
have to get close to work it. But he had nothing to lose.

And luckily, climatic conditions were perfect for it.

It started as a thin ground-mist. But, as the watery sun climbed
the grey sky, fog began forming.

Herrera cursed angrily as it grew more dense. "Keep close
together now. Of all the luck!"

Soon they were walking with their hands on each others' shoulders, blasters ready, peering into the impenetrable fog.

"Herrera?"

"Yeah?"

"Are you sure we're going in the right direction?"

"Sure. I took a compass course before the fog closed in."

"Suppose your compass is off?"

"Don't even think about it."

They walked on, picking their way carefully over the rock-strewn
ground.

"I think I see the ship," Paxton said.

"No, not yet," Herrera said.

Stellman stumbled over a rock, dropped his blaster, picked it up
again and fumbled around for Herrera's shoulder. He found it and
walked on.

"I think we're almost there," Herrera said.

"I sure hope so," Paxton said. "I've had enough."

"Think your girl friend's waiting for you at the ship?"

"Don't rub it in."

"Okay," Herrera said. "Hey, Stellman, you better grab hold of my
shoulder again. No sense getting separated."

"I am holding your shoulder," Stellman said.

"You're not."

"I am, I tell you!"

"Look, I guess I know if someone's holding my shoulder or not."

"Am I holding your shoulder, Paxton?"

"No," Paxton said.

"That's bad," Stellman said, very slowly. "That's bad, indeed."

"Why?"

"Because I'm definitely holding *someone's* shoulder."

Herrera yelled, "Get down, get down quick, give me room to shoot!" But it was too late. A sweet-sour odour was in the air. Stellman and Paxton smelled it and collapsed. Herrera ran forward blindly, trying to hold his breath. He stumbled and fell over a rock, tried to get back on his feet—

And everything went black.

The fog lifted suddenly and Drog was standing alone, smiling triumphantly. He pulled out a long-bladed skinning knife and bent over the nearest Mirash.

The spaceship hurtled towards Terra at a velocity which threatened momentarily to burn out the overdrive. Herrera hunched over the controls, finally regained his self-control and cut the speed down to normal. His usually tan face was still ashen, and his hands shook on the instruments.

Stellman came in from the bunkroom and flopped wearily in the co-pilot's seat.

"How's Paxton?" Herrera asked.

"I dosed him with Drona-3," Stellman said. "He's going to be all right."

"He's a good kid," Herrera said.

"It's just shock, for the most part," Stellman said. "When he comes to, I'm going to put him to work counting diamonds. Counting diamonds is the best of therapies, I understand."

Herrera grinned, and his face began to regain its normal colour "I feel like doing a little diamond-counting myself, now that it's all turned out okay." Then his long face became serious. "But I ask you, Stellman, who could figure it? I still don't understand!"

The Scouter Jamboree was a glorious spectacle. The Soaring Falcon Patrol, number 22, gave a short pantomime showing the clearing of the land on Elbonai. The Brave Bisons, number 31, were in full pioneer dress.

And at the head of Patrol 19, the Charging Mirash Patrol, was Drog, a first-class Scouter now, wearing a glittering achievement badge. He was carrying the Patrol flag—the position of honour—and everyone cheered to see it.

Because waving proudly from the flagpole was the firm, fine-textured, characteristic skin of an adult Mirash, its zippers, tubes, gauges, buttons and holsters flashing merrily in the sunshine.

GHOST V

"He's reading our sign now," Gregor said, his long bony face pressed against the peephole in the office door.

"Let me see," Arnold said.

Gregor pushed him back. "He's going to knock—no, he's changed his mind. He's leaving."

Arnold returned to his desk and laid out another game of solitaire. Gregor kept watch at the peephole.

They had constructed the peephole out of sheer boredom three months after forming their partnership and renting the office. During that time, the AAA Ace Planet Decontamination Service had had no business—in spite of being first in the telephone book. Planetary decontamination was an old, established line, completely monopolized by two large outfits. It was discouraging for a small new firm run by two young men with big ideas and a lot of unpaid-for equipment.

"He's coming back," Gregor called. "*Quick*—look busy and important!"

Arnold swept his cards into a drawer and just finished buttoning his lab gown when the knock came.

Their visitor was a short, bald, tired-looking man. He stared at them dubiously.

"You decontaminate planets?"

"That is correct, sir," Gregor said, pushing away a pile of papers and shaking the man's moist hand. "I am Richard Gregor. This is my partner, Doctor Frank Arnold."

Arnold, impressively garbed in a white lab gown and black horn-rimmed glasses, nodded absently and resumed his examination of a row of ancient, crusted test tubes.

"Kindly be seated, Mister—"

"Ferngraum."

"Mr. Ferngraum. I think we can handle just about anything you require," Gregor said heartily. "Flora or fauna control, cleansing atmosphere, purifying water supply, sterilizing soil, stability testing, volcano and earthquake control—anything you need to make a planet fit for human habitation."

Ferngraum still looked dubious. "I'm going to level with you. I've got a problem planet on my hands."

Gregor nodded confidently. "Problems are our business."

"I'm a freelance real-estate broker," Ferngraum said. "You know how it works—buy a planet, sell a planet, everyone makes a living. Usually I stick with the scrub worlds and let my buyers do their decontaminating. But a few months ago I had a chance to buy a real quality planet—took it right out from under the noses of the big operators."

Ferngraum mopped his forehead unhappily.

"It's a beautiful place," he continued with no enthusiasm whatsoever. "Average temperature of 71 degrees. Mountainous, but fertile. Waterfalls, rainbows, all that sort of thing. And no fauna at all."

"Sounds perfect," Gregor said. "Micro-organisms?"

"Nothing dangerous."

"Then what's wrong with the place?"

Ferngraum looked embarrassed. "Maybe you heard about it. The government catalogue number is RJC-5. But everyone else calls it 'Ghost V'."

Gregor raised an eyebrow. "Ghost" was an odd nickname for a planet, but he had heard odder. After all, you had to call them something. There were thousands of planet-bearing suns within spaceship range, many of them inhabitable or potentially inhabitable. And there were plenty of people from the civilized worlds who wanted to colonize them. Religious sects, political minorities, philosophic groups—or just plain pioneers, out to make a fresh start.

"I don't believe I've heard of it," Gregor said.

Ferngraum squirmed uncomfortably in his chair. "I should have listened to my wife. But no—I was gonna be a big operator. Paid ten times my usual price for Ghost V and now I'm stuck with it."

"But what's *wrong* with it?" Gregor asked.

"It seems to be haunted," Ferngraum said in despair.

Ferngraum had radar-checked his planet, then leased it to a combine of farmers from Dijon VI. The eight-man advance guard landed and, within a day, began to broadcast garbled reports about demons, ghouls, vampires, dinosaurs and other inimical fauna.

When a relief ship came for them, all were dead. An autopsy report stated that the gashes, cuts and marks on their bodies could indeed have been made by almost anything, even demons, ghouls, vampires or dinosaurs, if such existed.

Ferngraum was fined for improper decontamination. The farmers dropped their lease. But he managed to lease it to a group of sun worshippers from Opal II.

The sun worshippers were cautious. They sent their equipment, but only three men accompanied it, to scout out trouble. The men set up camp, unpacked and declared the place a paradise. They

radioed the home group to come at once—then, suddenly, there was
a wild scream and radio silence.

A patrol ship went to Ghost V, buried the three mangled bodies
and departed in five minutes flat.

"And that did it," Ferngraum said. "Now no one will touch it at
any price. Space crews refuse to land on it. And I still don't know
what happened."

He sighed deeply and looked at Gregor. "It's your baby, if you
want it."

Gregor and Arnold excused themselves and went into the ante-
room.

Arnold whooped at once, "We've got a job!"

"Yeah," Gregor said, "but what a job."

"We wanted the tough ones," Arnold pointed out. "If we lick this,
we're established—to say nothing of the profit we'll make on a percentage basis."

"You seem to forget," Gregor said, "I'm the one who has to
actually land on the planet. All you do is sit here and interpret
my data."

"That's the way we set it up," Arnold reminded him. "I'm the
research department—you're the troubleshooter. Remember?"

Gregor remembered. Ever since childhood, he had been sticking
his neck out while Arnold stayed home and told him why he was
sticking his neck out.

"I don't like it," he said.

"You don't believe in ghosts, do you?"

"No, of course not."

"Well, we can handle anything else. Faint heart ne'er won fair
profit."

Gregor shrugged his shoulders. They went back to Ferngraum.

In half an hour, they had worked out their terms—a large percentage of future development profits if they succeeded, a forfeiture
clause if they failed.

Gregor walked to the door with Ferngraum. "By the way, sir,"
he asked, "how did you happen to come to us?"

"No one else would handle it," Ferngraum said, looking extremely
pleased with himself. "Good luck."

Three days later, Gregor was aboard a rickety space freighter,
bound for Ghost V. He spent his time studying reports on the two
colonization attempts and reading survey after survey on supernatural phenomena.

They didn't help at all. No trace of animal life had been found
on Ghost V. And no proof of the existence of supernatural creatures
had been discovered anywhere in the Galaxy.

Gregor pondered this, then checked his weapons as the freighter spiralled into the region of Ghost V. He was carrying an arsenal large enough to start a small war and win it.

If he could find something to shoot at...

The captain of the freighter brought his ship to within several thousand feet of the smiling green surface of the planet, but no closer. Gregor parachuted his equipment to the site of the last two camps, shook hands with the captain and 'chuted himself down.

He landed safely and looked up. The freighter was streaking into space as though the furies were after it.

He was alone on Ghost V.

After checking his equipment for breakage, he radioed Arnold that he had landed safely. Then, with drawn blaster, he inspected the sun worshippers' camp.

They had set themselves up at the base of a mountain, beside a small, crystal-clear lake. The prefabs were in perfect condition

No storms had ever damaged them, because Ghost V was blessed with a beautifully even climate. But they looked pathetically lonely.

Gregor made a careful check of one. Clothes were still neatly packed in cabinets, pictures were hung on the wall and there was even a curtain on one window. In a corner of the room, a case of toys had been opened for the arrival of the main party's children. A water pistol, a top and a bag of marbles had spilled on to the floor.

Evening was coming, so Gregor dragged his equipment into the prefab and made his preparations He rigged an alarm system and adjusted it so finely that even a roach would set it off. He put up a radar alarm to scan the immediate area. He unpacked his arsenal, laying the heavy rifles within easy reach, but keeping a hand-blaster in his belt. Then, satisfied, he ate a leisurely supper.

Outside, the evening drifted into night. The warm and dreamy land grew dark. A gentle breeze ruffled the surface of the lake and rustled silkily in the tall grass.

It was all very peaceful.

The settlers must have been hysterical types, he decided. They had probably panicked and killed each other.

After checking his alarm system one last time, Gregor threw his clothes on to a chair, turned off the lights and climbed into bed. The room was illuminated by starlight, stronger than moonlight on Earth. His blaster was under his pillow. All was well with the world.

He had just begun to doze off when he became aware that he was not alone in the room.

That was impossible. His alarm system hadn't gone off. The radar was still humming peacefully.

Yet every nerve in his body was shrieking alarm. He eased the blaster out and looked around.

A man was standing in a corner of the room.

There was no time to consider how he had come. Gregor aimed the blaster and said, "Okay, raise your hands," in a quiet, resolute voice.

The figure didn't move.

Gregor's finger tightened on the trigger, then suddenly relaxed. He recognized the man. It was his own clothing, heaped on a chair, distorted by the starlight and his own imagination.

He grinned and lowered the blaster. The pile of clothing began to stir faintly. Gregor felt a faint breeze from the window and continued to grin.

Then the pile of clothing stood up, stretched itself and began to walk towards him purposefully.

Frozen to his bed, he watched the disembodied clothing, assembled roughly in manlike form, advance on him.

When it was half-way across the room and its empty sleeves were reaching for him, he began to blast.

And kept on blasting, for the rags and remnants slithered towards him as if filled with a life of their own. Flaming bits of cloth crowded towards his face and a belt tried to coil around his legs. He had to burn everything to ashes before the attack stopped.

When it was over, Gregor turned on every light he could find. He brewed a pot of coffee and poured in most of a bottle of brandy. Somehow, he resisted an urge to kick his useless alarm system to pieces. Instead, he radioed his partner.

"That's very interesting," Arnold said, after Gregor had brought him up to date. "Animation! Very interesting indeed."

"I hoped it would amuse you," Gregor answered bitterly. After several shots of brandy, he was beginning to feel abandoned and abused.

"Did anything else happen?"

"Not yet."

"Well, take care. I've got a theory. Have to do some research on it. By the way, some crazy bookie is laying five to one against you."

"Really?"

"Yeah. I took a piece of it."

"Did you bet for me or against me?" Gregor asked, worried.

"For you, of course," Arnold said indignantly. "We're partners, aren't we?"

They signed off and Gregor brewed another pot of coffee. He was not planning on any more sleep that night. It was comforting to know that Arnold had bet on him. But, then, Arnold was a notoriously bad gambler.

*   *   *

By daylight, Gregor was able to get a few hours of fitful sleep. In the early afternoon he awoke, found some clothes and began to explore the sun worshippers' camp.

Towards evening, he found something. On the wall of a prefab, the word *"Tgasklit"* had been hastily scratched. *Tgasklit.* It meant nothing to him, but he relayed it to Arnold at once.

He then searched his prefab carefully, set up more lights, tested the alarm system and recharged his blaster.

Everything seemed in order. With regret, he watched the sun go down, hoping he would live to see it rise again. Then he settled himself in a comfortable chair and tried to do some constructive thinking.

There was no animal life here—nor were there any walking plants, intelligent rocks or giant brains dwelling in the planet's core. Ghost V hadn't even a moon for someone to hide on.

And he couldn't believe in ghosts or demons. He knew that supernatural happenings tended to break down, under detailed examination, into eminently natural events. The ones that didn't break down—stopped. Ghosts just wouldn't stand still and let a non-believer examine them. The phantom of the castle was invariably on vacation when a scientist showed up with cameras and tape recorders.

That left another possibility. Suppose someone wanted this planet, but wasn't prepared to pay Ferngraum's price? Couldn't this someone hide here, frighten the settlers, kill them if necessary in order to drive down the price?

That seemed logical. You could even explain the behaviour of his clothes that way. Static electricity, correctly used, could—

Something was standing in front of him. His alarm system, as before, hadn't gone off.

Gregor looked up slowly. The thing in front of him was about ten feet tall and roughly human in shape, except for its crocodile head. It was coloured a bright crimson and had purple stripes running lengthwise on its body. In one claw, it was carrying a large brown can.

"Hello," it said.

"Hello," Gregor gulped. His blaster was on a table only two feet away. He wondered, would the thing attack if he reached for it?

"What's your name?" Gregor asked, with the calmness of deep shock.

"I'm the Purple-striped Grabber," the thing said. "I grab things."

"How interesting." Gregor's hand began to creep towards the blaster.

"I grab things named Richard Gregor," the Grabber told him in its bright, ingenuous voice. "And I usually eat them in chocolate sauce." It held up the brown can and Gregor saw that it was labelled "Smig's Chocolate—An Ideal Sauce to Use with Gregors, Arnolds and Flynns."

Gregor's fingers touched the butt of the blaster. He asked, "Were you planning to eat me?"

"Oh, yes," the Grabber said.

Gregor had the gun now. He flipped off the safety catch and fired. The radiant blast cascaded off the Grabber's chest and singed the floor, the walls and Gregor's eyebrows.

"That won't hurt me," the Grabber explained. "I'm too tall."

The blaster dropped from Gregor's fingers. The Grabber leaned forward.

"I'm not going to eat you now," the Grabber said.

"No?" Gregor managed to enunciate.

"No. I can only eat you tomorrow, on May first. Those are the rules. I just came to ask a favour."

"What is it?"

The Grabber smiled winningly. "Would you be a good sport and eat a few apples? They flavour the flesh so wonderfully."

And, with that, the striped monster vanished.

With shaking hands, Gregor worked the radio and told Arnold everything that had happened.

"Hmm," Arnold said. "Purple-striped Grabber, eh? I think that clinches it. Everything fits."

"What fits? What is it?"

"First, do as I say. I want to make sure."

Obeying Arnold's instructions, Gregor unpacked his chemical equipment and laid out a number of test tubes, retorts and chemicals. He stirred, mixed, added and subtracted as directed and finally put the mixture on the stove to heat.

"Now," Gregor said, coming back to the radio, "tell me what's going on."

"Certainly. I looked up the word 'Tgasklit'. It's Opalian. It means 'many-toothed ghost'. The sun worshippers were from Opal. What does that suggest to you?"

"They were killed by a home-town ghost," Gregor replied nastily. "It must have stowed away on their ship. Maybe there was a curse and—"

"Calm down," Arnold said. "There aren't any ghosts in this. Is the solution boiling yet?"

"No."

"Tell me when it does. Now let's take your animated clothing. Does it remind you of anything?"

Gregor thought. "Well," he said, "when I was a kid—no, that's ridiculous."

"Out with it," Arnold insisted.

"When I was a kid, I never left clothing on a chair. In the dark, it always looked like a man or a dragon or something. I guess everyone's had that experience. But it doesn't explain—"

"Sure it does! Remember the Purple-striped Grabber now?"

"No. Why should I?"

"Because you invented him! Remember? We must have been eight or nine, you and me and Jimmy Flynn. We invented the most horrible monster you could think of—he was our own personal monster and he only wanted to eat you or me or Jimmy—flavoured with chocolate sauce. But only on the first of every month, when the report cards were due. You had to use the magic word to get rid of him."

Then Gregor remembered and wondered how he could ever have forgotten. How many nights had he stayed up in fearful expectation of the Grabber? It had made bad report cards seem very unimportant.

"Is the solution boiling?" Arnold asked.

"Yes," said Gregor, glancing obediently at the stove.

"What colour is it?"

"A sort of greenish blue. No, it's more blue than—"

"Right. You can pour it out. I want to run a few more tests, but I think we've got it licked."

"Got *what* licked? Would you do a little explaining?"

"It's obvious. The planet has no animal life. There are no ghosts or at least none solid enough to kill off a party of armed men. Hallucination was the answer, so I looked for something that would produce it. I found plenty. Aside from all the drugs on Earth, there are about a dozen hallucination-forming gases in the *Catalogue of Alien Trace Elements*. There are depressants, stimulants, stuff that'll make you feel like a genius or an earthworm or an eagle. This particular one corresponds to Longstead 42 in the catalogue. It's a heavy, transparent, odourless gas, not harmful physically. It's an imagination stimulant."

"You mean I was just having hallucinations? I tell you—"

"Not quite that simple," Arnold cut in. "Longstead 42 works directly on the subconscious. It releases your strongest subconscious fears, the childhood terrors you've been suppressing. It animates them. And that's what you've been seeing."

"Then there's actually nothing here?" Gregor asked.

"Nothing physical. But the hallucinations are real enough to whoever is having them."

Gregor reached over for another bottle of brandy. This called for a celebration.

"It won't be hard to decontaminate Ghost V," Arnold went on

confidently. "We can cancel the Longstead 42 with no difficulty. And then—we'll be rich, partner!"

Gregor suggested a toast, then thought of something disturbing. "If they're just hallucinations, what happened to the settlers?"

Arnold was silent for a moment. "Well," he said finally, "Longstead may have a tendency to stimulate the mortido—the death instinct. The settlers must have gone crazy. Killed each other."

"And no survivors?"

"Sure, why not? The last ones alive committed suicide or died of wounds. Don't worry about it. I'm chartering a ship immediately and coming out to run those tests. Relax. I'll pick you up in a day or two."

Gregor signed off. He allowed himself the rest of the bottle of brandy that night. It seemed only fair. The mystery of Ghost V was solved and they were going to be rich. Soon *he* would be able to hire a man to land on strange planets for him while *he* sat home and gave instructions over a radio.

He awoke late the next day with a hangover. Arnold's ship hadn't arrived yet, so he packed his equipment and waited. By evening, there was still no ship. He sat in the doorway of the prefab and watched a gaudy sunset, then went inside and made dinner.

The problem of the settlers still bothered him, but he determined not to worry about it. Undoubtedly there was a logical answer.

After dinner, he stretched out on a bed. He had barely closed his eyes when he heard someone cough apologetically.

"Hello," said the Purple-striped Grabber.

His own personal hallucination had returned to eat him. "Hello, old chap," Gregor said cheerfully, without a bit of fear or worry.

"Did you eat the apples?"

"Dreadfully sorry. I forgot."

"Oh, well." The Grabber tried to conceal his disappointment. "I brought the chocolate sauce." He held up the can.

Gregor smiled. "You can leave now," he said. "I know you're just a figment of my imagination. You can't hurt me."

"I'm not going to hurt you," the Grabber said. "I'm just going to eat you."

He walked up to Gregor. Gregor held his ground, smiling, although he wished the Grabber didn't appear so solid and un-dreamlike. The Grabber leaned over and bit his arm experimentally.

He jumped back and looked at his arm. There were toothmarks on it. Blood was oozing out—real blood—*his* blood.

The colonists had been bitten, gashed, torn and ripped.

At that moment, Gregor remembered an exhibition of hypnotism he had once seen. The hypnotist had told the subject he was putting a lighted cigarette on his arm. Then he had touched the spot with a pencil.

Within seconds, an angry red blister had appeared on the subject's arm, because he *believed* he had been burned. If your subconscious thinks you're dead, you're dead. If it orders the stigmata of tooth-marks, they are there.

He didn't believe in the Grabber.

But his subconscious did.

Gregor tried to run for the door. The Grabber cut him off. It seized him in its claws and bent to reach his neck.

The magic word! What was it?

Gregor shouted, "*Alphoisto?*"

"Wrong word," said the Grabber. "Please don't squirm."

"*Regnastikio!*"

"Nope. Stop wriggling and it'll be over before you—"

"*Voorshpellhappilo!*"

The Grabber let out a scream of pain and released him. It bounded high into the air and vanished.

Gregor collapsed into a chair. That had been close. Too close. It would be a particularly stupid way to die—rent by his own death-desiring subconscious, slashed by his own imagination, killed by his own conviction. It was fortunate he had remembered the word. Now if Arnold would only hurry...

He heard a low chuckle of amusement.

It came from the blackness of a half-opened closet door, touching off an almost forgotten memory. He was nine years old again, and the Shadower—his Shadower—was a strange, thin, grisly creature who hid in doorways, slept under beds and attacked only in the dark.

"Turn out the lights," the Shadower said.

"Not a chance," Gregor retorted, drawing his blaster. As long as the lights were on, he was safe.

"You'd better turn them off."

"No!"

"Very well. Egan, Megan, Degan!"

Three little creatures scampered into the room. They raced to the nearest light bulb, flung themselves on it and began to gulp hungrily.

The room was growing darker.

Gregor blasted at them each time they approached a light. Glass shattered, but the nimble creatures darted out of the way.

And then Gregor realized what he had done. The creatures couldn't actually eat light. Imagination can't make any impression on inanimate matter. He had *imagined* that the room was growing dark and—

He had shot out his light bulbs! His own destructive subconscious had tricked him.

Now the Shadower stepped out. Leaping from shadow to shadow, he came towards Gregor.

The blaster had no effect. Gregor tried frantically to think of the magic word—and terrifiedly remembered that no magic word banished the Shadower.

He backed away, the Shadower advancing, until he was stopped by a packing case. The Shadower towered over him and Gregor shrank to the floor and closed his eyes.

His hands came in contact with something cold. He was leaning against the packing case of toys for the settlers' children. And he was holding a water pistol.

Gregor brandished it. The Shadower backed away, eyeing the weapon with apprehension.

Quickly, Gregor ran to the tap and filled the pistol. He directed a deadly stream of water into the creature.

The Shadower howled in agony and vanished.

Gregor smiled tightly and slipped the empty gun into his belt.

A water pistol was the right weapon to use against an imaginary monster.

It was nearly dawn when the ship landed and Arnold stepped out. Without wasting any time, he set up his tests. By midday, it was done and the element definitely established as Longstead 42. He and Gregor packed up immediately and blasted off.

Once they were in space, Gregor told his partner everything that had happened.

"Pretty rough," said Arnold softly, but with deep feeling.

Gregor could smile with modest heroism now that he was safely off Ghost V. "Could have been worse," he said.

"How?"

"Suppose Jimmy Flynn were here. There was a kid who could really dream up monsters. Remember the Grumbler?"

"All I remember is the nightmares it gave me," Arnold said.

They were on their way home. Arnold jotted down some notes for an article entitled "The Death Instinct on Ghost V: An Examination of Subconscious Stimulation, Hysteria, and Mass Hallucination in Producing Physical Stigmata". Then he went to the control room to set the autopilot.

Gregor threw himself on a couch, determined to get his first decent night's sleep since landing on Ghost V. He had barely dozed off when Arnold hurried in, his face pasty with terror.

"I think there's something in the control room," he said.

Gregor sat up. "There can't be. We're off the—"

There was a low growl from the control room.

"Oh, my God!" Arnold gasped. He concentrated furiously for a few seconds. "I know. I left the airlocks open when I landed. We're still breathing Ghost V air!"

And there, framed in the open doorway, was an immense grey creature with red spots on its hide. It had an amazing number of arms, legs, tentacles, claws and teeth, plus two tiny wings on its back. It walked slowly towards them, mumbling and groaning.

They both recognized it as the Grumbler.

Gregor dashed forward and slammed the door in its face. "We should be safe in here," he panted. "That door is airtight. But how will we pilot the ship?"

"We won't," Arnold said. "We'll have to trust the robot pilot—unless we can figure out some way of getting that thing out of there."

They noticed that a faint smoke was beginning to seep through the sealed edges of the door.

"What's that?" Arnold asked, with a sharp edge of panic in his voice.

Gregor frowned. "You remember, don't you? The Grumbler can get into any room. There's no way of keeping him out."

"I don't remember anything about him," Arnold said. "Does he eat people?"

"No. As I recall, he just mangles them thoroughly."

The smoke was beginning to solidify into the immense grey shape of the Grumbler. They retreated into the next compartment and sealed the door. Within seconds, the thin smoke was leaking through.

"This is ridiculous," Arnold said, biting his lip. "To be hunted by an imaginary monster—wait! You've still got your water pistol, haven't you?"

"Yes, but—"

"Give it to me!"

Arnold hurried over to a water tank and filled the pistol. The Grumbler had taken form again and was lumbering towards them, groaning unhappily. Arnold raked it with a stream of water.

The Grumbler kept on advancing.

"Now it's all coming back to me," Gregor said. "A water pistol never could stop the Grumbler."

They backed into the next room and slammed the door. Behind them was only the bunkroom, with nothing behind that but the deadly vacuum of space.

Gregor asked, "Isn't there something you can do about the atmosphere?"

Arnold shook his head. "It's dissipating now. But it takes about twenty hours for the effects of Longstead to wear off."

"Haven't you any antidote?"

"No."

Once again the Grumbler was materializing, and neither silently nor pleasantly.

"How can we kill it?" Arnold asked. "There must be a way. Magic words? How about a wooden sword?"

Gregor shook his head. "I remember the Grumbler now," he said unhappily.

"What kills it?"

"It can't be destroyed by water pistols, cap guns, firecrackers, sling-shots, stink bombs, or any other childhood weapon. The Grumbler is absolutely unkillable."

"That Flynn and his damned imagination! Why did we have to talk about him? How do you get rid of it then?"

"I told you. You don't. It just has to go away of its own accord."

The Grumbler was full size now. Gregor and Arnold hurried into the tiny bunkroom and slammed their last door.

"*Think*, Gregor," Arnold pleaded. "No kid invents a monster without a defence of some sort. *Think!*"

"The Grumbler cannot be killed," Gregor said.

The red-spotted monster was taking shape again. Gregor thought back over all the midnight horrors he had ever known. He *must* have done something as a child to neutralize the power of the unknown.

And then—almost too late—he remembered.

Under auto-pilot controls, the ship flashed Earthward with the Grumbler as complete master. He marched up and down the empty corridors and floated through steel partitions into cabins and cargo compartments, moaning, groaning and cursing because he could not get at any victim.

The ship reached the Solar System and took up an automatic orbit around the Moon.

Gregor peered out cautiously, ready to duck back if necessary. There was no sinister shuffling, no moaning or groaning, no hungry mist seeping under the door or through the walls.

"All clear," he called out to Arnold. "The Grumbler's gone."

Safe within the ultimate defence against night horrors—wrapped in the blankets that had covered their heads—they climbed out of their bunks.

"I told you the water pistol wouldn't do any good," Gregor said.

Arnold gave him a sick grin and put the pistol in his pocket. "I'm hanging on to it. If I ever get married and have a kid, it's going to be his first present."

"Not for any of mine," said Gregor. He patted the bunk affection-ately. "You can't beat blankets over the head for protection."

SOMETHING FOR NOTHING

But had he heard a voice? He couldn't be sure. Reconstructing it a moment later, Joe Collins knew he had been lying on his bed, too tired even to take his waterlogged shoes off the blanket. He had been staring at the network of cracks in the muddy yellow ceiling, watching water drip slowly and mournfully through.

It must have happened then. Collins caught a glimpse of metal beside his bed. He sat up. There was a machine on the floor, where no machine had been.

In that first moment of surprise, Collins thought he heard a very distant voice say, "There! *That* does it!"

He couldn't be sure of the voice. But the machine was undeniably there.

Collins knelt to examine it. The machine was about three feet square and it was humming softly. The crackle-grey surface was featureless, except for a red button in one corner and a brass plate in the centre. The plate said, CLASS-A UTILIZER, SERIES AA-1256432. And underneath, WARNING! THIS MACHINE SHOULD BE USED ONLY BY CLASS-A RATINGS!

That was all.

There were no knobs, dials, switches or any of the other attachments Collins associated with machines. Just the brass plate, the red button and the hum.

"Where did you come from?" Collins asked. The Class-A Utilizer continued to hum. He hadn't really expected an answer. Sitting on the edge of his bed, he stared thoughtfully at the Utilizer. The question now was—what to do with it?

He touched the red button warily, aware of his lack of experience with machines that fell from nowhere. When he turned it on, would the floor open up? Would little green men drop from the ceiling?

But he had slightly less than nothing to lose. He pressed the button lightly.

Nothing happened.

"All right—*do* something," Collins said, feeling definitely let down. The Utilizer only continued to hum softly.

Well, he could always pawn it. Honest Charlie would give him at least a dollar for the metal. He tried to lift the Utilizer. It wouldn't lift. He tried again, exerting all his strength, and succeeded in raising one corner an inch from the floor. He released it and sat down on the bed, breathing heavily.

"You should have sent a couple of men to help me," Collins told the Utilizer. Immediately, the hum grew louder and the machine started to vibrate.

Collins watched, but still nothing happened. On a hunch, he reached out and stabbed the red button.

Immediately, two bulky men appeared, dressed in rough work-clothes. They looked at the Utilizer appraisingly. One of them said, "Thank God, it's the small model. The big ones is brutes to get a grip on."

The other man said, "It beats the marble quarry, don't it?"

They looked at Collins, who stared back. Finally the first man said, "Okay, Mac, we ain't got all day. Where you want it?"

"Who are you?" Collins managed to croak.

"The moving men. Do we look like the Vanizaggi Sisters?"

"But where do you come from?" Collins asked. "And why?"

"We come from the Powha Minnile Movers, Incorporated," the man said. "And we came because you wanted movers, that's why. Now, where you want it?"

"Go away," Collins said. "I'll call for you later."

The moving men shrugged their shoulders and vanished. For several minutes, Collins stared at the spot where they had been. Then he stared at the Class-A Utilizer, which was humming softly again.

Utilizer? He could give it a better name.

A Wishing Machine.

Collins was not particularly shocked. When the miraculous occurs, only dull, workaday mentalities are unable to accept it. Collins was certainly not one of those. He had an excellent background for acceptance.

Most of his life had been spent wishing, hoping, praying that something marvellous would happen to him. In high school, he had dreamed of waking up some morning with an ability to know his homework without the tedious necessity of studying it. In the army, he had wished for some witch or jinn to change his orders, putting him in charge of the day room, instead of forcing him to do close-order drill like everyone else.

Out of the army, Collins had avoided work, for which he was psychologically unsuited. He had drifted around, hoping that some fabulously wealthy person would be induced to change his will, leaving him Everything.

He had never really expected anything to happen. But he was prepared when it did.

"I'd like a thousand dollars in small unmarked bills," Collins said cautiously. When the hum grew louder, he pressed the button. In front of him appeared a large mound of soiled singles, five and ten dollar bills. They were not crisp, but they certainly were money.

Collins threw a handful in the air and watched it settle beautifully to the floor. He lay on his bed and began making plans.

First, he would get the machine out of New York—upstate, perhaps—some place where he wouldn't be bothered by nosy neighbours. The income tax would be tricky on this sort of thing. Perhaps, after he got organized, he should go to Central America, or . . .

There was a suspicious noise in the room.

Collins leaped to his feet. A hole was opening in the wall, and someone was forcing his way through.

"*Hey*, I didn't ask you anything!" Collins told the machine.

The hole grew larger, and a large, red-faced man was half-way through, pushing angrily at the hole.

At that moment, Collins remembered that machines usually have owners. Anyone who owned a wishing machine wouldn't take kindly to having it gone. He would go to any lengths to recover it. Probably, he wouldn't stop short of—

"Protect me!" Collins shouted at the Utilizer, and stabbed the red button.

A small, bald man in loud pyjamas appeared, yawning sleepily. "Sanisa Leek, Temporal Wall Protection Service," he said, rubbing his eyes. "I'm Leek. What can I do for you?"

"Get him out of here!" Collins screamed. The red-faced man, waving his arms wildly, was almost through the hole.

Leek found a bit of bright metal in his pyjamas pocket. The red-faced man shouted, "Wait! You don't understand! That man—"

Leek pointed his piece of metal. The red-faced man screamed and vanished. In another moment the hole had vanished too.

"Did you kill him?" Collins asked.

"Of course not," Leek said, putting away the bit of metal. "I just veered him back through his glommatch. He won't try *that* way again."

"You mean he'll try some other way?" Collins asked.

"It's possible," Leek said. "He could attempt a micro-transfer, or even an animation." He looked sharply at Collins. "This is your Utilizer, isn't it?"

"Of course," Collins said, starting to perspire.

"And you're an A-rating?"

"Naturally," Collins told him. "If I wasn't, what would I be doing with a Utilizer?"

"No offence," Leek said drowsily, "just being friendly." He shook his head slowly. "How you A's get around! I suppose you've come back here to do a history book?"

Collins just smiled enigmatically.

"I'll be on my way," Leek said, yawning copiously. "On the go, night and day. I'd be better off in a quarry."

And he vanished in the middle of a yawn.

Rain was still beating against the ceiling. Across the airshaft, the snoring continued, undisturbed. Collins was alone again, with the machine.

And with a thousand dollars in small bills scattered around the floor.

He patted the Utilizer affectionately. Those A-ratings had it pretty good. Want something? Just ask for it and press a button. Undoubtedly, the real owner missed it.

Leek had said that the man might try to get in some other way. What way?

What did it matter? Collins gathered up the bills, whistling softly. As long as he had the wishing machine, he could take care of himself.

The next few days marked a great change in Collins' fortunes. With the aid of the Powha Minnile Movers he took the Utilizer to upstate New York. There, he bought a medium-sized mountain in a neglected corner of the Adirondacks. Once the papers were in his hands, he walked to the centre of his property, several miles from the highway. The two movers, sweating profusely, lugged the Utilizer behind him, cursing monotonously as they broke through the dense underbrush.

"Set it down here and scram," Collins said. The last few days had done a lot for his confidence.

The moving men sighed wearily and vanished. Collins looked around. On all sides, as far as he could see, was closely spaced forest of birch and pine. The air was sweet and damp. Birds were chirping merrily in the treetops, and an occasional squirrel darted by.

Nature! He had always loved nature. This would be the perfect spot to build a large, impressive house with swimming pool, tennis courts and, possibly, a small airport.

"I want a house," Collins stated firmly, and pushed the red button.

A man in a neat grey business suit and pince-nez appeared. "Yes, sir," he said, squinting at the trees, "but you really must be more specific. Do you want something classic, like a bungalow, ranch, split-level, mansion, castle or palace? Or primitive, like an igloo or hut? Since you are an A, you could have something up-to-the-minute, like a semiface, an Extended New or a Sunken Miniature."

"Huh?" Collins said. "I don't know. What would you suggest?"

"Small mansion," the man said promptly. "They usually start with that."

"They do?"

"Oh, yes. Later, they move to a warm climate and build a palace."

Collins wanted to ask more questions, but he decided against it. Everything was going smoothly. These people thought he was an A, and the true owner of the Utilizer. There was no sense in disenchanting them.

"You take care of it all," he told the man.

"Yes, sir," the man said. "I usually do."

The rest of the day, Collins reclined on a couch and drank iced beverages while the Maxima Olph Construction Company materialized equipment and put up his house.

It was a low-slung affair of some twenty rooms, which Collins considered quite modest under the circumstances. It was built only of the best materials, from a design of Mig of Degma, interior by Towige, a Mula swimming pool and formal gardens by Vierien.

By evening, it was completed, and the small army of workmen packed up their equipment and vanished.

Collins allowed his chef to prepare a light supper for him. Afterward, he sat in his large, cool living-room to think the whole thing over. In front of him, humming gently, sat the Utilizer.

Collins lighted a cheroot and sniffed the aroma. First of all, he rejected any supernatural explanations. There were no demons or devils involved in this. His house had been built by ordinary human beings, who swore and laughed and cursed like human beings. The Utilizer was simply a scientific gadget, which worked on principles he didn't understand or care to understand.

Could it have come from another planet? Not likely. They wouldn't have learned English just for him.

The Utilizer must have come from the Earth's future. But how?

Collins leaned back and puffed his cheroot. Accidents will happen, he reminded himself. Why couldn't the Utilizer have just *slipped* into the past? After all, it could create something from nothing, and that was much more complicated.

What a wonderful future it must be, he thought. Wishing machines! How marvellously civilized! All a person had to do was think of something. Presto! There it was. In time, perhaps, they'd eliminate the red button. Then there'd be no manual labour involved.

Of course, he'd have to watch his step. There was still the owner —and the rest of the A's. They would try to take the machine from him. Probably, they were a hereditary clique...

A movement caught the edge of his eye and he looked up. The

Utilizer was quivering like a leaf in a gale.

Collins walked up to it, frowning blackly. A faint mist of steam surrounded the trembling Utilizer. It seemed to be overheating.

Could he have overworked it? Perhaps a bucket of water...

Then he noticed that the Utilizer was perceptibly smaller. It was no more than two feet square and shrinking before his eyes.

The owner! Or perhaps the A's! This must be the micro-transfer that Leek had talked about. If he didn't do something quickly, Collins knew, his wishing machine would dwindle to nothingness and disappear.

"Leek Protection Service," Collins snapped. He punched the button and withdrew his hand quickly. The machine was very hot.

Leek appeared in a corner of the room, wearing slacks and a sports shirt, and carrying a golf club. "Must I be disturbed every time I—"

"*Do something!*" Collins shouted, pointing to the Utilizer, which was now only a foot square and glowing a dull red.

"Nothing I can do," Leek said. "Temporal wall is all I'm licensed for. You want the microcontrol people." He hefted his golf club and was gone.

"Microcontrol," Collins said, and reached for the button. He withdrew his hand hastily. The Utilizer was only about four inches on a side now and glowing a hot cherry red. He could barely see the button, which was the size of a pin.

Collins whirled around, grabbed a cushion and punched down.

A girl with horn-rimmed glasses appeared, note-book in hand, pencil poised. "With whom did you wish to make an appointment?" she asked sedately.

"Get me help fast!" Collins roared, watching his precious Utilizer grow smaller and smaller.

"Mr. Vergon is out to lunch," the girl said, biting her pencil thoughtfully. "He's de-zoned himself. I can't reach him."

"Who *can* you reach?"

She consulted her note-book. "Mr. Vis is in the Dieg Continuum and Mr. Elgis is doing field work in Paleolithic Europe. If you're really in a rush, maybe you'd better call Transferpoint Control. They're a smaller outfit, but—"

"Transferpoint Control. Okay—scram." He turned his full attention to the Utilizer and stabbed down on it with the scorched pillow. Nothing happened. The Utilizer was barely half an inch square, and Collins realized that the cushion hadn't been able to depress the almost invisible button.

For a moment Collins considered letting the Utilizer go. Maybe this was the time. He could sell the house, the furnishings, and still be pretty well off...

No! He hadn't wished for anything important yet! No one was going to take it from him without a struggle.

He forced himself to keep his eyes open as he stabbed the white-hot button with a rigid forefinger.

A thin, shabbily dressed old man appeared, holding something that looked like a gaily coloured Easter egg. He threw it down. The egg burst and an orange smoke billowed out and was sucked directly into the infinitesimal Utilizer. A great billow of smoke went up, almost choking Collins. Then the Utilizer's shape started to form again. Soon, it was normal size and apparently undamaged. The old man nodded curtly.

"We're not fancy," he said, "but we're reliable." He nodded again and disappeared.

Collins thought he could hear a distant shout of anger.

Shakily, he sat down on the floor in front of the machine. His hand was throbbing painfully.

"Fix me up," he muttered through dry lips, and punched the button with his good hand.

The Utilizer hummed louder for a moment, then was silent. The pain left his scorched finger and, looking down, Collins saw that there was no sign of a burn—not even scar tissue to mark where it had been.

Collins poured himself a long shot of brandy and went directly to bed. That night, he dreamed he was being chased by a gigantic letter A, but he didn't remember it in the morning.

Within a week, Collins found that building his mansion in the woods had been precisely the wrong thing to do. He had to hire a platoon of guards to keep away sightseers, and hunters insisted on camping in his formal gardens.

Also, the Bureau of Internal Revenue began to take a lively interest in his affairs.

But, above all, Collins discovered he wasn't so fond of nature after all. Birds and squirrels were all very well, but they hardly ranked as conversationalists. Trees, though quite ornamental, made poor drinking companions.

Collins decided he was a city boy at heart.

Therefore, with the aid of the Powha Minnile Movers, the Maxima Olph Construction Corporation, the Jagton Instantaneous Travel Bureau and a great deal of money placed in the proper hands, Collins moved to a small Central American republic. There, since the climate was warmer and income tax nonexistent, he built a large, airy, ostentatious palace.

It came equipped with the usual accessories—horses, dogs, peacocks, servants, maintenance men, guards, musicians, bevies of dancing girls and everything else a palace should have. Collins spent two weeks just exploring the place.

Everything went along nicely for a while.

One morning Collins approached the Utilizer, with the vague intention of asking for a sports-car, or possibly a small herd of pedigreed cattle. He bent over the grey machine, reached for the red button...

And the Utilizer backed away from him.

For a moment, Collins thought he was seeing things, and he almost decided to stop drinking champagne before breakfast. He took a step forward and reached for the red button.

The Utilizer sidestepped him neatly and trotted out of the room.

Collins sprinted after it, cursing the owner and the A's. This was probably the animation that Leek had spoken about—somehow, the owner had managed to imbue the machine with mobility. It didn't matter. All he had to do was catch up, punch the button and ask for the Animation Control people.

The Utilizer raced down a hall, Collins close behind. An under-butler, polishing a solid gold doorknob, stared open-mouthed.

"Stop it!" Collins shouted.

The under-butler moved clumsily into the Utilizer's path. The machine dodged him gracefully and sprinted towards the main door.

Collins pushed a switch and the door slammed shut.

The Utilizer gathered momentum and went right through it. Once in the open, it tripped over a garden hose, regained its balance and headed towards the open countryside.

Collins raced after it. If he could get just a little closer...

The Utilizer suddenly leaped into the air. It hung there for a long moment, then fell to the ground. Collins sprang at the button.

The Utilizer rolled out of his way, took a short run and leaped again. For a moment, it hung twenty feet above his head—drifted a few feet straight up, stopped, twisted wildly and fell.

Collins was afraid that, on a third jump, it would keep going up. When it drifted unwillingly back to the ground, he was ready. He feinted, then stabbed at the button. The Utilizer couldn't duck fast enough.

"Animation Control!" Collins roared triumphantly.

There was a small explosion, and the Utilizer settled down docilely. There was no hint of animation left in it.

Collins wiped his forehead and sat on the machine. Closer and closer. He'd better do some big wishing now, while he still had the chance.

In rapid succession, he asked for five million dollars, three functioning oil wells, a motion-picture studio, perfect health, twenty-five more dancing girls, immortality, a sports car and a herd of pedigreed cattle.

He thought he heard someone snicker. He looked around. No one was there.

When he turned back, the Utilizer had vanished.

He just stared. And, in another moment, *he* vanished.

When he opened his eyes, Collins found himself standing in front of a desk. On the other side was the large, red-faced man who had originally tried to break into his room. The man didn't appear angry. Rather, he appeared resigned, even melancholy.

Collins stood for a moment in silence, sorry that the whole thing was over. The owner and the A's had finally caught him. But it had been glorious while it lasted.

"Well," Collins said directly, "you've got your machine back. Now, what else do you want?"

"*My* machine?" the red-faced man said, looking up incredulously. "It's not my machine, sir. Not at all."

Collins stared at him. "Don't try to kid me, mister. You A-ratings want to protect your monopoly, don't you?"

The red-faced man put down his paper. "Mr. Collins," he said stiffly, "my name is Flign. I am an agent for the Citizens Protective Union, a non-profit organization, whose aim is to protect individuals such as yourself from errors of judgment."

"You mean you're not one of the A's?"

"You are labouring under a misapprehension, sir," Flign said with quiet dignity. "The A-rating does not represent a social group, as you seem to believe. It is merely a credit rating."

"A what?" Collins asked slowly.

"A credit rating." Flign glanced at his watch. "We haven't much time, so I'll make this as brief as possible. Ours is a decentralized age, Mr. Collins. Our businesses, industries and services are scattered through an appreciable portion of space and time. The utilization corporation is an essential link. It provides for the transfer of goods and services from point to point. Do you understand?"

Collins nodded.

"Credit is, of course, an automatic privilege. But, eventually, everything must be paid for."

Collins didn't like the sound of that. *Pay?* This place wasn't as civilized as he had thought. No one had mentioned paying. Why did they bring it up now?

"Why didn't someone stop me?" he asked desperately. "They must have known I didn't have a proper rating."

Flign shook his head. "The credit ratings are suggestions, not laws. In a civilized world, an individual has the right to his own decisions. I'm very sorry, sir." He glanced at his watch again and handed Collins the paper he had been reading. "Would you just glance at this bill and tell me whether it's in order?"

Collins took the paper and read:

One Palace, with Accessories..............................	Cr. 45,000,000
Services of Maxima Olph Movers........................	111,000
122 Dancing Girls..	122,000,000
Perfect Health...	888,234,031

He scanned the rest of the list quickly. The total came to slightly better than eighteen billion Credits.

"Wait a minute!" Collins shouted. "I can't be held to this! The Utilizer just dropped into my room by accident!"

"That's the very fact I'm going to bring to their attention," Flign said. "Who knows? Perhaps they will be reasonable. It does no harm to try."

Collins felt the room sway. Flign's face began to melt before him. "Time's up," Flign said. "Good luck."

Collins closed his eyes.

When he opened them again, he was standing on a bleak plain, facing a range of stubby mountains. A cold wind lashed his face and the sky was the colour of steel.

A raggedly dressed man was standing beside him. "Here," the man said and handed Collins a pick.

"What's this?"

"This is a pick," the man said patiently. "And over there is a quarry, where you and I and a number of others will cut marble."

"Marble?"

"Sure. There's always some idiot who wants a palace," the man said with a wry grin. "You can call me Jang. We'll be together for some time."

Collins blinked stupidly. "How long?"

"You work it out," Jang said. "The rate is fifty credits a month until your debt is paid off."

The pick dropped from Collins' hand. They couldn't do this to him! The Utilization Corporation must realize its mistake by now! *They* had been at fault, letting the machine slip into the past. Didn't they realize that?

"It's all a mistake!" Collins said.

"No mistake," Jang said. "They're very short of labour. Have to go recruiting all over for it. Come on. After the first thousand years you won't mind it."

Collins started to follow Jang towards the quarry. He stopped.

"The first *thousand* years? I won't live that long!"

"Sure you will," Jang assured him. "You got immortality, didn't you?"

Yes, he had. He had wished for it, just before they took back the machine. Or had they taken back the machine *after* he wished for it?

Collins remembered something. Strange, but he didn't remember seeing immortality on the bill Flign had showed him.

"How much did they charge me for immortality?" he asked.

Jang looked at him and laughed. "Don't be naïve, pal. You should have it figured out by now."

He led Collins towards the quarry. "Naturally, they give *that* away for nothing."

THE STORE OF THE WORLDS

Mr. Wayne came to the end of the long, shoulder-high mound of grey rubble, and there was the Store of the Worlds. It was exactly as his friends had described; a small shack constructed of bits of lumber, parts of cars, a piece of galvanized iron and a few rows of crumbling bricks, all daubed over with a watery blue paint.

Mr. Wayne glanced back down the long lane of rubble to make sure he hadn't been followed. He tucked his parcel more firmly under his arm; then, with a little shiver at his own audacity, he opened the door and slipped inside.

"Good morning," the proprietor said.

He, too, was exactly as described; a tall, crafty-looking old fellow with narrow eyes and a downcast mouth. His name was Tompkins. He sat in an old rocking chair, and perched on the back of it was a blue and green parrot. There was one other chair in the store, and a table. On the table was a rusted hypodermic.

"I've heard about your store from friends," Mr. Wayne said.

"Then you know my price," Tompkins said. "Have you brought it?"

"Yes," said Mr. Wayne, holding up his parcel. "But I want to ask first—"

"They always want to ask," Tompkins said to the parrot, who blinked. "Go ahead, ask."

"I want to know what really happens."

Tompkins sighed. "What happens is this. You pay me my fee. I give you an injection which knocks you out. Then, with the aid of certain gadgets which I have in the back of the store, I liberate your mind."

Tompkins smiled as he said that, and his silent parrot seemed to smile, too.

"What happens then?" Mr. Wayne asked.

"Your mind, liberated from its body, is able to choose from the countless probability-worlds which the Earth casts off in every second of its existence."

Grinning now, Tompkins sat up in his rocking chair and began to show signs of enthusiasm.

"Yes, my friend, though you might not have suspected it, from the moment this battered Earth was born out of the sun's fiery womb, it cast off its alternate-probability worlds. Worlds without end, emanating from events large and small; every Alexander and every amoeba creating worlds, just as ripples will spread in a pond no matter how big or how small the stone you throw. Doesn't every object cast a shadow? Well, my friend, the Earth itself is four-dimensional; therefore it casts three-dimensional shadows, solid reflections of itself through every moment of its being. Millions, billions of Earths! An infinity of Earths! And your mind, liberated by me, will be able to select any of these worlds, and to live upon it for a while."

Mr. Wayne was uncomfortably aware that Tompkins sounded like a circus barker, proclaiming marvels that simply couldn't exist. But, Mr. Wayne reminded himself, things had happened within his own lifetime which he would never have believed possible. Never! So perhaps the wonders that Tompkins spoke of were possible, too.

Mr. Wayne said, "My friends also told me—"

"That I was an out-and-out fraud?" Tompkins asked.

"Some of them *implied* that," Mr. Wayne said cautiously. "But I try to keep an open mind. They also said—"

"I know what your dirty-minded friends said. They told you about the fulfilment of desire. Is that what you want to hear about?"

"Yes," said Mr. Wayne. "They told me that whatever I wished for—whatever I wanted—"

"Exactly," Tompkins said. "The thing could work in no other way. There are the infinite worlds to choose among. Your mind chooses, and is guided only by desire. Your deepest desire is the only thing that counts. If you have been harbouring a secret dream of murder—"

"Oh hardly, hardly!" cried Mr. Wayne.

"—then you will go to a world where you *can* murder, where you can roll in blood, where you can outdo Sade or Caesar, or whoever your idol may be. Suppose it's power you want? Then you'll choose a world where you are a god, literally and actually. A blood-thirsty Juggernaut, perhaps, or an all-wise Buddha."

"I doubt very much if I—"

"There are other desires, too," Tompkins said. "All heavens and all hells. Unbridled sexuality. Gluttony, drunkenness, love, fame—anything you want."

"Amazing!" said Mr. Wayne.

"Yes," Tompkins agreed. "Of course, my little list doesn't exhaust all the possibilities, all the combinations and permutations of desire. For all I know you might want a simple, placid, pastoral existence on a South Seas island among idealized natives."

"That sounds more like me," Mr. Wayne said, with a shy laugh.

"But who knows?" Tompkins asked. "Even you might not know what your true desires are. They might involve your own death."

"Does that happen often?" Mr. Wayne asked anxiously.

"Occasionally."

"I wouldn't want to die," Mr. Wayne said.

"It hardly ever happens," Tompkins said, looking at the parcel in Mr. Wayne's hands.

"If you say so ... But how do I know all this is real? Your fee is extremely high, it'll take everything I own. And for all I know, you'll give me a drug and I'll just *dream*! Everything I own just for a—a shot of heroin and a lot of fancy words!"

Tompkins smiled reassuringly. "The experience has no drug-like quality about it. And no sensation of a dream, either."

"If it's *true*," Mr. Wayne said, a little petulantly, "why can't I stay in the world of my desire for good?"

"I'm working on that," Tompkins said. "That's why I charge so high a fee; to get materials, to experiment. I'm trying to find a way of making the transition permanent. So far I haven't been able to loosen the cord that binds a man to his own Earth—and pulls him back to it. Not even the great mystics could cut that cord, except with death. But I still have my hopes."

"It would be a great thing if you succeeded," Mr. Wayne said politely.

"Yes it would!" Tompkins cried, with a surprising burst of passion. "For then I'd turn my wretched shop into an escape hatch! My process would be free then, free for everyone! Everyone would go to the Earth of their desires, the Earth that really suited them, and leave *this* damned place to the rats and worms—"

Tompkins cut himself off in mid-sentence, and became icy calm. "But I fear my prejudices are showing. I can't offer a permanent escape from the Earth yet; not one that doesn't involve death. Perhaps I never will be able to. For now, all I can offer you is a vacation, a change, a taste of another world and a look at your own desires. You know my fee. I'll refund it if the experience isn't satisfactory."

"That's good of you," Mr. Wayne said, quite earnestly. "But there's that other matter my friends told me about. The ten years off my life."

"That can't be helped," Tompkins said, "and can't be refunded. My process is a tremendous strain on the nervous system, and life-expectancy is shortened accordingly. That's one of the reasons why our so-called government has declared my process illegal."

"But they don't enforce the ban very firmly," Mr. Wayne said.

"No. Officially the process is banned as a harmful fraud. But officials are men, too. They'd like to leave this Earth, just like everyone else."

"The cost," Mr. Wayne mused, gripping his parcel tightly. "And ten years off my life! For the fulfilment of my secret desires ... Really, I must give this some thought."

"Think away," Tompkins said indifferently.

All the way home Mr. Wayne thought about it. When his train reached Port Washington, Long Island, he was still thinking. And driving his car from the station to his home he was still thinking about Tompkins' crafty old face, and worlds of probability, and the fulfilment of desire.

But when he stepped inside his house, those thoughts had to stop. Janet, his wife, wanted him to speak sharply to the maid, who had been drinking again. His son Tommy wanted help with the sloop, which was to be launched tomorrow. And his baby daughter wanted to tell about her day in kindergarten.

Mr. Wayne spoke pleasantly but firmly to the maid. He helped Tommy put the final coat of copper paint on the sloop's bottom, and he listened to Peggy tell about her adventures in the playground.

Later, when the children were in bed and he and Janet were alone in their living-room, she asked him if something were wrong.

"Wrong?"

"You seem to be worried about something," Janet said. "Did you have a bad day at the office?"

"Oh, just the usual sort of thing..."

He certainly was not going to tell Janet, or anyone else, that he had taken the day off and gone to see Tompkins in his crazy old Store of the Worlds. Nor was he going to speak about the right every man should have, once in his lifetime, to fulfil his most secret desires. Janet, with her good common sense, would never understand that.

The next days at the office were extremely hectic. All of Wall Street was in a mild panic over events in the Middle East and in Asia, and stocks were reacting accordingly. Mr. Wayne settled down to work. He tried not to think of the fulfilment of desire at the cost of everything he possessed, with ten years of his life thrown in for good measure. It was crazy! Old Tompkins must be insane!

On week-ends he went sailing with Tommy. The old sloop was behaving very well, making practically no water through her bottom seams. Tommy wanted a new suit of racing sails, but Mr. Wayne sternly rejected that. Perhaps next year, if the market looked better. For now, the old sails would have to do.

Sometimes at night, after the children were asleep, he and Janet would go sailing. Long Island Sound was quiet then, and cool. Their boat glided past the blinking buoys, sailing towards the swollen yellow moon.

"I *know* something's on your mind," Janet said.

"Darling, please!"

"Is there something you're keeping from me?"

"Nothing!"

"Are you sure? Are you absolutely sure?"

"Absolutely sure."

"Then put your arms around me. That's right..."

And the sloop sailed itself for a while.

Desire and fulfilment ... But autumn came, and the sloop had to be hauled. The stock market regained some stability, but Peggy caught the measles. Tommy wanted to know the differences between ordinary bombs, atom bombs, hydrogen bombs, cobalt bombs, and all the other kinds of bombs that were in the news. Mr. Wayne explained to the best of his ability. And the maid quit unexpectedly.

Secret desires were all very well. Perhaps he *did* want to kill someone, or live on a South Seas island. But there were responsibilities to consider. He had two growing children, and a better wife than he deserved.

Perhaps around Christmas time...

But in mid-winter there was a fire in the unoccupied guest bedroom due to defective wiring. The firemen put out the blaze without much damage, and no one was hurt. But it put any thought of Tompkins out of his mind for a while. First the bedroom had to be repaired, for Mr. Wayne was very proud of his gracious old house.

Business was still frantic and uncertain due to the international situation. Those Russians, those Arabs, those Greeks, those Chinese. The intercontinental missiles, the atom bombs, the sputniks ... Mr. Wayne spent long days at the office, and sometimes evenings, too. Tommy caught the mumps. A part of the roof had to be re-shingled. And then already it was time to consider the spring launching of the sloop.

A year had passed, and he'd had very little time to think of secret desires. But perhaps next year. In the meantime—

"Well?" said Tompkins. "Are you all right?"

"Yes, quite all right," Mr. Wayne said. He got up from the chair and rubbed his forehead.

"Do you want a refund?" Tompkins asked.

"No. The experience was quite satisfactory."

"They always are," Tompkins said, winking lewdly at the parrot. "Well, what was yours?"

"A world of the recent past," Mr. Wayne said.

"A lot of them are. Did you find out about your secret desire? Was it murder? Or a South Seas island?"

"I'd rather not discuss it," Mr. Wayne said, pleasantly but firmly.

"A lot of people won't discuss it with me," Tompkins said sulkily. "I'll be damned if I know why."

"Because—well, I think the world of one's secret desire feels sacred, somehow. No offence ... Do you think you'll ever be able to make it permanent? The world of one's choice, I mean?"

The old man shrugged his shoulders. "I'm trying. If I succeed, you'll hear about it. Everyone will."

"Yes, I suppose so." Mr. Wayne undid his parcel and laid its contents on the table. The parcel contained a pair of army boots, a knife, two coils of copper wire, and three small cans of corned beef.

Tompkins' eyes glittered for a moment. "Quite satisfactory," he said. "Thank you."

"Good-bye," said Mr. Wayne. "And thank *you*."

Mr. Wayne left the shop and hurried down to the end of the lane of grey rubble. Beyond it, as far as he could see, lay flat fields of rubble, brown and grey and black. Those fields, stretching to every horizon, were made of the twisted corpses of cities, the shattered remnants of trees, and the fine white ash that once was human flesh and bone.

"Well," Mr. Wayne said to himself, "at least we gave as good as we got."

That year in the past had cost him everything he owned, and ten years of life thrown in for good measure. Had it been a dream? It was still worth it! But now he had to put away all thought of Janet and the children. That was finished, unless Tompkins perfected his process. Now he had to think about his own survival.

With the aid of his wrist geiger he found a deactivated lane through the rubble. He'd better get back to the shelter before dark, before the rats came out. If he didn't hurry he'd miss the evening potato ration.

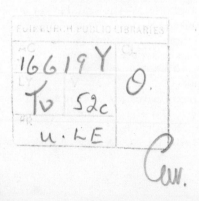